Advance praise for *I Buried Paul*:

"Bruce Ferber has captured lightning in a bottle, chronicling a generation's obsessive attachment to the Beatles. His love for their music and legacy is evident on every page. And as the poets said, 'With a love like that you know it can't be bad.' (Yeah-yeah-yeah.)"
—Bob Spitz, author of *The Beatles*

"Bruce Ferber's prose is music to my ears. *I Buried Paul* is very funny, and very insightful."
—John Densmore, *New York Times* bestselling author of *Riders on the Storm*, drummer in a famous rock band

"In his touching and funny novel, Bruce Ferber comes not to bury Paul McCartney but to celebrate his true believers, the dreamers who carry the torch of their youthful rock dreams well into pension age, and who refuse to sacrifice their passion despite high cholesterol counts and the possibility of embarrassing themselves. *I Buried Paul* is a tender paean to the music that changed us all, its revivifying and enduring power."
—Marc Weingarten, author of *The Gang that Wouldn't Write Straight: Wolfe, Thompson, Didion, Capote, and the New Journalism Revolution*

"Funny, heartfelt, ar̶ who loves music or has e̶
—Ben Loory, autho

"Reading Bruce Ferber's latest novel is like being told a great tale from your favorite and funniest pal—the one who really seems to know stuff—the one you trust—the one who gets you when nobody else does. Long live Paul."
—Jason Alexander, actor, director

"First, the good news: Paul isn't dead, and this isn't an autopsy. Rather it's a funny, moving novel about trying to find your way home from the Abbey Road of your teenage fantasy life, while simultaneously escaping the shadows cast by your father, your older brother, many failed relationships, and a world that doesn't like to see people doing what they love—such as making their own music. Reminiscent of Anne Tyler and Richard Russo (if either could keep a steady bass beat), Bruce Ferber writes humorous fiction for grown ups."
—Scott Bradfield, author of *The History of Luminous Motion*

"Funny, deep, and compulsive, *I Buried Paul* is a tribute to family, lifelong friends, and the Beatles tunes that unite them. Told with Ferber's trademark wit, literary verve and big-heartedness, it's a veritable magical mystery tour of growing up and finding love and meaning in a complex world."
—Michaela Carter, author of *Leonora in the Morning Light*

I
BURIED
PAUL

Bruce Ferber

THE
STORY
PLANT

Also by Bruce Ferber:

Cascade Falls
Elevating Overman
The Way We Work: On the Job in Hollywood (editor)

The Story Plant
Studio Digital CT, LLC
P.O. Box 4331
Stamford, CT 06907

Story Plant trade paperback ISBN-13 978-1-61188-328-2
Fiction Studio Books e-book ISBN-13: 978-1-945839-64-1

Visit our website at www.TheStoryPlant.com

First Story Plant Paperback Printing: June 2022
Printed in The United States of America

For Queen B, RIP.

"Information is not knowledge.
Knowledge is not wisdom.
Wisdom is not truth.
Truth is not beauty.
Beauty is not love.
Love is not music.
Music is the best."
—Frank Zappa

OKLAHOMA 1989

Milestones are seldom what they're cracked up to be, unless you're a charmed preppie who inherits the Hallmark gene. My first time kissing a girl turned out to be a mercy stunt, engineered by some douchey linebacker on the junior varsity. The most memorable thing about getting my driver's license was that I had no car, and my parents' station wagon was never available. When I put on the cap and gown for high school graduation, it felt like I was going to a Halloween party, dressed as a fraud.

As I went on to achieve my own versions of milestones, none of them would adhere to society's definitions or timetable. Instead, they appeared out of the blue like stealth jack-in-the-boxes. How was I to know that the fourth kiss from my third girlfriend would be the portal to life-changing sex? Or that on my first solo plane trip at eighteen, I'd be moved to First Class and treated like a VIP, despite having accomplished nothing? Or that shortly after the plane touched down, I would never again look at the world the same way.

It's not that I'm against the element of surprise. I'm just convinced it would be a lot less stressful to be the Hallmark guy.

Rarely has anyone so relished the opportunity to visit Bixby, Oklahoma, in August, where the average temperature hovers around ninety-one degrees with seventy-five percent humidity. But I hadn't come for the sod-growing convention or to attend prayer breakfasts at Oral Roberts University. My mission was to spend a week with my big brother, Eddie Kozlowski, lead guitarist for the popular, small-venue cover band, Traction. Fourteen years my senior, Eddie had invited me to join him on a leg of his Midwest tour, and, after shameless begging on my part, Mom and Dad agreed to let me go. They spent most of their Sunday mornings praying for Eddie to come to his senses and reconsider an intern position with Bob Snell, an accountant they knew.

As far as I was concerned, my brother surpassed Neil Armstrong in the role model department. Perhaps if Neil had once slept on the top bunk in my room, he'd have the edge, but I had witnessed firsthand how hard Eddie worked to become a rock star. Even though his band didn't write original material and might, on occasion, play a bar catty-corner to a wheat field, I was convinced that my brother had reached the Promised Land. He had figured out a way to not be a lawyer or a CPA and make a living doing the thing he loved most—which was the thing *I* loved most.

I'd never seen a better smile than the one on Eddie's face the day he pulled up to Tulsa International in the band's beat-up Econoline. To be fair, I couldn't make out his upper lip, given the Lemmy Kilmister mustache he'd been growing since the beginning of the tour, but it took more than facial hair to contain Eddie's spirit.

As I emerged from baggage claim, he shouted "Jimmy the K!", bolted out of the van, and proceeded to hug me so hard I feared for my upper vertebrae. "Look at that hair!" Eddie exclaimed, tousling my shoulder-length locks that paled in comparison to his layered Bon Jovi 'do.

I felt blessed to be included in his world, and not just because of the music. Most of my friends had complicated relationships with their brothers, but Eddie and I were always stoked to be in each other's company. Maybe we got along so well because the difference in age ruled out any sort of competition between us, but my guess is that even had we been twins, I could never compete with him.

"Gonna be a killer show tonight, little bro!" He slapped me on the back. "You're gonna love Oklahoma!"

I already did. The first night would be Bixby, the next, Tulsa, the following night, the college town of Norman, then Oklahoma City. You always heard about musicians hating the grind of the road, but to Eddie it was salvation. Before he started touring with Traction, he'd spent most of his life on Long Island, so, to him, each stop was a new adventure, no matter how small the town, shitty the club, or meager the crowd. Since I'd grown up just like Eddie, I felt the same way, even though my stint on the tour would only amount to seven days. "So, what are the motel rooms like?" I had to ask.

"Phenomenal," Eddie said. "Every night a clean bed, every morning a big-ass mess to remind us of all the partying we did."

"I wish I didn't have to go to college," I muttered, lost in the moment. My musical abilities couldn't hold a candle to Eddie's, but after sitting in his van for two minutes, I wanted to ride around in it forever.

"Plenty of time to play music," he assured me. "Your education is only going to help."

I thought of how happy Dad would be to hear Eddie's speech. Then it occurred to me that maybe they had cut a deal whereby I'd be allowed to visit, provided Eddie encouraged me to stick with my college plan. I decided to put the dark cloud of academia out of my mind, not wanting anything to spoil my first night on tour.

Soon we were driving through towns with names like Broken Arrow and Jenks, and, a few minutes later, pulling into the parking lot of the Bixby Holiday Inn. Eddie said that before we headed up to the room, he wanted to show me the lounge where he'd be performing that night. I followed him through the entrance and into a dark, smoky space out of a forties film noir. In front of us stood a nondescript bar populated by a couple of red-faced farmer-types who looked as if they'd been sitting there since the Korean War. The farmers glanced over in our direction, their expressions exuding "who invited this hippie scum?" Twenty years after the Summer of Love, these guys still held a grudge, wearing their entrenchment like a badge of honor. Eddie paid them no mind and led me to the other side of the bar where, at the center of the tiny stage area, sat a drum kit with the word "Traction" plastered across the kick drum beneath the Ludwig insignia. The guitar stands and mics were set up, the other instruments still in their motel rooms. "I think it'll be a good crowd tonight, Jimbo," he said, pumping his fist for good measure.

"How do you know?"

"I don't know. I just think it'll be good, and usually I'm right."

I wasn't about to question a professional. At the same time, I was clear-headed enough to recognize that a lounge in Bixby was not the most distinguished performance space for a guitar god to showcase his power.

What made my brother believe that a Holiday Inn thirty miles outside of Tulsa was worthy of his rock 'n' roll dreams? Eddie explained that there were a whole lot of Holiday Inns which, when you added up all the people who heard and enjoyed his music on a nightly basis, was nothing to sneeze at. "Keep your eyes on the prize, but while you're looking—rock on."

Normally the band didn't have dinner until after the show, but once we dropped off my suitcase in the room, Eddie asked if I was hungry. I said yes, and he took me out for pizza. At the restaurant, we were treated to a few more disdainful looks, after which I asked about Gene Klein, the rhythm guitarist and leader of Traction, who'd grown up in our neighborhood and had planted the rock 'n' roll seed in Eddie's head.

"Gene's Gene. Found his calling as a toddler and never looked back. In Red Cloud, Nebraska, he's like Van Halen."

"That's insane." It really was when you considered the history. Gene's father had been a Holocaust survivor whose approach to life was to be as invisible as possible, and here was his son, strutting his stuff across a swath of the country that viewed Jews as cheap novelty items. From my brother's point of view, Gene Klein was bigger than bigotry. Rock 'n' roll supremacy had made him an exclusive, in-demand party favor.

I offered Eddie a slice of pepperoni, which he refused, explaining that the grease would screw up his stomach and get in the way of the evening's guitar shredding. When I asked which songs the band would be playing, he said it would be cooler for me to be surprised by the setlist. Of course it would be cooler. My brother's ideas were always one step ahead of mine.

Eddie wanted to know about things at home. I told him it was the same as always: Mom and Dad worrying about finances, missing him, wishing they could have come along. Suddenly, we both burst out laughing. It went without saying that if our parents had the money for two more plane tickets, they would have gladly made me sacrifice my coveted week of freedom so they could observe their other son "wasting his life." A direct quote.

We returned to the motel, and Eddie excused himself to get ready for the show. Showers had to be taken, hair begged to be blown dry, outfits were in need of assembly. I volunteered to go down to the lounge while I waited for show time, and Eddie said I'd probably enjoy that more than hanging around the room.

It was an empowering feeling, returning to that divey place by myself, bellying up to the now farmerless bar; ordering the first of what would likely amount to four ginger ales. Little by little, the lounge started to fill up, an equal mix of Holiday Inn guests and local kids in their twenties, ready for a night on the town in the only place that could deliver one. Traction was billed to go on at 8, but at 8:45 or so there was still no sign of Eddie or the rest of the guys. I managed to exchange a few glances with a cute redhead, who'd arrived with maybe five girlfriends. After a few cat-and-mouse volleys, she wandered over to my table to introduce herself.

"Hey, I'm Toni."

"Jimmy."

"Usually, the guy comes over to my table and asks to buy me a drink, but I guess there's a lot of us, and you're kind of shy."

Shy and underage was the truth of it. "I would have come over to you but … I left my ID at home," I explained.

"That won't be a problem, since I have mine." Pulling her license out of her bra, Toni went on to tell me that I would be buying her a vodka tonic, and would I like to buy myself one as well?

"Sure," I said, as the beginning of Independence Week had gone from zero to sixty at warp speed. Still, when Toni held out her hand for the cash, it took me back to the mortifying Makeout Fakeout of 1985, and I began looking around for suspicious linebacker types. There didn't seem to be anybody matching that description, and the last thing I wanted was to come off as a dweeb, so I slapped a ten and a five in her hand. Around 9:15, just as Toni stepped up to the bar, the room went black. Two or three minutes later, the crowd started to murmur, wondering if what they assumed was the start of the show was, in fact, a power outage.

"Jimmy?" I heard Toni's voice shout out.

"I'm over here."

"I have your drink."

Power outage be damned, at least I wasn't getting punked again. "I'm holding out my arm," I told her, reaching around until my hand somehow connected with my drink. "Here's the chair," I instructed, guiding her to the seat next to me. Once Toni sat down, I found myself becoming intoxicated by whatever citrusy scent was emanating from her pores. I leaned in closer, figuring I could always blame an inadvertent head-bump on the dark.

"Cheers," she said, and after two near misses, we managed to clink glasses. Then, after only one near-miss, she kissed me.

In a split second, my priorities changed from desperately wanting to hear my brother's band to hoping the blackout lasted till morning. Having no clue as to when the lights would come on again, Toni and I acted as if we needed to accomplish as much as possible in Dark Time, however long that turned out to be. Deep, hungry kisses, the squeezing of breasts and seizing of crotches, all in what could've been five seconds or five minutes. Suddenly I felt Toni pull away. She dropped to the floor, unzipped my fly and set to work. Independence Week, Day One, had veered off the track and was now bound for the stratosphere. As much as I wanted to enjoy my good fortune, I was young and nervous. I tried deep breathing, which did the trick until my eighth or ninth inhale—when the stage lights came up. Toni jumped back to her seat and we both tried our best to compose ourselves. It turned out not to matter because nobody was interested in us anyway. All eyes were on Gene, who had launched into the opening chords of "Should I Stay or Should I Go?" Seconds later, Toni was up out of her chair, bouncing to the beat, and looking at me on the line: "you're happy when I'm on my knees."

It might have been a tiny room in Nowheresville, but to the Bixby crowd, this was the Roxy and the Bottom Line and the Fillmore all rolled into one. Gene took total command of the stage, and Eddie made him look even better, adding power chords, arpeggios—whatever managed to convey maximum energy without coming off showy. From what I could tell, the bass player and drummer didn't have a fraction of Eddie's talent or Gene's charisma. Their playing was serviceable enough, but they were poseurs. The crowd didn't seem to care as the band uncorked one pulsating delight after the next ("Addicted to Love," "Jump," "Vicious"), the adrenaline pumping faster with each successive tune. Then, just as the night looked as if it had peaked, Traction took it to the next level, dipping into the punk catalog. Eddie sang lead on the Dead Kennedys' "Too Drunk to Fuck," without ever uttering the f-word himself. He left that to the crowd, which gobbled up the bait.

Two hours went by in what seemed like twenty minutes, but the best was yet to come. Gene launched into the finale, a Ramones medley that started with "The KKK Took My Baby Away," and closed with a sick cover of "Blitzkrieg Bop." As the band took their bows, the crowd gave them a standing O, and Toni took advantage of the moment to give me a giant hug. We were several vodkas in by then, but she seemed a lot further gone, perhaps having gotten a head start earlier in the evening. "I loved that band so much," she said, her voice sounding grief-stricken at the thought of never seeing Traction again.

"They're the best," I said. "Wanna meet them?"

"You know these guys?" Toni sprang to full attention at the prospect.

"The lead guitarist is my brother. I'm sure there's gonna be a party after."

"Omigod, you're amazing." Toni's kiss was so intense, I wondered if it might be yet another portal to the beyond.

While I helped Eddie and the band break down the gear, Toni and her friends hung out in the bar, continuing to knock back cocktails. An hour and a half later, the whole bunch of us were hanging in Gene's room, which he shared with the bass player, a quiet, Bill Wyman-type who, for reasons I had yet to learn, went by the name "Spoon." Toni now seemed less interested in ushering me through uncharted portals than in getting to know the members of Traction. Much to her delight, Eddie was blasting Hüsker Du's "Celebrated Summer" on the boombox, and drummer Larry Lizzardo (né Kantrowitz) earned her applause when he announced that it was "party time." Although Eddie had prepped me for the nightly bacchanals of the road, I was nevertheless confused when Spoon whipped out what looked like a light bulb and a steel scrubber, not unlike the one our mother used to do the dishes.

My brother shot Spoon a disapproving look. "Can we not do this tonight, please?"

"You don't have to. Nobody does, unless they want to. Anybody?"

Lizzardo and the girls were eager to join in. The light bulb turned out to be a crack pipe, the scrubber, its filter.

Eddie told me to go back to his room. He needed to stay to make sure things didn't get out of hand. I told him I wanted to hang just a little while, since I was the one who had invited Toni and her friends. I was curious to see how the evening would play out, and if Toni would revisit the enterprise she'd initiated in the hallowed dark.

In addition to DIY crack opportunities, the room was fully stocked with all manner of alcohol and weed. This crowd was not only up to the challenge but would leave no trace. Spoon, Lizzardo and the girls chugged Wild Turkey in between hits, until a couple of them looked as if they were about to pass out. Somehow, they pressed on. I got up the nerve and went over to Toni to ask how she was doing, but rather than answer my question, she stood up, walked right past me, and planted her mouth on Gene's. Once she began heading in a southerly direction, I turned away, only to find Toni's friend, Robin, sitting on my brother's lap, and Spoon and Lizzardo starting to peel articles of clothing off the other girls. As things continued to get hotter, Eddie kept one eye on the groupies and the other on me, until I finally gave up on Toni and headed back to his room. Naturally, it hurt to get tossed aside on what had promised to be a triumphant first night of freedom, but a part of me understood. Toni was older, plus these guys had already invested the time and done the work. They were the band.

Was it really like this every night? I had to wonder. I wasn't crazy about the getting-wasted part, but the rest of it sure beat filling out 1040 forms with Bob Snell. I also knew that with my beginner's musical skills, it would be an arduous climb to get anywhere near the level I needed to be. Yet despite the odds, in that moment, I, Jimmy Kozlowski, the brother from the lower bunk, made a vow to work my ass off, become a real bass player, and maybe somewhere down the line, find a Toni who would walk past another guy to be with me.

GOOD EVENING, CEDARHURST

One night, stinking of Jack Daniels and about to play a casino gig in the bowels of South Jersey, I cornered a bunch of Red Hat ladies and begged them to see a Barry Manilow impersonator rather than the genuine article. The startled posse reacted with indignation and fright, both of which increased as I shadowed their synchronized waddle out of the buffet. But I was not to be deterred, as I had a compelling, sour mash whiskey-infused case to make that went beyond the obvious cost savings. Before they could pop their Tums, I looked them in the trifocals and explained why my approach was the only humane choice. "Ladies, we must remember that the Tribute Barry is just trying to make an honest living. The real dude willfully started that shit."

As airtight as the logic seemed at the time, my life up till that point had yet to be graced by the schmaltz-laden stylings of Manilow mimic Wayne Weinberg, whose wretched "Mandy" is oozing its way through the bar and underneath the crack of a tightly closed office door. On the other side, I sit with three other grown men in suits and wigs, stuffed in a glorified closet that reeks of sweat, stale cigar smoke, and bad Chinese takeout, replete with gaseous fallout.

The now legendary Gene Klein is mouthing the words to our set opener while his right knee convulses as if it's been electrocuted. The leg generally starts shaking about twelve minutes before he goes to work, and Gene-o's been at this for over fifty years. He calls it "Rock 'n' roll Parkinson's" and "part of his process," a regimen that also seems to include nitpicking perceived flaws in his fellow band members, moments before they take the stage.

Mikey's suit is too wrinkled. Prem's boots aren't shiny enough. I look like my mind is elsewhere.

"I didn't have to hire you, Jimmy," Gene loves to remind me.

For some reason, it never occurs to him that I didn't have to accept, that maybe I had higher aspirations than spending my evenings playing to beer drunks in a former titty bar that was more prestigious in its previous incarnation. But I shut my mouth because Gene is right. My mind *is* elsewhere, and these gigs are his life. He's almost two decades older than I am which, in rock 'n' roll years, makes him a corpse, minus the monied cadavery of a Jagger or McCartney. Yet despite being a Medicare recipient with twenty-five extra pounds and a squinty facial tic, the dude kicks ass. He hasn't lost a step vocally, his guitar playing is sweeter and more confident than ever; his onstage presence as assured as when he won his first talent show at age eight. From schoolboy to card-carrying AARP member, Gene Klein has invested his entire being in doing the only thing he was ever any good at—playing the gutsiest rock and roll he can summon. As a result, whenever one of his players gets sick of being insulted or micromanaged and quits the band, there is always an eager replacement waiting in the wings.

Wayne is midway through his bloated "Copacabana" finish when Gene turns to me and asks who else I'm working with these days. He knows I play with other bands and musicians and have a non-music shit-job to boot. Like most of my fellow tradesmen, I have no choice. I tell him I'm backing up a couple of singer-songwriters, filling in for other bass-player friends who have other gigs, and continuing to write original material. He registers a wistful smile when he hears about my writing, perhaps flashing back a half-century when he was sure he'd be composing hits of his own someday. Gene is living proof of how dreams get reconfigured, his vision of playing stadium shows now downsized to match his dive-bar reality. The way I look at it, he's still ahead of the game because, regardless of what never came to be, the man is doing what he loves, night in and night out.

Wayne finishes to a limp smattering of applause, indicating a less-than-full house. The good news is that he has been singing to pre-recorded tracks, so there won't be the usual wait to swap out gear before we go on. In a matter of minutes, club owner Carmine Coconato will introduce us, and the night will play out as the gods intended.

"Good evening, Cedarhurst!" Carmine shouts into the mic.

"This is Glen Cove, ya mook!" one of the patrons shouts back.

"Whaddya know?" Carmine barks. "We got one guy who's still sober!"

It's the man's go-to line, and the regulars are aware he expects a laugh. They graciously oblige.

"Well, you're in for a real treat tonight," he continues. "I can't think of a better way to finish off Hump Day … except for actual humping."

This draws two hoots and a half-holler.

"Maybe some of you are having a rough week at work, maybe you caught one of your kids swiping your weed, whatever. The point is, ladies and gentlemen, 'Help!' is on the way!"

And with that, two middle-aged men and two senior citizens pour out of the fart-clouded office and onto the small stage. Mikey takes his place behind the drums, I plug in my bass, and with the opening cry of "Help!" Gene morphs into a transcendent John Lennon. Patrons start to emerge from their "Mandy"-induced stupor. I egg them on, serving up my cute Paul smile and bouncing like a twenty-something bobblehead. The McCartney moves used to make me feel geeky and stupid, but I've grown to accept them as benign tools of the trade. Mikey, for his part, has the Ringo nod down pat and seems much happier since Gene agreed to let him play without the prosthetic nose. It is our Quiet Beatle who restores the crowd to full consciousness with the signature descending guitar run in the chorus. The sixth George in the storied history of the Help! tribute band, Prem Choudhary was born and raised in a small village twenty miles outside of Mumbai, and didn't set foot on American soil until the year 2000. While other tribute bands blanched at signing a GOC (George of Color), Gene Klein had the acumen to recognize "hiring Indian" as a pure Harrisonian move. What better way to honor the icon who introduced the sitar and tablas to American pop music than poach from the culture he had embraced with such fervor? Sure, it might invite the occasional purist (read racist) to heckle a dark-skinned Beatle, but the overriding factor was that this Indian mop top had the goods. Gene would never dare to say the words aloud, but it was not lost on him that Prem owned his lead on "While My Guitar Gently Weeps," while the real George had subcontracted his to Clapton. Gene's only real complaint with the Hindu guitarist, other than his lackadaisical attitude toward properly shined Beatle boots, was that he sometimes smelled of curry, one of Gene's allergy-inflaming archenemies.

Is Help! the best Beatles tribute band in rock 'n' roll history? Probably not. There's a European tribute band (also called Help!) whose "Eleanor Rigby" makes me want to bury ours. The more pertinent question is: are we the best Beatle band playing at ten o'clock on a Wednesday night in a Long Island strip mall? The guy who runs the falafel joint seems to think so.

As Prem and I harmonize with Gene on the "Help!" chorus, I notice a pretty, forty-something blonde checking me out. I know the whole flirting deal comes with being a Paul, but I'm not too far from fifty, which seems a little old to play the cute Beatle unless you're the actual McCartney—

who's earned the privilege of looking like somebody's hip grandma. I make a mental note that the blonde is drinking white wine rather than beer or a cocktail, and that it's been a while since I've attracted a groupie who wasn't knocking back Jägerbombs. There's something comforting in this. I'm looking forward to seeing her reaction to the next tune, where I take the lead vocal.

There appear to be sixty or so people scattered about the room, some of whom are regular Help! fans, and a whole bunch I don't recognize. The age range at our shows varies from the sixty-somethings who went to high school with Gene, to people in their twenties whose parents or grandparents loved the music, to the multi-generational flotsam who'd sit through a Hootie and the Blowfish tribute if there was well vodka. Our biggest fan happens to be a frail, eighty-nine-year-old. She (accompanied by her caregiver) occupies a corner booth at every one of our performances, and never fails to cast a beatific smile in Gene's direction. Gene returns the favor, grateful for the unconditional support of his loving mother, Marcia Klein. As we finish our "Help!" anthem, Marcia attempts to rise for a standing ovation, but is tamped back down for safety reasons by the caregiver.

At this point Gene welcomes the crowd in a thick Liverpool accent. Amazingly, it's not that awful, considering his normal speech lands somewhere between Judge Judy and a Queens cabbie who bought his medallion in 1965. "For our next number, I'd like to ask for a bit o' help. The people in the cheaper seats, clap your hands … and the rest of you, if you'll just rattle your jewelry …"

This yields mild laughter from the two patrons who recognize the John Lennon line from the Beatles' Royal Command Performance for the Queen Mother and Princess Margaret. Gene doesn't care if his patter is too inside baseball. He views it as essential history and part of the fun.

"Our next number will be sung by Paul. You'll remember it as the B-side of the "Elp!' single, which is from our second film, entitled …"

Gene cups his ear, waiting for the crowd to respond.

Marcia's caregiver, Lupe, shouts "Help!" She's been through Gene's basic training.

"That one knows her onions." Gene smiles. He looks over to give me the signal. "Paul?"

I love the first line of "I'm Down" because I get to belt it pretty much a cappella.

"You tell lies thinking I can't see; you can't cry 'cause you're laughing at me …"

It's me channeling Paul channeling Little Richard. I get to smile, wink, and howl at the blonde who's now on her second Chardonnay. I loosen up fast, unconcerned that I might be pushing too hard, or ignoring some of the other Paul fans in the house. In these moments, I get why Gene loves what he does. With all the shitty places real life takes us, when we're on this stage, singing these songs, the music never lets us down. Never. Even if we're playing "Taxman" to an audience of three, it's still fucking "Taxman," and nobody

27

can make it any less brilliant than it is—well, except Perry Parker from the Ronkonkoma Beatles, universally regarded as the worst of the grade-D Long Island tribute bands.

The further I get into "I'm Down," the more irresistible the Chardonnay blonde looks to me. My adrenaline has converted an amiable-looking possibility into a must-have sex partner who, I'm now convinced, cannot wait to strip off my Hofner bass. As I scream my way to the end, the object of my cuteness claps wildly. I finish it off with a wink, just for her.

Now it's "Taxman" time. Prem routinely nails the shit out of this one, but tonight he'll have to wait a few minutes to get started because Gene has written a special introduction to be delivered in his finest Liverpudlian. This is his first time trying out the new material.

"Next up we're going to hear from the Quiet Beatle. This is a song George wrote one day when we were suddenly in the green, y'know, and he couldn't believe how much we were handin' over to the government. The Labour Party slapped us with a 95% supertax, y'know, which wasn't gear at all. So, George called me and Paul into the studio, y'know—"

"We know!" shouts a three-hundred-pound beer guzzler in an Anthrax T-shirt. "Just play fucking 'Taxman'!"

Gene is taken aback, yet not enough to alter, much less forgo, his prepared text. He has an intro to finish. "As I was about to say, Paul did the guitar solo, I threw in some of me one-liners—"

The Anthrax guy isn't having it. "You didn't do shit, asshole. You're not John Lennon. You're a Jewish dude from Long Island—"

"And you're daft," Gene shoots back, refusing to break character.

"Fuck you, Klein." The big man starts to rush the stage, at which point Mikey leaps out from behind his drum kit to flash peace signs with both hands, while Prem offers multiple "namastes." Their well-meaning gestures have no effect on the approaching behemoth who seems intent on strangling Gene.

The caregiver moves to shield Marcia's eyes from what is about to be inflicted on her son. Then, just as Gene's vocal cords are about to be permanently retired, Carmine and his bouncer burst forth wielding matching taser guns. Several epithets later, Anthrax Man capitulates. As the bouncer escorts him out of the bar, Carmine corners Gene, informing him that "a little Liverpool goes a long way." Gene responds with a shrug, then turns into the mic and counts down: "1-2-3-4-1-2," Prem's signal to rip into "Taxman."

As always, the Mumbai native's rendition is a wonder to behold, Gene's minor quibble being that since Indians pronounce their w's as v's, it reduces the powerful last line to "you're vurking for no one but me." The show proceeds to our "Let it Be" finale without further incident.

On a scale of one to ten, I give the evening an eight. Musically, we killed it, but two points must be deducted for the unremarkable crowd size, and perhaps the first-ever attempted assault provoked by a fake John Lennon accent.

Mostly, I'm happy that Marcia Klein didn't have to see her son leave the building in a body bag.

Once my wig and suit are off, I head back to the stage to start packing up my stuff. I look up to see my boss giving his mom a big hug. Even though Gene Klein has zero chance of ever becoming a star, he will be treated like one as long as Marcia has breath left to give. I unplug my amp, wondering how much longer that might be, when I suddenly feel a soft tap on my shoulder. It's the Chardonnay blonde, whom I somehow lost track of after the near brawl. "Oh hey," I nod, trying to act nonchalant, as the real Paul undoubtedly would.

"Hey. I'm Amy."

"The wine drinker."

"You noticed."

"I'm the Observant Beatle, not just the cute one."

Amy smiles.

"James Kozlowski." I extend my hand and she shakes it stiffly.

"Also, the Formal Beatle. Very classy. I really enjoyed the show."

"Thanks. First time?"

"Yep. You guys are a lot better than that band from the Five Towns. What's their name?" she asks, tapping the recesses of her alcohol-addled brain.

"Norwegian Woodmere?"

"That's it. Their Paul was my chemistry teacher in high school. His 'Yesterday' is even more boring than his compounding labs."

"'Yesterday' isn't an easy one to pull off," I respond, opting to go the magnanimous route.

"You know, James—"

"Call me Jimmy."

"Okay. The whole time I was watching you—Jimmy—I kept thinking—"

"Maybe I was thinking the same thing." I smile.

"You look really familiar to me. I've never seen the band before, so it's got to be from somewhere else."

"I play all over with a lot of different groups."

"Maybe it was at a party."

"Sometimes I get called to play weddings—"

"Only one I've been to in a while was my sister's."

"Where was it? What kind of band?"

"Old Westbury. She didn't have a live band though. Just a DJ."

"Wasn't me then. Old Westbury, huh? I hate when people with that kind of dough hire a musician-killer instead of the real thing. No offense to your sister."

"None taken. It's not that she's cheap, by the way. The DJ she got is a house music heavyweight. Even did a couple of those Electric Daisy things in California. There were like three hundred people at this wedding. Amazing food, killer bar, trailers just for bathrooms—"

Now I know where she's seen me. The details are somewhat embarrassing, but it's a good bet she won't remember any of them.

"You okay?" Amy asks. "You look kind of funny all of a sudden."

"I'm fine. It's just, you know, the DJ thing is a sore point for people who do what I do."

"I'm sorry. I wish I hadn't said anything."

"It's fine, really. I'd better pack up this stuff. You can hang while I do it, if you want."

"I'm not going anywhere," she says, smiling.

We've been at this exact place before. She just doesn't know it.

WHEN JIMMY MET AMY

Back in the spring, Gene had wangled us a public parks date playing for the lawn-chair crowd at the Town of North Hempstead Mayday Madness, one of those gigs where the audience doesn't expect you to be any good because they got in for free. Even though we get paid for our work and people eventually discover that we *are* good, the mindset never wavers from: "Only a band of losers or middle-schoolers would stoop this low." Gene's standard response to such logic is to shake up the setlist at the last minute, which in this case meant dumping the "Let It Be" finale and having Ringo, a.k.a Mikey Ianucci, close with a song we hadn't done in five years: "I Wanna Be Your Man." Mikey wasn't thrilled with the switch, but acquitted himself admirably, despite having to sing through the rubberized schnoz Gene purchased at the 99 Cents Store. Once the show came to its merciful end, Mikey let out a huge sigh and told me how happy he was to have a day job.

Monday through Friday, Mikey runs Rest Easy, the service company built from scratch by his Sicilian immigrant father, Salvatore. For nearly half a century, the Ianucci clan has prided itself on being Long Island's premier supplier of construction site porta-potties, as well as luxury mobile facilities for corporate events and private outdoor galas. A few years back, Mikey asked if I'd be interested in picking up some extra cash delivering and monitoring "waste stations," as he likes to call them. After processing the fact that my responsibilities would include high-powered excrement removal, I realized that this was, in fact, the perfect side gig for me. My dad, the long-suffering bandleader, Lou Kozlowski, always told me to get a real job and play music for fun, but I couldn't handle a demanding career, plus the hours I needed to practice and hone my craft. If I wanted to be a great player, I'd have to subsidize my income in the most mindless way possible. What could be more ideal than the one profession that would never tempt me to leave music? Through sheer luck, I'd found a shit job that was literally … a shit job.

As the Mayday Madness crowd lumbered back to their cars, Mikey asked if I wanted to work an affair the following Saturday. It was in Old Westbury, and called for three "honey wagons," industry slang for fancy crappers on wheels. I immediately signed on, knowing I would make at least three times more than I did at the depressing park show. It would also be a nice change from having to wear the hot wig and sing "I Saw Her Standing There" to people who are either too lazy to stand, or too obese to try.

The bottom line is that the first time Amy laid eyes on my fabness, I was in Rest Easy coveralls, pumping a hundred pounds of fecal sludge through industrial hosing. It was probably around 2:00 a.m., and I remember telling her that we were packing up, so she needed to use the facilities in the house. She must have been pretty drunk because she hung around a while to watch me do my thing before going off to do hers. I guess I thought she was kind of cute, but how do you even begin to close the deal with a woman while siphoning gargantuan quantities of shit?

Here in Glen Cove, it's once again close to 2:00 a.m., and, thanks to the forty-five minutes spent in Carmine's office, I smell only slightly better than I did that night in Old Westbury. Amy doesn't seem to mind, though, and suggests we go somewhere to hang.

"You don't have to work in the morning?" I ask.

"That depends on how much insurance I want to sell. Who knows? Maybe I'll sell some tonight."

"So, you're hustling me?"

"Yes. But not for insurance."

"You put it all out there, don't you?"

Amy nods. "Doesn't always work out. I scared the crap out of Greg Agababian."

"Agababian? Isn't he the Armenian Paul from Eight Days a Week?"

"Uh-huh. Great bass player. But, to paraphrase John, his ticket ain't much of a ride."

I now realize that what's happening here is anything but a standard hookup. "Amy, are you into trying out different Pauls and comparing them?"

"Not every Paul. I mean, doing my former chemistry teacher would be like necrophilia. And it's slim pickins' when it comes to the Suffolk County McCartneys."

"I've got to say, you're not like most of the groupies who come around."

"You think I'm a groupie?" she snaps, either hurt, insulted, or both.

"Maybe that's the wrong word—"

"I happen to love the Beatles' music, especially Paul's. And I would guess that the people who play Paul have a similar affinity for his body of work."

"Okay—"

"So, you tell me, who do I have a better shot of connecting with? Those guys, or one more schmuck I meet on Match.com?"

It's a fair point. Like most everybody else, I tend to pigeonhole people because it's a lot less work than taking the time to explore who they really are. I decide to keep an open mind with Amy and see where the rest of the night takes us. "So, where do you want to go?"

"Home," she says. "I called an Uber."

"I have my car. Should I follow you?"

"Not unless you want to get the police involved."

"I thought—"

"You're an asshole, Jimmy. I don't care if your 'Here, There, and Everywhere' got a special mention in the *Williston Park News*. The real Paul would be sickened by your assumptions about women."

"I didn't mean anything by the groupie comment—"

"You should have thought of that before you opened your mouth. I could've been your Linda goddamn Eastman, for Chrissake. But we'll never know, will we?"

And off she goes to meet her Uber driver. It's a very weird thing being a fake Beatle, especially when you realize you've been doing this longer than any of the real ones ever did.

THE TERMS

I step out into the drizzly North Shore night to load up my Honda for the short drive to Albertson, a 0.7-square-mile suburb, one of fifty hamlets comprising the fifty-three-square-mile Town of North Hempstead, New York. It's kind of a weird place to be from because the mini-communities all blend into one another. Few have anything resembling a downtown, and, with as many as twelve hamlets to a single school district, kids grow up with little sense of hometown identity, or a desire to put down roots. Most of my high school buds went off to college and never came back, but there are still a few of us left. (Gene, Mikey, and me for starters.) We're only about eighteen miles from Manhattan, but good luck trying to pay the rent there, or anywhere in the city, for that matter. I'm lucky to have my basement apartment in Bill and Jan Girardi's little Cape Cod place off Willets Road. Bill was best friends with my brother, and I'm pretty sure he rents to me as a way of keeping some part of Eddie in his life. I'm grateful for that, as well as being allowed to adopt my rescue cat, Jaco.

Since it's such a cramped space and I own a lot of equipment, I have to make sure things are super organized to keep from feeling boxed in. Only after bass, amp, and pedalboards get returned to their rightful places do I allow myself to chill on the sofa with Jaco. It's not luxury living by a long shot, but that's by design. Small, inexpensive digs, an animal instead of a partner, a cat instead of a dog—these are the articles of containment I've deemed necessary to survive as a musician in today's world. The excesses of the past have been swapped out for proletariat resolve. No drugs for this modern-day rocker. A worker bee can't afford them. Sure, I'd like a bigger place, but the way I look at it, everybody has to make compromises in life. You weigh the middling versus the soul-crushing and cast your lot accordingly. The basement may be a little damp, and low on natural light, but it's quiet and peaceful, especially once the rest of the hamlet goes to sleep.

Like his namesake, the bass master Pastorious, Jaco can be an asshole at times, but that holds true of everyone I've ever lived with. In the grand scheme of things, I've had litter box turds kicked across my floor fewer times than I've had my wallet emptied for coke money. And tonight, the little bugger is golden, his purrs seeping into my brain like melatonin. I can feel my eyes start to close and am prepared to fall asleep in my T-shirt and jeans rather than disturb the blessed calm.

Tranquility is fleeting, as the stillness is broken by the ringtone on my phone. I look at the screen and see it's Gene, the one person I know who never seems to sleep and presumes nobody else does either. I consider not picking up ... but what if it's an emergency?

"Hey, man, what's going on?" I whisper, hoping the muffled voice conveys my wish to keep the conversation brief.

"Nothing much," he says. "Just wondering what you thought."

The postmortem call. Gene needs to recap every performance, and I'm his sounding board. He used to wait till the next day, but lately he can't seem to live without immediate feedback.

"I thought we were great, Gene. Really solid."

"You don't think the audience was distracted by the heckling?"

"It was one guy. And most people were too drunk to give a shit."

"Maybe we weren't doing enough to connect with the audience."

"Some things are out of our control. We just have to be the best musicians we can be."

"That's not enough," Gene scolds. "The Beatles were way more than good musicians."

I want to remind him that we're *fake* Beatles, and that while the bar needn't be set to rock bottom, neither should it be unattainable. I know this is the last thing he wants to hear, so I pivot. "How's your mom?"

"Marcia's good. She thought you could've smiled more on 'I'm Down,' incidentally."

"Gene. If I'm down, and I'm *really* down like the song says, why would I smile?"

"Because you're Paul," Gene reminds me. "Paul smiles."

The critique, of course, has nothing to do with his mother. This is Gene being Gene: not particularly pleasant during business hours, balls-out excruciating at two forty-five in the morning. I need to end this conversation ASAP.

"Tell Marcia 'thanks.' I'll act less down the next time I sing 'I'm Down.'"

"I don't know. Sounds like lip service—"

"It's the best I can do at the moment. Unless you want me to come over, wake up your mother and her caregiver, and sing it to them right now."

"The caregiver doesn't sleep when my mother sleeps, just so you know, and that won't be necessary. Don't forget. It's almost time to order our new Beatle boots, so I'll need a check."

"I'll give it to you next week; I promise. JP Murphy's, Tuesday night, right?"

"Right. So, Jimmy, what would you think about doing a UK tour?"

"Sounds awesome. I'm in."

"I'll get to work on it. See you Tuesday."

After Gene hangs up, I realize that this is the third or fourth time he's brought up a prospective UK tour. I always tell him it's a great idea, even though there's no way it will ever come to pass. First off, he won't leave his mom, who's not allowed to fly, and, secondly, who in England is clamoring to pay hotel and airfare for a Grade-B Beatles Tribute band from Long Island? The strangest part of it is that every time Gene brings up the tour, he acts as if it's something he's just thought of in the moment.

In addition to having grown quirkier over time, Gene has gotten more intense in his commitment to the band. Help! has evolved into his tribute religion. I, on the other hand, am on the verge of becoming a lapsed Paul. As much as I love the two-hundred or so songs the Beatles officially recorded, Help!'s been playing the same eighty for the last ten years, and I'd welcome a break. I'd probably hang it up entirely if Gene and I didn't go back over four decades. Somewhere along the line, I became the accidental consigliere, a position of vital importance in his world.

My world, on the other hand, would have no trouble weathering the breakup, and might well improve as a result of having more time for my own projects. It's not like I owe Gene undying loyalty or anything. If you take one look at the history, you'd wonder why I have anything to do with the man. Gene Klein was the only person my father actively despised, his dying regret having been that he didn't get to see "the fuck-up," as he had dubbed Gene, buy the farm before he did. Lou's logic was that since the fuck-up had been a magnet for every casualty rock 'n' roll had to offer, there was no justice in his having emerged unscathed. Dad couldn't see that Gene had been wounded plenty. Or maybe he could, but didn't feel the wounds were big enough, or cut as deep as Gene's transgressions warranted.

My take is different. What Lou perceived to be narcissistic and evil, I recognize as damaged and vulnerable. And even though I'm in no way obligated to be Gene's therapist or babysitter, the essence of who he is speaks to me on an elemental level. How could I not be moved by someone who lives for music and *on* music, knowing how fragile that bargain is should any part of the arrangement breakdown. In a way, it's like I'm waiting for a horrible train wreck I hope never happens, knowing full well that in rock 'n' roll, the odds of a collision are right up there with death and taxes.

A DAY IN THE LIFE

I'm not a big morning person, but since most of my workdays don't start before happy hour, I set aside time between 10 a.m. and 1 p.m. for writing and laying down scratch tracks. A musical bonus of our digital world is that you can have a studio in your laptop and record a bunch of songs on your phone before you even get out of bed. The many downsides come later, when you need to refine the songs for the album, have to scrape to pay other musicians to play on it, and then, God forbid, try to break even on the thing. At my age, I have no illusions about being discovered and becoming an overnight sensation. I never really expected it when I was younger, so at least my dreams didn't have to go through a drastic reinvention like Gene's. Yet, even with diminished expectations, they still seem as far away from being realized as they did when I was eighteen.

The goal has always been to record at least one album of kickass original tunes—original, not merely because I wrote them, but in the sense of not sounding like everything else that came before. Given the amount of music that pre-dates me, and the availability of it on every streaming service, this is a tall order. How do you turn heads when the complete catalog of every brilliant artist is a swipe away? The other obstacle is "supporting player syndrome." When the majority of your work is for someone else's team, you develop the self-image of a journeyman, which makes you question if you have the ability to create something of your own. I've learned to clear these stifling thoughts from my head because otherwise I'd never finish a measure or write a word. Whatever the odds, I'm not ready to admit that my career has peaked with Cute Paul.

The past few mornings, it's just been a pad, a pencil, and an acoustic guitar. I'm trying to come up with the right lyrics for the bridge to a song called "SSRI," a sonically punk-ish, lyrically Randy Newman-ish tale of a Neo-Nazi who realizes the error of his ways thanks to Prozac. Suffice it to say, I don't know of anybody else out there who's rhyming "shameless, evil white-trash exhibitor" with "Selective Serotonin Reuptake Inhibitor." Whether it's genius or career suicide, nobody will ever confuse me with Ed Sheeran. I start to contemplate how I might work "Mengele" into the chorus when the phone rings. Gene's calling again, but this time I won't pick up. The antidote to neediness is setting boundaries, and, with Gene, voicemail is my first line of defense. He doesn't like texting or email because he thinks they're too impersonal, yet he refuses to understand that most business doesn't need to *get* personal.

I come up with the idea for a descending bass line to connect the chorus with the bridge, but halfway through my first pass, the phone chimes again. It's a text from Prem saying he's done with Gene and wants out of the band. Against my better judgment, I go back and listen to Gene's voicemail, a slow-burning rant that begins with how ungrateful some people can be, and ends with the assertion that India should return to British Rule. As usual, I must determine how serious today's squabbling is and whether I need to get involved. On paper, these guys are more than able to navigate their own paths. Prem and Mikey both make enough money to tell Gene to piss off, and, in fact, do so on a regular basis, but some intangible always seems to call them back to the wigs and Nehru jackets. Gene, without question, is a piece of work, capable of sending anybody off a cliff at any moment. Challenging the legitimacy of India's independence could be the last straw.

I text Prem, who writes back that he's in a meeting—probably discussing the 140-million-dollar defense contract his engineering firm has just landed. He does, however, manage to text that he has no more time for Gene and his bullshit, but would love to discuss other musical opportunities with me at some point. I tell him to give it a night before making his final decision. He doesn't text back.

Having already dipped my toe in fetid Help! waters, I expose myself further by calling Gene. Before I get two words out, he's commanding me to be at his house in an hour to meet with a new George. He says he's close to poaching Dennis O'Malley from the Brian Epstein Massacre, a relative newcomer to the Beatles tribute scene. I inform him that I have other plans today and, more importantly, that O'Malley's chops are light years away from Prem's, which is the God's-honest truth. Gene tries to sell me (and himself) on how O'Malley working with us will up his game. I counter that there may not be much of an "us" left without Prem. Mikey is tired of the revolving-door Georges and, frankly, so am I.

"You're saying you'll quit if I lose Tommy Tandoori?"

"His name is Prem and, based on what you just called him, I should leave whether he goes or not."

"Excuse me. I hired you to be the cute Beatle, not the PC one. And I didn't have to hire you in the first place."

"Maybe it would have been better that way," is what slips out of my mouth.

Control freaks like Gene are not big fans of insubordination, so the hint of a full-on insurrection doesn't sit well at all. "I can replace the three of you this afternoon."

"If that's what you want, go for it. No hard feelings."

"What I want is a little support from my brothers."

After his barrage of haranguing and insults, he plays the family card, one more infuriating salvo from the twisted psyche of Gene Klein. This time, though, he's out-harangued himself and given me the perfect opening.

"I agree that a great band is a band of brothers," I say.

"Of course it is. The Beatles. From the beginning through *Pepper.*"

"Here's the thing, Gene. Who was the oldest brother?"

"John, of course."

"Then you know that as the oldest brother, it's up to you to set an example for the rest of us."

This is met with a long pause on the other end.

"Gene? You still there?"

"Why can't an Indian learn how to say his fucking W's?"

"Again? You have got to lay off the pronunciation shit."

"That's what he said. And that I shouldn't have signed him up for an English class without his permission."

"What? The guy has a full-time job. Besides, everyone understands what he's saying. I think he's doing great."

"Fine. I'll call him and work things out."

"Thank you. I'll see you Tuesday night."

"Just one more thing. I need your opinion."

"What, Gene?"

"Doesn't it bother you that Mikey's nose is too small?"

"I'm hanging up now. Say hi to Marcia."

Another crisis averted. Unfortunately, my concentration is now shot and I'm out of writing mode for the rest of the morning. I'll practice a little bass and record the line I came up with for later noodling. Then maybe some lunch, a little catnip time with Jaco, and it's off to the next gig.

The Pineview Nursing Facility is twenty miles east in the Suffolk County hamlet of Dix Hills, former home to the Secatogue Indians, John Coltrane, 50 Cent, and Lou Kozlowski in his declining years. Three times a week, I made the pilgrimage to Pineview to visit my dad, bearing witness to his gradual loss of words before the ultimate descent into silence. Seeing the former accordion player and bandleader, who must have emceed close to three thousand weddings, involuntarily transform into a Benedictine monk bordered on the surreal. But as unjust a hand as Lou had been dealt, what sent me over the edge was the spectacle of seeing him treated like a three-year-old.

Nowhere was this more apparent than during "activity time," when the less-than-industrious aides whipped out the jigsaw puzzles recommended for "Ages 3 and Up," and, on Thursday afternoons, when a middle-aged acoustic guitar player named Ricky stopped by to serenade the mostly unresponsive residents. Ricky always opened his act with the "Hello Song," an insipid, toddleresque roll call during which he'd greet each person by name and ask the others to wave to the recipient of the individual "hello." From there he'd segue into "The Alphabet Song," his "A-B-C-D-E-F-G" as torturous as giant nails on a blackboard, a sound scientists determined to be the same frequency as a human scream.

After Lou's death, I made it my mission to go gunning for Ricky's job, a curious pursuit in that unpaid volunteerism would not generally be described as a cutthroat business. I believed this to be a special circumstance, however, as Ricky's performances insulted me across multiple platforms. As a musician, I was horrified that his singing voice could be as off-key as his cheap, out-of-tune guitar. As the son of a dementia patient, I believed that addressing the audience as if they were babies, whether they were cognizant of the fact or not, was disrespectful to the contributions these folks had made in their lifetimes. One week after Lou was in the ground, I went storming into the administrator's office to present her with an impassioned plea for human dignity and explain why I deserved the job over Ricky.

Less than halfway into my tirade, Christina Pierce said "okay," which, despite my lack of respect for Ricky, seemed a tad cold. I didn't learn until six months later that Ricky had already given notice in order to take a paying gig on a Carnival cruise ship. I shuddered to think of the poor passengers slogging through the at-sea days, stuffing their faces to the drone of "A-B-C-D-E-F-G." While Ricky surely had a more adult repertoire for such situations, envisioning the damage he'd inflict on actual music was too frightening to consider.

So, what was my take on performing for folks bereft of physical and mental abilities? Christina wanted to know.

"Aim high," I said. "Give them old standards from their youth and you might make a connection to the people they were. Sing them the funniest lyrics, the prettiest melodies, the catchiest, most rhythmic shit you can think of." I didn't actually say "shit" because I wanted the gig, and Christina, a former Certified Nursing Assistant, now had a desk job that encompassed monitoring HR infractions. Nevertheless, I think she responded to my passion. Part-time Activity Room Singer was the kind of job that usually got filled by unemployed do-gooders who brought little sense of urgency to the table. Because I was so much more qualified than my predecessor, I took the liberty of leaving out one detail in my speech to her, figuring she'd never know the difference. My plan, which I've now followed for three years running, was to use these one-hour sessions to beta-test some of my original material. The thinking was that since Christina came from the Philippines, she'd assume the songs were hits in the States that she'd missed, and from my semi-conscious audience's point of view, who could say? The Pineview rec room was a far cry from open mic night at the Bluebird, but it was my chance to play to a crowd that was bigger than Jaco, comatose or not.

Over time, I've come to love the way the vocals sound in this large, open space. Today's setlist begins with a Help! staple, a tune I'd grown tired of playing in bars that took on new meaning here. While the residents don't exactly jump up out of their wheelchairs for "Hello, Goodbye," there are a few smiles and head-nods. And the message is spot on—you may think you want to give up and say goodbye, but I'm here to tell you it's not over, and saying hello.

From there I segue into the 1930s standard, "The Sunny Side of the Street," covered by everybody from Louis Armstrong to Rod Stewart, and, for my money, even more likable than "Hello, Goodbye." After that is when I go rogue, strumming the opening chords of "Angel," the song I wrote for the daughter who doesn't know she's mine. There was an agreement many years ago, but it didn't include a clause barring me from writing about the relationship that might have been. Sometimes I feel myself start to tear up when I perform it, so I always gauge where my head is at before taking the leap.

"You're not an apparition,
Not a superstition,
You're a straight-up first edition ...
An angel and you're mine."

Whenever I sing this verse, it's impossible for me not to imagine what the angel looks like at that moment, as opposed to the way she might have looked the last time I sang it. As I head into the instrumental break, I close my eyes and picture her climbing a jungle gym. Then I remind myself that she's old enough to have graduated college. Relationships are confusing enough, but when they're conjured in a vacuum? Pick your rabbit hole.

I power my way to the third verse, checking the room for some sign that I'm getting through. Ninety-seven-year-old Malcolm never even looks up, his energy focused on petting the stuffed kangaroo he holds in his lap. Violet, an eighty-eight-year-old brain cancer survivor, just stares into space. Neither has spoken in the entire time I've worked here. Nora, a relatively new resident, seems to be nodding to the music, but it could also be Parkinson's.

I go back into the chorus and see a man they call "The Colonel" flashing me a broad grin. I'm gratified that my lyrics have touched somebody, until I realize that they have nothing to do with the man's newfound happiness. His cause for celebration is having executed a long-awaited bowel movement. The Colonel is rushed out of the room by a CNA before the smell grows any fouler. No question, this is the most unique venue I've ever played.

When the song ends, I look up to see Christina standing in the doorway, shooting me an approving smile I'm going to assume has no correlation to bodily functions. Either she thinks "Angel" is an American standard or it's good enough not to matter. Christina is in her late thirties, I think. From what I've gathered, she's married to a much older man who brought her to the states when she was eighteen. She's pretty and smart, certainly smart enough to wait six months before revealing her true motivation for having hired me. I'd like to know more about her, but, then again, I already know more about her than I do about the angel in my song. Maybe I need to write one called "Off Limits," which could apply to most of the people and things I care about.

After saying goodbye to my Pineview fans until next week and hauling Eddie's '68 Gibson Hummingbird out to the car, I appraise the performance as slightly above average, my score elevated by the smile from Christina. Others might count the Colonel's bowel movement as an additional victory, seeing as how it took the music to finally give the man relief, but connecting those dots seems a bit desperate to me. Soon I will be back on the Long Island Expressway, en route to my last commitment of the day. Larry Lizzardo, former drummer of Traction, and current Mortuary Director at Larry's of Bethpage, has a son in the entertainment business who wants to meet with me. I'm not quite sure what it's all about, but after an hour of singing to a phalanx of oxygen machines, I can use an infusion of youthful energy. Larry described Barry as a kid with "a ton of ideas," which usually means there is no money being made, but maybe I'm projecting. After all, what could be a better motivator for success than seeing your father deal burial plots and coffins?

I pull up to the Roslyn Diner in my '89 Civic, watching a well-heeled young couple exit a brand-new S-Class Mercedes and walk through the front door. I always blanch at a scene like this, not to begrudge other people their wealth, but because some part of me wants them to be older before they get it, or at least not show it off till then. The other side of the coin, I suppose, is that couples like this give hope to people like Barry Lizzardo Kantrowitz that they won't wind up like the Old Man in the mortuary. Or me.

I enter the diner as I've done countless times before—with my parents, or Eddie, or high school buddies late at night—but never for an actual meeting which, in this case, will probably amount to giving an enthusiastic kid some friendly but useless advice. I look around for a young Lizzardo, whose father I haven't seen in over ten years. Swarthy and bug-eyed are my guideposts, but nobody seems to fit that description. A moment later, I hear "Mr. Kozlowski?" coming from a booth in the corner. It's the young man with the S500, and his companion, who looks like she's maybe seventeen. She has a laptop in front of her and is typing away.

"Barry?" I ask.

Barry nods, and I go to join them in the booth.

"This is Jenna, my assistant," he says.

The blonde extends her hand to shake. "Nice to meet you, Mr. Kozlowski."

"Jimmy," I say, taking a seat and feeling very, very old.

"So stoked you could make it." Barry smiles, radiating sincerity, and a certain amount of charm.

I tell them I'm happy to be there, though I'm not exactly sure why I've been asked. Jenna enters this response in her laptop. I order a coffee. They each ask for herbal tea, after which Barry launches into a description of their company, Table of Content.

"The name really says it all. We want to generate and acquire massive amounts of content to put out to the universe."

I've never been fond of the word "content" to describe any sort of creative endeavor. For me, it turns music into margarine, film into fiberboard, poetry into polyester. Yet I recognize that this is the new world order. What are the parameters that define "content" anyway?

"We have twenty-six web series in some phase of development," Barry announces. "We're also heavily into internet promotional opportunities and staging interactive mini-plays on Zoom."

Jenna peers over her laptop. "And we just made a first-look deal with Skechers."

"The shoe store?" I have to ask.

Barry nods. "They're getting into streaming original content."

"About shoes?"

Barry explains that Skechers is the advertiser. The footwear powerhouse is seeking online programming that clocks in at six minutes or under, appealing to fourteen- to twenty-two-year-olds. He and Jenna seem quite excited about the possibilities. I make an effort to understand why but come up empty-handed.

"It seems like you've got your business model figured out," I tell them. "I don't think you need any help from me."

Barry begs to differ. "With all the projects we have in the hopper, we're eventually going to be in the position to hire a music director. Somebody we can turn to for cues and riffs, maybe even some original songs. I thought of the guys my dad knew, and you were the first one who came to mind."

I tell Barry I'm flattered, which I kind of am, but every "project" they describe to me sounds like white noise—more unnecessary pollutants to unleash into an already toxic bullshit-sphere. Plus, Mercedes or not, most, if not all, of these grand plans still reside in the aforementioned hopper, which means no money in the short term, and a ridiculously small back end should the music find a streaming home down the line.

I don't verbalize any of this to my hosts. Rather, I suggest they recruit somebody in their demographic who can connect with their target audience. This is my polite way of saying that it takes someone from their age group to divine enthusiasm from what I have come to perceive as the End of Art. The almighty notion of "content" is nothing more than a mask that disguises commerce as enlightenment. It's mega-depressing, an insult to visionaries like Jaco, Dylan, Trane, Yo-Yo Ma; Lennon and McCartney, for God's sake.

We finish our beverages and I wish them the best of luck. Once the Mercedes peels out, I grapple with the likelihood that my curmudgeonly failure to embrace "content" will doom me to living in a basement apartment for the rest of my days. Then I invoke an image twenty years into the future ...

Barry and Jenna's content business has become a multi-million-dollar operation, streaming shit that nobody remembers after the six minutes are up. Meanwhile, Gene Klein, now mid-80s, continues to shuffle from bar to bar, plying his Beat-le-centric trade in scuffed-up boots and a mangy, tattered wig.

At first glance, it's a mighty dismal vision, but things start to brighten once I remind myself that Gene's cheesy getups were never meant to be anything more than window dressing. The mop top paraphernalia is a tool to help him create (or re-create) something of musical and emotional value that has nothing to do with commerce. Twenty years down the line, he is not forgotten because he's still true to his art. Gene Klein wins the future.

NIGHTTIME

After a sorry bowl of microwave pho and some quality time with my low-maintenance pet, I decide to pop into Russo's, an upscale jazz club in Cold Spring Harbor. The vibe is a welcome change from my usual haunts; plus there's nothing like Gershwin to get me out of my own head. Not only do these songs embody the real meaning of "content," but also tonight's performer, Tracy Marks, is one of the select few who's worthy of them. Tracy's an exceptional singer and actress, yet, despite having landed a couple of respectable roles on Broadway, she's virtually unknown outside the Long Island area. In this business, you can win a Grammy one year, and the next find yourself bussing half-eaten plates of jalapeño poppers. Tracy is a few months shy of her forty-fifth birthday and has already racked up accomplishments that include beating ovarian cancer, raising a daughter by herself, and reducing grown men to tears with a gut-wrenching mezzo soprano. She also dated me for a while, but we went back to being friends, mostly because I couldn't get past being intimidated by her massive talent.

Russo's has never been known for its booming amplification, but Tracy's voice carries almost a full block beyond the restaurant. It's not so much the volume that hits you, as the clarity. In my world, that kind of power beats every triple-stacked Marshall at a Metallica show.

I walk in, happy to see the tables filled, as well as an empty stool waiting for me at the bar. Since the high-end cocktail scene is at least two tax brackets above mine, my MO at these kinds of places is one Manhattan followed by a whole lot of water. I barely take my seat when I get a phone call, perpetrated by the recently anointed Gene Klein. With each muffled ring, I remind myself that while he may, indeed, win the future, he's still annoying as hell in the here and now. I turn off the phone because I don't want tonight to be about Help! personnel conflicts, or the setlist for some high school reunion he's signed us up for. I'm here for Tracy, and the chance to spend my downtime in a different musical space.

I recognize Steve Tatham, the keyboard player, and Joey Barnes, the acoustic bassist, both of whom I've gigged with on occasion. Not that it's a surprise, but Tracy looks stunning tonight, her auburn hair flowing down the shoulders of a curve-enhancing red sequined dress. She bends down, her face inches away from one of the older male patrons, and sings "I've Got a Crush on You."

I picture the guy having a heart attack but deciding it was worth it. Meanwhile, I sip my Manhattan at a very un-Manhattan-like pace, the idea being to make the drink last as long as possible. I'm not fooling anybody. Bartenders can spot a piker a mile away, and this one doesn't seem thrilled about the real estate I'm hoarding. Next to me are a couple of businessmen congratulating themselves on what the market did for their portfolios today, while occasionally glancing over to admire Tracy's cleavage. She's used to such attention, because in addition to being blessed with a killer voice and sharp intellect, Tracy inhabits a body that's off the hook. Crazy as it sounds, it was this glorious combo that drove me to break up with her, a classic case of "how could a club like that want me as a member?" One day, I'm going to get myself some serious therapy.

The businessman next to me leans over to start up a conversation. "Man, I'd like to fuck her," appears to be his take on "hello."

I nod my head for reasons I still can't explain. Anxious to get off the topic, I ask the bartender for my second glass of water now, as opposed to waiting until the first one's finished. He says nothing, handing me eight ounces of disdain with a spritz of pity.

"You don't seem very excited about the idea," the businessman persists.

"About what idea?" I ask, pretending I have no clue what the guy's talking about.

"You gay or something?"

"I've seen Liza Minelli eighteen times. Maybe we should move on."

The businessman is done with me, but his friend feels the urge to add his two cents.

"That Liza bitch looks like a man. I guess you like that."

The smug asswipes go back to their stock talk. I'm relieved because I can now lose myself in a 1928 Gershwin romantic fantasy, thanks to the resplendent Tracy.

Some part of me wants to tell the asswipes that when I was dating the object of their lust, she asked me to move in with her. But why? What would be gained by basking in a macho conquest I didn't have enough self-worth to sustain? I settle for a big sip of the Manhattan. As the glass comes down from my mouth, Tracy spots me. She flashes a smile so broad I find myself wondering whether my presence is what propels her joyful ending to the song.

The audience responds with well-earned enthusiasm. Tracy turns and whispers something to Steve and Jeff, then goes back to the microphone to address the crowd. "Thanks, everybody. You don't know how grateful I am to be able to play for you tonight." She clasps her hands, prayer-like, a favorite onstage thank-you among actors and musicians. "As a way of showing that gratitude, I have a little treat for you."

"Yeah, baby!" yells one of the old farts, as if he has suddenly been transported to a triple-X strip club abutting the airport. The guy's wife gives him a shove.

Unfazed, Tracy presses on. "I have a good friend in the audience who's a fantastic bass player."

The shout-out is very sweet of her, but I would have been quite content to slow-walk my Manhattan in obscurity.

"He doesn't know I've been learning this song, but it happens to be one of his favorites. I'd like him to come to the stage and play it with us. Ladies and gentlemen, give it up for Jimmy Kozlowski."

Why did she have to do this? I haven't touched my acoustic bass in months, and I'm certainly not in a place where

I want to play one in public. But I'm cornered. The entire room is looking at me.

I start to move toward the stage, feeling lightheaded and a little nauseous. Then, much to my relief, I see Joey reach down to the floor, pull an electric bass from its case, and extend it in my direction. It lands in my hands just as Steve switches his keyboard to synth mode and plays the opening notes of Zawinul's "Birdland." This is the Weather Report tune that convinced me there were no rules for what you could do on a bass guitar, as demonstrated by Jaco. Jazz singer Jon Hendricks wrote lyrics for it later, which is where Tracy comes in. She and I are about to enter the holy temple together. If we do our job right, the place will need a new roof by the time we're done.

Tracy is barely through the first verse when the crowd is up on its feet, seduced by a rhythm that, minus a drummer, falls on the shoulders of the bassist, a.k.a. me. Steve's keyboard playing is on-point and Zawinul-worthy, but the real joy is drinking in what's being created by Tracy. She makes the notes sound so effortless that by verse two, I want to reapply for membership in her club.

Once the bridge ends, it's time for my solo. I do my best to channel Jaco, but without his fretless bass and peerless genius, I'm at a bit of a disadvantage. No one seems to be viewing me critically, however, except maybe the old fart who wanted Tracy to show him her treats. As I make my way up the neck, I close my eyes and lose myself in the progression until I land on an improvisational island I never want to leave. After building to an intrepid cluster of sixteenth notes and harmonics, I suddenly hear the whole room applauding, and see Tracy coming over to give me a kiss. I look out at the businessmen by the bar, who are now shooting jealous glares in my direction.

I love Tracy for having learned this song, and, even more, for letting the two of us make it our own. It's the way playing music should be. The way life should be. Satisfaction of this magnitude comes in small doses, so I'm grateful when it surfaces. For all I know, tonight could turn out to be one of those jack-in-the-box milestones.

In what seems like less than a heartbeat, the song and the moment are over, and I'm making my way back to the bar. The businessmen are gone, evidently having conceded the evening to their homosexual competition. What's more, the bartender now meets my gaze with something bordering on respect. As a nod to his capitulation and the gratitude that fills me, I order another Manhattan. I will stay until Tracy's finished, so I can properly thank her for being a musical champion, for always reaffirming why I decided to give up everything else to do this.

I turn on my phone to check for messages. There's a voicemail from Prem, another from Mikey, and eleven from Gene. It would be easy to step outside and listen, but the sheer number of messages from the culprit assures me he is still alive, and that whatever the problem is can wait till morning.

Tracy starts singing "Someone to Watch Over Me." The audience is as silent as Christmas snow dusting the Sheep Meadow. Everybody, including the wives and girlfriends, wants to be that someone.

I Buried Paul

The band's second set ends around midnight. I shake hands with Joey and Steve and give Tracy a long hug. As I do, I feel tears on my cheek.

"You have time for a drink?" she asks.

By this hour, we're able to get our own private table in the bar area. My status continues to rise, thanks to the company I keep. Complimentary tapas are set down before us, but sampling them will have to wait until I find out what's going on with Tracy. The first thing I think of is that the cancer's back. I can't imagine what else could be making her so upset after the consummate performance she just turned in.

"I'm sorry," are the first words from her mouth.

Since she hasn't wronged me in any way, this is the apology of someone who equates sharing her troubles with being a burden on others. I assure her that no matter what's going on, I'm interested, and available to help.

"Deanne—" Tracy starts sniffling at the sound of her daughter's name.

"She's a freshman at SUNY Stonybrook, right?" I interject, mostly to keep her talking.

"She was. She started cutting again—"

I knew that Deanne had dabbled at hurting herself in high school, but freshman year of college had apparently brought it out in full force. Tracy says she's getting treatment at a residential facility in Hauppauge and, according to the staff, is making little, if any, progress. Her father has been of no help either emotionally or financially, and Tracy is freaked about money. She can't afford the copay, so if the situation doesn't improve, they'll have to transfer Deanne to a state facility on an austerity budget, with the failure rate to prove it. I offer to kick in whatever I can. Tracy appreciates my concern, but she and I both know my contribution can only move the bar fractions of an inch.

The logic of the situation is incomprehensible to me. Here we are, two responsible adults, seasoned artists who just kicked the living shit out of "Birdland," and we're powerless to help a sick young woman get well. I mention the idea of putting together a Go Fund Me page, but the notion of taking money from other people is too horrific for Tracy to wrap her head around. At least for now.

It might not be much consolation, but Tracy seems to appreciate the opportunity to talk about her dilemma with someone she trusts. She wants to know what's going on in my life.

"We don't have to talk about me," I say. Not a lot has changed since we saw each other what … six months ago?

"I want to know about you," Tracy insists. "Deanne is all that's on my mind, all the time. I need to hear something different. Anything."

I figure I'll give her a laugh with one of my work-related absurdities. "You won't believe this one. Gene thinks he's going to book a UK tour for us."

Tracy nods. "I know all about it."

"What?" I'm mystified as to how anyone other than the poor suckers in Help! would be privy to such nonsense.

"Gene calls me," Tracy says.

This strikes me as more horrific than *stealing* money from other people. "Why the hell would he call you?"

"That one time I came to see you guys at JP Murphy's? I gave him my number and he's been asking me out ever since."

"You and Gene?" I'm about to start screaming.

"I don't date him. He just wants to talk, and I listen."

With all the shit this woman is going through, she's kind enough to indulge a man whose conversation is like a trivia game where every answer is "Gene Klein." It's doubly irritating because, on some level, I believe his pestering her is about me. The Help! gigs, plus his constant phone calls and voicemails, somehow aren't enough. He must now make his presence known in my attempted moments of respite from Gene World and all its baggage.

Tracy and I close the place a few minutes after two, capping the night with multiple shots of grappa, dispensed by the formerly dismissive bartender who now refers to me as "brother." In truth, the two of us were done drinking an hour ago, but once we finished talking about Tracy's daughter and Gene's narcissism, we allowed ourselves some time to acknowledge the gift of a killer gig in a welcoming venue. In Musician's Heaven, these are the two key ingredients—with some good weed and spicy chicken wings thrown in at the after party. But the time has come for us to return to our lives and face the real music.

As Tracy and I head outside to the parking lot, I recoil at the sight of her ancient Toyota Corolla, a hot mess of faded paint, pockmark-like dings, and hideous patches of rust. The image of this sparkling beauty standing beside a decaying junk heap strikes me as yet one more indignity. How could anyone who produces such brilliant work be forced to climb into that piece of shit? We hug each other goodbye. Tracy says she's sorry for having upset me earlier by bringing up Gene. I tell her it's nothing she needs to worry about; the only things that matter are Deanne's welfare, and Tracy having the means to help her.

My concern and caring are genuine, but, if I'm being honest, what's hitting me hardest right now is the omni-presence of Gene Klein. His invasive ubiquity has shaken me to my core.

By all accounts, Gene Klein emerged from the womb screaming not for milk, but attention. This template would remain the default into adulthood, with Gene breaking the glass ceiling of neediness whenever his ego felt like a snack. My dad claimed there were reel-to-reel tapes of him singing "Besame Mucho" to his grandmother at three years old, and that Grandma Tessie's greatest pleasure was shuttling the little boy between the synagogue and the B'nai B'rith to show him off to her friends. This early, Yiddish-savvy gaggle of groupies fed the beast a sumptuous buffet of praise, which Gene grew to regard as a barometer of his self-worth. Legend had it that the only time he failed to get a standing ovation from Tessie was the afternoon he came home from kindergarten singing "Oh, Tannenbaum." Talent was one thing, but a Jewish kid singing a Christmas song, even one bearing no mention of Jesus, Mary, or the verboten Bethlehem, was beyond the pale. From that day forward, Gene's holiday season precociousness would be limited to Hanukah-oriented material, which would culminate in his own surf guitar version of "The Dreidel Song."

There are plenty of kids whose parents and grandparents parade them around as props, turning diaper-clad tykes

67

into models, spelling whizzes, or, in cases like Gene's, entertainers. Then, as the kids grow up, the business of real life takes over and the parades begin to wane. Waning, however, was not an option in the Klein household. The minute Tessie aged out as her grandson's head cheerleader, mother Marcia stepped in to make sure Gene entered every talent show and seized all promotional opportunities that presented themselves. Whenever the suits in the Alexander's Boy's Department went on sale, she snapped them up for her son to wear when he performed at school assemblies. When she went to get her hair done, she brought him to her stylist for showbizzy cuts worthy of a headlining act. Later, when Gene formed his first band at age twelve, his father, Phil, joined the team, buying a van to schlep all the equipment so the kids could play at birthday parties. Other parents, my own foremost among them, frowned upon such rock-star treatment, especially, the "Dad-as-roadie" concept. They believed it spoiled the boy and, even worse, took away his motivation to concentrate on schoolwork.

These naysayers, who assumed it their middle-class duty to judge all human behavior by the neatest and most universal of standards, missed the point. Gene Klein wasn't a normal boy. His parents, to their credit, had somehow recognized that he was ADHD before the diagnosis had been invented, and that serious academics would have no place in his future. Phil and Marcia's thinking was that if the choice were between musician and office worker, their son should go after the thing he loved, and settle later if it didn't work out.

My dad had no patience for such harebrained thinking. As leader of the Lou Kozlowski Orchestra, a key player on the Long Island wedding-band circuit, he knew how tough the music business was. The moment he heard that Phil Klein was enabling his son's bid for stardom, he proclaimed it a fool's errand. A musician could never find enough work if all he played was rock 'n' roll.

Lou would live to eat these words. After years of ranting about how the Kleins were creating a monster, he turned out to be the one who let the monster out of the cage.

As the Brits staged their invasion and the Beatles exploded into every household, wedding and Bar Mitzvah bands found themselves under growing pressure to include rock music at their events. My father resisted it for a year or so, then, after one feeble attempt at playing "I Saw Her Standing There" on a piano accordion, knew he had to do something. Nobody wanted to see an old guy in a toupee aping a twenty-three-year-old sex symbol. It was my brother, Eddie, a few years younger than Gene, but well aware of his talent, who gave Lou the idea of paying the kid to play a set at the affairs that requested rock 'n' roll. Dad explained that it was morally unsound to encourage a career choice guaranteed to end in heartbreak. Then Mom reminded him that hiring Gene would be hundreds of dollars cheaper than adding any extra adult musicians, and that they needed to save every penny possible for Eddie's and my college funds.

Lou agreed to a test run at the Feinman Bat Mitzvah the following Saturday. The other members of the Kozlowski Orchestra approached the new addition with trepidation but, much to everyone's surprise, the girls went crazy for Gene, a few even tugging the bottom of his Alexander's pant leg. The precocious kid's appeal resulted in the orchestra getting calls for life-cycle events all over Nassau County. Soon, fourteen-year-old Gene Klein was working every weekend, riding the coattails of "Sunrise, Sunset" to blaze his own superstar trail. The Gene phenomenon inspired half the boys in school to learn the guitar, my brother being the most ambitious of the lot. Eddie's plan was to get so good that Gene wouldn't be able to resist inviting him to become a bandmate.

My father's role in facilitating the ascension of Gene Klein, and the distance it would eventually create between him and his firstborn son, would haunt him for the last twenty years of his life. No matter how many times my mom and I told him not to be so hard on himself, Lou would insist that a person had to own his mistakes. But how was he to know it would be a mistake? What if it wasn't really his mistake, and somebody else was to blame? What if nobody was to blame, and it was simply one of life's unfair tragedies?

One of the things I learned watching my father was that when bad shit happens, the pain has to go somewhere, and there are people who take it upon themselves to absorb every last drop. Lou needed to run the show, whether he was leading an orchestra, or processing grief.

I was a newborn when Gene World started to become our world, but a few years later, my head would be filled with the sounds of Eddie practicing his guitar, which he did upwards of four hours a day. The more he practiced, the more I heard Lou and Irene argue. Mom didn't have that big a problem with Eddie's new passion, but to Dad it was as if the Japanese had launched an attack on nearby Roslyn Harbor. As a musician himself, one would think some part of Lou had to respect Eddie's dedication, as well as his increased understanding of music theory and chord construction. Yet the more Eddie played, the further apart he and Dad grew. I would later learn that, as much as Lou loved music, turning it into a job defined by rules and repetition made it as tedious to him as working on an assembly line. In some respects, it was worse. At least assembly-line workers didn't have to hustle for new gigs every week.

It didn't take long for my father to figure out that Eddie idolized Gene and hoped to join him someday in the quest for rock 'n' roll stardom. This fanned the flames of Lou's already existing resentment of Gene, and the tension began to surface in front of the guests at various Bar and Bat Mitzvahs. On more than one occasion, as Gene sang "Satisfaction," doing his best Mick Jagger imitation, Lou stood behind the teenager and imitated the imitation, which garnered cheap laughs from the grown-ups in the crowd. Eventually, Gene was made aware of the fact that he was being mocked. This led to my dad getting summoned to Phil Klein's house for a sit-down.

Phil said he couldn't understand why Lou would want to make fun of a kid. Lou told him he didn't mean anything by it, but there was no question he meant plenty. He now realized that adding Gene to the mix had been a high-stakes gamble. The more Gene succeeded, the less interest Eddie would have in getting a college education which, to Lou's way of thinking, was the only ticket out of singing "Volare" for the rest of one's life. Phil, of course, hadn't been briefed on the danger of Eddie being negatively impacted by Gene, and, even if he had, his job was to protect his son. He told Lou that he considered this treatment of Gene a form of abuse, and warned him that if it continued, the teenage heartthrob would have to stop working with the orchestra.

There was nothing that would have pleased my dad more, short of rock 'n' roll's speedy demise as an alleged art form. In the ideal world, Lou would have fired Gene, or pushed the envelope one more time to make Gene quit, but he wasn't in the position to do either. This spoiled, hustling kid, whom he considered a terrible role model for his eldest son, was the one bringing in new business—business that would eventually help get Eddie a college degree, assuming he and Irene managed to keep the boy on track.

As much as Lou hated going against his principles, he sucked it up and left Gene alone to soak up the screams of hormonal Bat Mitzvah girls. In the long run, it was more important for Lou to regain Eddie's trust, so he would be able to point his son in the right direction. Meanwhile, Eddie got better and better on the guitar, which my father finally decided to acknowledge. Dismissing his son's hard work had only alienated him further, so why not come at it from a more positive place? According to my mom, things improved for a while. College wasn't mentioned in every other sentence, and, for the first time in years, Eddie felt like everybody was on the same team, looking out for each other's best interests.

The more Dad laid off, the better my brother did with his schoolwork. The lack of parental pressure also had an exponential effect on Eddie's playing. He started to get into jazz and came home one day with a hollow-body Gibson electric that the salesman at Knopf's, the local music shop, had agreed to lend him. Nobody was more surprised than Lou when, from behind the closed door of our bedroom, he heard a Wes Montgomery-esque version of "Volare." The one song that represented his most hellish musical Groundhog Day now sounded brand new. Against all odds, his son had turned stale into fresh, hackneyed into innovative. Lou was impressed.

Mom thought the revelation might inspire Dad to get more enjoyment out of music again. For a while he did, throwing some deep cuts into the mix along with "Moon River" and "The Girl from Ipanema." The Lou Kozlowski Orchestra was still running on autopilot, but with just enough new ideas to keep it from growing mold. Dad even reached some form of détente with Gene, the two bonding over their love of the Yankees. Then, one Saturday night, after what must have been Lou's two-thousandth performance of "Thank Heaven for Little Girls," one of the guests announced that the Yanks had just clinched the pennant. As the band took a break, Gene made his way over to Dad and the two of them high-fived. Gene decided that since Lou was in such a good mood, it would be the perfect time to have a talk. Dad assumed the boy was going to ask for permission to play a longer set, which was not an uncommon occurrence. But, that night, Gene had something else in mind. He announced he was quitting the orchestra.

Lou's first reaction was that another wedding band must have swooped in and poached his protégé, but this was not the case. Gene explained that he'd gone as far as he could in this type of work and needed to concentrate on putting together his own band. He was a determined sixteen-year-old who now had his parents' permission to drop out of high school. He had also landed an agent who, according to Gene, believed in his talent and recognized his charisma.

For all Lou's grumbling about Gene and rock 'n' roll, he had grown comfortable with the new arrangement. Business was rolling along at a nice clip, the work plentiful, and the clients happy. They had the system down pat, calibrating the ratio of grown-up music to rock as the individual party demanded. On a few occasions, Lou would even ask Gene to add a guitar part to one of the orchestra's more upbeat MOR tunes. Apparently, there was also a night when Gene turned to Lou for advice about a girl, a subject matter he found difficult to broach with his own father. Lou gave him the same thoughtful counsel he would have given his own sons, and Gene thanked him for it.

Not wanting to fix something that wasn't broke, Lou suggested a compromise, whereby Gene could sit out a fair percentage of gigs in order to concentrate on his own music. Gene thanked him for the offer but said he'd made up his mind. All my father could do was wish him well. The Lou Kozlowski Orchestra would weather the storm and play on.

Play on they did, but, over time, the work became more sporadic. Dad hired a few different Gene wannabes, but none who could reel in an audience like the original. Mom was sure Eddie would lobby to fill in, but it turned out my brother had no interest in being the cool fish in a very uncool pond. He was determined to display his chops elsewhere, in situations where they mattered. Soon, disco and DJs started to happen. A new musical paradigm was taking shape, forcing old schoolers like Lou, and up-and-comers like Gene, to re-assess how and where they fit in. Lou thought about becoming a music teacher. Gene set his sights on creating a supergroup that would play basketball arenas and sixty-thousand-seat stadiums. Mom worried about money. And I thought about how I could be as much like my older brother as genetics—and our parents—would allow.

OVERLOAD

The rain is hitting in thick, steady streams when I turn onto my street. The phone rings, but there's no need to look at the screen because I can feel the caller zeroing in on me as a host body. I check anyway, my suspicion confirmed. It's two-fifteen in the morning. Who does this? And why should I put up with it? My car makes an abrupt about-face and speeds off in the direction of Cliffside Terrace.

Gene's subdivision, built a few years later than the development where I grew up, or currently reside, was once considered a crown jewel among Long Island tracts, with slightly bigger lawns, lusher foliage, and houses boasting a few hundred more square feet than the previously established norm. Today, with both McMansions and homelessness encroaching on the suburban dream, Cliffside doesn't seem so jewel-like.

I park at the curb in front of 35 Maple Drive. I see a light on in one of the upstairs rooms. It's Gene Klein's bedroom, where he once slept in his crib and now lays his head more than six decades later. As pathetic as that might appear, there are two important caveats to consider. The first is that Gene is not the kid who never left home, but the rock 'n' roll maverick who struck out on his own at seventeen and traveled cross-country probably forty times over, living everywhere from the Haight to a YMCA in Evanston, Illinois. The second caveat is that the reason he's back in his old twin bed is to help his mom. With Phil Klein long gone, Gene believes it is his responsibility to make sure Marcia has a decent quality of life in her declining years. And if that means sleeping on the mattress where he lost his virginity to Gail Marmorstein in the eighth grade, so be it.

I pick up my phone, ready to call and order his ass outside when I see the light go off. Better to let him, and me, get some sleep than address a lifetime of neediness at this ungodly hour. I start to turn the car key when a first-floor light comes on. I can make out a few shadows, one of which looks to be Gene's mom, sitting up in bed. I hear her moan, maybe in pain, perhaps in confusion. I then see another shadow walking toward her, which I assume must be the caregiver. I soon realize it's Gene because he's carrying a guitar. He starts to play, but I can't make out the song. What I can piece together is that, as he strums, the moaning dies down.

Why am I still here? I'm exhausted, I've had too much to drink, and I'm still thinking about how I let a gem like Tracy get away. I should cut my losses and step on the gas. But I keep staring at the window; if that isn't bad enough, I feel my left hand open the driver's side door, daring me to step out. Is this really where I've landed? Have I spent almost fifty years on the planet, only to end up a voyeur? I'm now tiptoeing forward on the Klein's front lawn. It appears I have.

When I reach the hedge below Marcia's window, the song Gene is playing becomes unmistakable. "You've Got to Hide Your Love Away" is one of his signature re-creations, rendered with such feeling and precision that it never gets old for me, no matter how many times I hear him sing it. Tonight, it takes on a different kind of significance. When she's gone will Gene be able to go on? Or will he feel two-foot small?

As hard as it was for me to lose both my mom and dad to different, but equally cruel, diseases, there is something otherworldly about this only child's bond with the woman who has devoted nearly every waking hour to him since he made his entrance.

Marcia reaches her arms in the air to hold her son's head as he sings to her. He manages to keep the verse going while she looks to be clutching his skull for dear life. Even in shadow, the emotion of the picture is riveting: a woman with little time left being comforted by her only living descendant, who, himself, is on Social Security.

I feel a vibration coming from my pants pocket. I take out my phone to turn it off for the night when I notice the screen reads: "Gene Klein." How can somebody be comforting one person and pestering another at the same time? I consider that I might be hallucinating; that it really is the caregiver on the other side of the window, and there is no guitar or singing. I step a little closer to the glass. Unless I'm delirious, Gene is, indeed, performing for his elderly mom.

So, who is the Gene Klein on the phone?

A more rational person might wait till he got home, or the following morning, to sort it out, but this is too bizarre for me to ignore, even for a minute. I move away from the window and slightly into the neighbor's shrubs, so no one will hear when I play back Gene's voicemail. I look at the screen, almost afraid to tap the icon in the bottom right corner, but I forge ahead …

"Hey, guys, it's Gene. Sorry for the group message. I just want to make sure everybody's got their marching orders for JP Murphy's on Tuesday. Sound check at six-thirty. We're gonna talk boots, and I'll also need a fifty percent deposit for the Sgt. Pepper outfits. Jimmy, don't be late again. Mikey, I found a more breathable nose. Prem, don't forget it's 'You're *working* for no one but me.' Gonna be a killer show. UK Tour details to come!"

A fucking robocall. As if he weren't enough of a control freak, Gene has now taken a page from telemarketers to get under our skin 24/7. The most disturbing part is that since the man's tech savvy is limited to plugging his guitar into an amp, some malevolent enabler must have taught him how to do this.

In one fell swoop, the pathos of a son serenading his ailing mother has been snuffed out by a Help! infomercial. I must get away from this place before I burn down the house, or worse. I sprint back toward the car, but not fast enough. The window from Marcia's room has opened, and Gene is sticking his head out.

"Jimmy, I've been calling you all night. Glad you stopped by."

He is not only wide awake, but fully expecting me to come inside so we can shoot the shit, as if it's something people do at his hour.

Jesus Christ. How did I set myself up for this? "You know, I'm really tired," I say, producing an oversized faux yawn for emphasis. "I should go home."

"You can't," he says. "I just told Mom I saw your car out there and she's gonna be really upset if you leave."

"Where's her caregiver?" I ask, knowing that whatever the answer is will have no bearing on Gene's demand.

"It's Lupe's night off. Just me—and now you."

"Doesn't your mom need to rest?"

"That's what she does all day long. Now she wants to hear 'I'm Down.'"

Screaming like Little Richard at 2:30 a.m.? In what psycho fun house are these people living? "I don't think that's a good idea, Gene."

"It's a great idea! It'll make her feel so much better to hear you sing. Especially if you take her performance notes and smile more."

If I haven't completely bottomed out, I'm hard-pressed to think what that looks like. I can't do this. I must put my foot down.

Suddenly, I see Marcia popping her head out the window and waving at me. "Hi, Paul!"

I wave back, managing to force a smile through my fury. It's not that I don't feel for Marcia, but her failing health doesn't negate the other sickness happening here.

"You're cuter when you're wearing the wig," she says. "Can you put it on?"

"Next time," I say, hating myself as I feel my legs begin to trudge up the walkway.

When Gene opens the door, I notice he's wearing his *Revolver*-era Lennon wig and granny sunglasses. In the middle of the night.

"Pleased as punch you're here," he greets me, in his best Liverpudlian, which only enrages me further.

As I walk in, I feel the strength leaving my body, and, once the door closes behind me, I know I have already committed to three encores.

We walk down the hall to Marcia's room. I start thinking about Eddie, and how he would never let Gene run roughshod over him like this. Then again, he was Gene's right-hand man for almost fifteen years, so there was no way he could have avoided putting up with some of this insane shit. The thing to keep in mind is how much times have changed. Today's music business would be unrecognizable to my brother, and even a self-assured guy like Eddie would have to make compromises. Or maybe I'm blowing smoke up my own ass to justify my passivity.

"Say hello to Paul McCartney," Gene announces to his mother.

Gene is as surprised as I am to see that Marcia is now lying down, with her eyes closed. He rushes to her side to feel for a pulse. He nods. She's still among us. "All ready for 'I'm Down?'" he asks his mom. She doesn't stir.

"Maybe we should let her sleep," I say. It's an obvious and sensible suggestion, so I assume Gene will argue otherwise.

He proves me wrong, switching gears as if his mother isn't even there. "Let's go in the living room and I'll fill you in on the UK."

"Why don't we save it for Tuesday?" I suggest. "That way you don't have to repeat the same information to the rest of the band."

"I don't mind—"

"It's late, Gene. I really have to go."

"Fine. Can I talk to you about something else?"

I can only imagine what's next. He's probably decided to add a Hamburg leg to the trip when we finish up in England. "What's going on?"

"My mom. Sometimes she hears music that isn't there. It can be completely quiet, and she'll say, 'Listen, isn't that beautiful?' I tell her I don't hear anything, but she insists it's real."

"What kind of music does she hear?"

"Usually songs she liked to dance to. Sinatra, Tony Bennett. Stuff your dad played. Apparently, there are these people who have musical hallucinations."

"So strange. I remember there was some book about that."

"I guess imaginary songs are better than imaginary flesh-eating demons," Gene says.

I nod my head, about to extend my sympathy, when he offers to fire up a pot of coffee. "It won't take long," he assures me. "And I can give you a little UK sneak preview."

"I have to get back." I hold firm. "I can't wait to hear about it on Tuesday though."

Without a doubt, Gene thinks I'm abandoning him, but there's not much I can do about Marcia's situation. I need to return to my basement and reconnect with my warm and only mildly judgmental cat.

BACK BEATS

I started to become familiar with the relationship between music and stress as early as five years old. I'd be watching TV, or trying to figure out a puzzle, when my father would suddenly start yelling at my mom and waving sheets of paper in her face. I would later learn that these papers were called "bills," and that Lou Kozlowski spent many of his waking hours in abject fear of not being able to pay them. His anxiety seemed to increase with each passing year and came to a head when he ordered my mother to produce receipts for every purchase she made. Irene sucked it up and remained a calm presence, providing my father with all the documentation he requested until one day, when he lambasted her for taking two shirts to the dry cleaner rather than laundering and ironing them herself. According to Eddie, she cried for a week about how demeaning it was to be held accountable for the ever-prudent decisions she made in managing our home.

Sometimes the tension would follow me to school. I'd look at other kids and wonder if their dads also yelled about bills, but, in time, I concluded that they didn't have to, because mine was yelling for them. One of Lou's favorite pastimes was sounding off about Billy Fenster's father driving a brand-new Cadillac, or Mrs. Fenster wearing a full-length mink coat. I wasn't clear on what other people's cars and clothes had to do with anything. Didn't we have a car and winter coats too?

It would take years for me to understand that even though Lou seemed to fit in with the other dads in the neighborhood, he saw himself as an outlier. Mom explained that, in my father's mind, he could never be like one of them because he was a musician. The rest of the dads worked in business or had concrete skills for which there was always demand. It wasn't compulsory for a neighbor to hire a band for a party, but if a pipe leaked before the guests were about to arrive, that neighbor needed a plumber, who didn't have to jump through hoops to get the job.

Lou Kozlowski had made the choice to earn his living doing something he enjoyed, and that he was good at. To many, being able to pull off such a feat would be cause for celebration, but, for whatever reason, it made Lou feel like he was cheating. Some part of him regretted not having been trained for a more serious, button-down career that, mind-numbing though it might be, carried the promise of steady money. As a result, every time he had to struggle to book gigs, Lou would curse his own lack of gumption. Then, when things got really slow, he'd begin to view himself as an inadequate provider, a bad husband and someone unfit to be a father. If he felt the browbeating still fell short, he'd up the stakes by reviling his chosen career path, until he despised the very thing that was once his passion. Ultimately, the act of playing music became more abhorrent to him than the shame of not being able to pay his bills.

The one constant in my father's life was his determination to keep Eddie and me from becoming professional musicians. He threw himself into the endeavor with everything in his arsenal, attempting to bribe us with apartments and cars he couldn't afford, and hookers he couldn't morally justify, if only we'd agree to relinquish our foolish dreams. Eddie and I didn't think they were foolish at all. Our game plan, put into motion many years apart, was to become so accomplished at our crafts that Lou would have no choice but to bless whatever decisions we made.

There was no doubt that Lou recognized Eddie's extraordinary development as a guitarist. He would also see my bass playing improve as I grew up. But in the end, no matter what level of skill either of us might attain, nothing we could do, short of quitting the business and getting full-time jobs, would ever appease him. Lou Kozlowski's destiny was to leave this earth castigating himself for not being able to prevent his sons from becoming his biggest failure.

The spring of 1976 marked the beginning of the end. Eddie was in his second year at Nassau Community College, working toward an accounting degree while continuing to hone his guitar chops. At first, Lou was cautiously optimistic about the career-hobby balance, but, as he saw Eddie improving by the day, he worried that the prospect of doing other people's taxes would never be able to compete with the chance to entertain them. He knew whereof he feared because he'd been stricken by the same bug, having only a fraction of his son's talent.

Still, Eddie had applied to finish his undergraduate degree at both Adelphi and Hofstra and been accepted by both schools, pleasing Lou and Irene no end. Hoping to capitalize on the good news, Dad decided that it would make a lot of sense to connect Eddie with Bob Snell. What could be better than a summer internship to get the boy into the swing of junior year accounting classes? He'd been a client of Bob's for years, and Eddie was a smart, personable young man who knew how to talk to grown-ups, so the match seemed like a slam-dunk. Channeling Dad's eagerness, Mom proposed the bold notion that they invite Bob Snell and his wife, Charlotte, for Sunday brunch.

We were not the kind of family that anyone would describe as brunch people. That form of eating was reserved for fancy folk like the Fensters. The Kozlowskis were the Froot Loops and frozen waffle crowd, which is why Eddie found it odd to see Mom hauling out a crisp white tablecloth for something other than Christmas or Easter. I thought that maybe I was going to get presents or something, but my brother eyed the scene with suspicion, no doubt having identified the inauthenticity of it all. The set-up was bad enough, but did they really need to kiss an accountant's ass?

For someone to whom the concept of brunch was as exotic as hitting the spa for a mud bath, Irene rose to the occasion, creating the illusion that we ate all our meals using three forks apiece. The Froot Loops were relegated to the deep recesses of the pantry in favor of cheese omelets, bacon, home fried potatoes, Pillsbury dinner rolls, a fruit and cheese platter, and Sara Lee coffee cake. The Snells couldn't get over the beautiful spread. I was too young to have any recollection of the conversation, but my brother would later tell me that the topics ranged from term vs. whole life insurance, to cement vs. asphalt driveways, to Bob Snell's pride in having recently outfitted his home with central air conditioning. Eddie said that despite his best efforts to be polite and not doze off, he was fully zoned out by the time Dad raised the possibility of an internship. Suddenly, he and Mom were smiling and patting him on the back, but the last thing he recalled hearing was Bob Snell's wistful ode to freon.

Amid my parents' exuberant hosting activities and Eddie's awkward reaction came the ringing of the telephone. One thing I do remember, all these years later, is the feeling that, somehow, we were going to be saved by the bell. (I would later find out that it did, indeed, provide a life raft for one of us.) Lou asked Eddie if he'd answer it, and Eddie bolted from the table like a death row inmate whose sentence had just been overturned. Legend has it the call went something like this:

"Hello, Kozlowski's." That was the way Mom instructed us to always answer the phone.

"Hey, Eddie, how're you doing?" came the enthusiastic voice on the other end.

"Good. Who's this?"

"It's Gene."

"Gene Klein?"

"That's how they make out the checks."

"Hey, man, how're you doing?"

"Working hard. I'm in Iowa. Got four back-to-back gigs here."

"Wow. You're calling long distance. I don't want to waste your money. I'll get my dad."

"Eddie, I want to talk to you."

"Me?"

"Don't act so surprised. You're still shredding the shit out of that Strat, aren't you?"

"Doing what I can."

"That's what I figured. Listen, my lead guitarist's wife is having a kid, so he doesn't want to work the road anymore. I was wondering if maybe you—"

Concurrently, Bob Snell stood up from the table to point out where the vents would be positioned should Lou and Irene follow his lead and embrace central air conditioning. Lou nodded his head with apparent conviction, but anyone who knew my father understood there wasn't a chance in hell of him incurring such an expense. He was sucking up to Bob Snell in order to seal the deal on an internship Eddie never wanted.

"I'm in," my brother blurted into the phone.

Eddie later told me that he felt no need to hear the tour details from Gene. There was plenty of time to get into the small stuff. The most important thing in that moment was to make the commitment and secure a hard out from a summer in hell. Gene asked if he thought Lou would be okay with the proposal, volunteering to talk to him about it himself if need be. My brother didn't see an upside to having Gene fight his battle. The guy wasn't exactly Lou's favorite person to begin with, plus, the way Eddie saw it, if he was going to defy the wishes of his parents, it was on him to take the heat. He wrote down Gene's phone numbers for the Travelodges where he'd be staying for the next four nights, and said he'd get back to him. Once Eddie hung up, he realized that he was in such shock, he forgot to thank the first person in his life to offer him a paycheck for playing music.

I remember the strange look on my brother's face when he rejoined us at the table.

"So, who was on the phone?" Mom asked.

"Oh, just a friend of mine from school," Eddie said.

"I hope you didn't tell him about the internship," Lou said. "He might get jealous."

Bob Snell blushed, emitting the bullshit "aw, shucks" humility of a two-bit kingmaker. Eddie found the exchange repulsive. Obviously, this wasn't the time to let the cat out of the bag, but, on the other hand, when would there be a good time?

Bob turned to Eddie. "You'll be working eight o'clock to four-thirty, with a half-hour for lunch. Of course, some of us like to work through lunch because we enjoy what we do."

"See, Eddie," Lou piped in. "It's an incredibly exciting opportunity."

"Granted, it's not rock 'n' roll," Charlotte Snell chimed in, with a giggle. Bob seemed to enjoy her joke, or whatever it was supposed to be.

Eddie looked to Mom and Dad to see if they were going to join in, but somehow they had the good sense to stay mum. Even so, he couldn't let the remark go by unchallenged. "What's that supposed to mean, Mrs. Snell?" he asked.

"What's what supposed to mean?" Bob said, as if no words had been uttered.

"Your wife," Eddie answered. "She made a comment about rock 'n' roll. I didn't understand it."

"Oh, it was nothing," Charlotte answered. "Our daughter told us you play rock guitar, and that's great, but it's not something you can make money at."

"Amen to that," Lou seconded.

Eddie was incensed. These Snell people, and now his father, were passing judgment on something they didn't know anything about. "I disagree," he said. "If you're a good enough musician, there'll be work for you."

Charlotte smiled. "Well, luckily, you won't have to worry about that."

As to what happened next, I remember Eddie quietly stating his future plans, the Snells saying they had to leave, and Lou Kozlowski hurling a lamp through the living room window.

CRAFT WORK

The weekend gets off to a promising start. Sunny skies, temperatures expected to reach seventy or so, and not a peep out of Gene. I'm somewhat curious to know how his mom is doing today, but not curious enough to interrupt a productive morning of writing. "SSRI" has taken another step forward, and now features a screaming punk bridge that name-checks Boormann and Himmler. I'm under no illusions about the song's chances of making it to the final album, but I also believe it's important to unpack this stuff, if only to make room for the next batch of ideas that pop into my head. As for the cool bass run I came up with the other day, I'm pretty sure it's adaptable enough to be integrated elsewhere should "SSRI" prove a casualty of overreaching.

I check my watch to make sure I haven't lost track of the time. I'm supposed to be at Prem's by noon, having agreed to play some non-Beatles music with him and one of his friend's sons, some eighteen-year-old jazz pi-ano prodigy. I know the kid must be the real deal because Prem, in addition to having an encyclopedic knowledge of music, has impeccable taste. I can't wait to get in the room with them and see what kind of sparks fly.

I'm sure there are those who would doubt the kind of artist who writes an anti-Nazi punk tune in the morning and fills out an impromptu jazz trio in the afternoon. Aren't we supposed to have our own specific brands? That's fine, if you're Bono or Beyoncé, but for us commoners trying to make the rent, being a versatile, hirable musician demands a broad education and diverse skills. There are plenty of hacks who care only about what's selling in the moment, but the visionaries are the ones who know the history. Awareness of the music that came before informs the insights that generate original work.

First things first, I need to get Jaco back inside. He's mostly an indoor guy, but when I'm home during the day, I try to let him see some of the world. The thought of any living thing spending its entire life indoors, eating, pissing and shitting, is way too depressing, especially since I know so many people like that.

I go to the screen door, which opens onto the backyard, and start calling his name. No Jaco in sight. I step out and see a rabbit scurry into the yard behind ours. Still no Jaco. Realizing this could take a while, I go back inside to get my phone so I can call Prem in case I'm delayed.

I return to the backyard, only to see my feline friend standing in front of me, a dead brown bird stuffed in his mouth. He looks damn pleased about it, too, a definite swagger emanating from this little shit of a hunter-gatherer. "Drop it," I say to no effect. Needing to get the show on the road, I grab the skin on top of his neck. The cat's mouth pops open with a squeak and a gasp, after which the expired prey plops to the ground. As Jaco scurries back into the house, I weigh the possibility of him throwing up a pile of avian innards all over my bed. That will have to be addressed later, because now I must deal with the deceased. I've never bothered to learn much about identifying birds, but on my way to get a shovel out of the tool shed, I wonder what I'm about to bury.

According to the pictures on Google, I will be administering last rites for a sparrow, identified as female because of its brown color, the males being black and gray. Both genders of these sweet-looking creatures have been classified as pests, ostensibly so annoying that there is a company specializing in their extermination called BirdsBeGone. com.

From their website:

> Sparrows are a social and aggressive species that often attack other species of birds. Their nests clog gutters, vents, and damage air-conditioning units. Their feces are corrosive, destroying homes and other buildings. Sparrow droppings may also lead to slip and fall accidents. Sparrows carry and transmit a large variety of diseases that can be passed to humans and introduce a variety of other parasites like ticks and mites to your property.

In that context, not only has Jaco performed a public service, but one worth actual money. It occurs to me that if BirdsBeGone would give him a steady gig, I could take some time off from playing with Help!

Having grasped the odiousness of what I'm about to inter, I consider going back in the house for some plastic gloves. I'm anxious to get to Prem's, though, so I settle for handling the shovel carefully. I manage to scoop up the corpse without having to bend down and touch it. I carry it over to the hedge, drop it on the ground, and start digging up dirt. Two shovels in, I hear a voice call out.

"Hey there, Jimbo. Anything I can help you with?" It's my landlord, Bill Girardi, who may not be pleased about this tiny monster being laid to rest on his property.

"Jaco killed a bird. I thought I'd bury it. If it's okay with you."

Bill looks down to appraise the dead. "Goddamn sparrow. We should wipe out every one of those vile pieces of shit, but of course we can't. You know, Save the Whales, climate change and crap."

I don't have time to debate the health of the planet. I just need to know my next move. "So, I shouldn't bury it here?"

"Dig away, brother."

"I'll clean off your shovel when I'm done," I assure him.

"No need. She's been a lot worse places than that, let me tell you."

I'm not exactly sure what that means, but the images it evokes, plus the fact that he's referred to his shovel as "she," tell me I've already heard too much. Two more shovels full of dirt and I can pack my gear in the car.

"Listen, Jimmy, I've been meaning to talk to you," Bill says.

The tone of voice is calm, but ominous. It's either going to be a rent increase, or the more dire possibility that he now wants to use the basement for one of his kids or his mother-in-law, which would send me scrambling for a new place to live.

"What's up, man?" I ask, trying to sound casual.

"I don't know if you remember, but I told you a while back that we're throwing a little dinner party tonight for Jan's friends from work."

"Oh yeah, sure," I reply, having no recollection of the conversation. "Don't worry, I'll be out of the house. You won't be hearing any rumbling bass or anything."

"We were kind of hoping you'd be around. Jan had this idea that it might be nice to have some sort of entertainment at the party, and she was wondering if you could do some songs with your guitar. Background music, or what have you. Of course, we'd pay you."

"I couldn't take your money, Bill."

"We can't ask you to work for free."

I tell him that I don't have a gig till ten tonight, so I'd be happy to come by and play a few songs. But I refuse to take his money. He says "fine." He'll just deduct it from my rent.

Life surprises me all the time, but rarely for the better. I'll take it, even from a climate-change denier. "Thanks, Bill. What time would you like me to be there?"

"How's cocktail hour? Say around six?"

"See you then." I start back to the basement when Bill calls out.

"Jan loves the Bee Gees. You do any Bee Gees?"

"No," is my rapid response. My repertoire covers a wide range, but there are certain places I just can't go.

"Good. I hate the Bee Gees." Bill heads into the house.

Prem lives in one of the newer enclaves in the Albertson-Searingtown area, meaning the homes were built in the late seventies. They're another few hundred square feet bigger than the ones in Gene's development but situated on smaller lots. As I pull into the driveway, I'm graced by a breeze infused with cumin, cardamom, and whatever else goes into the heavenly food cooked behind these walls. Once I'm out of the car, the aromatic opiates are joined by the inviting opening bars of "In Walked Bud" coming from inside. It's one of my favorite Monk tunes, now being played on an electric piano, with Prem's electric guitar vamping in the background.

Bass in hand, I arrive at the front door, where I'm greeted by Prem's wife, Jaya, a reserved, thirtyish woman dressed in a traditional sari. Jaya informs me that she's preparing lunch for us, which should be ready in an hour or so. It's hard to know what to be more excited about, Monk or masala. I enter Prem's studio to find Raji Balakrishnan working his magic at the vintage Fender Rhodes. He's eighteen, looks thirteen, and, if you add those two numbers together, you get a good idea of how mature his technique is. Prem greets me with a big smile, something I haven't seen out of him at our recent Help! gigs. His playing seems looser and more adventurous which, I guess, makes sense. Whenever we're onstage together, the man is stuffed into a suit, tie, and boiling hot wig. This is what freedom sounds like.

Normally, Monk's work calls for an acoustic double-bass like the one in Tracy's band, but since Raji has gone electric, it's a perfect fit when I plug in to join them. It also helps that "In Walked Bud" is one of the more straight-ahead Thelonious compositions, light on the master's trademark dissonance, odd rhythms, and asymmetry. It's still a worthy challenge for Prem and me because we don't usually get to play in F minor, with diatonic chords alternating between F natural minor and F melodic minor. Plus, since Prem's job leaves him little time to explore a musical life outside of Indian George, he laps up every drop of this new adventure. As I watch Raji take a solo, I'm impressed by his ability to integrate Monk's percussive style with his own more fluid approach. I also wonder how it's possible for someone this young to bring such a lived-in feel to a composition created out of the black experience in the 1950s.

In a shy whisper, Raji asks what we'd like him to play next. We tell the kid we want him to lead the way, that we're here to step out of our comfort zones and dive into his groove. He smiles, turns to his Nord keyboard, and, a few seconds later, we're in hip-hop land—pounding drums, Kendrick Lamar samples, and a classic audio clip of Gil Scott-Heron's "The Revolution Will Not Be Televised." Raji puts a chunky piano riff on top of the flute part. Prem adds a blistering guitar section. I harmonize with the pre-recorded bass track, a bottom-heavy take on the Allman Brothers' melody and harmony lead guitars. The results are bumpy at first, but Raji's sharp instincts motor us through. By the time the song's over, Prem and I aren't thinking whether the revolution will indeed be televised. We're just thrilled to have been a part of the conversation. Raji segues into Steve Wonder's "Too High." There aren't any samples, so I assume we're going to play it as an instrumental. It's then I learn the kid has pipes. Bashful Raji is a ferocious vocalist. The mind-blowing wonders continue with each song he pulls out of his hat, the choices ranging from Radiohead to the O'Jays.

The next stunner appears at the kitchen table, in the form of Jaya's tikka masala, basmati rice, homemade samosas, and raita. I surrender to their glory, managing a long enough pause between bites to ask Jaya if she's ever worked as a professional chef. She laughs, informing me that she's a dental hygienist, which was also her profession in India. My praise of her cooking earns me a doggie bag to take home.

After expressing my thanks to both Prem and Jaya for their hospitality, I shake Raji's hand, telling him what an exceptional musician I think he is. He responds with a barely audible, "It was nice playing with you." The poor guy should just sing all his sentences. That voice could win a Grammy for ordering a burger at a drive-through. Prem walks me out to my car, reminding me that we'll see each other Tuesday night at the bar. I try to gauge whether he's dreading yet one more Help! gig, but he seems fine. I'm not in a funk about it either. A brief reprieve from the Fab grind has put everything in perspective. Gene's peculiar behaviors aside, all of us revere the Beatles, and he makes sure we represent them to the best of our abilities. If Prem and I don't want to be defined by our jobs as Fake George and Fake Paul, we need to fill our cups with these challenging musical side trips. A change of pace will both expand our creative horizons, and provide necessary refuge from the boss's all-consuming zeal.

As I drive home, I remember the promise I made to Bill and Jan Girardi. In a few short hours, I will be singing sixties soft rock to people in their sixties as they nibble on cocktail franks. The combination is fitting in that I have similar feelings about soft rock and cocktail franks. Each is an homage to the overexposed and uninspiring, neither approaching the league of "In Walked Bud" or tikka masala. Nevertheless, a promise is a promise, and a landlord is somebody you don't want to piss off.

Jan Girardi has been an office manager at the Long Island Power Authority for twenty-some years, going back to when it was called the Long Island Lighting Company. She was one of the first of my brother's friends to settle into the kind of life he was determined to avoid. Her husband, Bill, held onto his dreams a bit longer, trying his hand at photography before starting up an aluminum siding company. I've never once wondered what it might be like to spend an evening with Jan and her co-workers, but tonight I'm about to find out. Since utilities are included in my rent, I won't be able to add anything to a conversation about rising electric bills, but, as a hired gun whose purpose is to supply inoffensive background music, I shouldn't have to worry about making small talk. Immunity from obligatory chit-chat is one of the unsung benefits of the work I do.

The party is already into the booze and weenies when I arrive. Jan offers me a glass of Long Island Power Iced Tea, which she describes as an amped-up version of the standard (already potent) stuff. I tell her I never drink on the job, which gets a laugh from most everyone in the group. I'm not quite sure why until I remember that most people don't think what I do is real work. While I've made peace with being ignored or heckled, the lack of respect for what it takes to make a career in music still gets under my skin. I'd like to move past my annoyance and start playing, but Jan insists I meet Ellen, from customer relations, Hal, from the advertising department, Mary, from marketing, and their respective spouses. Mary and her husband, Harry, have brought their twenty-two-year-old daughter, Gracie, with them. Gracie has even less interest in being at this party than I do. She takes her glass of Power Tea to a BarcaLounger at the far end of the room, where she can drink and text in peace.

I assume my place on the designated folding chair and kick off the set with "Peaceful Easy Feeling," a beloved 1972 hit that has always struck me as hippie elevator music. Bill and Jan throw a couple of mildly appreciative nods in my direction, but none of the others acknowledge any sound being generated beyond their own chatter. Gracie never once looks up from her phone. I settle into my role of doing what could just as easily be done by an Amazon Echo, and without the bitterness. Every musician has played plenty of gigs like this, but tonight, as I go through the motions, it's painful. I can't pinpoint why.

Whatever the reason, I must find a way to make the rest of the hour more palatable. I put together a bunch of softish rock songs I like, beginning with "And I Love Her." A reliable crowd-pleaser at all our Help! shows, this earnest McCartney composition gets no reaction from the Power Authority crowd. Likewise, the Stones' "Wild Horses," and JT's "Fire and Rain." As I progress to Sting's "Fields of Gold" and hear Bill Girardi mumble something that sounds perilously like "body shots," I realize why I'm spiraling into a funk. Much as my dad started to resent being a musician when the money got tight, I get angry and depressed when the work feels hacky or unimportant. What's also distressing is that the high of this afternoon is being eaten away by a vibe that oozes mediocrity. That feeling that there was no limit to life's opportunities is evaporating into the ether as Jan Girardi recites her recipe for ham roll-ups.

After Sting fails to impress, I get the idea to take a page out of my Pineview Nursing Home playbook. Since nobody's listening anyway, I'll play "Angel," which always has meaning for me no matter what anyone else thinks. It will be ironic if this turns out to be the tune that finally gets people to pay attention.

"Angel" doesn't come close to stirring anyone other than me. What's interesting, though, is that the feeling I get from the song is different from any other time I've played it. I realize it's because I'm watching Gracie, who would be around the same age as the young woman I wrote this for. As I sing, I imagine Gracie's face morphing into a combination of mine and the face of the angel's mother, someone I hardly remember since we had our one-night stand over two decades ago. It's an exercise in masochism, yet it still beats the image of Bill and Jan's guests sucking tequila off each other.

I find myself wondering what the angel in my song might be doing on a Saturday night. Is she engaging with the world, or staring at her phone like Gracie and most everybody else her age? I'd just like to know is all. Why shouldn't I know how my daughter's doing? Hasn't enough time passed for me to be able to get some idea of who this person is?

Suddenly, I see Gracie look up at me.

"Are you okay," she asks.

"Yeah," I reply.

I feel a lone teardrop escape from my eye.

LAST CALL

The one positive of nobody paying attention to your performance is that you can slip out unnoticed when the work is done, which is exactly what I plan to do at the Girardis' after my cover of "Sugar Mountain." Bill's body shots proposal has been gathering steam, with Gracie's father volunteering to take her home, so he can come back and play unfettered. Once he and Gracie leave, Bill suggests a cocktail comprised of tequila, and Gracie's mom.

As I pull out of the driveway, I wonder how it was possible for the Girardis to have been two of my brother's best friends. I can't think of any life experience that would turn Eddie into a sixty-something soft-porn swinger. And I certainly don't want to think about the things that might unfold over the next few hours. Thankfully, I'm now on my way to the last gig of the night, a twenty-minute set I've agreed to play with a young singer-songwriter named Ben Gardner, who approached me one Wednesday after a Help! gig. It's at Shores, a chill lounge near the water in Sea Cliff, with tonight's lineup comprised of open-mic-night regulars. I plan to waltz in, do my thing, and go home to my cozy basement, where I will arm myself with noise-canceling headphones should I need to block out unsavory sounds from upstairs.

The club is dimly lit when I arrive, so it takes a few seconds for me to realize just how sparse the crowd is for a Saturday night. Usually there's at least somebody on the bill who brings a bunch of friends, but not tonight. Either that or the popular acts have already performed or haven't shown up yet. I spot Ben and wave. He rushes over, looking as nervous as if he were a headliner at Coachella. "We're on in like ten minutes," he sputters. "You gonna be okay?"

"I'll be fine, man. How're you doing?"

"I'm cool. I just don't know whether to open with 'White Lantern' or 'Desdemona's Dream.'"

I'm not sure what to tell him because, while I know the basic chords, I haven't taken the time to analyze the substance of the songs. In the interest of calming his nerves, I help make the decision. How about "White Lantern?"

"You're right. Grab them first, let them think later."

I'm unaware how that theory applies to either of these songs, but at least he now has a game plan.

As it turns out, we're not called to the stage for another half-hour. When I go to plug in my bass, I see that our audience of twenty-somethings has dwindled to maybe eight people, one of whom is a sound guy, another an off-duty waitress. Crowd size be damned, Ben steps up to the mic and proceeds to break the cardinal rule of performing: show before you tell. Rather than play, he talks, and keeps talking—about his songs, how he came to write them, why he hopes the audience enjoys them and, most egregiously, how they should feel free to sing along with the choruses should they have the urge. Every audience member, to a person, is texting for the entirety of his long-winded introduction. Apparently, they didn't get the memo that this singer-songwriter's insights were so profound, they should be on the edge of their seats waiting to hear them. No one is waiting to hear Ben Gardner. The tragedy of it is not that he is about to become background noise, but that he has no clue as to why.

Finally, Ben strums the opening chord to "White Lantern," a navel-gazing summation of a relationship gone sour. It's not awful, and Ben's voice is pleasant enough, but the song that was intended to "grab them" falls as flat as Lizzardo's kid talking about the twenty-six projects he has in development. The rest of the tunes are of a piece in terms of their blandness, varying in tempo but not originality. When the set ends to a tiny smattering of applause, I make the fastest possible move to put my bass away, hoping to execute as covert a departure as I managed at the Girardis'. My hopes are dashed when I see Ben coming toward me.

"Well," he says. "I think they liked it."

"Yeah," I nod, always terrible at waxing poetic about shit I have to make up.

"I think next time I'll start with 'Desdemona's Dream,'" he says.

Ben is either oblivious to what just went down, or doesn't give a shit what anyone else thinks. The latter is an admirable quality in a unique artist, but instant death for a pedestrian archetype of what passes for talent in America's bars, coffeehouses, and YouTube videos. Ben Gardners are everywhere, perhaps because there is such an insatiable appetite for the dreaded "content" that it takes years for them to realize their imagined profundity will never translate to actual income. Eventually they disappear, only to be replaced by a whole new crop of Ben Gardners.

Watching this Ben pack up his guitar, I feel a sadness come over me. As clearly as I was able to recognize that Raji had the goods, I know in my heart that Ben does not. He's a nice kid who's looking at a boatload of heartbreak. If I had to guess, I'd say he's got three to five years before he arrives at his "Come to Jesus" moment. I think about taking him somewhere for a sit-down, telling him how hard the business is, and that he'd be better off finding a real job and playing music on the side.

On the verge of making this altruistic gesture, I realize I've turned into doomsayer Lou Kozlowski, who foisted the identical lecture on Eddie and me. What's the difference between my dad pissing off his kids and me pissing off this one? Maybe I have a bit more talent than Ben? Who's to say? It's not like I'm rolling in the dough. Is it really my place to put the kibosh on someone else's dreams, even if I think the chances of them coming true are slim to none?

I decide it's not. Minuscule though the percentages may be, it's possible that Ben's songwriting will get better, and his stage presence will improve with maturity and experience. At least the guy is making an effort to put himself out there and do something original. Ben Gardner's not the one wearing wigs and Nehru jackets.

I arrive at my house, thankful to be home, and relieved that the cars from the Girardi party have vacated the premises. I speculate that the aging and battered bodies could only withstand a limited amount of shots and cut their losses. Whatever precipitated the party's early end, it's a blessing after a day like this. When I walk inside, Jaco throws me his best sneer, which I deserve for being such an absentee parent. I pet him until it seems like we've reconciled. Then I weigh the proposition of diving into Jaya's leftovers. I decide to save them for tomorrow so I can extend that piece of euphoria for one more day.

After washing up and getting into bed, I'm surprised to feel as wired as I did after Tracy's show last night. My head is clogged with the abundance of singer-songwriters, the inadequacy of the health care system, and the questionable sanity of my fake Beatle boss. After rehashing all three sets of problems, I have no new insights or fixes for any of them. I start thinking about Gracie, wondering how the rest of her night went. Did she think less of her parents after observing the way they interacted with my kind but creepy landlord? Did she meet up with her BFF after her father went back to the party? Did the picture of seeing me cry affect her in any way?

I now understand that the cause of my restlessness is Gracie or, rather, what Gracie represents. Other triggers have driven me to this headspace before, but I'd always rid myself of such thoughts since there was no realistic way to act upon them. Tonight feels different. What always seemed either impossible, or destined to end badly, now demands to be explored.

As much as I dislike social media, Facebook is usually the quickest way to find somebody you haven't seen in over twenty years. The obstacle in my case is that the woman I got pregnant was named Laurie Miller, and there are hundreds of Laurie Millers, not counting the "Lauras," or Lauries/Lauras who go by their married names. Some of them don't even have pictures, and the ones my age look a quarter-century older than anybody I might remember. I do recall that we met at a gig somewhere in Florida, maybe Tampa, and that she might have had freckles on her nose. Not a whole lot to go on, but I devise a plan that will at least make me feel as if I've done something.

I'll start with the Laurie Millers, then go on to the Lauras, and finish up with the ones who've added a married name after the "Miller." When I spot one that's even a vague possibility, I'll send a private message stating my name, where we met, and to contact me if she happens to be that Laurie Miller.

I get through about twenty Laurie Millers, including two in Florida, contacting everyone who looks to be within ten years of my age group. I'll do another batch tomorrow night. Even though I'm resigned to failure, the spontaneous decision to push the button has an energizing effect. It's kind of like the album I'm putting together. Even should nothing come of it, doing the work has intrinsic value. And if a song about drugs and Nazis merits that kind of commitment, trying to find the daughter I've never met deserves everything I've got in me. I wish I could have arrived at this place sooner, but Laurie Miller and I had a deal. Now I need to know which Laurie Miller, and whether the terms are negotiable.

CIRCLE THE HONEY WAGONS

I'm up bright and early the next morning for a daytime porta-potty gig that has the potential to go till the end of the week, according to Mikey. An independent film starring people I've never heard of who apparently merit fancy toilets is shooting at the Planting Fields Arboretum in Brookville. The auteurish director has kept the script closely under wraps (not that he'd be looking for notes from the toilet guy), but from the tidbits I've gleaned, there are zombies involved, as well as a murder in the Dahlia Garden. All I know is, it's a four-hundred-dollar payday, so who's dead or undead is as crucial to me as whether the Dow spikes or tumbles. I have no skin in the game. Another positive is that the arboretum is a pretty place to chill, even if my job is to pump shit. There's also plenty of downtime. I'll try to be productive, though it's never easy for me to mix my separate worlds. I work best with defined parameters, so if there aren't any rules in place, I make my own. Mikey has never forbidden me from bringing my guitar along, but, in the interest of being professional, I leave it at home. I do have my notebook with me, in case a lyric or a new idea for a song appears out of the blue, and this time I also packed a book I started reading, *Love in the*

Time of Cholera. It's a fitting choice given that the classic symptom of cholera is diarrhea.

I know it sounds odd, but my days as a maintenance man are often more relaxing than the music gigs. Set up, monitor, tear down, and pray for no mechanical malfunctions in between. There's an elegance to the simplicity that makes me feel centered. Today's assignment, however, will not be as calming as usual for reasons having nothing to do with the tasks, or lack of them. The antsiness I already feel is a direct result of the curiosity I set in motion on Facebook. Once I dragged myself out of bed at 4:30 this morning, the possibilities began filling my brain: Has anyone responded? What if it's the wrong Laurie Miller? What if the right Laurie Miller saw it, but refuses to reply? What if there's some sicko Laurie Miller out there who has nothing better to do than troll me, and is after money? What if the real Laurie writes back and it turns out my angel is a druggie or a cutter like Tracy's daughter? What did I get myself into?

My obsessiveness seems to be fostering an addiction I despise in others. I'm now checking my phone every two seconds.

Four hours into the shoot, I still have no return message from any of the Laurie Millers. My hope is that the lack of responses will help me to move on and focus on the job at hand. I'm thankful to see the full cast and crew arrive, many of whom engage me in conversation on their trips to and from the restrooms. I chat with the co-stars of the movie, a James Dean look-alike who doesn't know anything about James Dean, and a former model who played a waitress in the last Martin Scorsese film. At some point, she tells me that she stopped one of this director's takes so she could tell him how Scorsese might approach the scene. The director was less than appreciative, so she now thinks she's going to be fired. She asks my opinion, but I've yet to meet the man, and I'm only half-listening anyway. I've temporarily let go of the Laurie Miller situation, but now I'm wondering how Tracy's doing, and thinking about Christina at the Pineview Nursing Home.

Having blown my chance with Tracy, I find myself fantasizing about what it would be like to have one with Christina. Never mind that she is happily married and someone with whom, at least on the surface, I have little in common. It's perfect. Why would I seek out a relationship that made sense? I'm drawn to Christina not just because she's attractive and easy to talk to, but because she was so kind to my dad during his two-year stint at Pineview. When she smiled at Lou and he hugged her as if she were his own, it made me wish he'd had her for a daughter instead of me and Eddie for sons. For one thing, Christina never played a musical instrument, which would have eliminated all those years of anger and regret.

I'm thinking that maybe I should take out the Márquez book, as the thoughts I'm having are not particularly helpful. First I need to check on the restrooms to make sure they haven't been decimated by any troublesome reactions to craft service's breakfast burritos. Everything seems to be under control, so I'm able to barrel through the honey wagons at a good pace. Then, just as I'm cleaning the last one, I hear somebody calling my name from outside.

The voice is unmistakable. Gene Klein has shown up at my porta-potty job, no doubt to impart wisdom he feels cannot wait until our pre-gig meeting tomorrow night. I weigh the idea of locking myself in the restroom until he goes away. For five minutes or so, I try that, preferring the smell of shit in a tank to this man stalking me. When it sounds like the coast is clear, I open the door and see no sign of Gene. I go to get my book.

"Jimmy," Gene calls out, stepping out from behind a shrub. He seems uncharacteristically subdued.

"Hey, Gene," I reply, with an equal lack of enthusiasm. "Didn't expect to see you here."

"I didn't expect to be here. You didn't answer your phone, so I went to see Mikey and asked if he knew where you were."

What the hell? Mikey threw me under the bus?

"He claimed not to know until I told him it was really, really important, and that I wouldn't make him wear the new fake nose tomorrow night."

"What's so important, Gene? You need to bust my chops about 'I'm Down' again?"

"My mom's in the hospital."

"Oh, geez, I'm sorry."

Gene looks pale as a ghost. "She was having trouble breathing last night, so we took her to the Emergency Room. Doctor said there was fluid in her lungs. She's doing a little better now. In her own room at North Shore. Claimed she heard a jazz group playing 'Satin Doll' out at the nurse's station."

"I'm glad to hear she's on the mend. Anything you need me to do?" The minute the words leave my lips, I know they're about to be twisted into something Gene wants as opposed to what Marcia needs.

"As a matter of fact, there is," Gene says. "I want you to promise you're going to make the trip to Liverpool with me."

"What are you talking about, Gene? Did you seriously book a UK Tour? How could you even do something like that with your mom in this kind of shape?"

"It's complicated," Gene says. "It's going to take a few steps to get us there, but I just want to make sure you're in. I'd love to have the whole band there, but I know Mikey has this business and Tommy Tandoori has some bullshit he needs to be around for—"

"Prem designs missiles for Lockheed."

'Whatever. I need my Paul to be part of the package. I can farm out George and Ringo if I have to."

"I'm trying to wrap my head around this, Gene. Your mom is in the hospital with serious health issues, hearing music that isn't there, and it's more important to visit me at my toilets to talk about a pie-in-the-sky UK tour? It makes no sense."

"It will, once I lay out the specifics for the whole band tomorrow night. Plus, I'm sure you know how much Marcia wants you involved."

"Marcia is fighting for her life. How could she possibly give a shit about a bunch of old men taking their cosplay overseas?"

"I may be the heart of this band, but she's the soul."

They're both out of their fucking minds. "Fine. If that's what it takes to make everybody happy, I'll go with you to Liverpool. Can I get back to my toilets now?"

"You don't sound very excited about it."

"Does it matter? I said 'yes.'"

"See you tomorrow night at JP's." He scampers off like a teenager about to play a Battle of the Bands in his middle school gym.

I finally get the book out of my backpack when I feel the phone buzzing. History tells me to expect Gene, but when I pull it out of my pocket, I find a text from Mikey that says "I'm sorry."

I don't blame him. I'd name names too if I had a pit bull like Gene barging into my office and breathing down my neck. I start to put the phone back in my pocket when it buzzes again. It appears I have another notification, this one from Facebook Messenger.

It's from Laurie Miller.

While part of me doesn't want to go near this until the toilet work is done, waiting to read a message from the possible mother of my daughter would require the patience of Job, who had a lot less down time than I do. I take a deep breath and click the icon. Laurie's message is not quite what I'd hoped for.

What the fuck do you think you're doing?

Then it sinks in, and I can't help but smile. The first Laurie Miller to respond to me is pissed off big time, which means she has something invested in my request. Bullseye.

The joy is fleeting, however, as the message goes on to remind me that I was the one who wanted to wash my hands of the situation (which is absolutely true), so how dare I try to make contact all these years later?

What Laurie is conveniently leaving out is that she had a fiancé at the time of our tryst and was convinced he'd break up with her if he found out the baby wasn't his. Thus, in the interest of protecting us both, we forged a deal based on damage control. She was already in a committed relationship but happened to get a little drunk and cheated. I was an immature rock 'n' roller and poor. The idea of

116

erasing me from the picture was the most practical and humane solution for all. At least it seemed so at the time.

According to Laurie, nothing has changed.

> Steve would be devastated if he found out
> Gaby wasn't his.

Gaby. The angel has a name.

> I'm sure you understand.

I do. Sort of. I'm not the kind of person who wants to tear apart anyone's family. On the other hand, Gaby is an adult now. Doesn't she have a right to know who her birth father is?

I consider the possibility that I'm being selfish. If Gaby's happy with her life and the father she thinks is hers, why risk creating chaos where it needn't exist? Exposing the truth at this point would be all about me, a guy who, despite having carved out a Spartan musician's lifestyle, never thought he'd wind up forty-nine and alone. It's not like I think of myself as lonely, or even alone in the world, but there is something brewing that I can't ignore. With no wife or significant other, both parents and a sibling gone, I'm hungry for a connection with someone who's closer than a buddy, an ex-girlfriend, or the leader of a Beatles tribute band.

I read further into Laurie's message.

> Since she's now an adult, it's obviously Ga-
> by's legal right to know who her father is.

I'm heartened. Laurie understands that this is not some random musing; that my request has legitimate meaning for both father and daughter.

Gaby isn't her real name, by the way.

So much for her keen sensitivity. The woman is treating me like a predator on the loose, which, I've got to say, isn't the best feeling in the world.

> Put yourself in my position. I don't know anything about you. I would hope you're a nice person. I'd like to think I turned out okay, and that Steve and I have been good parents to Gaby and her three sisters.

My daughter has three half-sisters. I waste no time wondering whether the other siblings all look alike and if "Gaby's" ever noticed she's different. I read on.

> I've always known that I would have to tell Gaby the truth one day, but, so far, there's never seemed to be a good time. And even if there had been, I wasn't planning to claim I knew who her dad was. How would I have found you anyway? I couldn't remember your last name. I'm not sure you ever gave it to me.

That seems impossible. How could I have not told her my last name, especially if she went as far as letting me know about the pregnancy? I suppose with all the drugs and alcohol swirling around, anything was possible.

Laurie provides me with one final paragraph.

> If this is really important to you, I'll need to do some thinking. I would ask you to please consider my family's situation as it is now before doing anything rash. The last thing I would want is for you to try to contact her before I get a chance to sort this out. I hope you can be patient. I'll be in touch.

It's a lot to absorb, and I also need to consider the consequences. I decide it might be a good idea to write down the pros and cons of pursuing this further, which I can start doing right now in my lyric notebook. I'm about to remove it from the backpack, when the director of the film approaches.

"You the toilet guy?" he asks.

"At the moment I am."

"Honey Wagon #4 smells like a goddamn sewer."

"Might that be because it's a collection vessel for … sewage?"

"Don't be a wiseass. Just clean it the fuck up." He starts to walk away.

Having been around far too many prima donna musicians, I can't let him off scot-free. "Scorsese doesn't talk to people like that," I call out. "Maybe that's why his actors never complain about his direction."

The director turns and starts back toward me. "What did you just say?"

"Pretty much that you're a little shit making a zombie movie that will be forgotten by next summer."

"I'm gonna have you fired," the director shoots back, rattled.

"All good. I've hosed out way more important toilets than yours."

A megaphone calls the director back to set. He gives me a parting glare.

It occurs to me that I might have gotten Mikey's company in trouble. I'll have to clean up that mess later because my mind is elsewhere, in a place it has never been. If the word from Laurie turns out to be positive, it could change everything.

HERE'S MY CARD

By the time I wake up the next morning, I've received messages from three additional Laurie Millers, including one hawking her XXX webcam. I take some comfort in knowing that the porn star who specializes in "old school bondage" is not the mother of my child, yet I do spend a few unhurried minutes absorbing the virtual tour of her "toy closet," featuring over two hundred vintage whips.

I also get a call from Mikey, informing me that my services will not be needed on set today. It seems the reason for my dismissal has nothing to do with being fired by the director, but with the director being fired by the producer. The movie is shut down for at least the rest of the week. I suppose the lesson is that nobody's indispensable, whether you're an auteur, a mediocre singer-songwriter, or a guy doing volunteer work with a bunch of old people.

The cancellation has freed me up for Pineview rec room duty, where the crowd now anticipates my first song with the eagerness of calves waiting to become veal. I know by now that blank stares are part of the bargain, so, instead of taking it personally, I focus on the work. On the way over, I felt like I wanted to start with a different welcome song instead of "Hello, Goodbye," but I was hard-pressed to come up with a worthy substitute. Then, right as I turned into the Pineview driveway, the gods shone down on me, reminding me of a tune Eddie used to play in our room. In addition to being catchy, the lyric entreats the listener to participate—perfect for trying to engage an audience that either shows up checked out or gets there in a hurry without the proper musical intervention. Excited about putting my theory to the test, I strum the opening chord and start singing.

"Hello, I love you, won't you tell me your name?
Hello, I love you, can I jump in your game?
Hello, I love you, won't you tell me your name?"

Nothing. This audience makes the Girardi crowd's reaction look like a mosh pit. I remain undaunted, repeating the chorus over and over until I detect one of the women starting to stir.

"Nora!" she suddenly shouts out.

"Barney!" another resident chimes in.

You gotta love the Doors. I never get to the rest of the lyrics, because I want to see how many reactions I can squeeze out of the first three lines. I manage to add a Barbara, a Jenny and a Cecil to my tally, expanding the two-minute hit to nearly eight minutes before concluding that I've exhausted every possible participant. It's an unqualified breakthrough, which will earn "Hello, I Love You" a regular spot in the rotation.

One of the things I like about this job, besides the opportunity to honor my dad's memory, is the present nature of the task at hand. It's hard to obsess over less talented musicians making seven figures when you're working with people who could cross over to the other side at any moment. Your voice could be the last voice they hear. Ergo, I feel a deep sense of responsibility to my audience, whether they're calling out their names or gazing off into space. Today I'm graced with a bonus. A good number of visitor/relatives are sitting with their loved ones. These guests tend to prompt the residents to get with the program and participate to the best of their abilities. Most of them also seem to appreciate the effort I put into what I do, which helps prevent my enthusiasm from flagging. On some days, when there are no visitors and everyone is off in the clouds, I'll drift off to my own dark places. I'll occasionally channel my dad and berate myself for having to cobble together so many C-grade gigs just to pay the rent. I'll wish I were one of the Ben Gardners—that way, I would have been forced to switch careers before I hit thirty.

The key to maintaining a good attitude in this game is being able to recognize, and hang onto, the snippets of magic that cross your path. My duet with Tracy, jamming with Raji. Even Gene's "You've Got to Hide Your Love Away." There is no dollar amount you can put on the alchemy created in those moments. Today I can add Nora, Barney, Barbara, Jenny and Cecil's responses to that list.

The visitor/relatives' unwavering support is making the hour fly by. I'm particularly grateful to a thirtyish hipster-type, who I'm guessing is Violet's grandson. He's taken it upon himself to play the cheerleader role, encouraging the group to sing along on "Yellow Submarine," and applauding after every song, clapping the loudest for the one I wrote about my daughter. I know it's a good tune, but I'm still surprised that it appears to be his favorite. It usually takes more than one listen for an audience member to get excited about a new piece of music.

I close the set with "So Long, Marianne," the Leonard Cohen confessional that took up residence in my soul the first time I heard it. The narrator informs us that he and Marianne met when they were "almost young." She held onto him like he was a crucifix. He says he'd like to live with her, but he can't because she makes him forget things like praying to the angels. He's saying "so long" while, at the same time, declaring that this is the time to laugh and cry about all they experienced together. I can't think of a better song to illustrate the paradoxical nature of relationships. It's also a perfect closer, because the listener can either ruminate on that theme, or use it to say goodbye, which is perfect in this context.

Challenging myself to compile a meaningful setlist is another reminder of the value in what I do, even when others don't see it. It got me through the Girardi party, and it means the world here, as the songs reflect my deep respect for the residents, as well as the workers who care for them.

I wave goodbye to Nora, Barbara, Cecil, and the rest, as they are wheeled back to their rooms. Violet's grandson stops to thank me for my efforts. "That was really awesome, Jimmy."

I'm surprised he knows my name. I don't think I mentioned it this afternoon.

"I really loved that one ballad you played. I'm guessing it was an original?"

I nod my head. "Angel."

"Christina was right about you."

"Christina?"

"Normally I visit my grandma on Mondays, but Christina told me how good you were, and I should come on a Tuesday when I could hear you."

I'm bowled over. Not only does Christina think I'm good, she's advertising it.

"I produce a bunch of different acts, and I'm always looking for new voices," he continues.

"I'm not exactly what you'd call 'new,'" I respond with a laugh.

"How many albums have you recorded?"

"Of solo work? None."

"Then you're new. I'm Donny Delgado."

His name doesn't sound familiar, but nobody can keep track of all the new music. "Jimmy Kozlowski." We shake hands.

Donny takes out his business card. "Give me a call sometime, Jimmy Kozlowski. I'd love to chat. Maybe see you perform somewhere."

"At an under-ninety-nine venue?"

Donny smiles. "I'm not into ageism."

"Obviously not, if you're handing me your card."

"It's a card. And this is a hunch. Neither of 'em cost much, but who knows? Could be a big payoff. Worse comes to worst, you seem like a good dude. See you." Donny waves and heads out.

Is it possible that, against all odds, I've just been discovered at age forty-nine, in a nursing home? I suppose stranger things have happened, but I can't think of one. Any way you slice it, Donny is a different sort of grandson than the ones I usually run into here. I need to go to Christina's office to thank her.

I walk down the hall and see that her door is closed. Vera, the receptionist, says she's talking to a woman about admitting her husband, and could be a while. I ask Vera for a piece of paper and an envelope, which she is happy to supply. Since I don't have Christina's cell number or email address, I decide to write out a thank-you note, which Vera can give to her after her meeting.

Composing the note takes a little longer than anticipated, as I find myself obsessing over how to sign off ("Sincerely?" "Warmly?" "Fondly?"), and whether to include my cell number and/or email address. I go with "fondly" and start scribbling every bit of information I can think of, minus my list of prescription medications and blood type. I put down my home address, but then think better of it. What if Christina went to look for me, knocked on Bill's door by mistake, and wound up becoming one of his tequila treats? A ridiculous thought, seeing as how she has no reason to come to my house, but I'm not about to take any chances. I stuff the letter in the envelope and hand it to Vera. She shoots me the sly smile of someone who's been handed the most secret of love notes.

Maybe I'm imagining that, too. As I leave Pineview, I wonder whether it's time for me to have sex with somebody who's actually available. There are a few sure bets spanning various tiers of maintenance, or I can venture into the unknown, and further complicate my life. Honestly, as much as I crave the feel of another body, there's a lot to be said for flying solo. Every outing is a command performance, and nobody breaks your balls for saying the wrong thing when it's over.

This doesn't prevent me from fantasizing that Christina will open the letter and call me on my drive home. I want her to hear my voice, thanking her for sending Donny Delgado my way. Then I'm struck by the thought that maybe Donny is as attracted to her as I am, and that he showed up for my set to score some points. I regroup, realizing I'm so busy mooning over Christina, I haven't bothered to Google Donny to check out what he's done. Whether he's a for-real producer. It's also conceivable that I hesitated because I've become more jaded over the years and tend to discount the career-changing carrots that are sporadically dangled before me. The self-fulfilling negative prophecy is that if anything big was going to happen, it would have happened by now. Contemplating new possibilities is always tricky. In a way, it's easier to be Gene Klein, whose entire world is his band and his mother. The more moving parts you add, the more avenues there are for disappointment. The greatest first line ever written doesn't just apply to families. Each unhappy musician is unhappy in his own way.

THE BIG TIME

According to Google, Donny Delgado is an up-and-comer. That I've never heard of him, or the acts he produces, likely means he's even more successful than I think he is. With five hip-hop releases under his belt, Donny's also dabbled in EDM, and is most recently responsible for the debut album from a twenty-five-year-old, butt-shaking chanteuse who's being marketed as the Guatemalan Shakira. I'm not sure what young Donny sees in me, but, endgame aside, the prospect of working with him is a hell of a lot more attractive than pumping out musical pablum for Barry Lizzardo's content business. To have a prayer of making it happen, though, I need to lay a lot of groundwork. First off, I must arrange a night to showcase my original material. Finding a venue shouldn't be a problem, but crafting the right setlist into something seasoned and polished is another story. I'm too old to be perceived as an *enfant terrible*, so I'll have to shoot for "battle-scarred artiste." It's a formidable task. Thanks to my other obligations and a career-long case of front-man insecurity, I haven't done an entire set of my own material in at least ten years. For now, my solution is to tape Donny's business card next to the trackpad on my laptop in the hope that it will motivate me each time I open it.

From what Eddie told me, he and Gene had their own Donny Delgado in the late seventies, a rock 'n' roll critic from Chillicothe, Ohio, named Marshall Haberman. Haberman had made it his mission to get their band (at the time known as The Cracks) a contract with Columbia Records. After seeing them at a local beer bar, he penned an essay for the *Chillicothe Gazette* proclaiming that he, much like Jon Landau, had also seen "rock 'n' roll future." The critic didn't dispute that Bruce Springsteen would be the headliner of the future—his prediction was that the Boss's opening act would be a Long Island quartet known as The Cracks. Even though it was common knowledge that Springsteen didn't tour with an opening act, the *Gazette* piece was syndicated throughout the country, resulting in twenty gigs the band would never have booked otherwise.

Haberman went on to become the manager of The Cracks, and, at the end of what was jokingly referred to as "The Springsteen Tour," sat Gene and Eddie down to issue them their marching orders. Columbia Records wasn't going to be interested in an act whose bread and butter was Deep Purple and T. Rex covers, so if they wanted to be anything more than a bar band, they needed to write original material, and great material at that. Gene and Eddie took his words to heart, making a vow to write songs that were worthy of the venerated red Columbia label.

Unfortunately, the hopeful resolve of this newly minted songwriting partnership would be mitigated by Gene being both a control freak, and the poster boy for the still-yet-to-be-diagnosed ADHD. The bandleader's lethal potpourri of behavioral disorders would put a serious crimp in their Leiber-Stoller and Lennon-McCartney dreams. Gene had many subjects he wanted to write about, from love, to religion, to space travel, but, due to his hyper nature, he was only capable of generating disparate fragments that proved unusable. Eddie's more stable presence gave him a leg up on crafting a coherent song but, by his own later admission, the product lacked a compelling original voice. Still, he managed to churn out enough for a debut album, which Gene declared cause for celebration. As a token of his thanks, he invited Eddie to Manero's, a local steakhouse where we'd sometimes go with the family on special occasions. Eddie felt relaxed and grateful to have his contributions recognized. Then, just as the medium rare filets hit the table, Gene revealed the impetus for his generosity. He begged my brother not to tell Haberman that he wrote the songs himself because he felt it would do serious damage to the "Gene Klein persona."

Not only did Eddie find the "persona" description melodramatic, but he was also aware that if he complied, he'd be giving up half his royalties. He complied anyway, unable to bear the thought of the man who brought him into the music industry becoming any more of a neurotic head case than he already was.

I was unlucky enough to be in the room the first time Eddie played one of his originals for Dad. Lou sat on the sofa, quietly absorbing the three verses, chorus, middle eight, and guitar solo of "Give It All to Me," a tune I was excited about for no other reason than it was written by my brother. When the song ended, Dad paused for at least thirty seconds before uttering a word. That the word happened to be "eh," didn't help matters. Eddie looked like he was about to kill Lou and proceeded to go off on him in a way I'd never seen anyone dare to attempt. It scared the shit out of me. He called him a terrible father, a mediocre talent, bitter, and jealous of everybody else's successes. What made it even worse for Lou, according to Mom, was that the amped-up nature of my brother's reaction sounded more to him like Gene than Eddie. Out-of-control unraveling had never been a part of my brother's emotional make-up.

Another father might have taken a little time to let the incident pass, and try to work things out, as Irene suggested, but Lou was a firm believer in tough love. He kicked Eddie out of the house, telling him that if he wanted to destroy his life and write terrible songs in the process, he was on his own.

Meanwhile, Marshall Haberman, while far more positive about the Cracks' original material, hadn't gotten them a meeting with Columbia Records, or with any label for that matter. Gene began to grumble about how hard "they" had worked on these new songs, that maybe they needed to find a new manager who could deliver on his promises. Eddie, perhaps out of loyalty, or maybe because he didn't truly believe he was churning out A-level stuff, impressed upon Gene to remember that Haberman was the one who had taken them this far. Gene agreed to give the manager a little more time to peddle their wares.

Nobody was more surprised than Gene when Haberman burst into a rehearsal with the announcement that he was getting them a meeting at Columbia with a young A&R guy named Jeff Morton. There was no set date yet, but Morton assured him it would take place over the next couple of weeks. Eddie managed to keep his cool when Gene remarked that "their" songwriting hard work had finally paid off. My brother was less concerned with Gene taking the credit than with how Lou would eat shit when he heard about their record contract.

Eddie and Gene took turns checking in with Haberman to make sure he nailed down the meeting before their next tour. Since the manager was the one who booked the tour, he obviously knew the schedule, but it was fast approaching, and the band was anxious to find out what Columbia had to say. When another two weeks passed without hearing anything, they started getting pissed off, and feeling ignored. Haberman hadn't returned either of their calls for five days. Five days became ten days, which turned into two more weeks.

In an ironic twist, the first person to find out about the manager was Lou. Somebody looking for Eddie had dialed our house, thinking he still lived at that number. The man who'd cut my brother out of his life had to break it to him that Marshall Haberman had died of a massive heroin overdose.

The one silver lining to the tragedy was that it created an opening for Lou and Eddie's relationship. They started talking again, and Eddie began sleeping at the house between tours. Gene, on the other hand, mourned the manager's loss for maybe an hour and a half, then went on to inform my brother that their priority should be to contact Jeff Morton. The Cracks were the same band, with or without Haberman. Eddie reminded him that it wasn't professional to just pick up the phone and call an executive at Columbia Records, but maybe they could write him a letter. This, of course, meant that Eddie would have to write the letter for Gene to approve. After eight drafts, Gene and Eddie went to the post office to make sure their missive wouldn't be lost by some irresponsible mail carrier.

The return address was Gene's mom's house, so, every night, he'd check in with her from the road to see if they'd gotten a response. One night, after an uneventful gig in Elkhart, Indiana, Gene told him he had some news. Instead of receiving a reply from Jeff Morton saying he couldn't wait to meet them, their letter had been returned to sender, adorned with a handwritten scrawl that read: "No one by that name at this address." Gene postulated that perhaps Morton had defected to Atco or Polygram Records, and that Columbia wasn't forwarding his mail because they didn't want to enable any new deals he was interested in making. The truth was that since neither he nor my brother had any big-name contacts in the music business, and the internet had yet to exist, there was no concrete information to go on; any theory was pure speculation. Adding to the frustration was that they still had a slew of road gigs ahead of them, so it would be a while before they'd be able to get to the bottom of it.

When Eddie and Gene finally learned the truth, it only made things worse. They knew Haberman had a glib, schmoozy side, but neither of them would have pegged him to make up a meeting, or, worse, make up a person. Gene saw this as the ultimate betrayal, and took it hard. The unexpected blow began to chip away at his self-image and ever-reliable ambition. Soon, he lost all interest in playing original material. What was the point, if this was where all that hard work took you?

Eddie didn't necessarily feel as if every manager and recording opportunity would produce the same lack of results, but he'd grown tired of shouldering the songwriting burden himself. That was why, when Gene suggested they take a break from writing to focus all their efforts on booking tour dates, Eddie jumped at the idea.

It's important for me to remember that my situation is different. Delgado isn't Haberman until proven guilty. And my original material, some of it written years before I had anything to do with Gene, might even be good. I must remain open to that possibility and do whatever is in my power to see this through.

BEATLE BUSINESS

The schedule for tonight's gig starts with our 5:30 p.m. band meeting, followed by a 6 p.m. set-up, 6:30 sound check, and a first set start time between 7:30 p.m. and 8. Prem, Mikey, and I usually straggle in ten or fifteen minutes late, which forces our leader to be more succinct in trumpeting his latest agenda and current list of complaints. Gene usually shows up around 4:30 to soak up the vibe, using the extra time to write down the important wisdom he needs to impart. Tonight, however, the rest of the band is present and accounted for by 6, with no trace of the boss in sight. We assume he's busy with Marcia, either in the hospital or back home, on the chance she's already been released.

The guys and I start arranging our equipment onstage, each of us remarking how much more relaxed it is without Gene there to supervise. I talk about the ups and downs of putting together my album. Prem shows us the '57 Les Paul Sunburst he just added to his guitar collection. Mikey reveals that he had his hearing tested, and he's losing some of the high end. None of these topics would have had a prayer of surfacing with Gene around, because as much as he romanticizes being a band of brothers, he is incapable of sharing, or listening, thanks to his lifelong run as the center of attention. Gene's psychological makeup also precludes Help! from functioning as a strict, patriarchal unit, as he lacks every qualification to be a father.

The boss finally shows up at 6:10, pre-dressed in the John wig and white suit from Abbey Road. He already gave us the heads-up that he wants to focus on later Beatles material tonight, but this is the first time he's ever showed up in 1968 wardrobe. He seems even more fidgety than usual, especially when I ask how Marcia's doing.

"She can't make it tonight," is his response, the tone suggesting that he has no intention of elaborating on the subject. He plugs in his amp, sets his microphone, places his guitars on stands, and hurries Prem, Mikey, and me to a table so we can begin our meeting.

"We're gonna start with Setlist #7," is his first surprising announcement. We've opened with later Beatles stuff before, but I don't think we've ever begun a show with Setlist #7. Gene must be feeling his oats tonight, because the lynchpins of this set are two Lennon wailers: "Yer Blues," and "Everybody Got Something to Hide 'Cept for Me and My Monkey." I appreciate that he's decided to channel his intensity into the music and look forward to hearing him sing these tunes. I also know that if we're doing Setlist #7, he's going to tell me to be more animated on "Helter Skelter," like he always does.

Gene is true to form on the "more animated" front, and I am equally so when I nod "okay." Mikey is lucky enough to get a pass on aftermarket noses, and Prem manages to escape without an elocution lesson. The introductory business completed, we arrive at the "open your checkbook" portion of the meeting.

Gene begins with an enthusiastic pitch for a Beatle boot manufacturer whose footwear has a more authentic look than what we're currently wearing. He feels that given the quality of the leather, they're a steal at $150 a pair. While I don't dispute the craftsmanship, it still seems like throwing away money. I make the argument that the boots we have are decent enough and, besides, how many people are looking at our feet? Prem and Mikey shoot me the evil eye. They're willing to cave on this one in order to spare us all a miserable evening. In the interest of keeping the peace, I fold.

The next item on Gene's agenda isn't as well received. Unlike many of the current tribute bands, Help! has yet to appear wearing Sgt. Pepper outfits. We've been able to dodge this bullet up till now, because Gene has always considered the available products to be cheesy. Fifty or seventy-five dollars got you something that looked like a cheap Halloween costume, as opposed to the silk ensembles worn by the Beatles, and it was beneath the leader of Help! to have his band come off like a bunch of trick-or-treaters. Now, he explains, there are garments worthy of our professional consideration. An exclusive haberdasher in London can provide us with bespoke Sgt. Pepper suits for a mere nine hundred pounds apiece. All we need to do is get measured by a local tailor, email the lengths to the UK, and in six weeks we'll be a Lonely Hearts Club Band.

Mikey, who makes more money in one year from his toilet business than Help! will earn over its entire lifespan, refuses to shell out that kind of money so our Fake John can feel classy. Gene is disappointed in his drummer. "You're saying you'd be comfortable looking like a clown?" he asks Mikey.

"I'm saying you're the guy who wants me to wear a rubber nose. What's more clownish than that?"

"Apples and oranges," is Gene's comeback.

Prem is no more enthusiastic than Mikey, which incenses Gene further.

"Seriously? You, with all your big defense contracts, want to do this on the cheap? I don't need to tell you that Sgt. Pepper is a military man," he reminds Prem.

Finally, Gene looks at me, knowing he won't get anywhere since I was the one who raised an objection to the $150 boots. He shakes his head at the three of us, aghast that we would even consider presenting as anything less than a top-level tribute band. "All I'm saying is 'Rain' didn't get to Broadway wearing fifty-dollar Pepper suits."

Mikey is not about to let this remark pass. "The Fab Faux don't wear any costumes, and they're the best Beatles tribute band ever."

"Don't throw those elitists in my face," Gene fumes. "They have like sixteen people onstage to make them sound that way. How am I gonna be able to pay sixteen ungrateful cheapskates?"

"Almost time for sound check," I remind the boss, a reliable tension-cutter.

"I have one more item I need to talk about," he says. "It won't take long."

The idiotic UK Tour. He probably got me to commit in advance so he could use it as bait to sign up the others.

"As you know, it's been my dream to show the world outside Nassau and Suffolk counties just what this amazing band is capable of. Now we're going to have the opportunity to do just that."

I dread what's coming next. If he expects us to spring for nine hundred pounds on costumes, how much is a UK Tour going to cost? Nobody in their right mind is going to pay for this band's airfare and hotel.

"I've heard all your concerns, and, based on your reactions to the Pepper suits, I'm sure you're questioning the expense of crossing the pond. I'm here to tell you, you can put that worry out of your minds."

Mikey is the first to speak up. "You're saying you got us booked to play in England?"

Prem wants to know when. He'll need to coordinate the dates with his work.

I'm still not buying that anybody else is paying, but I'm curious as to what they're supposedly paying for. "Will we be playing just in Liverpool or all around England?"

"Liverpool for now. The rest depends on whether or not we win."

"Win what?" Mikey throws up his hands. "What the hell are you talking about, Gene?"

Gene smiles and proceeds to hand us the printouts he's been hiding under his Help! agenda legal pad. The headline of the page reads:

Battle of the Beatles Tribute Bands!
August 13–14

"Marcia already paid our entrance fee," he announces with delight. "Jimmy's committed, but I need to know where the rest of you stand ASAP, so I can make other arrangements if necessary."

According to the flyer, the weekend contest is to be held in the town of Liverpool, New York, a bedroom community outside of Syracuse. Gene explains that a local music promoter came up with the idea of using the town's name as a marketing tool to lure a bunch of the world's cover groups into participating in what he promises will be a major annual event. The winning band will, indeed, get flown to Liverpool, England, and perform at the Cavern Club, as well as three other UK venues.

Mikey's not thrilled. "It's a Battle of the Bands, for Chrissake. I've hated those since I was a kid."

Prem has never experienced a Battle of the Bands and is somewhat intrigued by the idea. "Is it like *American Idol*? or *The Voice*?" he wants to know.

"It's even better," Gene says, "because everybody in competition is a Beatle." He turns to include the rest of us. "Now you see why the Pepper outfits are so important. You don't want to go in handicapped."

Mikey tells him the contest looks like even more of a scam than the nine-hundred-pound custom suits, which doesn't go over well with our Beatle-in-Chief.

"I'll take either of those scams over a career in excrement. You don't want to come, there are plenty of drummers who do."

Mikey glares at me. "Did you really agree to this?"

I want to tell him I was roped in under duress, but I'm certain this would just make things worse.

Prem asks what the cut-off date is for him to give his answer.

"Yesterday," Gene says. "But since I didn't tell you till today, talk to your wife, take a few days to think it over. I will warn you, though, you'll need to up your game on those 'W's' if we're going to stand a chance with 'Taxman.'"

Mikey rolls his eyes, which doesn't escape Gene.

"So, you're not going?" Gene barks.

"Why would I want to? You just insulted the highly successful company my family started forty-six years ago."

"I'm sorry if I offended you. But, be honest, don't you love music more than you love shit?"

"I don't love shit, you dickhead! Why would you even say that?"

"I'm sorry. And you're in no way obligated to come with us if you don't want to."

"I'm entitled to free will? That's very generous of you."

Gene's not done. "Look, Mikey, I love Help!, and, for my money, the four of us are the ideal lineup for this battle. But I can't force it on you. The thing is—"

"What, Gene? What's the thing?" Mikey says, girding himself for the next insult.

Gene sighs. "I just want to say that, even though I know I'll have my choice of drummers, the only one I'd choose to sing 'A Little Help From My Friends' is you. That's all. I'm gonna go comb my wig." Gene repairs to the dressing room.

I look at Mikey. Unless I'm crazy, I think he's softening.

It's unclear whether Gene's excitement about the contest, or the challenge of playing his first local show without Marcia to cheer him on, has changed the dynamic. Either way, tonight's John Lennon is fire. No corny introductions, no Liverpool accent, just a punch to the gut that rocks hard, and rings true. Consciously or not, Gene has put his "boots-and-suits" bullshit aside to channel what drew him to the music in the first place.

"Yes, I'm lonely. Wanna die …"

In the context of Gene's current situation, this cry from the soul confronts his impending loss with even greater depth than "You've Got to Hide Your Love Away." Even Mikey, who most nights projects a Ringo-like "I just play the drums" detachment, seems emotionally invested. It's hard to ignore the conviction with which Gene plays each guitar note, or the monster intensity of his vocal attack. I'm curious as to whether Gene himself recognizes that this is a different kind of evening. I get my answer when he decides to change up the set order, and go straight from "Yer Blues" to "Everybody's Got Something to Hide …"

JP Murphy's is a similar crowd to Carmine's in Glen Cove, but tonight even the Jägerbombers sense that attention must be paid to the man in the white suit. I, for one, would have no objection to Gene singing every song, and I doubt the audience would mind either. Another interesting side note is that our regulars have come to recognize Marcia, and those who weren't already aware of her absence are made so when Gene switches out "I Dig a Pony" for the Lennon solo track, "Mother." The whole place rises to its feet. Gene's read on the song is remarkable in that he makes John's primal cry for help *his* cry, which the crowd feels to its core. I start thinking about my dad, wishing he could have witnessed this performance. Perhaps he would have finally been able to see the value in an artist who was able to dig deep, and communicate in such a raw, vulnerable way. At the very least, maybe he would've stopped reciting all the horrible ways he hoped Gene would die.

After three mega-doses of ferociousness, Gene decides to lighten things up with the Lennon version of "Stand By Me" from the Phil Spector-produced *Rock 'n' roll* album. The evening's rocky start has made a one-eighty turn, and become the most interesting Help! show in a long time. Gene finishes the second chorus, and signals to Prem that he'd like a guitar solo. Prem is happy to oblige. Just as he begins, I see a group of Asian women enter and head for a table. One of them looks up to smile at me, and I realize it's Christina from Pineview, who appears to have shown up with a bunch of friends. I'm sure I never mentioned that I was playing anywhere tonight, so I'm both surprised and touched that she sought me out. I'm also pleased that giving Christina my contact info turned out way better than her knocking on Bill Girardi's door by mistake.

Gene turns to me, asking for "Back in the USSR," followed by a set-ender of "Helter Skelter." I'm smart enough to recognize that however I might try to match Gene's passion, the night belongs to him. Whatever catalyst propelled him to these heights has paid enormous dividends, rendering the crowd putty in his hands. I am the beneficiary, as the audience is so revved up, their appreciation spills over to me, whether or not I deserve it. The closing bar of "Helter Skelter" gets them on their feet, applauding, with Christina leading the charge. It's a kick to see this straitlaced nursing-home administrator having the time of her life. I'm not totally sure what to make of it, or if there is anything more than what's on the surface. If my job was welcoming guests to God's waiting room, listening to a bunch of fake Beatles might well be the highlight of my life.

After Gene tells the crowd we'll back in twenty, I deposit my Hofner bass on its guitar stand and make a beeline over to the table of my appreciative-looking guests. Christina stands and gives me a big hug.

I think I might be blushing. "What a fantastic surprise!" I tell her. "Thank you so much for coming. How did you even know I was—"

"Your website," she replies. "But there weren't any pictures of you in a wig." She gives it a close look and giggles.

"I have four more of these suckers. I hate to tell you, but this is the best of them."

"It's good quality," says one of her compatriots, a serious-looking woman with long, dark hair.

"Thank you, Christina's friend."

"This is Jasmine," Christina chimes in. "And this is Rosamie, and Darna."

"Pleased to meet you," I say. "It's so nice of you all to come out."

Rosamie and Darna offer the sweetest of smiles. Jasmine, however, retains her studious pose.

"Is the wig human hair?" she wants to know. "It looks to me like it came from an Indian or Sri Lankan head."

"I'm really not sure," I say. "Gene does all our wig-ordering."

"Who's Gene?"

"He's the guy who plays John."

"Who's John?"

Jasmine is obviously not too familiar with the Beatles. Rosamie is a little more so, and Darna momentarily mistakes them for another old band, which I finally figure out is the Monkees. I sit down to join the group, and learn that all three of Christina's friends are in the caregiving business as well, working at other nursing homes or with private clients. They each wear wedding bands which, fairly or not, leads me to wonder if they also came into the country by marrying Americans. I order a round of beers and chicken wings for the table, earning me generous thank-yous from all but the circumspect Jasmine, who throws a noncommittal nod in my direction. I'm about to go into a little Beatles history, as well as their cultural significance, when I see Gene heading in our direction, probably to reprimand me for something I have no idea I did.

"Evenin', luvs," he says, hauling out the old Liverpudlian for their benefit.

"Are you John?" Jasmine asks.

"Indeed I am. And you would be?"

"Yoko," Christina offers.

I laugh. Nobody except Christina and Gene knows what I'm laughing at. Gene doesn't seem to find it funny.

"You do look a bit like Yoko," he tells Jasmine.

"Who is Yoko?" she asks with a blank stare.

A comment such as this would normally cause Gene to lose it, as he expects everyone with a pulse to possess a substantive knowledge of Beatles lore. Inexplicably, he seems to be holding his shit together. I introduce him to my friend Christina, who goes on to introduce her three friends. Christina lets him know how much they're enjoying the show, but Gene is barely paying attention. He can't take his eyes off Jasmine.

"I like your hair," he says.

"It's mine," she answers. "Came with me from the Philippines. Where is yours from?"

"My wig? The UK, of course. It has to be authentic."

They move from hair talk to Gene asking Jasmine what she does for a living. Jasmine tells him she's a caregiver for a blind man who is about to turn a hundred next month. Gene, probably on account of his experience with Marcia, seems awed by Jasmine's ability to take on such a task.

"I like to help people," she says.

Gene spends the rest of the break chatting up Jasmine. I do my best to entertain Christina's other friends, hoping they'll be impressed by how nice I am, and later sing my praises to the ringleader of the group. I don't expect it to go anywhere, but I guess a part of me wants Christina to acknowledge that she feels something, even if all options are off the table. When I ask the women if they miss the Philippines, Rosamie looks as if she's about to cry. She describes her hometown, idyllic in every way barring the lack of work and crippling poverty. She sends money back to her family but hasn't been back in over four years. She's saving every penny to make a trip home. Darna says she was in Manila last year and has no interest in returning for a while.

"What about you?" I ask Christina. She shrugs, saying her husband doesn't like to go back, so she doesn't visit all that often.

"Is that okay with you?"

She nods that it is. I don't believe her. I think she's being kind, because that's who she is.

I check my watch and see it's about time for the second set. I call out to Gene and tip my head toward the stage. He holds up his finger to let me know he needs another minute. I see him shake Jasmine's hand as if they've just sealed some kind of deal.

I tell Christina and the others that I'll see them after the next set. When Gene follows me to the green room, I ask him what it was I just saw.

"Great stuff, Jimbo. Jasmine is somebody who likes to help, and I came up with a way for her to help us."

"The band?"

Gene nods and grins.

Backstage, we're informed that it's going to be a late-Beatles second set, and that Gene intends to start with "Come Together." He then lets us know that Jasmine has been hired to assist him for the rest of the evening. Prem, Mikey, and I are at a total loss as to what this means. As we leave the Green Room to take our places, the answer reveals itself. At the foot of the stage, right beneath where Gene will be singing, sits Jasmine, whose new part-time job is to stare at him adoringly. Prem and Mikey exchange incredulous looks, but let it go, as they have music to play. We kick off "Come Together," with Jasmine fixating on Gene in unblinking worship. She's a natural, as proven by her ability to hold this pose for the entirety of the song. I've experienced kismet in various forms, but this, to the best of my knowledge, is the first time a Long Island Jewish John has found his Filipina Yoko. I'm also pretty sure the pairing is the only sideshow of its kind to grace any Beatles tribute band worldwide.

I look out at the audience, which seems to find nothing odd about the scene. I can't imagine what Christina and the others think, seeing their friend bow in servitude to a guitar player, but whatever their feelings are don't stop them from swaying to the beat and scarfing down their chicken wings. The most insane part of the picture is the pride Gene takes in having a subservient fake girlfriend. His performance simmers with a sexuality that hasn't surfaced since his bands with Eddie. I'm curious as to whether he intends to make Jasmine his actual girlfriend, which could be a problem since she wears a wedding ring. Deciphering the inner workings of Gene's strange mind will have to wait, as I need to get ready for "Maxwell's Silver Hammer" and "Oh, Darling!"

We end the night with the *Abbey Road* medley and an encore of "I Saw Her Standing There." Not a soul has left the room for the duration of our performance. Gene's response to the hearty applause is a rare (for us) arena-rock-like move, summoning the band members to put our arms around each other and take a bow. The rest of us think it's cheesy and over the top, but who cares at this point? As good a show as we delivered, it's another day in the fake Beatle salt mines, and we're ready to pack up and go home. Gene, however, wants us to take additional bows, during which he blows kisses to Jasmine. She responds with a beatific smile, her first display of emotion since she arrived.

Before I start to deal with my gear, I go over to Christina's table to thank her again for coming by. If I'm being honest, just as Jasmine playing Yoko pumped up Gene's testosterone, Christina's presence has raised my hopes. Whether she showed up as an act of friendship, or another fun night on the town with her girlfriends, I am grateful to have her in my life.

"I hope you enjoyed yourselves," I say.

"We did." Christina smiles. "You're amazing." Her steadfast gaze makes the words seem like they are personally directed, as opposed to band directed.

Is it a big tease? Maybe she really does feel something.

"I think Jasmine had the best time," Rosamie exclaims, looking toward the stage.

Sure enough, Gene is placing a couple of bills in Jasmine's outstretched palm.

Truth be told, I'm less interested in the absurdity of Gene paying a stranger to stare at him than in trying to decipher Christina's current state of mind. I want to tell her she's amazing as well, but I'm too self-conscious to follow through. Since thanking her for coming one more time would border on ridiculous, I float an alternate superficial pleasantry. "I can't wait to play at Pineview next week," I say, a double meaning there for the taking.

"I can't wait to hear you," she answers.

I'm not any closer to knowing what to think. There isn't time to worry about it, as a gleeful Jasmine comes skipping over to us, grinning from ear to ear. "I just made forty dollars," she announces. "This Yoko lady had an easy job."

Three new fake-Beatles fans and one new fake-Beatles employee head out to their car. I can't imagine what Gene is thinking right now, but nothing would surprise me. In my ideal world, he and Fake Yoko hole up in a hotel room for a week to protest whatever the hell they want, and I get a vacation from the neediness so I can deal with my own stuff. I have an album to record, a set to put together, and something with the potential to be bigger than both.

I note the symmetry of not only being a fake Beatle but having a fake daughter. Technically, she's a real daughter with a fake name, but the idea that I can't be trusted with the truth doesn't help matters. I check my messages. There's an email from Laurie Miller. I'm ecstatic upon seeing the subject line: "The Next Step," but this time, I'm smart enough to wait until I'm home before getting into the specifics of how she wants me to proceed. It turns out to be a wise move because just as I put the phone back in my pocket, I'm accosted by Gene.

"Incredible, right?" he asks, with a smile.

"You killed it, Gene. Powerful stuff."

As much as he loves praise, his mind is elsewhere. "I'm talking about Yoko. How great is this gonna be?"

"That depends on how much people like Yoko. If they think she was the one who broke up the Beatles, it might not be so great."

"The 'Get Back' documentary shot that full of holes. Plus, you gotta look at the whole picture. It's a big wide tribute world out there, and Help! needs to stand out from the pack. This adds a layer of authenticity that none of the other bands can claim."

I tell Gene to step back a second and reexamine the authenticity gambit. "Jasmine isn't only not Japanese, she has no idea who the Beatles were."

Gene shakes his head. "You saw her performance. She feels it from within. I think Marcia's gonna love her, don't you?"

I don't know what to say, but it doesn't matter anyway. Gene's going to do what Gene wants, and I will be much better served by agreeing, and getting myself out of here. I look over at the empty stage, realizing that Prem and Mikey have beaten me to it. "Give Marcia my love," I tell Gene, the only sincere thing I can think of to say.

"Right-o, mate," he responds in his British accent. "Yoko's gonna slay them in Liverpool."

THE NEXT STEP

I get home around 1:30, the first order of business being to show some love to the furry blob whose mild anger-management problems are totally on me. Considering the number of hours the dude is forced to spend with only a pathetic-looking bowl of kibble for company, it's amazing he's this well-adjusted. A few forkfuls of canned salmon seem small compensation for a life sentence in a basement.

My second task is to turn on the computer and read Laurie's email in a quiet space on a bigger screen, so I can fully absorb whatever she's decided to fling at me, good or bad. As the laptop boots up, I start thinking about when might be a good time for me to fly to Florida, assuming "Gaby" still lives there. With a busy month of gigs, a setlist to put together for Donny Delgado, and a commitment to what is destined to be a bizarre weekend in Liverpool, New York, I know it will be a challenge to find a workable couple of days, even before taking Gaby's schedule into account. On the other hand, as the one who initiated contact, it's my responsibility to make this happen.

I click on Laurie's email and am surprised to see it's only a few lines long. You'd think a daughter meeting her birth father for the first time would call for a more extensive dialogue. Once I start reading, I understand the reason for the email's skimpiness.

> Hi Jimmy,
>
> I'm still uncomfortable talking about this to Gaby because I don't feel I know you well enough. Could you give me more information, so I can be sure this is the right thing for my daughter? It's a dangerous world out there, and Gaby is still young, so I want to do everything I can to protect her. I'm sorry if this is an inconvenience, but I'm sure you'd feel the same way in my position. Thank you, Laurie.

Her daughter? I get that she raised this girl, but refusing to acknowledge any involvement on my part strikes me as particularly insensitive in light of our previous communication. Laurie's also dead wrong about how I would feel in her position, because I'd never take a "predator until proven normal" stance toward someone I have no reason to fear. I won't bring up either of these things because they would only slam the door shut, possibly forever. The wiser, albeit more demanding choice is to compose a heartfelt letter providing Laurie Miller with a more in-depth picture of who I am. I hate this idea. As a musician, I've spent so much time trying to justify my existence that the idea of having to prove my worth to this person makes me want to put my fist through a wall. But there are only two options here: suck it up or give it up.

I haven't pulled an all-nighter since I quit playing the road, but my gut tells me the sun will come up before I complete My Life in Cliff Notes. In keeping with the theme of going back in time, I open the cabinet above the kitchen sink and retrieve a bottle of single malt Glenlivet, my constant companion back in the touring days. Whenever I needed a little extra loosening up, it was Highlander liquid manna that did the trick. Recalling that some of those situations progressed from loose to sloppy, I promise myself to not hit "send" until I've had a few hours of sobriety.

I take a couple of quick shots and get started, but it's almost an hour before I compose the first sentence. Eventually, the words begin to come together.

Dear Laurie,

I know it's been a lifetime since our night together and the agreement we made a few months later. Memories can be deceiving, especially those of a musician like me who, at twenty-two, was known to dabble in substances I've long since abandoned. Despite the fogginess of my youth, not only did I never forget your last name, but there was another thing that stuck just as vividly (aside from the fact that you were really pretty).

It seems almost inconceivable today, but after you told me you were pregnant, the two of us discussed it rationally, determined how we thought the future should play out, and trusted each other enough to forgo signing documents. In retrospect, you could say we were a couple of dumb kids who didn't know any better. I prefer to think there was something in our respective characters that told us everything would turn out all right. From the little you've told me about Gaby and your family, it appears we were correct.

Please know that the last thing I'd want is to screw that up. Should you decide to tell her who I am, I will continue to respect her relationship with you, as well as the one she's built with the father who raised her. All I'm after here is a connection. Perhaps seeing her birth father in the flesh will be meaningful to her as well.

As for what my life is like, the road isn't my thing anymore, but I'm still a musician, doing the work I love. Other fun facts? I've been playing in a Beatles tribute band for over ten years, working with the same guy my brother used to play with. I'm also putting together a solo record, and I volunteer at a nursing home. If you need more, I'm happy to provide you with my driver's license, health insurance information, and latest credit report, which is pretty damn clean because I no longer owe or borrow anything. I'd love to know more about your life, too—not in a background-checky kind of way. I'm just interested in where people land once they figure out who they really are. If you don't want to talk about it, that's cool too. I wish you and your family nothing but the best.

Sincerely,
Jimmy Kozlowski

The letter is finished just before sunrise, the bottle, slightly after. I remember to follow my own advice and wait a few hours before sending. When I read it over, the words seem honest enough, but I've skirted one key point—that I have no one left. The last thing I want Laurie to think is that I'm looking for some kind of replacement family. It's not like I expect my daughter to pick up and come live with me so we can make up for all our years apart. My goal is to get one more shot at a caring, invested relationship. To have somebody out there who gives a shit. To be there for that somebody any way I can: as a sounding board, a fresh perspective, a source of compassion. I never got there with Tracy. I only fantasize about it with Christina. And I lost it with the one person other than my mother who always had my back. For twenty-nine years, I've been looking to fill the hole left by Eddie Kozlowski, who was always there to remind me of the possibilities.

GOODBYE

In the fall of 1990, as the popularity of the Lou Kozlowski Orchestra continued to wane, my mother took it upon herself to find gainful employment. The goals were to put Lou at ease and, more importantly, to get herself out of the house. Eddie was on the road most of the year with Gene, and I was a sophomore at SUNY Albany, which left Irene free to take advantage of her long-awaited opportunity to explore the world. Some people backpacked across Europe, others became tellers at the Reliance Savings Bank on Willis Avenue in Albertson.

To Irene, who had spent thirty-plus years as a pro-bono nurturer and anxiety-deflector, enrolling customers in the Christmas Club (zero interest, WTF?) seemed no less exciting than serving as Ambassador to the United Nations. Back in those halcyon, pre-ATM days, people *liked* talking to their bank tellers. Irene got to meet all kinds of new folks, many of whom she would come to regard as friends. Sometimes people she knew would step up to the window and feel embarrassed by her finding out how much money they had in their accounts, but once Irene realized this, she made a conscious effort to put all her customers at ease and avoid judging them on the worth of their passbooks. She also resolved never to share the numbers with Lou, who knew for a fact that a few of the neighbors were Reliance Savings customers. The only time Irene broke confidentiality was the day Charlotte Snell walked in to withdraw fifteen dollars from a passbook account that clocked in at $67.12. It made no sense to her. Even if this were merely her "allowance" savings, how could the big-shot accountant, who they had lobbied for Eddie's internship, let his wife traffic in chump change? The mystery was compounded by Charlotte's polite and unflustered manner throughout the transaction. Lou half-joked that Bob Snell must have spent his entire fortune on air conditioning.

Mom's new career provided the bonus of being able to start conversations with her husband that were outside the realm of so-and so's new Cadillac, Eddie wasting his life, and the constant disappointments of the music business. My father didn't necessarily appreciate her newly collected tales of the nun who spoke Pig Latin, or the former dentist who became a muffler repairman, but he liked seeing his wife happy, and admired her willingness to roll up her sleeves and pitch in. By the time I came home for Christmas break that year, the atmosphere in the house seemed appreciably lighter, as if an environmental response team had expunged ancient layers of emotional asbestos. Lou still had his complaints, but the bitterness had taken a substantial dip. Word had it, he'd even agreed to treat Irene to a Caribbean cruise, an unheard-of splurge in previous years.

When Mom asked if I was dating, Dad seemed relieved to hear that there was nobody serious. Even with all the progress he'd made, my concentrating on schoolwork and getting a degree remained his number-one priority. My priority for this visit was to keep the mood calm and bright. Hence, I stayed mum about Bloodshot, the new band I had joined, which was fast making a name for itself with the crazed fraternity and sorority parties we played almost every weekend. There was nothing to be gained from a Christmas that shattered their illusions about the "good son." Better they continued to think of me as the pimply, shy kid as opposed to the popular SUNY Albany bassist who now had his pick of the finest debauchery options. I no longer had to spend hours mapping out how to start conversations with girls because they were the ones who initiated the small talk before getting to the things I'd witnessed on Eddie's Oklahoma tour. If my brother was a bona fide a rock star, I could now be categorized as "rock star lite." I was getting a taste of the great life while continuing to please my parents.

Eddie and I didn't have the chance to talk much, as he was always on the road, and the cell phone was still a few years away. Occasionally, a pay phone he dialed would get through to my dorm and I'd grill him on the gigs and the fans. Sometimes he sounded tired, but he was always happy to hear my voice, as I was to hear his. On some calls, I'd ask him to recite every city and venue he'd be playing, so I could write down all the information. It wasn't as if I'd be joining him in places like Nebraska anytime soon, but knowing I'd be able to find him gave me comfort.

When Eddie called the house on Christmas morning, Lou happened to be the one who picked up. I prepared myself for the fireworks certain to ensue, but as I heard my father's side of the conversation, I felt proud of him for the first time since I was a kid. His tone was one of interest and concern, as opposed to his boilerplate derision. Somehow, in my absence, Lou had managed to look inward and find empathy. When he closed the conversation with "Merry Christmas, son," I thought I detected a tear in the corner of his eye. He handed the phone to Irene, who started bawling the minute she tried to speak. I could tell that my brother was asking her a bunch of questions, but Mom could only sniffle back the answers.

Sobbing was where personal growth ended for Lou, as he still hadn't arrived at the place where he could deal with overt displays of emotion. The best he could do was give Irene an awkward pat on the back and sit down on the couch to watch the Dallas Cowboys piss off all of New York by beating the Giants, yet again. When Mom finally finished weeping her love for Eddie, she handed the phone to me, and went off to the kitchen to check on her infamous candy-cane-shaped snickerdoodles.

"Merry Christmas, bro," I began. "How's the weather in Cleveland?"

"Raining and Merry Christmas to you. You really do keep track of everywhere I go."

"Something to keep me busy," I said, downplaying my need to live vicariously through him. "How's the road treating you?"

"It's the road," Eddie answered, sounding a bit less enchanted with it than he once was.

"How's Gene? And don't just tell me 'He's Gene.'"

"How 'bout this, then? He's Gene, only more so."

I was hungry for real news. Some rock 'n' roll epiphany I hadn't heard before. Or maybe just that my brother was still excited about the music. Nobody with that much God-given talent should see his gifts become old hat. "Tell me you're still loving it all," I finally blurted out.

"I'm cool with it," Eddie's replied. "But it's like any other job you take. You kind of want a sense of what's next. Where things are going."

I told Eddie I understood. I went on to give him the scoop on Albany and the latest with Bloodshot. "We're no Traction, but the kids seem to like us. I'm in with some good players too."

Eddie was happy for me. "I'm gonna come hear you guys!" he crowed, as if he was ready to jump on a plane to Albany so he could catch a fraternity gig.

"We're putting in the work—getting better," I added, not wanting to raise his expectations.

"I'm definitely gonna do it," Eddie said. "And, I got a little Christmas present for you, Jimmy the K. But you don't get it till April."

"That's cool. I still haven't gotten anything for you. Is it a surprise?"

"Yep. But I'm telling you about it now. Traction just booked some new tour dates, and one of them is in Albany."

"Unbelievable! I can't think of a better present than seeing you guys. I'll bring half the school."

"That's not the surprise, Jimmy."

I was at a loss. "It sounds like a pretty big one to me."

Eddie proceeded to lay out the whole picture. "Traction is going to play at this dive bar called Pauly's Hotel—"

"I know it well. Got dragged there to some disco night two weeks ago."

"I think you're going to enjoy this show a little more. Especially since you and your band are going to open for us."

"What???" I couldn't believe what I was hearing.

"I told Gene to make it a condition of booking the gig. It worked."

"Holy shit!" I screamed, drawing glares from both the snickerdoodle-maker and Cowboy-hater. "That is the most amazing thing ever. Thank you so much!"

"I gotta go, Jimmy. Merry Christmas."

"Merry Christmas," I answered in a whisper, all I had left after that news.

As I hung up the phone, Lou stared me up and down. "What's the most amazing thing ever, Jimmy?"

"Eddie's gonna play Albany!" I left out the second part, convinced it would not seem quite as amazing to Lou as it had to me.

When I got back to school in January, I made a point of stopping into Pauly's Hotel to double-check that Traction and Bloodshot were on their official calendar. They told me they had nothing printed up for events that far in advance, but that some band called Traction was indeed booked to headline on April 1. Nobody seemed very psyched, which pissed me off until I realized that there were a million cover bands, and it was hard to get excited about any of them until they showed you what they could do onstage. To the event organizer at Pauly's, Traction was just another come-on for beer and wings.

The guys in Bloodshot, on the other hand, were crazy stoked about the booking. I had talked about Eddie from Day One, and played them every recording I had of him, including the cassettes made in our bedroom. Kyle Morris, our lead guitarist, compared Eddie's tone to Jimmy Page's, which was the highest form of praise. I had also briefed the band on rock 'n' roll savant Gene Klein, so the idea of getting to share the bill with the two of them motivated Bloodshot to rehearse like demons. In preparation for April, we went from one practice a week, to two or three, and even four, on occasion, working to put together twenty to thirty minutes of the tightest material we could. The only dilemma was whether to include any of our originals in the mix. Traction, by that point, had gone back to an all-cover setlist, so was it presumptuous for an opening act made up of college kids to present itself as a band that aspired to more? I assured the guys that Eddie and Gene wouldn't be fazed either way—they were pros through and through. The best argument against doing originals was that they weren't that great. The case "for" was that a couple of the tunes ("Gone Wishing" and "Red Cells") had developed somewhat of a cult following among the local groupies, one of whom happened to be the girl I'd been seeing for a couple of months.

Jolie Reese showed up at rehearsals from time to time, usually with one of the other band members' girlfriends. This could be distracting, but it was also a great confidence-builder. What could be more empowering for a twenty-year-old rocker than locking eyes with a denim-clad nymph who believed in you? The truth was that outside of practice sessions and gigs, Jolie and I didn't have all that much to say to one another. She was a hometown Albany girl who smoked way more weed than I did, and had enrolled in college only because her parents insisted on it. She was a psychology major, but the vibe she gave off was of someone whose future would be defined by a boring job, and a couch potato husband who cheated on her. It wasn't that Jolie was depressed, or a depressing person. She was smart, loved to sing and dance, and didn't have a mean bone in her body. What she lacked was the motivation to convert these admirable qualities into anything productive or rewarding.

She did, however, give the best head known to man. One night in my dorm room, she was on track to produce perhaps her finest work, a piece of artistry I had already christened the *Penis de Milo*. Awestruck by Jolie's perfectionism, I was preparing for a meteoric finale when something strange happened. All of a sudden, I began to feel a sense of future outrage on her behalf. I pictured myself confronting Jolie's inevitably boring husband, telling him he should stop cheating on her and appreciate what he's got. Then, midway through my imaginary rebuke of a nonexistent person, I heard a sharp rap on the door.

"Hey, Jimmy, you in there?" shouted a voice from the hallway. "It's Rick."

Rick was my RA. He was totally cool about having girls in the room, so there was no reason to be concerned.

"Can I talk to you later?" I asked. "A little busy at the moment."

"Your dad's on the phone. Says it's important."

"Okay, thanks, Rick."

What could that be about?

Jolie, bless her heart, promised to finish what she'd started after I talked to Lou, but something told me to ask for a rain check. I gave her a long, fond kiss goodbye.

"Thank you, Jimmy." She smiled and went on her way.

Her thanking *me* for a kiss? This girl was doomed, no question.

As I picked up the hall phone, it occurred to me that neither of my parents had ever called with any kind of emergency, and that when they normally got in touch, Mom was always the first one on the line. Whatever this was about seemed different than business as usual. Mom had looked healthy and happy at Christmas, enjoying her new life of trying to ignore other people's net worth. Maybe Lou had just been diagnosed with something awful and wanted to tell me himself.

"Hey, Dad," I said into the mouthpiece, trying my best to be cheery.

"Hi, Jimmy," he replied, absent his usual piss-and-vinegar inflection.

"Good to hear from you. What's up?"

"Jimmy—"

Now he didn't sound like my father at all, mostly because he was full-on crying, and I'd never seen or heard him do that.

"What's wrong? Is Mom okay?"

"Yeah. She's fine—"

I heard my mother shrieking in the background. "She doesn't sound fine. What happened?"

Lou attempted to get out the words, but, somehow, it seemed even harder for him to speak than it was for Mom when Eddie called over Christmas. Finally, I was able to make out some of what he was trying to say. "They found him ... in bed."

"Found who in bed? What's going on?"

"In the motel," he said, between Mom's shrieks.

Maybe it was on account of Mom's hysteria, or Dad sounding like a different person, but it took a few steps for me to put the pieces together.

After three more stabs at articulating the information, Lou managed to convey that Gene had just called from Nebraska to tell them Eddie had died of an overdose.

I tried to process the information, but it didn't compute. Not Eddie. Eddie was the smart one, the practical one. He was the guy who kept the others from going off the rails; the guy who always made sure he was on a path that made sense.

According to Gene, the band had been partying the previous night with a combination of drugs and alcohol, but nothing more excessive than usual. If those details were intended to reassure my father, they had fallen well short. Hearing the worst news of his life only reignited Lou's early antipathy toward Gene, this time with violent intensity. "That little asshole killed my son!" he screamed into the phone.

In that moment, pinning the blame on Gene was the only place Lou could go, the handy alternative to holding his Number One son accountable for becoming one more rock 'n' roll casualty.

I didn't know who to blame or what to think. I *couldn't* think, because none of it was real to me. This was my brother. My hero. He still had a surprise he needed to make good on. Pauly's Hotel was expecting both Kozlowski brothers on April 1.

Powerless to form any thoughts that resembled logic, I searched for something comforting to say to my dad, but I was in the same state of shock he and my mom inhabited. The only thing I could think to say was, "Are you sure about this?"

Part of me knew it was stupid, but when you're numb, you don't always come up with the most coherent questions, especially when you don't want to hear the answer.

"Your mother and I are flying to Omaha tomorrow for the autopsy, then we'll bring him home," Lou said. "If you want to come, I'll wire you money for the ticket."

"Of course I want to be there."

I didn't want to be there at all. I'd taken a few psychology classes and knew all about "closure," but if I stayed in Albany, I could pretend for a little while longer that this was just a bad dream, and my world hadn't been blown to shit. But I knew pretending wasn't going to cut it. I needed to be in Nebraska for Eddie, who meant everything to me, whether as a role model or a corpse.

I asked Lou if Irene wanted to get on the phone, thinking it might help to hear one son, present and accounted for, but she was too distraught to even lift the receiver. As bad as it felt to me, I could only imagine the grief of a mother who'd loved her son so much, she cried at the mere sound of his voice. I suggested to Lou that perhaps it would be better if just the two of us went, to spare Mom some of the anguish.

"She doesn't want to be spared," Lou said.

I knew exactly what she meant. Even though I hadn't yet experienced it in an adult relationship, my instincts told me that the only accurate measure of love was the willingness to withstand an equal measure of pain.

"You can do me one favor, though, kid," my father added.

"Whatever you need."

"Make sure I never see Gene Klein's face for as long as I live. Otherwise, you'll be visiting me in the slammer."

"Okay," I said, seeing no point in pursuing the subject. "I'll start checking into flights."

Hanging up the receiver, I took a moment and looked around the cinderblock hallway. Why did I bother to go to college? Why did it matter?

Lou would probably say, "So you don't wind up like your brother," which is exactly what he said to me when Eddie was alive. There was too much to take in. A vibrant young soul had been stopped in his tracks at the age of thirty-four. Why would he let that happen? Unless it really was somebody else's fault. Eddie had sounded tired in that last phone call. Was he unhappy? Depressed? Was there some part of him that wanted to go out that way?

There would be plenty of time to search for answers in the days and years ahead. Soon, my roommate would be walking down the hall on his way back from the library. If I didn't get my act together before then, I'd have to explain why I was on the phone with the airlines, booking a last-minute flight to Omaha. As I turned back to the phone, it rang again before I could pick up the receiver. Probably Mom wanting to check in.

"Hello?"

"Hey," said the voice on the other side, which sounded nothing like my mother, and exactly like Jolie. "I just wanted to see what was up. Everything okay?"

"Yeah," I lied. "Everything's fine."

Maybe if we'd had more mutual interests than sex and rock 'n' roll, I could have talked about what happened, but probably not. This was all new to me, and I hadn't a clue how to sort out my muddled thoughts and feelings. For all I knew, Jolie wanted me to ask her to come back over. I didn't.

"I guess I'll see you around," she said. "Maybe tomorrow or something?"

"Maybe." I couldn't even be honest enough to tell her I wouldn't be there.

Now, not only did I hate the cruel fate that had befallen my brother, I hated myself.

FULL BORE

My head finally hits the pillow, but sleep doesn't seem to be in the cards, as there is a raucous, story-slam competition raging in my head. The competing plot lines feature the paranoid woman I impregnated, the married woman I covet, and the mercenary who has unknowingly agreed to impersonate the most hated character in all of Beatledom. While I'm lucid enough to realize that the endings to these stories can't yet be known, common sense does little to quiet the internal chatter. The chaos is compounded by a flashback of my brother's bloated body at the Omaha morgue.

The only way out at this point is the little jar on my nightstand. I'm about to pop a double-dose of Ambien, but just as I unscrew the childproof cap, I hear a thumping noise from upstairs. Joining the insomnia jamboree are the unsettling sounds of my landlords, Bill and Jan Girardi, engaging in early morning sex play, the imagined visual now even less appealing on the heels of the Body Shots Incident. Dialogue-wise, the combination of Bill's "take it all," and Jan's old-school "fuck me, Daddy" are enough to drive anyone to a vow of celibacy. That said, props to the Girardis for continuing to do their thing flesh on flesh. For the last six months, my bedtime partners have mostly appeared via video, courtesy of the fine folks at Porn Hub. To make things worse, the rote nature of the Hub's slight variations on a theme has become mind-numbing. The other night, I chose to go offline and imagine a hotter, less predictable plotline, which also felt like a chore. It's not that I've lost interest in sex, but these days it takes a lot of work to come up with even a bare-bones fantasy.

I start to consider that maybe I haven't been functioning quite as well as I think I have. The whole trick to living the contained musician's life is the belief that you're getting enough out of it. I can't seem to stop myself from wanting more. Why else would I stay up all night composing a letter that will most likely be dead on arrival? In the past, I would never have considered a move so fraught with landmines. I guess it doesn't feel so good to be on the verge of turning fifty, having mastered only one life lesson—low expectations. It's a useful tool to keep me from feeling devastated when I don't get the high-end gig I want, or when I'm forced to accept a shitty one for embarrassing pay, but it's also a curse. The presumption of diminished returns makes it harder to take a leap of faith, even on opportunities that have the potential to turn things around.

Case in point, Donny Delgado. A producer walks into a nursing home, and, rather than being the set-up for a joke, winds up daring me to get at it; do something that could become something bigger. Granted, the odds are never in your favor, but when you're putting everything you've got into the work you love, odds don't matter. Being able to power through the self-doubt, go deep, maybe mine a few specks of gold—that's a win right there, even if Donny Delgado turns out to be the spawn of Marshall Haberman. In my pre-low-expectations twenties, I would have jumped at the challenge, rehearsing and recording demo tracks late into the night until I collapsed in a puddle. Not so for the pushing-fifty Jimmy. I'll put something together, for sure, but at a much more deliberate pace. After so many career disappointments, I don't want to expend so much energy that I'll feel like a fool if I get burned.

At the same time, I know that if I do want something more, I need to leave my comfort zone. The kind of gamble I took with Laurie Miller must find its way into my music, and, on a personal level, with Christina. I don't want to break up a marriage. I just want to know what she's thinking. Since sex doesn't seem to be my priority right now, the idea of developing a friendship seems plausible. She might think otherwise, but I'll never know unless I ask.

As Jan Girardi adds "Make me come, Daddy" to the repertoire, I decide to kick into high gear, both with my set for Delgado, and trying to get closer to Christina. I leap out of bed, grab my Stratocaster, and crank the amp loud enough to drown out any future noises from the Girardis. Three power chords later, I'm not thinking about insomnia. I've got work to do.

I hit it hard for two and a half hours and get half my setlist figured out. Then, just to make it official, I shoot off an email to Delgado, informing him of my progress. Putting it in writing is my insurance policy, the theory being that since I've announced my commitment, I must now deliver on it. My hope is that Donny will send back an encouraging response, which will provide just the jolt I need to finish the work.

I close the laptop, wolf down a quick bowl of cereal, and jump in the car to make my way to Pineview Nursing Home. No guitars in the trunk this time, because it's not a workday for me. I'm going to see Christina. My feeling is that not waiting the seventy-two hours until I *have* to be there makes a statement about how important she is, even if I'm the only one who interprets it that way.

I know Christina has a busy schedule, admitting new residents and working overtime to keep the old ones (and their families) happy under trying circumstances. I don't intend to stay long. I just want to see her face while the exhilaration and craziness of last night are still fresh in her mind.

I spend the better part of the drive rehashing how I'm responsible for my own loneliness, having closed myself off from relationships to create the life I thought I wanted. I wasn't always resistant to romance. Before Tracy but after Jolie, there was Kirsten Walters, a girl I'd had a monster crush on in high school but was too insecure to approach. A cheerleader and 4.0 student who played the oboe and got accepted to Princeton, she never once acted like she knew who I was. Then, one year, we both happened to be home from college on spring break and found ourselves in the same aisle at the old Nescott Drug Store on Willis Avenue. She looked even more beautiful than I remembered, but, somehow, under the fluorescent lights in the 2-liter soda section, she suddenly seemed accessible. Without hesitation, I offered a casual hello, and Kirsten returned the greeting. She indicated that she knew who I was all along, and said I seemed different now.

Of course I was different. High school nerd Jimmy Kozlowski had become rock star lite, a respected bass-man who, by now, had been with enough girls that the likelihood of a drug store rejection was no longer a life-or-death issue. Besides, word on the street was that Ivy Leaguers were uptight and snooty, so who needed that shit anyway? As it turned out, Kirsten was not only down-to-earth, but on the rebound from a boy named Blake, whose family epitomized the patrician sense of entitlement she had grown to despise. Thanks to the Blake-ster, I had an epic spring break, Kirsten's resentment being the motivator for my exhaustive good fortune.

I also fell madly in love with her. No matter how confident I'd become at college, winning the affection of someone I'd long written off as unattainable was like a first date with heroin. I was prepared to do anything for Kirsten Walters, even offering to trade in my bass for a cello, so we could better complement each other when she played the oboe. Kirsten then informed me that she gave up the oboe three years ago and that she had no interest in a serious relationship. She confessed that she'd been using me for sex, which, while flattering, also hurt my feelings. How come it always had to be like that? The minute you were finally ready to love somebody, they didn't love you. It was the flipside of my relationship with Jolie, except that when I thought about it, there was no real evidence of her having loved me either. Girls seemed to like fooling around with me, but would any of them ever feel what I felt for Kirsten?

Reeling from the loss, I came to a decision. From that point forward, rock 'n' roll babes were the least damaging way to go. They fed your ego, and you went home happy— at least happy enough to get you to the next gig, or the next class, when the weekend was over. From then until Tracy, and after Tracy, my life would become a revolving door of non-relationships, producing varying degrees of sexual satisfaction and nothing in the way of emotional attachment.

Arriving at the nursing home, I step up to the reception desk and let Vera know I'm there to see Christina. "I don't have an appointment. I was in the area and just wanted to say hi."

"No passing notes this time?" Vera winks.

She's on to me, even though, at this stage, there's not a whole lot of red meat there. She buzzes Christina and tells me to have a seat. "Ms. Pierce will be right with you." Vera seems to be enjoying this.

I sit down and start thinking about what I'm going to say once I get waved into the office. There are plenty of opening lines I can go with.

So glad you came to the show. I just wanted to thank you. What did your friend Jasmine say on the way home? Hey, if you want to come to another show, we're playing at Carmine's in Glen Cove next week …

I look down and see my knee twitching like Gene Klein's. I'm a nervous teenager, about to ask a girl to his first dance. Starting the conversation shouldn't be a problem. What's tricky is figuring out how to tell her the real reason I'm here—that I want her in my life, on whatever terms she chooses. Realistically, I won't be able to get that far in a drive-by office visit, but if I can score a good vibe, it might set up whatever is to happen next.

Coffee? Lunch? A walk somewhere—

"Mr. Kozlowski—" Vera clears her throat.

I think she's been trying to get my attention while I've checked out.

"Ms. Pierce is ready for you."

I take a deep breath and walk through the door to Christina's office. She seems as relaxed as I am nervous, greeting me with a smile that cries out for a hug. Considering the HR-appropriateness of such a move, I hang back, only to find Christina hugging me. She's wearing a silk blouse, black velvet pants, and tailored yellow sport coat—the essence of administrative aphrodisia.

"What brings you by, stranger?" she says, seemingly not bothered by the interruption.

"I was in the area—"

"Doing what?" She's direct. Gotta love that.

"Visiting you."

"That's so nice. Have a seat."

"Thanks." Now I'm directly across from her and starting to feel more comfortable. "So, did you have a good time the other night?"

"I told you I did. Are you here to make sure I wasn't lying?"

"I'm here to make sure I wasn't dreaming," are the words that tumble out. *Did I really just say that?*

"I was there all right. Gene is a funny guy. He already hired Jasmine for next Wednesday night."

"Carmine's in Glen Cove. Are you going?" I ask, hoping she's decided to become a regular.

"I have to see what the hubby wants to do."

She calls him "hubby," which hits me like a punch to the gut. Her being forced to take his white bread last name, "Pierce," was bad enough. I don't know that she was forced, but the assumption fits in nicely with the "loveless marriage" fantasy I'm constructing.

"Just let me know," I say, doing my best to act nonchalant. "I'm sure I can get you comped for some drinks."

"That's really kind of you. You're a great bass player, Jimmy."

I like hearing her say my name. "Thank you, Christina." I'm making full eye contact and she's not turning away. "Listen. I was wondering—"

Her phone buzzes. She picks up, raising her index finger to let me know she'll only be a second. "Uh-huh, Uh-uh … thanks, Vera, I'll be right there." Christina hangs up the phone and rises from her desk. "I have to put out a fire between the activities director and Resident Services," she says. "What were you wondering?"

"Nothing important. I thought maybe you'd want to have coffee sometime, but you're busy and that's okay. I don't mean to—"

"Eight thirty tomorrow morning," she announces. "Starbucks on Commack Road. Don't be late." Christina graces me with one more smile, then shoots out the door. I don't get up right away, so shocked am I that following my impulse has received a positive response. When I do leave the office, my look of satisfaction does not go unnoticed by Vera.

"She's married, you know," the receptionist says.

"She's my boss," I snap back. "I'm not an idiot."

I am an idiot, but not because she's my boss. I suppose if I were a mental health expert, writing up a file on Jimmy Kozlowski, the report would go something like this:

"The patient is unable to function like a normal human, gravitating toward extremes in both the professional and personal arenas. Kozlowski lives below his means as a security blanket, and only seeks out relationships he knows have zero percent chance of developing into anything real."

Maybe I do go to extremes, but, when you think about it, how is a basement apartment any less "normal" than a car-bon-sucking McMansion? And why is nurturing a chaste friendship any less real than a marriage that turns chaste as soon as the kids pop out? My alter-ego therapist might then ask why my leg twitches in anticipation of seeing a woman I'm allegedly not pursuing in a sexual way. I'd answer that while I appreciate her sexuality, I intend to block these thoughts out of respect for her situation. The therapist might say it's the obstacle that excites me, not Christina. I'd then fire the jerk and storm out of his office, only to feel sheepish later because "he" is me.

The only thing I'm sure about is that I can't let any of these questions stand in the way of tomorrow. I will be at Starbucks, 8:30 sharp, ready to learn everything I can about this woman before she goes off to work.

The minute I get home, I collapse on the bed and sleep for almost six hours before crawling out from the covers to check voicemails and messages. Nothing from Donny Delgado or Laurie, ten voicemails from Gene, two from Prem and one from Mikey. The fast version is that Marcia now feels well enough to make a return engagement to Carmine's next week, and Gene wants to surprise her with a Help! rendition of "Strawberry Fields Forever," replete with freshly mixed sound effects. Prem, in response to Gene's pestering phone calls, apparently took a few hours off work to edit digital files, but Gene is still calling to ask for changes. Mikey's message, on the other hand, says there's a toilet job next Monday afternoon if I want it. I decide to ignore all of it for now and harness the energy I got from Christina to refine my solo set.

The '64 Gibson LG-1 acoustic sounds mega-sweet right now, especially in the DADGAD tuning I use on a couple of the songs. The mandate is not to fall into the Ben Gardner trap of playing too many slow ones in a row and put the audience in an emo coma. I have upbeat tunes, but I need at least one more to balance things out. I open my notebooks, prepared to scour a thirty-year-old back catalog, when an idea falls from the sky. I strum the opening chords of "Gone Wishing," the old Bloodshot standby that always seemed half-baked to me. I start filling in the missing pieces, replacing a B major chord with an F-sharp minor, a D with a G-minor 7, changing up a few lyrics that always sucked, reworking it over and over until I feel like I've arrived at something worthwhile. I now have a setlist that clocks in at almost sixteen minutes. I'm on my way. It's been a helluva twenty-four hours by a contained musician's standards—or anyone else's for that matter.

After addressing the various Help! idiocies and saying yes to the toilet job, I hit the gym. I'm no stranger to working out, but I'd be lying if I claimed the timing of this visit had nothing to do with the reaction I got at Pineview. Dopey as it is, some part of me wants to feel young and studly when I walk into Starbucks tomorrow morning, and lifting some decent-sized weights is my best shot at deluding myself. Worst case scenario, I'll tire myself out and be well rested for my long-awaited one-on-one with my boss slash fan.

I awaken to a cool, but sun-drenched morning, rife with promise. Jaco eyes my enthusiasm with suspicion as he watches me get dressed. He's never seen me in an outfit this painstakingly curated or, quite possibly, this clean. I've gone for the Oxford shirt, sport coat, and jeans look, a business-casual complement to whatever ensemble Christina will have chosen to wear to work.

I arrive at Starbucks a little early because I want to see her make an entrance. She's always at Pineview by the time I get there, so a different vantage point strikes me as appealing. Before going inside, I pick out the perfect empty table in the corner where nobody will bother us. Then, just as I walk in, I hear "Hey, you" from the other side of the room. I turn to see someone I might not have recognized had she not opened her mouth. Christina's in sweats, wears no make-up, and has her hair in a ponytail. All natural, and damn cute.

"Look at you," I say, sitting down. The table is nowhere near as private as the one in the corner, but with her on the other side, it's still the best seat in the house. "I thought I was the only one who got to go to work in sweats."

Christina laughs. "Don't be silly. It's my day off. I drop my son off at school, then I come here after my morning run."

Her son. I knew she had a kid, but hearing her say it out loud makes it harder for me to entertain the things I swore I wasn't going to think about in the first place. The good news is, I've been here less than two minutes and she's already given me a killer smile and a window into her life. Plus, how cool is it that she wanted to see me on her day off? I ask what I can get for her. She wants a Grande latte, and I order the same.

As we wait for our drinks, the small talk begins. I thank her for meeting me. She thanks me for inviting her. I ask how the rest of her day went after she raced off to put out the fire. She asks what I did after I left Pineview. I'm sensing she knows we're biding time until the order's ready, and we can get to the real stuff, uninterrupted, but I've been wrong before.

I carry the coffees to the table, sit down, and cite some newspaper article I read that got me to stop putting Splenda in my beverages, spitting out statistics involving lab rats.

After Christina nods her head and I run out of bullshit factoids, she makes the breakthrough move. She wants to know if I miss my dad.

I feel like an idiot for having been the one to prolong the chit-chat. "I miss him a lot," I tell her. "Even though he wasn't the easiest guy to have as a father."

"He knew how much you loved him," Christina replies.

How he'd ascertained that is anybody's guess. By the time Lou came to Pineview, his dementia had progressed to the point where he'd lost all his words. But I believe her, a) because I want to believe everything she says, and b) because she formed a bond with Lou that was unlike her relationships with the other residents. It made sense once I learned that she'd lost her own father around the time mine was admitted. She cried at Lou's funeral, which was where she learned that I have no family left.

For a second, I wonder if this could be a "pity" coffee, but I put the thought out of my head. Why ruin any part of this morning with hypothetical ego-shaming?

"How's your mom doing?" I ask, wondering if I'd have a connection with her like Christina had with my dad.

Christina looks down and shakes her head. She says her mother died a couple of months ago, and she went back to the Philippines to bury her.

I tell her how sorry I am. "I had no idea. I remember you were gone for a week or two, but I thought you were on vacation."

"I didn't want to bother anybody with my personal stuff. It's hard enough keeping people's spirits up at that place."

"What was it like going back?"

"Hard. Sweet. So many good memories. I have a large family. Lots of little cousins. I plan to go back and live there one day. When I'm old."

"Is it beautiful, where you're from?"

"It is." She describes her journey home, first landing in Manila, then riding in a Jeep for four hours to get to the small village where she grew up. From the way she's talking, it doesn't sound like Hubby went with her, but I'm not about to open that can of worms. Instead, I ask her to tell me about the town.

Christina pulls out her phone and shows me pictures. The place where she was born and raised looks poor, yet the beach and the color of the ocean rival the finest Caribbean resorts. There's an adorable shot of her in a bathing suit, guiding two of her cousins into the water. No husband in sight.

I try not to linger too long. "I guess you like the beach, growing up there and all."

"More than anything. No matter how stressed out I get, I breathe that air, feel the sand between my toes, and I'm good again."

I tell her that from my experience, she seems to be the least stressed-out person I've ever met. Christina explains that Pineview is owned by a big corporation. The administrators are always under pressure to fill every bed, and get every bill paid. She says that despite having worked there for ten years, she still loses sleep over a caregiving facility that values the bottom line above all else.

I could be in love.

"What?" she asks, catching me staring.

"I don't know. I was just thinking about something."

"Which was—"

I'm not sure how to answer this. I could make up some crap about Gene or the next gig, but I don't want to. "Maybe we should go to the beach," is all I can think of.

"It's forty-five degrees outside," she says. But she doesn't say "no."

"The beach is fun when there's nobody around," I tell her.

"That's crazy talk, mister."

It may be, but I think she's getting a kick out of it. "I promise to get you back in time to pick up your son."

"Jimmy, I can't—"

The second time she's said my name. Suddenly, I see her eyes looking down at her wedding band.

"It's okay," I assure her. "We've known each other for four years now. I swear on my father's memory, I'm not going to do anything stupid."

"If it's forty-five degrees here, it's gonna feel like thirty-five there. That sounds pretty stupid to me."

If anyone had told me that the admissions director of my late father's nursing home would be riding shotgun in my car, educating me on seabirds of the Philippines, I'd have suggested an on-the-spot drug test. But here we are, headed for Jones Beach, the six-and-a-half-mile summer madhouse that becomes the most blessed of sanctuaries once the off-season begins. I ask Christina if she's ever been there in the fall or winter, to which she replies that she's never visited at all. I can't believe it, knowing she grew up by the water, and has lived on Long Island for over a decade. She explains that Hubby isn't all that crazy about the beach.

"How can you not love the beach?" I ask, immediately regretting my bald, dismissive tone.

"Jack's not a big outdoors guy."

Hubby's name is Jack. Jack Pierce. Hubby sounds dull as shit.

"Wifey," on the other hand, is a ball of fire who has been waiting way too long to play this particular version of hooky. As the beach comes into view, Christina practically bounces out of her seat with excitement. "The place is so empty and clean! But what's the deal with all the trash cans?"

As admirable as it is that the county tries to keep things tidy, the endless, symmetrical rows of metal receptacles are a bit disconcerting if the objective is to commune with nature. "Damage control," I explain. "Summer without these things would get really nasty. I guess you don't have beaches like this in the Philippines."

Christina hasn't heard me, as she's already opened the passenger door and is sprinting toward the cans. Before I know it, the improbability of winding up at the beach with her has yielded something even more improbable. Like a spirit that's been locked up for centuries and suddenly set free, Christina is dancing figure eights around the garbage cans as she makes her way to the shoreline. The profound implication of the scene is not lost on me. Thanks to Hubby Jack's aversion to the outdoors, Fake Beatle Jimmy is the one who gets to witness the personification of pure joy.

I walk toward the water to meet up with her, making a straight-line diagonal route through the cans, yet keeping my distance so as not to disrupt a one-show-only performance. While I know she isn't doing this to entertain an audience, it takes nothing away from the thrill of *being* the audience. I'm touched that Christina feels comfortable enough around me to let me watch her dance.

She reaches the water's edge a minute or so before I do. When I catch up with her, she's smiling, but shivering. I take my sport coat off and drape it over her sweatshirt.

"You don't have to do that. You must be freezing."

"I'll be warm when I'm dead." It takes me a second to realize that it doesn't work that way, unless hellfire happens to be in my future.

A flock of seagulls swoops overhead. Christina stares at them till they pass.

"You like birds," I ask, back in moderate small-talk mode.

"I do. What about you?"

"I never thought much about them. Until my cat killed a sparrow the other day and I had to bury it. I felt really bad about it, but then I found out that sparrows are categorized as pests. People exterminate them."

"People exterminate people," she reminds me.

"True."

"People suck, let's face it."

"You don't really believe that. I don't think you could do your job if you did."

"You're right. I like some people."

I thought I detected a wink, but I'm not sure. "Sometimes the people I like decide they don't like me."

"What do you do that's so bad?" she asks.

"Nothing. That's the beauty of it. I just have to be me."

Christina laughs. "Come on. You're a nice guy."

"Get to know me better and see what you say then."

"Okay," is her matter-of-fact answer.

Was it matter of fact, or was she flirting? I consider putting my arm around her, using the cold as my excuse. Just as I'm about to try, she turns away.

"Look, Jimmy!" she cries, pointing to a bird she seems thrilled to have spotted. She says it's a blue heron, which reminds her of the great-billed herons in the Philippines. I think about asking her if Jack Pierce likes birds, but if he doesn't, bringing it up might upset her. Better to keep finding ways to make her happy.

We talk a little about Gene and Jasmine, and where that might be headed. I tell her I'm recording an album. She says that in addition to having never played a musical instrument, she can't carry a tune, and that the only creative thing she's ever been able to do is draw. I tell her I'd like to see some of her drawings. She says they're not good enough to share.

"I'll bet they are. I'll ask you again sometime."

She glances at her watch. "We should get back."

Even though I know we weren't planning to camp out for the night, there's no part of me that wants to be anywhere but here. "This was amazing," I say, hoping she'll get that I'm talking about being with her.

"It was incredible. You were right about the beach in winter."

Bruce Ferber

I think about taking her hand as we walk to the car, but I wimp out at the last second. Maybe next time. If there is a next time. My last image of this one will be the wind blowing Christina's obsidian-black hair, the silky strands reaching out to brush against my cheek.

They feel like kisses.

ONWARD

Prem's meticulous effects work for the Help! debut of "Strawberry Fields Forever" is locked and loaded for the Carmine's gig, right down to Gene's garbled "I buried Paul" gibberish at the end. The only hitch is that Marcia Klein has turned out to be a no-show for her own surprise. There's obviously a new wrinkle to her story, but a muted and evasive Gene offers up nothing regarding his mother's status. He also looks ten years older than he did last week at JP Murphy's, and the facial tic has kicked into overdrive.

Nobody is surprised by the announcement that our premiere of "Strawberry Fields" will be postponed until Marcia's return, but we are taken aback when Jasmine arrives for Yoko duty, only to be sent home without pay. Gene's rationale is that he's in an early-Beatles mood tonight so, realistically, Yoko would have no reason to be there. Never mind that Jasmine had to spring for a round-trip Uber to receive this news.

The rowdy Carmine's crowd doesn't notice (or care) what kind of mood Gene Klein is in. As long as there's watery Bud and "Roll Over Beethoven," the man could have a massive heart attack and be impaled on his Rickenbacker. My focus is on the front entrance in anticipation of

Christina's arrival, with or without Hubby. A peripheral glance over at the bar has also alerted me to the presence of Amy, the Paul groupie who previously toyed with the idea of adding me to her McCartney collection. Tonight, she's ditched the Chardonnay in favor of Jägerbombs, and is knocking them back with Sean McNeil, the front man for the Wings Tribute Band, "Feathers," and, coincidentally, manager of a Buffalo Wild Wings franchise in Massapequa.

For reasons unknown, Amy starts giving me dirty looks the moment I begin harmonizing with Gene on "You Really Got a Hold on Me." Maybe she senses that I'm thinking about another woman, and it pisses her off. The Paul that got away. I'm picturing what kind of outfit Christina will be wearing when she walks in the door, as well as the body language between her and Hubby should he wind up tagging along.

After we finish the first set, take our break, and move on to the next group of songs, I make peace with the likelihood that my Jones Beach buddy has opted out of the evening's festivities. The noteworthy takeaway from tonight will be that Gene, for the first time since I joined the band, has managed to commandeer a tight, professional performance devoid of Liverpudlian patter, criticism of his fellow band members, and post-game noodging regarding the next rehearsal date.

As thrilled as the other guys are to have dodged the pointless drama and fake-nose talk, I'm not sold on what has gone down. I don't enjoy Gene's dysfunctional calisthenics any more than the next person, but somehow their absence is even more troubling. To me, this new cool professionalism is a form of surrender—the first step toward soullessness. Once the job is reduced to checking the required boxes, you might as well be draining porta-potties forty hours a week. I never want to treat music like grunt work, and for Gene that applies a hundredfold. Leaving it all onstage is his passion, so if that disappears, he goes from playing a hollow body to being one. As colossal a jerk as Gene can be, it would pain me to see the bright-eyed only child, born with a setlist in his head, fade into oblivion.

As we tear down and pack up, I make one more attempt to engage Gene in conversation, but the most he'll give me is a half-hearted assurance that he expects Marcia to be back in action soon. Seeing as how Marcia stopped being able to walk unassisted over two years ago, the term "back in action" is relative. The bigger point is that I lack the tools either to ascertain Marcia's prospects for recovery or recharge Gene's enthusiasm. The only path that makes sense for me now is to focus on the things I can control.

The one saving grace of being a poverty-stricken music veteran organizing a solo project is having a community of talented friends who are ready to roll up their sleeves and summon brilliance. My supporting cast for the Donny Delgado showcase comes together in a hurry, with Prem taking over the guitar parts so I can play bass, the young prodigy, Raji, on keyboards, and the ever superb Tracy doing background vocals. There won't be any drums for the gig, but once we get into the studio to record the album, Mikey has agreed to do the honors. As for Gene Klein's role? Being kept in the dark about everything so he doesn't feel threatened by an "underling" having the gall to record an album independent of the group (which will never record anyway, because who would buy a Beatles cover band album?). Part of me feels bad about hiding this side project from him, but I can't risk the overwhelming odds of intrusion.

Prem has offered his home studio for rehearsals, which means awesome acoustics and more of Jaya's cooking. Tracy is especially pumped to sing with me, which always bodes well. Things really clicked on "Birdland" at Russo's, so the hope is to expand on that musically and see where it goes from there. Since she asked to ride over together, I invited her to come to my place an hour or so before rehearsal. That way, she can fill me in on the situation with her daughter, and maybe I can help her work through the nuts and bolts of what needs to be done.

Tracy shows up wearing jeans and a Bob Marley T-shirt, looking happier than I've seen her in years. I'm pleased to find out that Deanne's doing a lot better in rehab and is expected to be back home soon.

"And," Tracy continues, "there's more good news."

Finally. This woman has gotten the acting role or record contract she deserved all along. "If it's Broadway, I expect to be comped," I tell her.

"It's not Broadway."

"Touring company? Record Contract? Backup singer?"

She shakes her head, "no," to all three. Then she takes a long pause and I know where this is headed. "I've met someone," she says, unable to keep herself from grinning.

I smile back, hoping she's not paying attention to how phony it must look. "Wow. That's so great. I'm really happy for you."

"You don't have to bullshit me, Jimmy."

"I'm not bullshitting!"

"Come on. That was a 'fuck you' in a smile costume."

"But I *want* to be happy for you. That's good, right?"

Her open look tells me she knows I'm trying. "Jimmy the K," she says, pulling me into a hug that makes things better and a whole lot worse. A body shouldn't be allowed to feel this good if you can't have it anymore.

"So, who's the guy?" I ask, one more epic fail in my attempt to sound casual.

"Gene Klein."

Once my face displays just enough horror, Tracy bursts out laughing.

"Don't play those kind of games with me," I say.

"Sorry, I couldn't resist. His name's Wes. He's one of the docs at Deanne's facility. Really solid guy. You'd like him a lot."

"I'm sure I would." *Wes. Short for Wesley? Westworld? I don't see her with a Wes.*

"Are you gonna be okay?" Tracy asks.

"I'll be fine." *Hey, it's not like I don't have another woman in my life who I also can't be with.* "We should probably get going."

I start gathering my gear, making sure to pick up my acoustic as well as the bass, in case I want two guitars on any of the tunes. As I reach down to grab the Gibson, the phone rings. I tell Tracy that whoever it is, I'll call back later, but when I see the screen, I'm stopped cold by the area code. It's the same as Laurie Miller's in Florida, but she's calling from a different number.

"I'd better get this," I say, grabbing the phone. "Hello?"

The voice on the other end sounds sort of like Laurie, but not exactly. "Hi, is this Jimmy?"

"Yeah, who's this?"

There's a long silence, then: "It's Kaylie Miller. I think you know me as Gaby."

"Oh, my God—it's you." I'm crazy flustered. "Thank you. Thank you so much for calling. I can't believe it's—" I feel myself starting to hyperventilate.

"It's okay—"

"I'll be fine in a second. It just had to take a lot for you to—wow."

Tracy sees how emotional I am, and steps away to give me as much privacy as is possible in a 16 x 20 apartment.

"It is kind of weird," Kaylie admits. "But my mom told me everything, and you sound like a good guy."

"I am a good guy." I see Tracy looking at me. "Apparently, there are better guys out there, but I do the best I can."

"I'm sure you do fine," Kaylie says.

I gather my courage. "Listen, maybe this is too awkward or too soon, but would you ever want to meet?"

"Sure," she replies without hesitation, "but I'm pretty busy with the new job I just took." Kaylie explains that she recently moved from Florida to Los Angeles and is working as a marketing consultant for a boutique clothing company. "Do you ever get out West?" she asks.

"Oh, yeah. I mean, not for a while, but you never know. I could be back out there anytime."

The truth is, I haven't been to Los Angeles in twenty years, and the odds of me getting any work on the West Coast at this point are slim, but what would be so bad about taking a trip out there to visit my daughter?"

"They're talking about me doing some traveling for the company," she says. "So, who knows? Maybe I'll get to New York."

"Or we could even meet in the middle," I offer.

"Great. So, this is awesome, right? We have each other's numbers, so now we can text."

"Absolutely. Easy on the emojis, if you don't mind. I find them a little depressing."

"Hashtag fist bump," Kaylie responds. "Hey, um— could you send me a picture? I'm sorta curious."

"I don't know if you want a picture," I say. "You might get scared of what the future looks like."

She laughs. "I just texted you mine."

My phone dings, and, just like that, twenty-five years after a random, substance-filled hook-up, my daughter's face pops up on the screen.

"Wow, you're beautiful." I blurt out. "You look just like your mom." The latter isn't obvious from the pictures of

Laurie I've seen on Facebook, but no sane person would connect this adorable face with mine.

"Thanks, Jimmy."

I feel a marked drop in energy. Did I really expect her to say "Thanks, Dad" after all these years of not knowing me? No, but I guess I wanted to hear it. "Okay," I relent. "I'll send you a picture as soon as I find one that doesn't make me throw up."

"If it makes any difference, I have a strong stomach."

"Obviously. You made it through this phone call."

"I'd better quit while I'm ahead," she says. "Ha ha. I should get back to work."

"Thanks for calling, Kaylie. So, so great to meet—I mean, not meet—you know what I mean."

"I do. Later."

I hang up. Tracy throws me a look. "Another ex-girl-friend? There's some symmetry for you. One door closes ..."

"Nice thought, except that's not who it was." I show her the picture on my phone. "I just got introduced to my daughter."

"Damn." Tracy pulls the phone closer for a better look. "She's gorgeous. You expect me to believe you had some-thing to do with this?"

"I know, right? I guess her mother finally decided I'm not a serial killer."

"Don't let it get to your head."

"Kaylie and I are going to keep talking."

"I'm happy for you, Jimmy."

"I appreciate that." I really do, because I know that, unlike me, she doesn't have to fake it.

Tracy and I walk up the steps to Prem's house, which smells like a Michelin-starred supper club in South Mumbai. Jaya greets us at the door and is immediately caught off guard by an enthusiastic hug from Tracy, who can't contain her visceral reaction to the aromas. Once Tracy realizes she's made Prem's wife uncomfortable, she apologizes for her forwardness. Jaya tells her not to worry about it. She was raised to be reserved, but wishes she were a little more outgoing.

"As long as Jaya likes your music, you get fed," I joke.

"In that case," Tracy says, "I'm going to sing the best I've ever sung in my life."

"Hopefully it will be good enough," Jaya deadpans, before shooting Tracy a smile.

As we enter the studio, Raji is busy at the keyboard, riffing on "Night and Day." Tracy's impressed right away, filling in with vocals as soon as there's an opening. Raji nods in appreciation, and, once Tracy's verse finishes, she looks over to Prem. His guitar break doesn't disappoint. We all get loose in a hurry. It's an auspicious start to a session I hope gives me the confidence to book time for the showcase.

After we finish "Night and Day," I talk about the feeling I want to convey in my seven-song set. "It's kind of Nick Drake meets Parliament Funkadelic."

"That makes absolutely no sense," Prem is quick to point out.

I concede that while it may be a bit of an exaggeration, it serves a purpose. "The lyrics need to be heard, but not at the expense of sleepy, predictable arrangements. I don't want us to be music to text by."

"I get it," Raji nods, and, in a matter of seconds, he's funking up the first verse of "Gone Wishing." I'd already emailed the scratch tracks to everybody's Dropboxes, and it appears Raji took the time to listen. He's raising the bar for all of us.

"That's what I'm talking about right there," I tell everybody.

Tracy asks when I want her to come in with the background vocals, Prem suggests a guitar break after the second verse, and, soon enough, everybody's on the same page. We're all set to go when my phone starts buzzing. I'd meant to turn it off, but, on the other hand, it could be Kaylie calling back. If it is, I'll tell her I'm in a session, and get back to her later.

Looking at the phone, I see it's not Kaylie, but the more obvious culprit.

"I need to talk to you now. Call me," is the message from Gene Klein.

I relay his command to the others. Prem and Tracy tell me to ignore Gene until the session's over. Raji agrees. He doesn't know the man. He's just anxious to start playing. I agree to wait till later and turn off my phone. Then Prem's phone buzzes. Gene.

"Where are you guys?" is his next ploy to get to me. Prem turns off his phone.

Finally, I count it down and Raji kicks off an intro that's light years funkier than what he played just minutes before. A smiling Tracy loves the way this kid's fingers are moving and nods her head in anticipation of the moment when she gets to do her thing. Suddenly, the smile leaves her face, and she removes a buzzing phone from her pocket. She pulls it out to find her own text from Gene Klein that reads:

I need Jimmy now.

Tracy holds up the screen for me, then puts away her phone, and turns to me. "Please don't make it about him tonight. We're here to play your music."

And we do. After two more swings at "Gone Wishing," the song is so tight I feel like we could record it right now. We probably would if we didn't have six more tunes to work through. I'm proud of myself for not giving in to Gene's demands, yet I can't help but wonder: What if something happened to Marcia? If she suddenly died of heart failure, who else could he go to besides me?

We nail down three more songs. Raji and Tracy get the idea to add a cool middle-eight to "Hunger Game," a recent song I wrote about Jaco's sparrow conquest. When we finally take our first break, I get out my phone to check the messages. There are twenty-one from Gene. I look up to see Prem staring at me. He comes over and takes me aside.

"I don't understand," he says. "Why do you put up with it?

"His mom could have—"

Prem cuts me off. "Let's say she died, okay? What can you do about it right now? Why should you have to drop

199

everything to accommodate him? Besides, you'd have to explain what you're doing, which would piss him off, or make up some story to justify your whereabouts, which is stupid. Either way it would interrupt the flow of what you're trying to accomplish."

"I know that, but—"

"Why do you care so much? Does this guy have something on you?"

"It's … a long story."

"That we don't have time to hear right now. We need to get you in shape for your big night."

"Thanks, Prem. I appreciate your support."

"And one more thing. If it makes you feel any better—if Marcia's dead, she'll still be dead in a couple of hours."

"Remind me not to use you for my funeral."

"Hey, you know the food will be great."

Thinking there would be strength in numbers, I borrowed our drummer's beater Jeep and drove all night from Albany so I could fly to Omaha with my folks, rather than meet them there. Lou and Irene were grateful for my effort, and further pleased when we got bumped up to First Class, just as I had been years ago on my trip to Tulsa. Mom called me their lucky charm, which also served as a not-so-veiled reference to the fact that I was still alive. As far as the flight went, what at first seemed like good fortune proved to be more cruel than lucky. The Tulsa upgrade had been the cherry on top of the excitement I'd already felt about getting to see Eddie in his element. This time, we were being offered warm nuts on a journey that would end with him coming home in a body bag. It was excruciating to watch Lou and Irene, who'd flown maybe twice in their entire lives, try to enjoy the airline's complimentary perks. Unlimited drinks and a hot meal were a transportation luxury they would have normally celebrated, but, in this context, indulging in such extravagance seemed like sacrilege.

A short time later, as we were flying over Harrisburg, Pennsylvania, Lou found a way to solve this conundrum by reframing it. Drinking whiskey would be repurposed from

201

a celebratory act to a means of anesthetizing himself. In this new approach, the flight attendant became the equivalent of an airborne pharmacist, refilling his prescription whenever he chose to press the "call" light. Irene, for her part, marveled at how helpful everyone was, and smiled each time a crew member passed by, which she thought was the polite thing to do. I wondered how my mother had the energy to be polite, much less smile, under the circumstances, but affability was Irene's stock-in-trade, and it had always served her well. If you could be upbeat and civil with a rude customer at the bank, why wouldn't you extend the same courtesy to an airline employee who was being nice to you? It was an attitude that won the day in most situations, the exceptions being Lou's tantrums and now—the unwinnable position of having a son pass way too soon.

The Omaha taxi driver would also turn out to be a case study in politeness, as would everybody at the morgue. While you'd probably never think to describe a place that examines and preps cadavers as "laid back," the atmosphere at the Douglas County facility had none of the angst-ridden urgency of the morgues on cop shows. Maybe it had to do with being in the Midwest, or the place not having much action that day, but when an employee named Cal asked if we were ready to see the body, it felt like a waiter asking if we'd had enough time to glance at the menu.

As Cal pulled back the sheet so we could identify my brother, I expected him to look like some grotesque blowfish, with thick, seaweed-like drool dripping down his chin. But he looked like Eddie—maybe a little puffier, a few days of stubble, but oddly at peace. I never would have bet on Lou being the first to burst into tears, but the sight of his lifeless Number One son reduced him to a blubbering mass. My mother was doing the comforting, in between sobs of her own. Her weeping was quieter, in keeping with an ever-accommodating public demeanor. I was still in too much shock to cry. Cal told us to take as much time as we needed and stepped away.

"Why couldn't you have listened?" Lou pleaded with his dead son.

Irene had to interject. "Maybe if you hadn't pushed him so hard."

"Don't defend what he did."

"What is wrong with you?" she snapped. "You can't stop wanting him to feel guilty. Even for dying."

"If he'd paid attention to me—"

"Nobody pays attention to you," she said, her voice as loud as I'd ever heard it. "With good reason."

The next thing I knew, Cal was poking his head in. "Everything all right in here?"

"We're fine," Lou told him.

It had taken the squabbling Kozlowskis of Long Island to unnerve the most genial of coroner's offices by inundating it with guilt and blame.

"Anything I can do?" Cal asked.

Lou nodded and pointed to the body. "Tell us how we get him the hell out of here."

Lou and Irene were led to a small office where they needed to fill out the required forms. I was told I could wait in the reception area, which I was more than relieved to do. I plopped down on a plastic chair and picked up a two-year-old *National Geographic* magazine. It was an interesting choice for a morgue, but a good one, as pictures of the Galapagos took my mind off formaldehyde and caskets. Eddie would have loved the giant tortoises, I thought to myself. I seemed to remember him having a turtle for a while when we were kids. The name "Harold" popped into my head.

"Hey," came a voice from the end of the hallway. I thought I recognized it, and when I turned to see who it was, I found myself standing up to greet Larry Lizzardo, who would soon be joined by Marcus Bates, the bass player who joined the band after Spoon went into rehab.

"I'm so sorry," Lizzardo said, pulling me into a bear hug. He smelled like a combination of sinsemilla and NyQuil.

"Me, too, man," Marcus said. "You're his brother, right?"

I nodded and shook the bass player's hand. "Jimmy Kozlowski."

"Eddie told us all about you," Marcus said. "Gene too."

"Gene talked about me?" I said, surprised.

"Says you're a hell of a bassist," Marcus replied.

"Aren't you guys supposed to be in Lincoln tonight?" I asked, their entire tour schedule locked in my head, like always. I figured they were contractually obligated, and would either have to play the gig without a lead guitarist, or find somebody to sit in.

Lizzardo informed me that Gene had canceled the rest of the tour, and all future Traction dates. Eddie's death had sapped him of the will to play. They were still staying at the motel, waiting to make sure we arrived safely before checking out. He said that Gene wanted to join them at the morgue to pay his respects but stayed away in deference to Lou. "Your dad said he'd smash him into a wall if he ever saw him again," Lizzardo added.

"I know. He blames Gene for fucking up Eddie's life."

"Gene's got his hands full fucking up his own life," Lizzardo said. "He had no time for Eddie's."

"My brother wasn't a druggie," I threw in, beginning to feel myself turning into Lou. "He never would have wound up here if he wasn't in this band."

"You don't know that. Besides, I get way more wasted than Gene," Lizzardo informed me. "How come your dad's not blaming me?"

"He doesn't know you," I say. "Should he be blaming you?"

"He could, unless you want to hear the truth."

Even though nothing Lizzardo or anybody else could say would bring Eddie back, I needed to know what went down. "Tell me what happened, Larry."

Lizzardo said it was a long story, and that it would probably be best if I sat down. We all grabbed chairs, and he began. "At the start of the tour, Bismarck, North Dakota, I think, Eddie met someone."

"A girlfriend?"

"Not exactly. We thought she was just a local groupie, you know, your typical road chick. But she turned out to be this crazy, new-agey priestess who got Eddie under her spell. Her name was Skybird, which should tell you something right there. Practiced this made-up religion that involved a lot of fasting, praying to spirit animals, bourbon, coke, smack. It would seem like a crock of shit to anyone on the outside. But if you were on the inside, man, you believed anything Skybird said. Me and Marcus totally dug her, but Eddie was the one who got way inside, real quick. He asked her to come with us to the next gig, and, pretty soon, she was riding on the bus with us from town to town. The only one who didn't seem to enjoy her company was Gene. We thought it was because it grabbed the attention away from him, but one day, in St. Paul, when Skybird had taken Eddie to go panhandling with her, Gene sat us down for a meeting. He said he was worried about Eddie's health, both physical and mental, and that all of us needed to keep close tabs on this chick to protect our brother. Me and Marcus tossed it off to Gene being overly dramatic, and acting out because he was jealous, but, not too long after that, Eddie started making mistakes on stage, and even missed a couple of gigs. Then one day, Gene found him weeping outside a motel dumpster, and decided enough was enough. He sent your brother to a local music shop for new guitar strings so he could get Skybird alone. Gene told her she was not only jeopardizing Eddie's health, but the band's ability to make a living. Skybird said she understood. That night, she made up some excuse to Eddie about needing to visit her mother in California for a while. Two weeks later, she showed up at our date in Madison and at the next one in Lansing. Just as Eddie had started feeling a little better, she came back to blow it up. Finally, Gene threatened the chick, telling her that if she came anywhere near Eddie again, he'd have her killed."

I had to interrupt. It seemed beyond far-fetched that the sheltered little boy who had once composed Temple Judea's rock 'n' roll Purim *shpiel* had morphed into Vito Corleone.

Lizzardo agreed that Gene wasn't crazy enough (or connected enough) to do anything like that. "He just wanted to scare her. It worked a little too well. One night, we were having a beer after this killer show at Johnnie's Bar in Cheboygan. The news came on, reporting that a body had been dredged from Lake Michigan. When they identified the woman as Gail Roberts, Eddie lost it. He was the only one who knew Skybird's real name. Marcus and I were pretty shook up too, but we did our best to console him. Gene didn't look as upset as we did, but he told Eddie he was sorry it happened. Eddie admitted he knew the chick was troubled, and it probably wasn't something any of us could have prevented. When we got back to the motel, Gene offered to stay on Eddie's floor, just to make sure he was okay. Eddie insisted he was fine. The next morning, Eddie didn't come out of his room, and Gene had the motel manager break down the door. It turned out Eddie had finished a whole bottle of Maker's Mark and swallowed half a bottle of pills. Gene gave him CPR, and managed to get him conscious, but by the time EMTs showed up he was gone."

I was stunned. "You're telling me Gene was trying to protect Eddie the whole time?"

"Let me put it this way. Gene spends most of his waking hours being a gifted, self-involved dick. He could take or leave anyone else in the band, but he loved your brother. Probably the only person he ever loved besides himself—and maybe his parents."

"How come nobody called us about what was going on with the girl? Until it was too late?"

"Gene did call. But he could never get your mom on the phone and your dad kept hanging up on him. Nobody knew how to get hold of you."

I was still trying to absorb all of it when I saw Lou and Irene step into the hallway. They looked in our direction, puzzled as to who the other guys were.

I called out to them. "Mom, Dad, these are Eddie's bandmates."

Irene started to come toward us, but Lou pulled her back and nodded at me. "Come on, Jimmy. We're going to get some dinner, then head back to the airport."

"We're sorry for your loss," Lizzardo called out.

"He was a great guy," Marcus added.

"We thought so," Lou replied, cold as ice. "Doesn't do us a whole lot of good now." My father nodded at me to join them.

I motioned that I'd be there in a second and turned to Lizzardo. "Tell Gene I said hello. And that I appreciate everything he tried to do."

"I'm sure that'll mean a lot to him," Lizzardo responded.

"Here's my number, if he ever wants to talk." I handed him my band's business card.

"Peace to you, buddy," Lizzardo said, reaching out to give me a farewell hug.

After saying goodbye to Marcus, I caught up with my parents, who were on their way out front to meet the taxi. I would soon learn that Eddie's body was scheduled to arrive at the airport two hours before our flight.

The cab ride was as chilly as Lou's reaction to Eddie's bandmates. After fifteen minutes of silence, Irene broke the ice. "It was sure nice of those boys to come by," she said. As someone who always tried to do the right thing, my mother felt it her duty to acknowledge when others acted in kind.

"Would've been a lot nicer if they kept him from killing himself," Lou said.

"They tried," I told him. "Gene did everything he could."

I'd barely finished the sentence when a boiling fury overcame my father. The mere mention of Gene's name had turned Lou's entire face broken-capillary red, which frightened the crap out of Irene. I thought he was going to throw me out of the moving cab right then and there.

"Did you talk to that motherfucker?" Lou had to know.

"I didn't."

"Good."

"But I wish I had."

Before I knew what was happening, Lou had me in a stranglehold, and Irene was screaming.

The cab driver proceeded to pull over to the side of the road. Evidently, even Nebraskans had a "polite" threshold. "Get out. All of you," was his unceremonious goodbye.

209

Irene tried to talk us back into the cabbie's good graces, but the man wanted no part of my father's temper. Thanks to Lou's refusal to listen to anything other than what he wanted to believe, three grieving Kozlowskis found themselves stranded in front of a Farmer Brown's Steakhouse in Omaha, Nebraska.

Luckily, we needed to eat.

THE MESSAGE

By ten o'clock, we've finished running through all seven songs in the set, and I couldn't be more pleased with the results. This combination of talent has managed to shape my work from over three decades into something both cohesive and emotionally resonant. Now it's time for the postgame feast.

As we race into the kitchen, Prem announces that our teetotaling chef, Jaya, has gone off to bed. He takes this as his cue to whip out a bottle of Amrut Double Cask Indian Whiskey, and a six-pack of Kingfisher beer. After three shots, the requisite chasers, and enough samosas to line our stomachs, the ad hoc Jimmy Kozlowski Band is on the express train to nirvana. Tracy contemplates shot number four, whispering in my ear, "I'm so proud of you, Jimbo." A nice surprise, but nothing compared to the one that takes place a moment later. Just as I dig into Jaya's sublime chicken korma, I feel Tracy's hand start creeping up my leg.

I'm about to bring up her new boyfriend when I remember that this is my night. If I'm not going to deal with Gene Klein until tomorrow, why should I worry about some rehab doctor who's known my ex-girlfriend for a minute and a half? After three years of serious dating, and twenty years of friendship, it's Tracy's God-given right to reward me however she chooses.

She chooses to finish her dinner, down a few more beers, and start singing to me while we pack up for the night and head out to the car. It's a drunken "Autumn Leaves," but a quality one, nonetheless. No matter how buzzed Tracy gets, she never slurs her lyrics.

We throw the guitars in the trunk. Then, without remembering that I should know better, I open the passenger door for her. Way back when we first dated, this became a major point of contention, with Tracy voicing various feminist arguments about how demeaning it was to be treated like a weakling, too fragile to get herself in and out of a car. Tonight, she doesn't seem to have a problem. In fact, by the time I get around to opening the door on my side, she's flashing body parts I had resigned myself to never seeing again. As much I'd like to get reacquainted, I know that, unlike her tipsy singing, these inebriated overtures demand some sort of discussion.

"Trace, I think maybe you've had a few more than—"

"I love what you did tonight," she says, inching closer to me.

"All of us were on. But that was just, you know, music."

"What else is there?" She pulls my hand to her chest.

I want to make a stronger case, but I need to revisit a past I could never quite believe was mine. I start by kissing her nipples, and graduate to swallowing as much of each breast as I can fit in my mouth. She closes her eyes and starts to moan. Even her moans sound musical. I don't know that I've ever heard a perfect D-sharp on Porn Hub.

I move up to kiss her lips. Two mouths reeking of beer and whiskey can't seem to get enough of each other.

"Fuck me right here," she says, biting my lip to prove the seriousness of her statement.

As lovely a thought as it is, there's also a strong argument against it. "This is Prem's neighborhood," I remind her. "Conservative Indian people."

"They don't fuck?"

"I don't want to do anything that would make Jaya uncomfortable."

She pulls away. "Don't want to burn that bridge. Her alu gobhi might be better than sex."

"A toss-up," I concede.

"Maybe not. Semen vs. cumin? Which would you rather have on your chicken?"

"Good point."

Once I pull away from the curb, I gently plant my right hand on her thigh. Its northward path might not be five-star Indian food, but still manages to earn two soulful D-sharps.

Then Gene calls for the twenty-second time.

"Jesus Christ!" Tracy shouts. "He wants to harass you to death."

"Unless something really happened—"

"Come on, Jimmy. I know the session's over, but do you really need to deal with that tonight?"

"You're right. He's completely out of my head."

She's not sold. "Okay, fine. Let's listen to his voice-mail."

"We don't have to do that."

"Play the voicemail, Jimmy."

I do. Gene's voice sounds weak. "Please call me," is all he says.

"This is the way he rolls," I explain. His voicemail messages are like cliffhangers, teasing you to find out what's going on.

"Let me ask you something," Tracy says. "If I weren't with you, planning to fuck you so hard you'll need crutches to walk tomorrow, what would you do right now?"

"Seriously? Wow."

"What would you do?"

"I guess I'd call him back. See what's what."

"Would it make you feel better to do that? Because I need you in optimum shape so you can mess me up as bad as what I'm gonna do to you."

"Hard to argue with that one. I'd just like to know he's okay."

"Then call."

I hit "call back." In yet one more odd twist, there's no answer. I wait for the beep and leave a message. "Hey, it's Jimmy, returning your call, just checking back with you. Hope everything's okay." I hang up and turn to Tracy. "I tried."

"Yes, you did. Are we done with Gene Klein?"

I nod. She puts my hand back on her thigh. But she knows something's up. "What, Jimmy?"

"Believe me, the last thing I want is to be able to walk unassisted tomorrow—but can we drive past Gene's house on the way home?"

"It would be the high point of my life," Tracy says, removing my hand.

"I'm sorry. We don't have to."

"Just go to his damn house. No guarantees what happens after."

"Understood."

Gene's place is pitch black and still. I walk around to the side of the garage and peek through the small window to see if Gene's van is there. It's gone. I reason that if he's at the hospital with Marcia, she's well taken care of, and I can contact him again in the morning. I look over at Tracy, whose boundless sexuality I appear to have single-handedly drained. We ride back to the house in silence, my hands at ten and two on the wheel. When we arrive, I channel the Irene Kozlowski polite gene and invite her in. "No expectations," I assure her.

Tracy looks at me and shakes her head. "You know, Jimmy, that's your goddamn problem."

"What is?"

"You *should* have expectations. The whole reason you and I couldn't get anywhere was that you never expected yourself to rise to the occasion. So, you didn't. Tonight, you probably walked into that studio with no expectations, but what did you do? You asserted your goddamn brilliance. I loved seeing that in you. But now … it's back to the old Jimmy."

"Fuck you, Tracy."

"Excuse me?"

"I said 'fuck you,' but what I meant to say was, I'm *gonna* fuck you. Right now. In this car."

"Yeah, right," she says, convinced I don't have the balls to risk upsetting the neighbors.

I proceed to apply some of the tricks I learned in the eight hundred hours logged watching Porn Hub, which has yielded maybe four minutes of teachable moments. These produce a refrain of heavenly D-sharps outside Bill and Jan Girardi's window, until the action progresses to going inside and fucking right underneath the Girardis' bedroom. Then, just for good measure, I get out the Glenlivet and do body shots off an ass sweet enough to give Bill Girardi the heart attack of his dreams.

As memorable as the night turns out to be, it delivers an equally arduous next morning, just as Tracy had promised. Struggling in both the movement and hangover departments, I make coffee, which Tracy gulps down as if it were room temperature.

"Doesn't it hurt to drink it so fast?" I ask.

"Don't know," she says. "I'll find out once I get the feeling back in my throat."

Now she's looking around the apartment. Based on her expression, I conclude that she views what happened last night as either a reckless mistake, or farewell intercourse. If this sorry basement is the best I can offer, who could blame her for trying out random doctors, any of whom must live above ground? Even so, I plan to stick with my own take on the evening. The music, the food, the woman I could have married so moved by my songs she had to give it up, doctor or no doctor.

I suppose there's a miniscule chance she just hates the apartment and has, despite herself, fallen in love with me again. Which would be weird because I have all these feelings for Christina that are probably going nowhere. I've known Tracy long enough that I can be direct, so I will be.

"Hey, what about that doctor you were seeing?"

"Wes? I'm going out with him tonight."

"Wow. You don't waste any time, do you?"

"What's that supposed to mean? Did you wake up and decide to sweep me off my feet?"

"I wouldn't put it that way. I think we're past feet-sweeping."

"Exactly. I'm always gonna love you, Jimmy. I'm just not ready to throw stuff against the wall and hope it sticks this time."

"Thank you for being honest."

"Thank you for taking it so well." She smiles. "Would you like to say goodbye to me one more time?"

"Are you kidding me?"

"I'm hung over and my whole body hurts," she says. "I don't have the energy to kid."

"But you have energy to …"

"I don't know. Nothing like a challenge, I always say."

Tracy chugs her second cup of coffee and puts me back to work.

COPING

Eddie's funeral was a modest affair, per Irene's measured sense of propriety and Lou's budget. The members of Traction wisely stayed away, allowing Dad to grieve with family and close friends, minus the reminder that rock 'n' roll and its practitioners had caused this senseless death. The one thing he hadn't counted on was having his equilibrium upset by the sight of Bob and Charlotte Snell. Even though Bob had remained his accountant and Lou still considered him a friend, everything had changed after the fateful brunch. Bob had clearly seen that Lou was furious at Eddie for snapping at Charlotte. He was also well aware that no one could have been more disappointed than Lou when his son turned his back on the internship. And yet, when the Snells came over to the reception line to express their sorrow, which Irene accepted with open arms, Lou thought he a saw smirk on the accountant's face—a look that said, "I offered that kid a life. Look at his dead ass now." Irene told Lou it was all in his head. I agreed, even though I still thought Bob Snell was a dick. I just didn't want my father to take on added freight, because there would be nothing to gain either from carrying it or releasing it down the line.

Later, back at the house, I assumed responsibility for entertaining my brother's friends who had stayed in the area. Since he'd been out on tour for so many years, and most of the people he hung with had scattered across the country, it wasn't a big crowd. I spent most of the time talking to Jan Girardi, who Eddie once dated, and was now married to their mutual friend Bill. She'd never traveled more than sixty miles outside of Long Island, was eight months pregnant with their fourth kid, and still hadn't stopped going to work every day. At one point, Jan took me aside and said that way back, she thought Eddie might propose to her. She confided that she would have said yes, but also recognized that my brother was destined for greater things than the unflashy Long Island life she was afraid to leave. Telling me these things made Jan start to cry. Bill came over and put his arm around her. He cried harder.

Obviously, the "greater things" for which my brother was destined did not include dying from an overdose at thirty-six years old. I tried to imagine an alternate reality in which Eddie had listened to Lou, taken the CPA route, pumped out rug rats with Jan, and wound up living to a ripe old age. On some level, I could picture him as a family man, paying the mortgage and taking his two-weeks-a-year vacations. He had a strong enough composition to make the most of any situation. Still, my guess was that after he tucked the kids in bed and went off to the den to fool around on his old, beat-up acoustic, he'd be thinking about the road not taken. Eddie used to talk about that poem—how you think of it as two roads that look kind of the same, but wind up leading to different places. He said that as wise as the words always seemed, they didn't come close to preparing him for *the* road—the one that makes or breaks musicians.

I stayed with my parents for two weeks after the funeral, long enough to see them get back to their routines. The bank was happy for Irene's return, but while she remained their most conscientious teller, she now found herself less captivated by her customers' life stories. "Sign here, sign there, have a nice day," was the new drill. By that time, Lou had already augmented his spotty band work with teaching basic piano skills to young kids. He'd lost all passion for music, and never loved little kids to begin with, but it was an easy way to bring in a few extra bucks. Occasionally he'd run into students who were so excited about playing the piano that they'd talk about becoming professional musicians. Lou would smile so as not to discourage them and leave it at that. While he still believed it his moral imperative to caution them, he knew that voicing the same argument he'd used on Eddie would only bring back memories he couldn't bear to relive.

I arrived back in Albany to a hero's welcome from the guys in Bloodshot. Unsurprisingly, they thought the best way for me to deal with the tragedy would be to dive into songwriting, rehearsals and booking more dates. I wasn't feeling it. Doing our regular Wednesday night bar gig and once-a-week re-hearsal was one thing, but beyond that, I preferred the quiet of my classes, the library, and even writing papers, to the precarious consequences of rock 'n' roll dreams. Was Eddie's death a warning sign? Or had Lou's haranguing finally beat-en me down? I'm sure both factored into my current state of mind, but a part of me just needed time to assess my next moves, now that I could no longer use my brother's life as a template. The guys in Bloodshot were disappointed with my dip in enthusiasm, but they put up with me either out of loyalty, or because I was the best musician of the bunch. That part of Eddie I would always try to preserve.

Eight weeks or so later, I was in my room studying for a psychology exam when the RA knocked on the door, the same RA whose last knock led to the news of Eddie's death. This time there was another call for me on the hall pay phone. He couldn't quite make out the name of the caller because there was a lot of noise in the background as the guy was talking. I prayed to God it wasn't Lou, calling to tell me that something else had befallen our already shattered family.

I went to the hall and picked up the receiver. I recognized the voice on the other end from somewhere, but couldn't quite place it.

"Jimmy, it's me. Larry."

"Lizzardo?"

"Wasted and at your service."

Lizzardo was calling to tell me that Traction was back together, and that as a tribute to Eddie, Gene decided to do the gig in Albany as their first comeback date. He was still good with Bloodshot opening for them.

I felt tears starting to well up. I didn't know what to say. "So, who'd you get to replace him?" was the main thing on my mind.

"Nobody yet," Lizzardo answered. "There's something else on the table, Jimmy."

"What do you mean?" I asked, clueless as to where this might be going.

"Gene wants Marcus to switch to guitar and you to play bass that night."

"Seriously?"

"Yeah. For the whole gig. As a way of honoring Eddie."

"That's amazing." It was both thoughtful and compassionate, which made it all the more amazing. Gene Klein, who'd spent his entire life being the poster boy for narcissism, had found a way to memorialize my brother that no funeral could ever match. The only question was, would I be able to get through it without breaking down?

Pun notwithstanding, the rebooting of Bloodshot's April gig with Traction was just the transfusion the band needed. The lethargy that had set in as a result of my waning interest had suddenly been replaced with a drive unlike anything we'd ever experienced. The guys knew how important it was for me to honor my brother by giving the performance of our lives. Plus, they saw how hard I worked on the songs in the Traction setlists, so I could do right by his bandmates. As the gig approached, the whole Bloodshot crew, including groupies, got the word out to friends, who then contacted their friends, who then repeated the process until Pauly's Hotel found itself hosting a show that was in such demand it had to turn away fifty people at the door.

Bloodshot exploded onto the stage, mixing three originals with the Replacements' "Bastards of Young," Elvis Costello's "Mystery Dance," and the Modern Lovers' "Roadrunner." My guys gave every ounce of themselves, and, by the time our thirty-minute set was up, they were completely drenched in sweat. In addition to helping me honor my brother, they wanted to prove they were as good a band as Traction. A world-class performance by Bloodshot would get me pumped up, and ready for my moment in the spotlight with the headliner.

I don't know that I was ready but, performance-wise, I'd never felt so in the moment. The eye contact I got from Lizzardo and Marcus made me feel as if I'd played with their band from its inception. Gene, on the other hand, who was allegedly apoplectic when Eddie died, and had instigated this memorial show, turned out to be all business. I kept waiting for some mention of the night's import (e.g.: what it felt like to pay tribute to my brother, how meaningful it was to have me stepping in to honor him, etc.), but that never came to pass either onstage, during the break between sets, or at the end of the show. Finally, I went up and thanked him for having tried to protect Eddie. He nodded his head, but appeared uninterested in exploring any of the emotions that had inspired the show in the first place.

"Eddie was the best guitarist I ever knew," was the most Gene could offer up. "'One Way Out.' Ever hear him play both lead guitar parts at the same time?"

"Incredible." I remembered my brother working on that for maybe eighty hours.

"Never met anybody else who could do that," Gene said. Then he walked away to pack up his guitar.

It occurred to me that maybe Lizzardo wasn't telling the whole truth. Maybe *he* was the one who had looked out for Eddie, had the deep emotional reaction, and come up with the idea to do this show. It was possible that Eddie had told him about the family's history with Gene, which spurred Lizzardo into creating a softer image of Traction's leader as a way of helping us heal. On closer examination, that didn't make much sense. Anybody who went through life as wasted as Lizzardo was probably incapable of such psychological strategizing. I decided that Gene probably did have all these feelings, but wouldn't, or couldn't, open up and express them—at least to me.

The net result was that a show hailed as one of the three most spectacular in Pauly's Hotel history wound up lacking the element of closure I desperately needed. As cool as it was to be able to fill in for Eddie by playing with his former band, Gene's silence regarding our collective loss killed any chance of catharsis. I thought the whole point of the memorial was to tie everything together, with Gene being the key link in a chain that had begun with my dad and ended with me. Since his close connection to my family went unexpressed, all we wound up giving our Albany fans was an entertaining show. I expected to come away from the night feeling like one of those people who walk for cancer to honor their loved ones; that by confronting tragedy with affirmation, I would be transported to a healthy place. In the end, I felt sadder than when I started.

ARRANGEMENTS

Now three days since Tracy's spirited acrobatics, my bones have been restored to factory specifications for middle-aged creakiness. Throbbing body parts aside, I couldn't have asked for a more satisfying finale to our unsolvable romance. An epic fuck from a living, breathing goddess, followed by the brutal honesty that brought her back to earth, put everything in perspective. Tracy had arrived at the "been there, done that" juncture, and, once she spelled it out, I realized I was in the same place. Nostalgia can creep up on a person without warning, especially if you go from being with someone like Tracy to living with a hairball-spitting sparrow-killer. It's only natural to gloss over the complexities of the previous relationship and pine for what was. Tracy closing the long-term door will only help me to move on. Now I can be cool with her dating Wes, or Les, or whatever his name is, and create my own future.

I've already contacted Shores, the club in Sea Cliff where I backed up Ben Gardner, and they're set to book us once I confirm the date with Donny Delgado. Possibly even cooler is that early this morning I got a text from my daughter, wanting to check in. I mean, I know tons of dads who never hear from their daughters unless they need something, and those are guys who put in the work to raise their kids. This morning, I'm energized and ready to go to Pineview, where I'll do my best to get a rise out of the old folks, and maybe a wink out of Christina. Life is good, except for one troubling piece of business. Nobody's heard from Gene since the night of our session at Prem's. In the "normal" scheme of things, it would be considered strange behavior for Gene not to call me at least three times a day, so having him AWOL for over seventy-two hours is a significant red flag. Tomorrow night we have our regular Help! gig at JP Murphy's, which I'm assuming is on, but I can't say for sure.

I've tried to make sense of the different possibilities. If Marcia's in the hospital, she's not at the same one that admitted her last time, as I've called both the main facility and the emergency room every day looking for her. If something's happened to Gene, Marcia would've had to be placed in someone else's care, but I have no idea who that person might be. Prem, Mikey and I have pitched various hypothetical Gene and Marcia storylines. *Did they take a spur-of-the-moment vacation? Pick up and move to an area with less tribute band competition? Maybe they drove off a cliff like a mother-son Thelma and Louise.* It speaks to the gravity of the situation that Fake George and Fake Ringo, so grateful to have been spared Gene's haranguing, are now concerned for his well-being. We make a group decision to go to the gig no matter what, hoping that, as always, this natural-born showman will come to claim his turf.

I always try to arrive at Pineview a few minutes early to increase my chances of catching Christina on the fly before it's time to perform. When I walk through the door, I play it cool, with a nonchalant wave to Vera as I head for the activity room. The receptionist has no intention of letting me off easy. Just as I make my way past her, I hear from behind me: "She's in meetings all morning."

I turn around to respond. "I assume you're talking about Christina?"

"Please," is Vera's eye-rolling reply. "She looks super cute today, by the way."

The receptionist has apparently decided to insert herself in the middle of something that isn't anything, and that, even if it were, would be none of her business. Up till now, Vera's game was being protective of Christina's marriage. Version 2.0 seems to be an attempt to torture me with what I can't have. *I've already got that one covered, thank you very much.*

There's not a lot of set-up time involved with my Pineview gig, seeing as how it's just an acoustic guitar and no microphone. Still, I like to review the material and think about throwing something new in the mix should I get the urge. I consider doing an unplugged version of the complete seven-song set for the showcase but think better of it. An unenthusiastic reaction, even from a crowd that is pharmaceutically comatose, would still be discouraging. My next thought is that since "Hello, I Love You" had been such a success, it might be fun to introduce another Doors tune.

"Roadhouse Blues?" "Love Her Madly?" Just gotta stay away from "The End."

I hear the sounds of various CNAs starting to wheel in their charges, and it looks like it's going to be close to a full house this afternoon. There are days when some of the residents are too tired to attend, but the current assemblage seems to be an eager, if not spry, group. The Powers That Be at Pineview have instructed me to begin on time no matter how many people are situated, so, as the clock strikes eleven, I begin "Hello, I Love You." As more residents trickle in. I get a head-nod from Lillian, an attempt at clapping on the beat from the Colonel, and, by the time the song is over, I've gotten four residents to tell me their names. Even though one of them is the wrong name, it goes in the books as a win. Instinct tells me to segue from there to a ballad, my spontaneous choice being Willie Nelson's "Crazy." This elicits a couple of smiles, as well as some vigorous snores, the unmistakable stylings of Rhona Epstein. It hadn't crossed my mind, but as I get to the line "crazy for loving you," I imagine Christina making an appearance at that exact moment.

My beach buddy is nowhere in sight. Instead, another wheelchair is making its way in, smack in the middle of the verse. You'd think that after all these years of performing, I would have gotten used to any kind of interruption, but the arrival of this wheelchair is jarring for reasons I don't immediately understand. I'm looking at something familiar, yet I can't identify why or where from. The woman in the wheelchair is asleep and, in her present state, looks like at least two other residents I've met, but the CNA who has wheeled her in is smiling at me as if we know each other. As I press on with my song and head into the bridge, I realize that the woman in the chair is Marcia Klein. The CNA behind her is none other than Jasmine, Gene's new Yoko Ono. This bombshell throws off the rest of my performance. I sing flat on one chorus and flub the easy intro of "And I Love Her." And why on earth would I play "Don't Get Around Much Anymore" for a roomful of invalids? Thankfully, this goes unnoticed by the audience, because ninety-five percent of them have joined Marcia and Rhona's slumber party. I expect Gene to walk in at any moment to offer on-the-spot criticism of my song selection, intonation, and wardrobe. But he doesn't show. The minute I'm through, I approach Marcia and Jasmine to find out what's going on.

"You play Beatles," are the first words out of Jasmine's mouth. "I'm getting to know their songs."

I note that Marcia is still breathing, which is the most animated thing she's done since her grand entrance. I need to get her attention, to see if the doting mother I've known for more than half my life is still in there. "Marcia. It's me … Paul. You know, the cute Beatle." I make a bunch of stupid Paul faces for emphasis.

No reaction. Time to bring out the big guns. I clear my throat and prepare to give it everything I have, careful not to project too much happiness as I wail the opening lines of "I'm Down."

I think I see an eye start to open, but it's probably wishful thinking. I ask Jasmine what happened.

Apparently, Marcia had a stroke and landed in the hospital. Jasmine, who had already started spending a lot of time with Gene, suggested he transition his mom to Pineview, the best nursing home on Long Island. She then offered to perform double duty, working as part-time care-giver, and part-time Yoko. Gene loved the idea.

"What happened to Lupe?" I had to ask. She'd been with Marcia for years.

"I don't know. You'll have to ask Gene."

"Who is where, exactly? I've been looking for him for three days."

"Gene's been staying at the Marriott Courtyard to be closer to Mom," she says. "Maybe he's getting some rest. He's here all the time."

"Is that so?"

"I'm supposed to go over there later to practice my part for tomorrow night. You could drop by. Room 303."

Practice her part? Doing what, exactly? "So, he is plan-ning to be at JP's?" I say, wanting clarification.

"Of course." Jasmine smiles. Then she looks down to check on Marcia. "How're you doing, Mom?"

Mom? She's calling Gene's mother "Mom"?

Marcia suddenly opens her mouth to speak. In the softest of voices, she says, "Listen … they're playing so beautifully."

"Who's playing so beautifully, Mom?" Jasmine asks.

Marcia registers the tiniest of smiles.

"I think she's hearing music," I say.

Jasmine speaks directly in Marcia's ear. "There's no music, Mom."

Marcia's smile fades. Part of me feels bad that she doesn't get to enjoy what seems like the most positive of available hallucinations.

"I'd better take her back to the room," Jasmine says. "Time for her meds. See you later, Jimmy."

Jasmine wheels Marcia off. I stand immobile, trying to make sense of what I've just witnessed. Somehow, some way, Gene Klein has done it again, marking his territory in another corner of what's mine. Of all the nursing homes on Long Island, he's found his way into the one that has touched my life, both during my father's illness, and now, as I attempt to give back to those currently in his shoes. Of course I want Marcia to get better, but I also need to be able to do my job. How long will it be before Gene starts bugging me to perform as a duet in the activity room? Insisting that he choose half the songs and split lead vocals?

"Hey, stranger," comes a familiar voice from behind, as I feel a tap on my shoulder that seems to linger just a little longer than necessary. I turn around to see that Vera was indeed speaking the truth when she kicked off her Jimmy Kozlowski Torture Campaign. Christina is glowing, wearing a conservative but curvy black dress falling just above the knee, black tights, boots, and a silver necklace that turns up the heat a few more notches. I wish I could enjoy the flawless picture, but I can't get over the feeling that my stabilizing home-away-from-home is about to get bulldozed.

"Hey," I nod, without my usual smile.

"Everything okay?' She knows me well enough to expect some excitement from her arrival.

"Not so much," I answer, unsure of how I intend to elaborate.

"You sounded really good from where I was standing," she says.

The words come out almost involuntarily. "You knew about this. And you never said anything," I blurt out, as if I've been stabbed in the back by an enemy I didn't know I had.

"Never said anything about what?" Christina asks.

"Gene. His mom. Coming here. You must have been the one to admit them."

"I was. But you know that's confidential information. I'm not allowed to discuss it with anyone outside the family."

"Jasmine wouldn't have known about Gene if it weren't for you. And you wouldn't have known about Gene if it weren't for me. Isn't that close enough for me to be considered family?"

She puts her hand on my shoulder again. "Legally, I can't count you as part of Gene's family. But if it means anything, I consider you close enough to be my family."

"Thank you." My head is spinning. What did she mean when she said she thinks of me as her family? Am I her brother? Her father? Her would-be incestuous lover, which I'd be down for, no questions asked.

Finally, after her hand has spent enough time on my shoulder for me to obsess about it for the next six months, she removes it. "I'm confused," Christina says. "I thought you and Gene were friends. Why would you play in his band if you don't like him?"

"I do like him. It's just that he takes up too much room. I hate the idea of him being around when I do my thing here. It's sacred space for me."

"Because of your dad."

"That's part of it." I'm staring at her now, wondering if she's going to fill in the blank.

"I want to do whatever we can for his mom," she says, not flinching from my stare.

"I know you do, and that's a good thing. This is my problem, and I'll have to work it out."

"I'll do whatever I can to help you with that," she says.

I want to kiss her right now, get us both fired, drive to some little beach town in Mexico, and live happily ever after. But I don't. "Would you want to have coffee again sometime?" is my weak substitute.

"No," Christina says.

I feel like a complete dumbass.

"I think we're ready for lunch."

I'm so taken aback by her response that all I can say is, "Are you sure?"

"I'm sorry. Do you want to talk me out of it?"

"No. Definitely not."

"Then shut up, and I'll let you know when I'm free."

I pretend to zip my lip.

She smiles, waves, and heads back to her office.

I think I'm on reasonably safe ground when I say that once-a-week volunteer gigs are seldom filled with this much drama. How is it possible for a world to be blown apart and reimagined within minutes of each other? I probably shouldn't spend too much time thinking about it, but I will. I'll also Yelp every restaurant within thirty miles of here to find the perfect spot to take Christina. There's no way of knowing what the situation is with Hubby, but maybe I don't want that information. She's the one who suggested upping the dining stakes, so she obviously feels comfortable with this next outing.

I try to get a handle on what she's thinking. Maybe I represent something she needs. I'm closer to her age than Hubby, I'm probably more entertaining, since it's what I do for a living, and the vibe I'm putting out is that I'm into everything about her, except the part that added more Gene to my life. I'm probably getting ahead of myself, but it wouldn't be the first time. The only thing you can predict about the future is that some of it will turn out good, and the shitty parts will be shittier than anything you could have imagined.

JIMMY JOINS THE BAND

Plenty of families have weathered tragedy and managed to rise from the ashes, but the Kozlowskis were not made of phoenix stock. 1991 would mark the beginning of a downward trajectory in the emotional and physical health of both my parents. In two years, Eddie's overdose would be followed by Irene's diagnosis of Stage 3 breast cancer. She would press on at the bank until she no longer had the will or the strength to be on her feet for the hours required. Then, once she left her job to spend her days either at home, or going to the doctor, Lou's Feisty Victim persona shape-shifted into Doting Caretaker, and when the situation advanced to hopeless, Doting Zombie, I made it my business to get back home as often as possible. Upon graduating college, I moved back in, setting up camp in my and Eddie's old bedroom.

If there were a surefire recipe for suicidal depression, having to sleep among the memories of my dead idol supplied all the necessary ingredients. To wit, I had no choice but to get rid of our old childhood furniture, Eddie's Hendrix, Clapton and Jimmy Page posters, and repaint the walls an awful, loud color I knew my brother would hate. I needed to stop thinking about how things were in order to deal with the business at hand. My first task was to switch

235

off with Dad, taking Mom for her treatments. This pleased her no end, as Lou had taken up permanent residence in a state of despondency, and she preferred the company of someone who was able to joke around.

"People with cancer can still laugh," she'd tell me.

To that end, I took her to the movies to see silly comedies like *City Slickers*, and *The Naked Gun 2 ½*. We'd go to lunch on occasion, but I'd usually have to prod her to eat. Irene said that since the chemo, foods that had been favorites her entire life now tasted like other things entirely. A hamburger had the flavor of chalk, eggs, a combination of phlegm and pepper. She thanked me for trying to make sure she got the proper nutrients. She also said that while she knew parent-child roles got reversed over time, she didn't expect it to happen to her so soon. I loved spending that time with my mom, especially since Dad was in no shape to be a nurturer. His bitterness toward the world had robbed him of the ability to comfort his wife.

The one area where Lou's focus remained steady was the importance of me getting a real job in a company that promised growth and benefits. He insisted he could handle all my mother's business, and that I needed to concentrate on my future. It seemed to escape him that my BA in psychology had failed to incite a bidding war for my services in the corporate world. His standard line was that Long Island had tons of companies that would be perfect for a smart college grad like me. Just to shut him up, I took a sales job with Orbit International, an outfit that described its mission as "The designing and manufacturing of subsystems and major components for prime contractors, government procurement agencies (both foreign and domestic), and R&D laboratories worldwide since 1957." The campus was located in a dreary business park way out on the South Shore. Needless to say, there weren't many Lightnin' Hopkins or Jane's Addiction fans in my new place of business. That I was miserable didn't seem apparent to Lou, or simply didn't matter.

I lasted maybe six months before coming to the realization that I had to get out, with or without my father's blessing. Mom had remained relatively stable, so I concocted a plan to preserve my sanity. One Friday, after turning in my resignation, I announced that Orbit had promoted me to a new position. Since I was now so familiar with Orbit's products, Corporate decided to bump me up to night manager of the parts division. I would be reporting for work at 6 p.m. and finishing by three in the morning. Occasionally, I would have to travel, visiting our manufacturing plants in South America and even China. As far-fetched a tale as this was, my desperation turned me into a skilled actor, or at least one passable enough to get Lou's seal of approval.

The other details of the new plan involved hooking up with as many Long Island musicians as I could, always having somewhere to hang when there wasn't a gig, and storing a bass and amp at a friend's place so I'd have access to them at all times. There were a few hiccups, especially in the beginning. The staff at the Roslyn diner got to know me very well, as I spent many non-gig hours hovering over endless cups of coffee. One gig-less Monday night, as I was treating myself to the Blue Plate Special, I looked out the window to see my father parking his car, and slowly helping my mom from the passenger side to the front door. I dashed into the kitchen and told one of the waiters to wrap up my food so I could come and pick it up a couple of hours later. Once I was sure Irene and Lou had enough time to get inside, I dashed out the back door of the kitchen.

There was something both disconcerting and unbearable about watching my parents from a secret perch where I couldn't wave, say hello, or assist my father in getting my mother situated in a booth. Without warning, they'd gone from being my family to fictional, stoic characters in a black-and-white movie. The man formerly my father was now being played by some wizened old coot from a Geritol commercial, and the person playing my mother looked like my grandmother. With distance, they not only seemed older, but more tragic. I resolved to spend some quality time with them the next morning, so they wouldn't feel like strangers anymore. I loved my mother as much as I could love anyone, at least at that stage of life. I wanted to feel the same way toward my father, but mostly I felt sorry for him. His narrow worldview was the reason I had to engage in this subterfuge. I also wondered if he might someday find peace in Eddie having gotten to do the thing he loved most and having done it really well. In my heart, I knew Lou would never change, and that I would have to take all responsibility for my own survival.

Eventually my convoluted machinations found their groove, as I hooked up with seven different bands and kept myself booked at least five nights a week. It wasn't Orbit night manager money, but I didn't have to pay rent, and I felt a sense of triumph whenever I was onstage. Some of the bands would book tours, which I had anticipated when I put the whole plan in motion. As far as Lou and Irene were concerned, a one-week swing through Massachusetts and Vermont was an Orbit International trip to Buenos Aires, to inspect air-conditioning parts for the Navy's new military transport planes. A two-night casino gig in Vegas was a visit to the Orbit campus in Fairfield, Iowa. It was a ridiculous ruse, but it kept everybody happy. Somewhere during this period, I met Tracy, who admired both my bass playing and my commitment to helping my parents. On the nights when we were without bookings, we'd huddle in her apartment listening to everything from Miles to Ella to the Beastie Boys. Most of the time I'd leave at three, so I could get back to my parents' house. The absurdity of it all had now added another color—the fake Orbit manager attempting to have an adult relationship while sleeping in the bottom bunk of his childhood bed.

Irene hung on for a couple more years, as did this arrangement. The moment she passed, Lou announced he was selling the house. I would have to find another crash pad during the weeks I wasn't flying to South America or Asia.

"You're making plenty of money, now," Lou said. "You probably want to buy a big house and have me move in with you."

I remained silent, which turned out to be the right move. After a few circuitous turns, Lou told me that while it was generous of me to offer, he'd probably feel more comfortable in a retirement facility with people his own age—as long as they weren't musicians.

Once we got him settled, I found my own apartment, and Tracy and I continued to flirt with falling in love, until I did and waited for her to join the party. Unfortunately, Tracy's eventual declaration of love timed out a little too neatly with her swift ascension as a singer and actress. While we both had chops, hers were star quality which, though unintended, became an ongoing source of friction. Everybody wanted to work with her, and double that number wanted to sleep with her. She handled it much better than I did. Thanks to my pissiness and jealousy, we suffered a record-setting number of breakups and reunions. The rapprochements were most notable for the alleged make-up sex that was merely a prelude to the further disintegration of our relationship. I began to feel happiest during the times we were apart, when I was on the road, playing with talented musicians and living the life of a C-grade rock star. In those days, "C" was still good enough to get you rent money, and plenty of hot women. I hooked up with as many as I could get my hands on, Laurie Miller among them. Post-Tracy, I followed in the footsteps of my brother, but armed with the hard-earned wisdom to stay away from bands that were too druggy, and bandleaders who were too controlling.

In one more cruel, "I told you so" blow, B- and C-grade rock 'n' roll would soon find itself afflicted with what I termed "Lou Kozlowski Orchestra Syndrome." A combination of DJ's, house music, hip-hop, and lower budgets conspired to turn talented young musicians into the equivalent of one more schmo playing "Volare" on the accordion. Holiday Inns in Omaha and Bismarck cut out live music. Neighborhood bars in Albany and Binghamton replaced acts like Bloodshot with free open mic nights. As baffling as it seemed, going out to hear rock 'n' roll from anybody other than big-name bands became a poor stepchild to "clubbing." Potentially even worse, something called the Internet was starting to make its presence known, with free bootleg sites like Napster ripping off the artists who owned the material. In a few years, legit CD revenues would be replaced by the paltry pennies of streaming. The writing was on the wall, even without knowing that rock was destined to be swept into the cultural dustbin by hip-hop. Anybody with foresight could see that the working musician's life, never easy to begin with, was about to become a whole lot harder. As I took it all in, Lou's voice began to echo in my head, admonishing me at all hours of the day and night for not heeding his warning. My only consolation was that I would be spared the live version of the lecture, because in-the-flesh Lou still thought I worked for Orbit International.

Then came the twist on top of the twist. Lou's cognitive abilities started deteriorating to the point where he was no longer even capable of giving such a lecture. The doctors' diagnosis was Alzheimer's, and, in a matter of months, a full-time caregiver was hired to stay with him in his apartment. Most of the times I visited, he seemed to know who I was, but, on other occasions, he would stare at the wall, muttering mostly unintelligible thoughts. His speech had become garbled, but I did manage to make out the words "Eddie," "Irene," and "bills" somewhere in the mix. It was painful to witness how, over the span of three years, my father had gone from indignant fighter to lonely shell, to befuddled ghost.

Managing my father's health care while trying to scrape together enough work to survive was a stressful balancing act. Guys I'd played with for years were hanging up their axes and selling Toyotas. A drummer I had worked with blew his brains out after getting paid twenty bucks for a four-hour gig. What kind of life was this? How was any musician supposed to fight back?

A good rule of thumb in situations like these is to look for answers from the people who have the most to lose. I wasn't smart enough to know that, but, in a strange turn of events, a potential answer found me. After having spent the afternoon with Lou, and making thirty-five dollars playing a business networking mixer, I zoned out in front of the TV to watch an episode of *Seinfeld* I'd taped. It was the one where Uncle Leo tells Jerry about all the great things his cousin Jeffrey does for the parks department, thereby implying that Jerry, the lowly stand-up comedian, is a loser. A little close to home, maybe, but the guy who played Leo always cracked me up. As Leo began one of his rants, my phone rang. I put the VCR on pause, never suspecting who the caller would be.

"Hey, how you doing?" came a somewhat familiar, but restrained, voice.

"Who's this?" I asked.

"If you don't want to talk to me, I totally get it."

"Gene?"

"I just wanted to see how you're doing, that's all."

"Fine. Great."

"Glad to hear it."

Whether he meant it or not, he sounded sincere, which I took as the "all clear" to tell him the truth. He seemed to be aware of my mom's passing but had no way of knowing about my father's condition. He told me how sorry he was, and that, even though Lou despised him, he remained grateful for all my dad had done for him. Then he started talking about the music business, and how much harder it had gotten for people to find work. Apparently, Gene had seen it coming and, in an effort to be proactive, came up with a solution he believed would generate long-term income.

"You selling municipal bonds?" I joked.

"I might be, if I hadn't found something better."

"Which is?"

A few years ago, Gene had done the math, and determined that it was the optimum time to get on the Beatles tribute band train. He had identified it as a burgeoning market that would retain or even grow in value beyond the Baby Boomers, and the market was not yet overrun. He also believed there were a lot worse things a person could do than make a living playing the greatest pop music ever written.

"So, you have a band already?" I asked.

"Yeah, for about six months. We're called 'Help!' Been playing exclusively in the Midwest, but Mom's having some health issues, so I've decided to move my base back to Long Island. It'll take some time to build up the business, but I feel pretty good about it."

"That's great, Gene."

"You working enough?" he asked.

"Yeah. I mean, there could always be more."

"'Cause I'm looking for a new Paul. You interested?"

"You want me to join your Beatle band?"

"If you're up for it. I've got a bunch of other bass players who want it, but you're my first choice. You don't have to tell me right now but say the word and it's yours."

"Wow. You're not doing this because of—"

"Guilt? No. Your brother was the best guitarist and the best guy I've ever worked with, but business is business. I'm asking you because you got game."

"Thank you."

"Think about it. If it's too weird because of your dad, I get it. We'll talk in a couple of days."

"Okay. Thanks, Gene."

I hung up, unable to ignore the fact that it *was* weird, on too many levels for me to name. Thankfully, I had some time to let things marinate. I picked up the remote and went back to Uncle Leo throwing his son's success in Jerry's face.

"You know what your cousin Jeffrey's doing now?"

Maybe Jeffrey had the right idea, working for the parks department. I'm in no position to judge.

IT'S ONLY LOVE

Leaving Pineview, I force myself down from the high of Christina having raised the mealtime ante in order to confront the more immediate issue—how to deal with Gene in his present emotional state. My choices are either stopping off at the motel and jumping into the fire or driving straight home and lying low until tomorrow night's gig. It's the Frost poem redux, with the asterisk that both roads lead to hell. There's no telling what might be going through Gene's self-involved brain right now, but his uncharacteristic lack of communication is not a good sign.

In theory, going to see him now means I get it over with. But the probability is, he'll want to keep me there till one in the morning in a two-hundred-square-foot space that reeks of General Tso's chicken—a hell all its own. This would seem to favor option two. If I wait, I get twenty-four more hours of peace—unless he starts calling me again tonight, in which case I'll regret not having settled things earlier, face-to-face. There's also the chance that a work night will find him back in evasive mode, which has its own sets of plusses and minuses. The healthiest thing would be for me to institute a third option, whereby I give myself permission to disengage from Gene's personal problems.

Justified or not, my conscience won't allow me to go cold turkey on this guy. You'd think there'd be some middle ground between my father's fatwa and me taking on the role of adult guardian, but the trouble is, there are no other Kleins to monitor the gravity of the situation, either on Marcia's end or Gene's. Marcia is obviously no longer in a position to take care of business, and Gene, being a rock 'n' roll savant, possesses few of the necessary life skills to negotiate a parent's aging and ultimate surrender. The only reason he's been able to deal with his mother's health up till now is that she's been in full control of her faculties, and capable of calling the shots.

When I try to imagine Gene's reaction to the new normal, I picture a fragile grade-school kid in an old guy's body. After all these years of nonstop adulation, how strange it must be for him to find himself without an advocate to applaud his every move. Granted, there were still a bunch of Gene Klein fans scattered about the heartland, but at the dawn of his career it had been his mother who anointed him a star, and, in its twilight, she who kept pushing him forward. The emptiness he must now feel triggers something in me, maybe because I've lost Eddie and my parents. In a way, I think it goes deeper than that. There are certain people who get in your heart, and it doesn't seem to matter how selfish or fucked up they are. You feel for them, even without knowing the specifics of their troubles. It's one of the better human instincts, and sometimes the least pleasant.

I take the elevator up to the third floor and exit onto an outdoor walkway reminiscent of every place I've crashed since becoming a professional musician. Gene's room is on the far end of the hall, so, along the way, I'm treated to standard motel audio of a man and woman screaming at each other, two babies crying, and something that sounds either like sex, or the Colonel from Pineview having a bowel movement. As I get to the end of the walkway, I hear something equally familiar, but far more comforting. Gene, accompanied by his vintage Epiphone acoustic, is singing "It's Only Love" with the passion of a twenty-five-year-old Lennon. *How is he still able to pull this off?*

I decide on executing my knock at the end of the song, but before he starts the next one. If he were to go right into "If I Fell," I'd never be able to interrupt, because it's that good. As soon as he hits the last chord, I spring into action with three firm raps.

"I already told you!" Gene shouts from inside. "I don't want the room cleaned!"

"Then I'll keep me fire engine clean," I respond, in adorable Paul-like Liverpudlian. "It's a clean machine."

Gene opens the door, looking neither particularly happy nor upset to see me.

"Hey, man, how're you doing?" he says, as if it's routine for me to show up at this strange motel, talking with a British accent.

I walk in expecting a disaster zone, but instead find a space that's methodically organized. On one side of the room sit neatly piled packages of adult diapers and cartons of Ensure, and on the other, two acoustic guitars, a Rick-enbacker, and a stack of Beatles biographies.

"I was just working on the setlist for Liverpool," Gene informs me. "I think they're going to flip for our 'Strawberry Fields,' don't you?"

"Uh-huh," is the best I can squeak out in my state of bewilderment. At this point, I should never be surprised by any of the places Gene's mind takes him, but nobody could have predicted this one. Rather than seeming fragile or ruffled as a result of seeing his mother reduced to a semi-conscious state, he is conducting fake-Beatle business as usual.

"I think the first thing we have to do is to distinguish ourselves from the hack tribute bands," he announces. "Don't you?"

"Sounds about right." What, exactly, distinguishes a "hack" group of mimics from the artful ones is open to debate, but I know what Gene means. Regardless, I can't go any further without addressing the elephant in the room. "Gene, I saw your mom. I'm sorry."

"Thanks. Shit happens. Jasmine says not to worry. Marcia will be back to her old self before we know it."

"Jasmine said that?"

"Maybe not those exact words, but I know my mom."

"What did the doctors say?"

"Who knows?"

"You didn't get any information from her doctors?"

"Yeah, yeah, I did, but it sounded like a bunch of mumbo-jumbo. They weren't super-positive, but it's their job not to raise your expectations, so they can make more money for themselves. You know Marcia."

This was true, but I didn't know her after a stroke, and neither did Gene. Yet it didn't prevent him from settling into a state of denial that not only allowed him to continue his work, but do so with a sunny attitude. I was now in the strange position of starting to feel better for him, while at the same time foreseeing a fall that would land so hard, he wouldn't be able to survive it.

"There's a lot of good news for us," Gene continues. "I've checked out all the bands that have entered the contest so far, and the only one that comes close to us has a fat Paul."

PC was never Gene's strong suit.

"Do you really think the judges are going to make their decision on the basis of weight?" I have to ask.

"Not knocking the obese. You can't have a cute Beatle who's fat is all I'm saying. It goes against the origin story. The thing Help! needs to decide is which way to lean. Should the set be half-early period, half-late, which is a logical way to go, or do we go bold with an all-late period set, where the tunes are more complex?"

I've been around Gene long enough to know I'm not being asked for an opinion. He's ruminating out loud until he arrives at his own, exhaustively analyzed, solution. There are no clear answers, as the deciding factors will boil down to the quality of the performances and the personal preferences of the judges. A kickass "She Loves You" will trump a sloppy "I Am the Walrus" all day long.

"Listen to this," Gene says, trading the Epiphone for a sixties Martin D-28 like the one Lennon brought with him to India. It sounds super sweet, especially when I realize what song he's starting to play. This is the first time I've heard him do "Happiness is a Warm Gun." The emotion Gene brings to Mother Superior jumping the gun is as potent as anything I've heard out of him. I give the thumbs-up and let him know that if he wants to include the song in our Liverpool set, it will make a fine addition.

Gene shakes his head, no. "Can't risk it. One of the judges might be Catholic and get all bent out of shape by the image of nuns with guns."

"But it's a classic Beatles song," I remind him.

"You don't have to tell me. But you never know what's gonna rub somebody the wrong way."

"Your call," I say, as if it could ever be otherwise.

Gene looks at his watch. "Hey, Jimmy, you can hang here if you want, but I should probably be getting back to the nursing home."

"Nah, I gotta head home," I say, thankful for the early release. "Marcia's lucky to have you."

"Thanks, man," Gene says, pulling me into a hug.

I take this as a positive sign, as it is, perhaps, the first such overture I've experienced from him. For all his grieving over Eddie, to this day he has never been able to express his sorrow to me personally. I start down the walkway when I hear his voice call out:

"Hey, I heard you play music at Pineview."

Here comes the ghastly pitch—the Klein-Kozlowski Band. "I volunteer an hour a week," I say, trying to make it sound as inconsequential as possible.

"I should come check you out. We'll have to see, though. I don't think Mom's gonna be in that place very long."

Unless Gene is thinking of moving her home and having two caretakers working around the clock, he appears to have embraced denial with a capital "D," which is also the first letter of "delusional."

"How long do you plan on hanging out at the motel?" I ask. "You only live a half-hour away."

"I know," Gene says. "I just need to be close to her for now. Besides, I'm getting a lot of good work done here."

The Rolling Stones had their chateau on the Côte d'Azur, Gene has a motel room in spitting distance of a bail bonds franchise. Dubious location aside, I can't argue with the quality of what I just heard or the fortitude of his spirit. The visit has proved far less unsettling than I'd feared. Marcia might be down for the count, but Gene is still Gene, which might serve him well after all.

CHANGES

The next few shows at JP Murphy's mark the beginning of what Beatles tribute historians will likely describe as Help!'s "late period," if they're being kind, "descent into the shitter," if they're fans of the truth. Mikey, Prem, and I knew it was inevitable that the closer we got to Liverpool weekend, the more intense and dictatorial our leader would become. In anticipation, we coordinated a pre-emptive response, a mix of acquiescence and resistance designed to get us to the finish line without spilling any blood. Yet despite our best efforts, the reprieve of Gene having shut up and done his job turned out to be a one-off, and things took a sharp turn for the WTF.

At our first gig post-Marcia-moving-into-the-home, the band would learn that Gene and Jasmine were officially an item. Like Pattie Boyd, she had left her husband to become the uncontested successor to the Gene Klein genuflecting throne. If the dual roles of Fake Yoko and Marcia's caregiver hadn't been suspect enough, the new arrangement cemented a high watermark for meta-enabling. Jasmine, who less than two months ago had possessed no knowledge whatsoever of the Fab Four, now walked around like she was the fifth fake Beatle. Fully committed to pleasing

Gene by becoming the consummate Yoko, the erstwhile silent worshiper installed herself as his emotional bodyguard, protecting "John's" interests in all aspects of his life. To no one's surprise, the shift was not popular with the people who had already suffered her boyfriend's excesses for years—namely, the band.

In the new Help! hierarchy, if any of us brings up a suggestion as far as the setlist or an arrangement, we now must suffer through Jasmine's opinion as well as Gene's. Naturally, since I'm the band's Paul, she has developed a unique distrust of me, and now questions my ulterior motives. I'm all for being authentic, but the idea is to mimic the Beatles' music, not add *their* personal jealousies to the shit we face in our own lives. This is meta-insanity.

As untenable as the situation is, it's a miracle the latest madness hasn't affected Gene's playing. Inexplicably, this Lipitor-popping mama's boy is at the height of his musical powers. For all I know, it helps him to have a fake Yoko filling the adoration gaps in Marcia's absence. I'm sure he's flattered to have somebody young who's both willing to do the job, and sleep with him.

Whether or not they have a sexual relationship has been a matter of conjecture between Prem and Mikey. Prem maintains that Gene and Jasmine are all about business, with neither of them projecting even the slightest hint of intimacy. Mikey points out the lack of touching, and that aging Gene stopped sleeping with aging groupies a long time ago. I'd have to agree that, to the outsider, they seem like they're doing a job as opposed to being in love. There is one area, however, where they've become familiar enough to give any couple a run for their money. Arguing appears to be very much in Jasmine's wheelhouse, as witnessed by the shouting matches she's had with Gene, both in rehearsal and before or after a gig. The gist of her griping is that Gene needs to make more money, which could be accomplished by letting her renegotiate the contracts for all our events. Gene tries to explain that we're working the bar circuit, not selling out stadiums for Live Nation or AEG. Jasmine has no idea what Live Nation is, or what the acronym stands for.

Mikey's on his last nerve. He isn't sure he's going to make it all the way to Liverpool, New York, much less travel with Gene to England should we win. Prem has responded to the lunacy by starting to put together a jazz band with Raji, which I think is a smart exit strategy. I was able to book a night for the Donny Delgado showcase, but it won't be for eight weeks since Donny's such a busy dude.

Marcia is presumably making baby steps with her speech and movement. Gene brought her home from Pineview after two weeks, somehow scrounging up enough dough to employ another full-time caregiver for the hours when Jasmine must tend to her Yoko chores. As for me, I'm grateful to have escaped Gene horning in on my volunteer work at the nursing home, but the less pleasing development is that I still haven't been able to have lunch with Christina. She's as friendly as ever, but between responsibilities with her kid, and being overloaded in the admissions office, we can't seem to nail down a date. Part of me wonders if she's having second thoughts. I get butterflies in my stomach whenever I walk into the building, but then, once I see her, I'm relaxed again. I do believe we'll get the chance to sit down and learn more about each other. I need to be patient is all. Besides, no matter what Tracy might think, this is where my low-expectations MO comes in handy. As attracted as I am to Christina, I'd rather spend the rest of my life seeing her on a regular basis with no sex than letting the friendship go by the wayside. I didn't form a bond with her because I wanted to be involved with a married woman. The connection grew organically, which could still happen with an unmarried woman if I ever find the right one.

I go over the calendar for the next two months, making note of the usual JP's and Carmine's gigs, plus a few Help! matinee shows at public libraries. I find a couple of other dates as well, where I'm filling in on bass for a buddy of mine who plays with an LGBT theater company. They're doing a gender-reversed version of "My Fair Lady" set in Little Italy, with cannolis from Ferrara's served during intermission. It should be a fun diversion from playing an eternally cute man-child whose band broke up before I was even born.

My reason for reviewing the booked dates is to examine the spaces in between. I'm thinking about a quick vacation, perhaps to Los Angeles, to meet my daughter. It seems like there are two long weekends that would work, provided, of course, that Kaylie really does want to see me. People say a lot of things, but, when push comes to shove, you never know. There's also the possibility, as I'm sure is the case with Christina, that she's busy for now, but will be available sometime in the future. The only way to get an answer is to put myself out there and make the offer. For a split second I wonder whether I need to contact her mother first, but since Kaylie is legally an adult and we've already been in touch, I decide against it. Plus, she seems so much nicer than her mother. I indulge myself in the flimsy notion that she got her agreeable disposition from me.

I text Kaylie, telling her I have some upcoming meetings in Los Angeles, which are to take place over one of the two Saturdays I've earmarked on the calendar. If there's a specific weekend that's better for her, I will reach out to my LA associates to weigh in with my preference. The work pretense is, of course, bullshit. I could probably book some meetings if I wanted to, as I know a few producers who moved out there, but we'd have nothing to meet about, unless I wanted to play them my seven-song Donny Delgado set. Out of loyalty to Donny, my lack of ambition, and having no desire to make the trip about business, this will not happen. I'll just wait to see what Kaylie has to say and make my plans accordingly.

I spend a quiet evening with Jaco, watching more *Seinfeld* reruns and re-reading the Charlie Mingus autobiography, *Beneath the Underdog*. Talk about a bass player. This cat did it all, from the Village Gate to Carnegie Hall, from the whorehouses to the psychiatric ward. Not to mention having come up with the greatest album titles of all time.

Mingus Ah-Um, *Pithecanthropus Erectus*, *The Black Saint and the Sinner Lady*, and, my personal favorite, *Mingus Mingus Mingus Mingus Mingus*. I put on that one as I read about his jaunt to Tijuana, where he banged twenty-six prostitutes in a single brothel visit.

Then Kaylie's text arrives.

> Either weekend gd. What part of town will U be staying?

This was an excellent question. It's been so long since I've been to LA that I'm not sure where I should stay, or where I can afford to. I shoot back:

> Whereabouts are you?

> Culver City.

Where, exactly, was Culver City? I remember the name, but not the area. A quick Google search tells me it's in West LA, not too far from the beach. I'll book an Air BnB, not in Culver City, but close enough to make my destination seem legit. I write:

> Somewhere in West LA.

> That's super close. You could even stay with me if you like. I have a 1 bdrm w/a decent fold-out sofa.

She's trusts me sight unseen. Night and day from the hell her mother put me through.

> That's really nice of you, but I don't want
> to impose.

> You're my effin' dad.

Shit's definitely getting real. Not only do I have a living, breathing daughter, she's infinitesimally cooler than anything I deserve.

I vacillate between renting the Air Bnb and staying with Kaylie. The last thing I want is to invade her personal space and have things get awkward. Once I book my flight, I pick up the phone so I can address the matter head-on. Kaylie reassures me her place is big, she's at work all day anyway, we'll be going out at night, and, as long as I don't mind sleeping on the couch, I should save my money and crash at her place. I tell her I will, provided she lets me take her out for a nice dinner. The deal is sealed. I will leave my little basement for adventures unknown on a Friday morning and treat myself to a weekend respite from the madness of Gene, Jasmine, and the looming possibility of Long Island's first fake Plastic Ono band.

Meanwhile, I have Mikey book me a bunch of comparatively high-paying porta-potty gigs to help fund my trip. In light of the Gene and Jasmine development, the toilet job's lack of ambiguity is as refreshing as its odors are nauseating. Except for working movie sets, it's an ego-less experience providing a necessary service that, when executed properly, is not subject to a thousand different opinions. And, while it's true that there are competing porta-potty companies, I doubt you'll find any middle-aged men dressing up like the original potty-makers from sixty years ago.

Prem, Mikey, and I are basically zoned out of Help!, doing whatever Gene wants while we mark time until Liverpool. Had we not already made the commitment, I'm not sure any of us would last until August. Jasmine has only gotten worse as her "power" has grown. I suspect that, behind closed doors, she may have crossed the line from argumentative to abusive, but I'm not about to go on that fishing expedition, at least for the time being. If it's true, I only hope the offenses are being aimed at Gene alone and sparing Marcia.

Part of me can't believe that Christina could be friends with someone like this, but I never got a real feel for how close they were. Everybody in the Filipino caregiving community seems to know one another, so there's no telling whether it's an actual friendship, somebody she once worked with, or an acquaintance from back home. I want to bring up the subject every time I go to Pineview, but we haven't had much opportunity to talk. I also want to tell her that I'll be going to LA to visit Kaylie. Since Christina was so close with my dad, I'm sure she'd love to know that I'll be spending time with the granddaughter he never got to meet. These are not things I want to text, or even talk about on the phone, so they'll probably have to wait for our phantom lunch date.

As I arrive at JFK to await my flight, I'm filled with excitement I didn't know a road-weary, middle-aged man could still have in him. While everyone else projects the appropriate misery of post 9-11 through COVID air travel, I've turned into a wide-eyed teenager, eager to spring for an overpriced cup of coffee and even more expensive bottle of water. My guess is that I'm rewarding myself for taking the leap into the unknown, for being open enough to bend the rules of containment. I'm also feeling proud of having assembled a packet of gifts for Kaylie—books by three of my favorite authors (T.C. Boyle, Russell Banks, Isabel Allende) and three heavy-rotation vinyl LPs (*A Love Supreme*, *Revolver*, *Fear of Music*). I have no clue what she reads or listens to, but at least she'll get some idea of who her pop is. I'm also kind of buzzed to see California again, this time with (it feels weird to say it) family. For whatever reason, the low-expectations default has refused to kick in, so it's a struggle not to raise my hopes too high. I'm just happy, as unthinkable as that now seems. Even being stuck in the middle seat doesn't faze me, despite the realization that the big guy on the aisle is about to spill into my personal space for five-plus hours. I have two J.P. Donleavy books and playlists from Talk,Talk, Soundgarden, and Johnny Cash. Game on.

Kaylie is still at her office downtown when I land at LAX. She has it all worked out, though, having texted me the gate code to her apartment building, and left the key under the front door mat. According to her instructions, the

Uber ride from the airport to Culver City will take twenty minutes, tops. There will be food for me in the fridge, coffee next to the Keurig machine, and my choice of alcohol should I need to take the edge off. She tells me to unpack, chill, prepare for my Saturday meeting, whatever I like. She'll be home around six, we have a dinner reservation at eight and, if I feel like it, we can meet some of her friends afterward for a nightcap. It appears I have a daughter who is both take-charge and confident, nothing like the fragile flower image put forth by her mother.

The Uber driver drops me off outside a newish apartment complex in a neighborhood well on its way to gentrification. The building seems like it's fully occupied, but there are few people around. The ones I do see look successful and under thirty-five. The lobby is so beautiful, hip, and immaculate, these tenants could eat their avocado toast right off the floor. I take the elevator up to the third level, open the door to Kaylie's apartment, and, in under five seconds, conclude that my daughter must never see where I live. Her digs, though not ostentatious in the least, suggest a life well-lived that will only get better. There are no Girardis upstairs. There are maintenance people to deal with dead-sparrow problems. There is youth. There is hope.

I put my bags down and start inspecting the apartment for details of Kaylie's life. Lots of pictures with groups of friends, none of any particular boy. The other thing I'm curious about is whether there are photographs of her with her mother. I'd already seen shots of Laurie on Facebook, but what I'm looking for here is some indication of whether the two of them have a good relationship. If she displays lots of pictures of herself with Laurie, I'll have my answer.

I don't find one. This makes me feel good, which then makes me feel bad for feeling good. Other stuff of note in the room? Nice but probably inexpensive abstract art, an old Yamaha acoustic guitar that looks as if it hasn't been played in fifteen years, and, most notably, a full bar. In addition to my daughter being successful enough to afford a place three times the size of mine, her apartment can double as a cocktail lounge. The liquor is top drawer across the board. I spot a half-full bottle of Glenlivet 18, which I've always considered too rich for my blood.

I'm not quite sure what I expected to find on this trip, but discovering that your twenty-five-year-old lives way better than you do messes with your head. I'm intimidated enough to polish off the Glen 18. My rarely exercised sense of decorum prevails, telling me it's better to be intimidated than sloshed when you meet your daughter for the first time. Out of habit, I pick up the guitar. The strings are completely rusted, so there's no point tuning it. I make a mental note to get a new set of light gauge while I'm here, so I can change them for her. "Be of Service" is always a wise mantra for the grateful houseguest.

Meanwhile, I've got a few hours to kill. I can read, go for a swim in the pool, maybe take a nap, so I'm rested for tonight. I decide to bag all those ideas in favor of taking a walk around the neighborhood. Hell, I didn't come to Southern California to do the same shit I do in my basement. I text Kaylie to let her know my plans. She tells me that Downtown Culver City is a five-minute walk from where I am and recommends a couple of cool bars and restaurants.

The downtown area seems to be populated by successful new media types. I walk into what I suppose is a gastropub, order an eleven-dollar beer, and people-watch. Apparently, there are a whole lot of folks who have the freedom to drink overpriced suds at three in the afternoon. A tall, twenty-something dude carrying a guitar walks in to talk to the owner. From what I can gather, he's supposed to play here tomorrow night and needs to get his start time straight. I wonder if the guy's any good. Based on nothing, I conclude that he's the West Coast version of Ben Gardner from Sea Cliff.

I try to imagine myself at that age, embarking on a music career in California without Eddie as my North Star, or Gene as my baggage. I can't picture it. On the other hand, if I'd gone to UCLA instead of Albany, I might have chucked music and turned into the very people I now observe: smiling as I pick at my tempura cauliflower; emitting, with each bite, the aura of a high-powered player with a cutting-edge career.

My little field trip is not turning out as I intended. I was looking for a relaxed jaunt into town, but the longer I sit here, the harder I am on myself. Stepping into one of these places is like entering a social media hologram where everybody is more successful than you are.

The fact is, I should be proud of the stuff I've done. A forty-nine-year-old working musician in New York? How many rockers can pull that off? I'm able to appreciate that when I'm back home, but in this deceptively sunny environment, I feel like a worthless piece of shit. Less than eight hours ago, I was so happy I bought a Bloody Mary for the guy whose spare tire was sharing my seat. Now I'm unmoored, feeling like I took on this mission without considering the potential pitfalls.

Leaving the bar, it hits me that my sudden mood swing has nothing to do with the sun, or the cauliflower eaters. I'm worried about what my daughter is going to think of me. The sad part of it is, I know I'd be a lot less anxious if her apartment had turned out to be a dump.

I regroup, identifying this sort of thinking as both stupid and unproductive. My answer is to hit a local music store where I can pick up some strings for Kaylie's guitar. I walk in, make a beeline for the basses, and try out a new Schecter Stiletto Studio 5-String. The guitar's black satin body is silky smooth, and the neck is super-easy to play. I fool around with Flea's riff on "Give it Away," which winds up impressing two music nerds who are carbon copies of the ones I see hanging out at Sam Ash on Long Island. My new fans, Lance and Junior, go on to regale me with torrents of gearhead minutia, providing unsolicited instruction on how I should set up my pedalboard. By the time I pay for my strings and head for the door, the boys are so deep into their Megadeth vs. Metallica argument, they don't even notice me leaving. The good news is that music has once again come to my rescue and restored my spirit.

I'm back in the apartment re-stringing the Yamaha when my phone buzzes. It's a "Hey, you" text from Christina, so the day continues to get better. She writes that she's free for lunch tomorrow, can I meet her? Of course I can't, but she asked, and I will employ this beacon of light to counter whatever pangs of self-doubt might resurface during my stay. I tell her where I am, who I'm visiting, and that it's great to hear from her. She's excited for me and says she's sure my daughter and I will adore each other. I want to hear Christina's voice right here, right now. I ask if she can talk on the phone, but she says there's a family coming in to meet with her, and she needs to prepare their application forms. She assures me we'll schedule something upon my return. I want to send one of those heart or kiss emojis that I normally can't stand. In this instance, they're the perfect substitute for a situation where you want someone to know how you feel, but it's too soon to write out the words. I stop myself from pushing the emoji button, hoping maybe she'll send me one first. She doesn't. She's married. My hunger to express real emotion with dopey graphics has passed. But Christina has made me happy, and nobody can take that away.

It's now a few minutes before seven. I've read, I've tuned, I've changed my clothes a couple of times, I've reconsidered breaking into the Glenlivet. I'm still feeling good, but now a bit fidgety in anticipation of the big moment. As I go to pour myself a glass of water, the door bursts open, and I hear a booming "Hey, hey!" I look up to see a long-haired, casually chic and vivacious young woman smiling at me. I go toward her, not entirely sure whether a hug is too familiar a first greeting, but she initiates it, and with gusto.

"You made it!" she squeals. "This is crazy, right?"

"Crazy good, I hope."

"Ya. You're like my dad."

"Technically I *am* your dad, not like him."

She giggles.

I'm trying to figure out if she looks even a little bit like me, but I don't see it at all. She's just a young, pretty girl who seems more excited to be alive than anyone I've ever known. "I wish we could have met sooner," I say.

"Me, too. But I probably wouldn't have had the fully stocked bar."

"Good way to think of it. You take lemons and make lemonade."

"Yup. And then I spike it." She laughs. This one is full-throated, pure and unguarded. "So, we could have a drink now, or I could go get dressed first."

"Whatever you like." I think she looks fine, but I'm not sure what kind of place she's taking me to. I've got my all-purpose outfit on—black jeans, white button-down, and casual sport coat I can throw on if called for.

"Getting dressed. You know how to make a Moscow Mule?"

"With or without the copper mug?"

"With. They're under the bar."

"Your beverage shall be ready upon your return."

"Nice." She smiles and heads off to change.

While I can't say that mixing a Moscow Mule was something I saw coming out of this first meeting, my amped-up, high-living daughter has already gone a long way toward making me feel relaxed, and at home. I think I remember how to do this: vodka, ginger beer, and lime, but I take my time in the interest of putting my best foot forward. When I'm done, I set the drinks on the bar, go over to the couch, and pick up the Yamaha, which can now be described as usable. The guitar sounds a little harsh but should mellow after a workout. I start fooling around with one of the songs for my upcoming showcase with Donny, making a mental note to talk to Prem about using his vintage flat-top Gibson.

Kaylie emerges in a short black dress, adjusting one of her earrings. She sees the two mugs sitting on the bar.

"Wow, you waited for me. You're way more polite than I am."

"How do you know I haven't already had my first drink?" I say.

"Like father, like daughter." She brings over the mugs. "You sound really good. I didn't know that thing was even playable."

"It wasn't when I got here. I put on new strings."

"That's so sweet of you." She hands me my mug. "Cheers!"

"Cheers." I'm blown away to be clinking copper with my own flesh and blood.

"Wow," Kaylie says, after her first sip. "Dad knows his alcohol."

"We use to be close friends."

She smiles and proceeds to take a seat beside me on the couch.

"So, when did you stop playing guitar?" I ask. "The strings felt like they were older than I am."

267

"Oh, I don't play. That belongs to some old, idiot boy-friend. I don't even remember which one."

"I'm sure he'll come back for it at some point."

"Ha. The guys I break up with don't ever come back."

"At least you're the one doing the break-ups."

"Usually. There've been a couple that went the other way. Most of them find me intimidating. Whatever." She takes a good-sized pull from the mug.

"I've heard dating is hard out here," I offer.

"As opposed to the chill scene in New York?" She eyes the naked ring finger on my left hand.

"Touché."

She takes a smaller sip from her mug. "So, you and Mom were some kind of one-night stand? Was that it?"

"It was."

"That's awesome." She downs the rest of her mule.

I'm confused by the joy she feels hearing this confirmation. "You know, most kids would be pissed to find out they were a product of parents fooling around, and that they never got to know their father."

"I'm getting to know you now. Steve's pretty cool too. I'm just happy to hear Mom wasn't always the way she is."

Perhaps I'm about to find out why there are no pictures of her in the apartment. "How is she?"

"I'll tell you after the next drink." Kaylie picks up her phone and orders our Uber.

There are probably a thousand restaurants on the Westside of Los Angeles, but my daughter wants me to have the full Hollywood experience, so we wind up at Musso and

Frank. The transition from mules to martinis is seamless, and, before long, the words coming out of my mouth seem as animated and confident as Kaylie's. It's not just the alcohol talking. Being around a young person this fearless and willing to put everything on the table is contagious. She tells me point blank that her mother is an uptight control freak who refuses to entertain anything approaching spontaneity. That's why Kaylie thinks it's so awesome that she once let herself go and hooked up with me. I tell Kaylie that, in retrospect, I'm sorry I agreed to stay out of her life. It was what her mom wanted, and I was poor and on the road all the time.

"Have you ever been married?" Kaylie asks.

I shake my head, no. "Never found the right situation."

"How could you? You're a rock 'n' roll guy. Having too much fun."

"I do my best." I'm having way too much fun now to get into the rules of containment.

"Yeah, I mean, that's where I'm at too," she says. "I love hanging with my girlfriends—you'll meet them later. We do epic shit: Vegas, Coachella every year, always plenty of options if I feel like hooking up."

By the second martini, it's clear my daughter has no dearth of sex partners. She's focused on career rather than marriage, made 85K last year, and is always on the lookout for a higher-paying job. Kaylie's a self-assured dynamo with the face of an actress and the ambition of a hedge-fund honcho. Maybe it's the booze, or a function of having gotten to know her a little better, but as impressive as she is, I'm no longer intimidated by the possibility of my daughter becoming a multi-millionaire businesswoman while I spend the rest of my life in a basement. What's even weirder is that as the ancient waiter she addresses like an old friend delivers our steaks to the table, I find myself looking around at the various characters and missing my basement. Curling up with Jaco. Working on my album. Kaylie, no doubt, would be unable to conceive of such a life, but I'm equally puzzled by this Hollywood tableau.

Kaylie says she's excited because her company's going to be sending her to Paris for work, and she's compiling a list of all the best clubs. She asks me for the names of the hot clubs in New York. I reply that the hottest club I frequent plays Beatles music to people on Social Security. I add that I'm the Paul of the band, figuring she'll get a kick out of that. Every kid these days seems to have grown up listening to the Beatles, before switching at age ten or so to hip-hop. Kaylie knows who Paul is, of course, but neither the Beatles, nor any of the music that moves me, are on her radar. (So much for the three albums I bought her.) She's all about Kendrick, Drake, Kodak Black, and 2 Chainz. It stands to reason, as these are the acts that generate income for today's music business, and Kaylie is in the thick of what's current and makes money. Kendrick and Drake also happen to be great.

Against my better judgment, I find myself wondering what her taste might have been had I been around while she was growing up. Under my influence, she might have grown up to love jazz, the *Abbey Road* medley, and maybe even learned how to play the guitar herself. It's also possible that she, too, would now be living in a basement.

We top out at three martinis and a glass of Cabernet. Kaylie leaves a little over half her steak on the plate. We tell Kaylie's waiter pal we're too full for dessert, I pay a dinner tab that's double my weekly fake-Beatle salary, and, the next thing I know, we're in another Uber, bound for an after-party at a club called Lash in East Hollywood. Our driver pulls up to a thirty-dollar valet stand, outside of which sits a flaming red Ferrari. Not your Carmine's crowd, that's for sure. We're dumped out at the end of a huge line waiting to get in, but Kaylie, no surprise, marches right past it, whispers something to the bald, three-hundred-pound dude behind the velvet rope, and we're ushered right in.

The dark, cozy space has plush leather sofas, wood wainscoting, and twenty-foot posters of a naked woman at either end of the room. It's as if the New York Yacht Club decided to join forces with a South Shore strip joint. The pounding, generic-sounding hip-hop is unrecognizable to me. I take it as a hopeful sign that no one is paying attention to this cut. The crowd is just making its way in, so another positive is that there's still breathing room. I ask Kaylie if she wants to snag a table while I order our drinks. She informs me that the tables are "bottle-service only" and have a three-thousand-dollar minimum. I tell her I'm okay with standing.

She smiles. "No worries. One of my friends will take care of it."

I look around at the patrons, who range from early twenties to forty or so. In theory, I shouldn't feel that old, as I'm maybe nine years past the top end, but not only do

271

I take on the mantle of dinosaur, I embrace it with every ossifying bone in my body. There's nothing like a posse of selfie-snapping Instagrammers to make you homesick for fake-Paul groupies with Long Island accents. I remind myself that I'm here to enjoy the time with my daughter who, at twenty-five, is a force to be reckoned with, even if I don't understand the purpose behind the force. I'm probably not about to learn, at least tonight, because when I turn around, Kaylie is handing me another martini. She introduces me to a suited-up guy named Brad, who has an Elvis-worthy pompadour atop his head, and a buzz cut covering the rest of it. He works in marketing for Netflix and wants (or pretends to want) to know what I do. Before I can answer, Kaylie steps in to say that I'm a brilliant musician who's played everywhere.

"Excellent. What's your name?" Brad asks, his phone at the ready so he can Google me.

"Jimmy Kozlowski. I'm pretty much a sideman."

"There you are," he says, having already found my website. "You play in a Beatles tribute band! My grandpa's in one of those."

And this is just the beginning. Little by little, the rest of Kaylie's squad arrives, one hot blonde after the next, as well as single-guy mover-and-shaker types: Chazz (restaurateur), Lorin (screenwriter), and Javier (Silicon Beach start-up owner). Javier buys the table, and I find myself jammed in between two of the blondes, who are extremely friendly given my prehistoric status. Although you'd never know it from the sloshed, giggly dialogue, these women are just as accomplished as the guys. Camilla, who's practically in my lap, works in the independent music business, licensing and streaming work from thousands of artists. She says her office receives thirty thousand new songs a day.

"Got to have the content," she says.

The dreaded "C" word again. I tell Camilla the thought of thirty-thousand songs times four minutes gives me a giant headache. She laughs. Camilla is apparently one of Kaylie's closest girlfriends and seems fascinated to be in the presence of a musician who's still kickin' it old school. By her third Cosmo, she's dying to hear me play, and says she'll be sure to come out to the Island the next time she's in New York. I manage to take it with a grain of salt, but her buzz-based handsiness is a little more difficult to ignore. I look up to see Kaylie deep in conversation with Javier and Brad. Something tells me she and I won't get to talk with each other until the Uber ride home. In the meantime, I'm not sure what I'm supposed to do next.

Camilla answers the question for me. "Let's go out to the patio."

"I didn't even know there was one."

"You didn't know a music company could receive thirty thousand songs a day."

"I didn't *want* to know that."

We step out onto the patio where there is a whole other bar serving a whole other set of happening millennials. Camilla asks me to buy her another Cosmo which, of course, I do. The music seems even louder out here, so I have to talk right in her ear when I excuse myself to find the men's room. She says she needs to go, too, and will direct me there. Cosmo in hand, she leads the way to what is evidently the gender-bending standard of Club Life Los Angeles. Common sinks for all, with individual stalls. Camilla whispers to me that it's not un-usual for people who pair off at the club to take advantage of the stalls if they can't wait till they get home. I start to think about how I'm going wriggle out of something that would be a whole lot of fun if I weren't visiting my daughter, when she turns and starts chatting up a guy at the sink. She thinks she knows him from somewhere. He guesses from another club downtown. She says no. He makes a joke about her drinking a Cosmo in the bathroom. She giggles. I go off to take a whizz.

Clichés be damned, by the time I open the door of my stall, the twenty-five-year-old who I thought wanted to fuck her best friend's father has disappeared, as has her buddy from the sink. It's just as well. There's an even chance she would have dumped him for me had I delayed my whizz and hung around to chat. *Yeah, I'll just keep tell-ing myself that.*

For a split second, I debate whether the polite thing to do in this sort of restroom is wait by the sink for the person who accompanied you. The co-ed moans coming from the middle stall bring my meditation on lavatory etiquette to a swift end. I feel like a drunk stranger in a very strange land. I can't wait to get away from this place. I fly out the door toward the main room, hoping Kaylie will have had enough, and we can head back to her apartment.

I arrive at our table to see the group has thinned out. Kaylie's stepped away, as have a couple of the guys whose names I've completely forgotten. I don't see them at the bar. They weren't in the john, so I assume they moved off to the patio. I'm about to go find them when Maura, another of Kaylie's "besties," engages me in a buzzed line of questioning as to whether social media is, in fact, a form of socialism. I remind her that companies like Facebook are behemoth capitalist enterprises whose concern is lining their own pockets, and that they are willing to compromise the privacy of the masses to attain this goal. Maura says she heard that, so she only uses Instagram. I don't have the heart to tell her they are the same company. I announce that I'm going out to the patio to find Kaylie and, in the spirit of my newfound politeness instinct, invite her to join me.

"Kaylie isn't out there," Maura says, taking a generous sip of her martini.

"I didn't see her anywhere else."

"She left. Said she'd meet up with you back home. She didn't know if you brought your house keys, so—"

Maura takes a set of keys out of her purse and hands them to me. I'm mystified. Granted, I've had too much to drink, and I'm in a bizarre, hedonistic environment, but it strikes me as a little odd that my daughter would abandon me on our first night together.

"Where did she go?" I ask.

"Wherever Brad and Chazz took her."

I plead martini-driven forgetfulness, and Maura reminds me that they are the Netflix guy and restaurant guy. "The three of them are super tight," she says. "Want to see pictures of my trip to Belize?"

Of course I don't, but my "no" doesn't materialize fast enough. She's already got the phone out and is scrolling

Bruce Ferber

through beach shot after beach shot, primarily of her in a bikini. It occurs to me that under normal circumstances, I would be a more than enthusiastic audience, but even for a guy who's toured with the whole spectrum of degenerate rock 'n' rollers, nothing about this night seems normal. I can't help wondering: Who are these people? What do they want? What are they getting for their money? Where are they going, other than on Instagrammable vacations?

I wonder if this is nothing more than the thought process of an old fart. Then I realize I'm okay with that. At least I'm *thinking*.

The return of Middle Stall Camilla is my cue to make a fast exit once and for all. I order an Uber, which is already waiting for me as I stumble out the door. The driver asks how my night's going. I tell him it's going great, but that I'm done conversing with anybody till the sun comes up, assuring him that it won't affect his tip. He seems relieved to be spared the small talk.

At three in the morning in a strange city, my brain supplying the heavy fog, the last thing I want is to be alone in an apartment full of somebody else's shit. I'm feeling even worse than I did at that stupid Culver City gastropub. Not only was this trip a mistake, the grand fantasy of bonding with my flesh and blood turned out to be just that. As friendly as she was in her texts and on the phone, I had no right to expect anything more, because I'm a stranger to her.

I have the urge to call Christina, who's probably getting up around now to go to work—she's usually at

Pineview on Saturdays. Even in my haze, I'm together enough to realize that this is a fantasy as well. What is Christina supposed to say that would make me feel any better? If I'm being honest, it doesn't matter what she says. All I want is to hear the voice of someone who's looking out for me. Whether it's true or not, I've decided that Christina is that person. Maybe I'll call her later, after she's in the office. For now, I have a sofa to pull out and a bed to make.

I manage to erase tonight's clubbing from my head and lull myself to sleep. Then, around 6:30 or so, I hear Kaylie come in. She's trying to be quiet, but her movements are too awkward and unsure to pull it off.

I sit up. "You're back. I wasn't expecting you so soon."

"I'm sorry."

"It's okay. I'm a light sleeper."

"I mean for tonight."

I see she's been crying. She looks terrible, her makeup smeared and smudged. "Sit down," I say, clearing a place for her at the end of the bed. "What happened?"

She gathers herself and goes on to explain. "Chazz wanted to hit a drag show. Then Brad wanted us to see his new loft downtown. We smoked, drank some more, and then …"

"What?"

"I guess I passed out."

"Why didn't you just stay the night?"

"The guys wanted to go out to breakfast. So, they woke me up and stuffed me into an Uber.'

"They didn't want to be responsible for you?"

She starts crying again. I'm not sure whether she wants to be hugged or left alone. I decide to go for it, figuring she can always push me away.

Kaylie melts into my arms, reeking of alcohol and weed. "How douchey was it of me to just leave you there?"

"Pretty fucking douchey," I say, hugging her tighter so she knows I'm not mad at her.

"I really screwed up," she says. "I mean, what do I do to come back from something this dumb?"

"First thing you need to do is get some sleep. We'll talk in the morning."

"It is the morning."

"The afternoon, then."

"You'll still be here?"

"If you stick around, you'll find out."

She smiles. "Thanks." Kaylie gives me a kiss on the cheek and goes off to the bedroom.

I send Christina a text saying that all is well, and that I'm just checking in. I go back to sleep for a couple of hours.

When Kaylie finally wakes up around 2:00 p.m., she's surprised to see that I have breakfast laid out on the table. Then, after expressing her profound gratitude, she says she needs to go into the office for a couple of hours, so it's got to be quick. I'm amazed this girl is even attempting to function after the night she had, but, to look at her, you'd think she went to bed at ten o'clock after a cup of hot tea. There's no mention of Brad and Chazz, her tears, or my having comforted her. It's as if we are in the same place we were yesterday.

"What time's your meeting?" Kaylie asks.

"Huh?"

"You said you were coming out here for producer meetings."

"Oh yeah. Those are later. While you're at work." Last night, as my head finally hit the pillow, I decided I would come clean with her about not having any meetings. But there's a distance now that stops me.

"I thought we'd do Italian tonight, if that's cool with you. Old school's my thing. Dan Tana's. I think Camilla's gonna be there with some guy she met last night."

The Middle Stall Guy. Fantastic. "Whatever you want to do is fine with me."

Kaylie makes herself a cappuccino, throws together a small plate of fruit, and excuses herself so she can get in the shower and start her day.

The rest of the weekend goes much as it began, minus any more all-night side trips. A lot of expensive eating and drinking with young, successful people who talk about nothing but new restaurants, resort vacations and which TV shows they should be bingeing. I know my daughter is deeper than that. The Jägerbombers at Carmine's are deeper than that.

How do I really know Kaylie is deeper? I don't. I want to believe she is because the whole reason I came out here was to get close to the only family I have left. Yet as much as I hate to admit it, Kaylie doesn't seem like my family. Perhaps it was unrealistic to expect a bond to develop over a three-day visit, but I think my miscalculation was more

extreme than that. I'd written a script for the wrong character. In my version of our family reunion, Kaylie was an
avid reader and music aficionado who couldn't wait to give
me the highlights of all the years I missed seeing her grow
up. She demanded to know everything about me, and we
had so much to say to one another that we both agreed I
hadn't booked a long enough visit. At the end of my stay,
I sang "Angel" to her. She cried and said I should move to
California so we could live nearby and make up for lost
time.

I wind up buying her a set of expensive moisturizing
products as a thank-you gift for letting me crash at the
apartment. I return the original gifts to my suitcase, and
fantasize about giving them to Christina someday. I look
over at the guitar, its pristine strings doomed to a rusty
future. Perhaps the idiot boyfriend will remember to pick
it up before that happens, but I wouldn't bet on it.

SHOWTIME

The return trip to New York is a more muted affair than the meeting-my-daughter premiere party I threw for myself on the flight out. This time I pass on the six-dollar airport water and mount an aggressive stance regarding middle-seat boundaries. If either of these fat window and aisle fucks so much as graze my arm while they're fiddling with their Excel spreadsheets, I will raise hell with the airline until they move me to business class.

One more fantasy, perhaps, but anger is one of my preferred tools for confronting sadness. A highly ineffective tool, mind you, but the only one I can summon as I think of all the hoops I had to jump through for Kaylie's mom, only to be back at square one. I suppose there's an argument to be made that the weekend wasn't a total bust. Kaylie seemed to like me. Maybe when she has a few more years under her belt, and a little more maturity, she'll be ready to skip a night of barhopping to talk to her old man about Coltrane. Of course, by then, I could be living at Pineview, listening to some fifty-year-old I call "kid" play "The Alphabet Song" on an out-of-tune guitar.

Thankfully, there was only one Gene Klein update over the weekend, a text from Prem informing me that the faux Two Virgins decided to stage a bed-in at Gene's house in the hope of attracting media attention. I picture Jasmine singing "Give Peace a Chance," then getting out from under the covers to give Marcia a sponge bath. According to Prem, the couple's stunt was met with across-the-board rejection by every news outlet from the *Williston Park Press* to the Roslyn Middle School newsletter.

Even though Gene has been a La La Land resident for quite some time, I have to wonder when he's going to see the folly of these latest shenanigans. As I consider the escalating wackiness, it is not lost on me that Jasmine's infiltration into Gene's life coincides with the potential recording of my debut album. Since the real Paul's first solo outing, "McCartney," was not greeted with the utmost affection by the real John, I am strategically positioned to be named the villain in the Help! saga. As to who might see the significance of this other than Jasmine and Gene, perhaps a grade school reporter will get scooped on a spelling bee story and need to fill the space.

I arrive back at my basement kingdom to find much of it bedecked with turds and kitty litter. I can't blame Jaco, because even though I told the Girardis I'd be away, I'm sure they never came down to check on him. Abandoned or not, the furry one greets me with enthusiastic leg-rubs, as if he knows I flamed out with an ungrateful relative and wants to remind me of his loyalty. I'm confident that it's only a matter of time before he, too, tires of how little this gets him.

Nevertheless, it's time to move on. I delay unpacking and turd-cleaning to text Christina and tell her I'm home. I email

Donny to let him know how much I'm looking forward to the showcase. Barely thirty seconds after I hit "send," he calls me. I ask how he's doing, but he skips the pleasantries, saying he wants to know whether we can do the show this weekend in Manhattan. He's got a club uptown that's ready to book us if I can put it together. Donny says he knows it's short notice but thought it might be worth a shot. I tell him I'll call the rest of the band and get back to him ASAP.

I'm fired up that a working producer thinks enough of me to bring us to the city. It occurs to me, however, that not doing the show on the Island means I won't be able to pack the house with friends, which could make for a less enthusiastic reception. A more honest reception may be what Donny is after. What's inarguable is that his club offers the advantage of real New York energy, which is lightning in a bottle if they happen to like you. None of it will matter if my ad hoc band turns out to be unavailable.

It seems Prem has a family obligation and Tracy's got a date with the doctor, but both are willing to beg out of their commitments to support me. As for Raji, this will be his first professional (albeit non-paid) gig, so he's over the moon about making his debut in Manhattan. Prem asks if I want to try to squeeze in another rehearsal beforehand, but the lack of time and conflicting schedules don't allow for it. Come Saturday night, the Jimmy Kozlowski Band will be winging it with whatever we've retained from our one and only session. There's something I like about the immediacy of it. I also know that the band will make up for any gaps with passion and chops. If we fall flat, it will be because my songs fail to connect with the audience.

I shudder to imagine my life after that kind of disappointment. More Gene and Jasmine? Continuing to chase the same married woman because I can't find someone suitable who's unattached? The possibility of sputtering on all cylinders is not only frightening, but all too real in my current frame of mind. If I'm to have any chance of success, I must find a way to extinguish these terrifying prospects, at least until after Saturday.

The Help! gigs for the week include Jasmine coming onstage to sing "Power to the People" with Gene, and Marcia being wheeled in for a curious, morbid finale of "Tomorrow Never Knows." It's as if Paul, George, and Ringo were drafted against their will for a creepy Beatles video game and have now scored enough points to get to the next level. The only plus of Jasmine running Gene's life is that it leaves him less time to check on the rest of our hourly comings and goings, which means my solo career is the furthest thing from his mind.

I'm starting to get pumped about Saturday night, and text Christina the details. I was originally planning to give them to her tomorrow at Pineview, but I can't wait that long. As it happens, she winds up in meetings the next day and I never get to see her, so the early tip-off turned out to have been the right move. I'm kind of surprised that she hasn't texted back yet, but she's got a lot on her plate. For all I know, she plans to surprise me at the gig, although since she never goes into the city, it's highly unlikely. I did write that under no circumstances should she mention the gig to Jasmine, because the last thing I want is for Gene to crash what could be the only solo opportunity I'll ever get.

The plan is for Prem and Raji to drive together with the gear while I pick up Tracy and go over the vocals and harmonies on our way into the city. When I arrive at her apartment, she's as enthusiastic as a third grader about to sing at her first talent show. She also looks like every teenage male's rock 'n' roll wet dream. I make an offhand remark about how her new doctor friend must be making her happy. She says her look doesn't have anything to do with him. What she's wearing, and how she feels, reflect her excitement about the project, and desire to support someone who's always been there for her professionally. I thank her for recognizing that.

I haven't been this far uptown in ages. Our Washington Heights venue, La Escollera, seems to be doing good business, with lots of customers streaming through the front door. Obviously these people have never heard of Jimmy Kozlowski, so perhaps there's some kind of happy hour special going on during setup and sound check. It wouldn't be the first time Tracy and I played for the cheap draft and slider crowd, so we know the ground rules—find a subtle way to engage without asking too much in return.

We get out of the car and enter the narrow, darkish space to find Prem and Raji already setting up their gear on the small stage. The other thing we notice is that everybody around us is speaking Spanish. Indeed, our audience seems to be ninety-five percent Hispanic. I never imagined Donny booking our first gig in a place where language might be a barrier. Tracy asks me to introduce her to the producer, but I don't see him anywhere.

We head over to Prem and Raji, who have all the equipment plugged in and ready to test.

"Hey, you guys got here early," I say.

"Good thing," Prem replies. "The club owner told us there are going to be so many people here, the fire department is watching the place."

"What's the deal?" Tracy asks. "Dollar beers? Free taquitos?"

"The deal," Raji tells her, "is Chuchita."

"Is that some kind of chicken?" Tracy asks.

The word sounds familiar to me, but I can't identify what it is.

"Chuchita is a singer," Prem tells us. "We're opening for her."

It all comes together. Chuchita is Donny's Guatemalan Shakira who, according to YouTube, already has a huge following in Latino communities outside the US. The question is, in what universe did Donny think the Jimmy Kozlowski Band would be a good fit for a Shakira-style audience? An old, white, first-time singer-songwriter warming up a Hispanic crowd who came to see sexy dance moves?

"I'm sorry," Prem says. "We'll give it our best."

Tracy puts her arm around me to soften the blow of the imminent fiasco that is to be my first, and probably last, solo gig.

After we finish our sound check, the busboy/emcee steps up to the microphone and introduces us as La Banda de Jaime Hoselowski.

Right from Prem's opening power chord on the upbeat "Bleed For You," I know we're good, especially considering we only had one rehearsal, and this is not our crowd. I can't wait to get to the chorus and hear Tracy's harmony, which I'm certain will get these people a little closer to where we want them. When we arrive there, she executes her vocal with a precision that, to my mind, deserves the kind of applause normally reserved for superlative instrumental breaks.

There are no applause. Or more than three people listening, for that matter. It's mostly talking and drinking, until the middle of the second chorus, when somebody decides to stream the Yankee game on his phone. So far, the most notable part of my solo debut is that the Cleveland Indians have apparently pulled ahead by a run. Just when I think it can't get any worse, we begin our second tune, "Lake Jane," at the exact moment a woman sitting at a corner table pulls a chihuahua out of her purse. She passes it around to be petted when it slips out of a customer's grasp and starts toward the stage. Tracy, the only one of us who's not playing an instrument, bends down to pick it up, and gets her finger nipped before the mangy little rat scurries back to its giggling owner. When the song is over, I turn to the band, ready to tell them we're done, and that nobody should have to endure this kind of treatment.

Then I hear Tracy's voice boom over the sound system. "Atenciones, hermanos y hermanas! Un poco de respeto por favor. Tocamos música hermosa. Escuchen ahora!" She gives her hair a confident flip, and her booty a fetching little shake. The room turns dead quiet. Tracy smiles and gestures toward me. "Señor Kozlowski, vamónos!"

We now play to a crowd of people who are on their best behavior, having been reprimanded by someone well-versed in the mechanics of playing "diva." Whatever they may think of the songs, Tracy makes sure to provide just enough eye candy to keep their attention from wandering. Part of me also thinks the situation has ignited her competitive spirit, and she wants the house to know she learned how to shake it before Chuchita was old enough to grow an ass. Tracy's expertise is incontestible, based on the looks she's getting from every guy in the room. There's also a tiny woman in a sequined mini dress standing in the back and nodding her head to the beat. It takes me a second to figure it out, but it seems Chuchita herself has become a fan.

While the mood in the room is on the upswing, the moment has lost none of its surrealism. My solo debut has been salvaged by my ex-girlfriend's surprisingly fluent Spanish and take-no-prisoners charm. Between our third and fourth songs, I ask where the Spanish came from.

"Dating that smug-ass Ché who toured with me in *Evita*," she says. "I guess he was good for something."

I offer a sincere thank-you and ask if she thinks we should cut one of my originals. My thought is, we can replace it with a cover of "Lady Marmalade," or something where she'll be able to keep the crowd interested. Tracy won't hear of it. "You got 'em now, Jimmy. Give 'em a chance to show you some love."

She's definitely "got 'em." I haven't an inkling as to where I stand. With no small amount of trepidation, I give the nod for us to go into "Angel," a ballad I now must judge at face value, with the romanticized version having been shot full of more holes than it took to fill the Albert Hall. I still think it's a good song, but I no longer picture my daughter as I sing it, and there is no shaking booty for the audience to look at. Nevertheless, the crowd is quiet. Either they don't want to risk Tracy's wrath or are legitimately into it. I'll find out when the song is over.

It's not Beyoncé applause, but it seems like they dug it, and Chuchita is smiling at me. I take this as my cue to talk to the audience and see where it goes. "I'd just like to thank the fabulous Chuchita"—I've seen her YouTube videos—I can honestly claim this—"for letting us open the show." At this point, Chuchita starts blowing me kisses and shouting "Te amo," which garners a standing ovation. Tracy set the table, and now Chuchita has given me the Guatemalan seal of approval.

The rest of the set goes smoothly, the entire crowd dancing along with Chuchita, who has made her way to the stage for a little mock girl-on-girl with Tracy. The crowd goes wild and demands another song before Chuchita takes the stage for her own set. I keep her there with us and call out "Lady Marmalade" for the encore. The Tracy-Chuchita combo sizzles, and the place goes insane. When we finish, Chuchita kisses me on the lips and tells me to get her number from Donny Delgado.

And where in God's name is Donny Delgado? I wonder.

Chuchita doesn't have any idea.

The band and I pack up our stuff. I am filled with gratitude for having survived what looked to be a career-ending disaster. Then, just as Raji starts toward the door with his keyboard, Donny walks in.

"Amazing show, Jimmy. Loved it!"

"What are you talking about? You weren't here."

"I saw every minute. It takes a skilled kind of performer to turn it around the way you did. Of course, your girl didn't hurt, but I was impressed with all of it. And how 'bout my Chuch', right?"

I tell him I'm confused. How could he have seen the show if he wasn't there? Donny explains that his new approach is to watch a gig without being in the room, which often makes the artist nervous. He points to various cameras in and around the stage and tells me he watched the whole thing on his phone in the car. It sounds insane to me, but the fact that he loved us makes the insanity more palatable. Still, I have to ask …

"Why would you book us for a Spanish-speaking audience?"

"Boot camp. You crushed it. Let me buy you guys dinner."

"Don't you want to stay for Chuchita?"

Donny holds up his phone. "She's coming with me."

Prem and Raji don't want to risk leaving their equipment in the car, much less at a speakeasy with a busboy for security. They plan to head home, volunteering to take my gear so I can enjoy the post-mortem with my over-the-moon producer. I thank them for their kindness, their time, and the incredible performance they turned in. They tell me how happy they are to see my music being recognized. The guys each give me a hug, and they're on their way. I make a mental note not to forget the moment, because, in the music business, this is about as pure as it gets.

Tracy and I follow Donny over to an Indian joint where we order the same alu gobhi, saag and masala that Prem's wife made for us the night of our rehearsal. Taj Palace's food can't measure up to Jaya's homemade cooking, but such failings are mitigated by the flowing Indian beer and the generous praise from Donny. He wants to produce my album. What's more, he insists that Tracy sing on it, and both of the guys record with us in the studio. Live gigs are also in the offing. He just needs to look at the calendar and find the right venues.

Listening to Donny reel off his plans for me is almost as surreal as the gig itself. After thirty-plus years as a sideman and band member, a volunteer gig at a nursing home has opened the door to my biggest opportunity ever. All I really expected out of the showcase was the thrill of getting to play my own songs with my favorite musicians. If Donny thought the material was good enough to record a few songs, fantastic, but I never dreamed of much beyond that. Yet it appears he sees us as a real band, fronted by my creative vision. I do wonder how I'm going to broach the topic of my supporting players having other commitments. There's a good chance Donny likes the material and the vibe enough that he'll be willing to fill in the missing pieces, but, either way, this isn't the time to throw cold water on our surprise love fest. I know Tracy will act as if she's totally available because she wants to lend her full support, and there's a decent chance she'll be totally available.

Our waiter comes by with the two additional bottles of beer Donny ordered for the table, as well as the check. Donny signs and tells us how much he's looking forward to working with us. Then he stands up, shakes my hand, and goes to give Tracy a hug. The producer is off to La Escollera to watch the end of Chuchita's set. He's floored by the audience reaction he's seen so far on his phone. "It's like they're worshiping Jesus, if Jesus twerked."

Donny scurries out the door. Tracy and I share a laugh, and pour ourselves another glass of beer. She raises hers for a toast. "To you, Jimmy. You've had some good karma coming to you for a long time."

"To you too," I say. "People always did think we were good together." We clink glasses. I assume she's going to start in on me for beating a dead horse; romanticizing something that never really worked to begin with. But she doesn't do that.

"We're still great together," Tracy says. "In the studio, on the stage. We're not bad in bed either. Don't ask me what else I'm looking for because every time I think I know, I get the rug pulled out from under me."

"Doctor whatever his name is?"

"Narcissist. Gone."

"I'm sorry."

"Don't be. Besides, tonight isn't about that. We're celebrating you."

"We wouldn't be celebrating if you didn't know Spanish."

"The booty didn't hurt either."

"It certainly did not. Chuchita's got nothing on you. Your voice was amazing tonight."

"Thank you." Tracy smiles and takes another swig of beer. "You know, Jimmy, the last time you sounded this good I fucked your brains out."

"Is that what you plan to do tonight?"

"No. But plans change."

SLOUCHING TOWARDS LIVERPOOL

When we get back to my car, I'm so buzzed and groggy, I need to find a way to keep from dozing on the drive back to the Island. My solution is to glance over at Tracy's body every few exits as motivation to stay awake. Unfortunately, by the time we hit the LIE, the booty-shaking Queen of Washington Heights is fast asleep and rocking some major mouth breathing. With enough alcohol, it's not a far trip from seductress to drooler.

The night is destined to end quietly, the fury of clawing at each other's flesh replaced by the two of us sharing a cup of herbal tea. I wind up talking about Christina, and how stupid I am for letting myself obsess on a married woman. Tracy says I shouldn't beat myself up, and that as a veteran of every bad relationship choice ever made, she's an authority. I thank her again for being the inspiring performer she is. She tells me I'm one of the main reasons she was able to get as far as she did.

Love. Respect. Music. Everything else is a distraction.

Any concern that my Washington Heights triumph would render me full of myself is nipped in the bud by the porta-potty gig I have the next day. People steal the toilet paper, tampons jam the bowls, and there's a major sewage

294

leak coming from one of the honey wagons. I'm literally up to my arms in shit when my phone starts ringing off the hook. I don't answer till later, after I get things under control. The urgent news is that Jasmine has drawn up the rehearsal schedule for Liverpool, which is now only a month away. She's talking about two sessions per week in addition to our regular slots at JP's and Carmine's. None of it makes sense because not only are we playing the same songs at our shows, we're performing them in front of live audiences, just like we'll be doing at the Liverpool competition.

When I call Gene to talk about the redundancy, he explains that the extra sessions are designed to focus on things like choosing the right stage patter, inter-band body language, costume checklists, and so on. Everything I've seen on the contest website suggests this is overkill. Yes, there is a significant prize involved, but the spirit of the event is to honor the music and have a great time. Many of the bands know each other, and the attendees are the fab equivalent of Trekkies.

The leader of Help!, on the other hand, is out for blood, a mission that only grows in intensity with each minute he spends around Jasmine. It becomes clear that this John and Yoko will accept nothing less than total victory and will do whatever it takes to achieve it.

The first rehearsal introduces a whole new brand of stupid, with Jasmine handing out script pages for the scene in the movie, *Help!* where the mop tops move into a flat together and John plops down on the couch in the sunken living room. I refer her to the contest guidelines which offer no opportunities for the bands to do any acting. She explains that reading the scene with each other before going out to perform will be a constructive bonding exercise. Mikey can't take it anymore. He tells her it's the shittiest idea he's ever heard. Gene, not wanting to raise the ire of his partner in delusion, suggests a compromise. "What if we each read it to ourselves the night before?"

"It's madness," Mikey replies, looking to Prem and me for confirmation.

"It doesn't seem like it's really necessary," I tell Gene, in my most sympathetic voice.

"Don't listen to them!" Jasmine shouts at Gene. "One of them is a stupid drummer, and the other thinks *he's* the genius behind this band!"

I have no choice but to jump in. "Jasmine, the actual Beatles were the geniuses behind this music. Not me. Or Gene."

"Tell me you've ever seen a better John Lennon than Gene," she barks. "I've watched every YouTube video of the real one, and I can't tell the difference."

I want to say this speaks to her faulty perception rather than Gene's excellence, and that he looks more like Billy Crystal than John Lennon, but I bite my tongue. For one thing, I'd have to explain who Billy Crystal is. Prem says there's no point in arguing. If we want to do our best in Liverpool, we've got to play our best. It's as simple as that.

Thankfully, Gene is itching to get to the music, and starts noodling with the opening riff of "Come Together."

Mikey and I add the bottom and it sounds super solid. That is, until Jasmine starts singing along with the verse.

Mikey throws his drumsticks across the room. "Seriously?" he asks Jasmine. "This is how we're going to win the contest?"

"It's only rehearsal," Gene points out. "She's not planning to sing it with us onstage. Right, luv?"

Jasmine responds with the least convincing nod I've ever seen. The rest of the rehearsal proceeds without further disruption. We sound fine. Any finer than we do on any other night? I sure as hell can't tell the difference. Gene's idea is to do two different five-song sets at each practice. Then, at the end of our rehearsals, he'll pick four from the eight that will take us from the first round all the way through to the finals, when we get there. (It's never *should* we get there.)

I haven't heard from Christina since I texted her about the Washington Heights gig, secretly hoping she'd make an appearance. Since she's decided to lie low for whatever reason, I never followed up to tell her how well it went. Based on a lifetime of ill-fated outcomes with women, my guess is her silence speaks volumes. She was probably flattered by the attention, but then became overwhelmed by it. Since I have no one to go home to except a cat, it's easy for me to savor an idyllic hour at the beach, and relive the moment in my head whenever I feel like it. From a married woman's perspective, if her relationship with Hubby is good, by the next day I'm a nice, but needy, hanger-on who wants something she can't give. If her relationship is bad,

I'm one more source of confusion that only adds to her angst. As I weigh each depressing side of the argument, I start to wonder if there really was anything between us. Whatever my conclusion turns out to be, there's no chance I will reach it before my next nursing home gig. Either way, I have a job to do, and I will try my best to brighten some Pineview lives for an hour.

In what has now become a disturbing routine, my arrival finds Christina wrapped up in meetings, behind closed doors. The thing that really tells me it's over is that I'm no longer getting teased by the receptionist. I don't even rate thirty seconds of sarcasm from my de facto tormenter. My gut tells me it's time to regroup and adopt a new outlook. Luckily, my history of disappointments has made pressing the reset button feel more like maintenance than trauma. I have no doubt that; in quiet moments, I'll daydream reruns of our beach day, but, for now, I must resume the position of a man who defines himself by music rather than relationships.

Strange as it seems, I give my most rousing performance to date of "Hello, I Love You," motivating six of the residents to say their names out loud, a personal best for me. Then, almost unconsciously, I go into "And I Love Her," making a mental note of how good it sounds in case Gene wants a McCartney ballad for Liverpool. I'm not thinking about Christina at all as I sing it, an apt beginning for my reset. The only thing that matters at this point is getting a few smiles and nods out of the group, which I accomplish.

Then, just as I finish the last guitar flourish, we get a late-comer being wheeled in by her grandson, Donny Delgado.

"I was hoping you'd be here," Donny says, flashing me a big smile. "I have some news."

Has he set up recording time? Found us a real label?

Having my producer show up unannounced with a smile on his face will provide additional fuel for the reset. I have something to look forward to besides being forced to play the cute Beatle into my seventies. Filling out the rest of my set with a mix of James Taylor, Hoagy Carmichael, Irving Berlin, and a couple of originals, my thoughts drift to the possible cover art for the Jimmy Kozlowski album that few will buy, but all will see on their streaming services. *Should it be a headshot? Me with all my basses and guitars? Maybe Jaco peeking his head out from behind an amplifier?*

I close with "Sunny Side of the Street." Donny motions that he'll come back to talk to me once he gets his grandmother settled in her room. As I pack up my guitar, I hear a woman's voice in the hallway that I'm sure is Christina's, but I don't turn to look. She knows my schedule, as well as the location, so if she wants to peek in and say hello, I'll be as polite and friendly as ever.

She doesn't, at least by the time Donny returns. He leads me over to a table that's sometimes used to feed residents who need extra help.

"Hell of a show the other night," is Donny's intro.

"It did turn out pretty well in the end. So … what do we got?"

"Some dates," Donny replies.

"Fantastic." *It's on.* "Which studio?"

"Not recording. Live shows."

"Wow, that was fast. How did you get it together so soon?"

"The tour was already in place," he says. "Chuchita wants you to open for her."

"Seriously? It was a fun night, but are we really compatible?"

"She loved you. That's all that matters. Hasn't stopped calling me because she wants to get this done. You in?"

"Of course—I mean, I'll have to check with the rest of the band."

"No worries. We'll get fill-ins for whoever can't make it. She's pretty adamant about signing Tracy though."

"I have to see. She's got a daughter, and some other obligations. When would we start?"

"Second weekend of August."

Suddenly, I feel all the blood start to drain out of my face. "Are you absolutely sure about the date?"

"The tour's been booked for a year. Is there a problem?"

"No, I mean … It's just that I have a commitment on that particular weekend."

"I'm sure you can move things around."

"It's not so easy," I tell Donny. "But any time after that, I'm yours, a hundred and ten percent."

"It's not about me, Jimmy. The boss doesn't like to hear 'no' for an answer."

"Musicians get booked. Chuchita knows that."

"She likes to get her way. What can I tell you? Needs to be in control."

"Should I call her? She told me she wanted you to give me her number."

"She always says that. Then she rips me a new asshole for giving out her contact info."

I suggest finding a replacement, just for the first weekend, but Donny is certain it won't fly. "Take a couple days to think about it," he says. He pats me on the back and makes his way down the hall.

It's beyond ridiculous that the woman won't work around one previously booked weekend, but, if I turn her down, I risk alienating the producer who may represent my future. *Haven't I paid enough dues to the dysfunctional Bank of Gene Klein?* There's nothing wrong with loyalty, but few could dispute my devoted years of service. Why blow off a decent payday and jeopardize a professional relationship when there are half a dozen competent Pauls who could replace me?

I decide to tell Donny I'm in, right after I explain the situation to Gene. I owe him that much.

ROLL UP

I place a business-like call to my Beatle boss, asking if I can stop by on my way home. Gene's response borders on rhapsodic. Though I haven't paid a casual visit to the man's house since I've known him, his narcissism shields him from the burden of subtext. *Who wouldn't grab any opportunity to see me and talk about what I'm up to?* Not wanting to show up empty-handed, I come armed with my list of six alternate Pauls, including the one who already messaged back to say he's interested. As soon as the opportunity presents itself, I will express my deep sorrow for having to miss Liverpool. Gene's reaction will hover somewhere between combative and enraged, but he should know better than anybody that business is business. If he chooses to take it personally, it will be his self-involved cross to bear.

Jasmine answers the door with the cold indifference of Lennon's *Let It Be* appendage facing the McCartney threat. "Come in. I was just on my way out."

I don't see or hear Gene. "Is he in Marcia's room?" I ask.

She points behind her. "Out back." Jasmine heads for the garage, disappearing faster than a Yoko solo album.

I move through the living room and into the den, where sliding doors lead to the backyard. Through the glass, I spot Marcia sitting in a wheelchair and Gene across from her, rocking back and forth. It looks like he's reading something. As I move closer, I hear him speaking in what sounds like Hebrew, and see his balding, wigless head sporting a yarmulke. He is praying.

Of all the unpredictable angles played by this fab eccentric, prayer is the most surprising. My assumption has always been that Gene believed *he* was the higher power. The picture I see before me, a plaintive worshiper reciting one blessing, and chanting another, belies that. I stand, frozen, not daring to intrude on this consecrated curveball.

Seconds later, Gene spots me through the glass. "Jimbo! Get out here, dude!"

I slide open the door to see Marcia sitting with her eyes closed, and Gene standing up to greet me.

"Just throwing down a little *shehecheyanu*." He turns to Marcia. "Mom, it's Jimmy."

She doesn't stir.

"Paul. Your favorite!"

Still nothing. Gene pulls up a chair for me, explaining that his mother is comforted by hearing the prayers she and his dad would recite in synagogue. He tells me that the *shehecheyanu*, offered in commemoration of special occasions, thanks the Almighty for the gift of life. I ask if today is a Jewish holiday. Gene says no. The special occasion is that Marcia is still breathing. He tells me that while it's been slow going, he believes she's getting better. He claims she even speaks every now and then and floats the possibility of her saying hello to me when she wakes up. As much as I want her to, I hope it doesn't happen before I get the chance to say my piece. I'm about to start in, but first I must ask a question. I want to know if the spirituality I've just witnessed was purely for Marcia's benefit, or if it's a part of Gene I never knew about.

"You mean, do I believe in God?" he asks.

"Yeah. Or whatever you choose to call it."

"I don't think God's a person, or some shape in a grilled cheese sandwich, but yeah. There's gotta be something bigger than us, right?"

"I don't know," I answer, ever useless in articulating my agnosticism.

Gene further explains his position. "I never thought about what those prayers meant when I was a kid, but I did feel something as I was saying them. Now, with what's at stake, I feel it that much deeper."

"It's understandable," I say, looking over at Marcia.

"We're on the verge of going to the UK, Jimmy. This is huge."

From there he launches into a checklist of Liverpool, New York particulars. Even had it occurred to him that I might have my own reasons for coming here, his obsession would have steamrolled over it. I weather a couple of gratuitous digs at his fake-John competition, until the briefest of pauses affords me an opening. "Gene, I've been offered a big opportunity," I say. "To make some real money."

He responds with a disapproving shake of the head. "Don't quit music, Jimmy. You're way too talented." The notion that I might be offered real money to play music doesn't even cross his mind, which is either his assessment of my limitations, or a reasonable assumption based on the last decade of working for peanuts.

"I met this producer who may want to record me. First, he wants me to go on tour with a singer he works with. It's four months."

"Four months? That's a lot of gigs you'll be missing. But hey, good on you. I'll make sure we have your fill-in lined up for when we get back from the UK."

What Gene perceives to be a courteous heads-up will be seen as anything but, once he realizes when my tour starts. I decide to work my way into it, beginning with a mention of the available Paul from the Lindenhurst band, Octopus's Garden. "You know, I was just talking to Brian McCalmont—"

"Great, great bass player," Gene interjects.

Yes!

"Too bad he's a supreme dick. Octopus's Garden just fired his ass. They were losing gigs because he refused to wear the outfits."

Five more Pauls to go. As I take the list out of my pocket, Marcia starts making sounds. Her eyes remain closed, and there are no identifiable words, but she begins gesticulating with both hands as the garbled utterances increase in volume. It seems like she's indicating something in the next yard over.

"It's okay, Mom," Gene says. "I'll tell them to quiet down."

"Tell who to quiet down?" I ask.

"She's hearing music again. It's making her agitated."

305

"I thought the music calmed her down."

"Depends what's being played. From what I can make out, sometimes it's loud, like heavy metal. She thinks it's hurting her ears."

Marcia cries out in anguish. Gene tries to calm her, initially with words, and then by going over to rub her shoulders. Despite his efforts, it seems like the anxiety is building. She holds her hands over both ears, but the imagined music must be piercing through. Her unintelligible mutterings become shouts. Gene tries to gently cover her mouth, so the neighbors don't start calling the police. She bites him. He lets out a yelp and tells me to go in the house and get Jasmine.

"Jasmine went out," I inform him.

"What do you mean she went out? She's supposed to be working."

"I guess she needed a break."

"It's okay," the devoted son repeats to his mother, determined to comfort her even though he is in pain. "Where the hell is Jasmine?" he yells, to no one in particular. Then he points to the cell phone on the table and orders me to call her. I notice some blood dripping from his left hand and ask if he has a first aid kit. This gets no reaction. He needs me to call Jasmine.

I do as he says but she doesn't pick up. As the blood continues to flow, Gene relents, telling me he thinks there are some Band-Aids in one of the kitchen drawers.

Each cabinet is messier than the next, but somewhere beneath a stack of ancient Yellow Pages lie a package of gauze, and a roll of adhesive tape. I gather them up, fill a bowl with warm water, grab a roll of paper towels, and make my way back to the yard. As I get closer, it seems the shouts have been reduced to whimpers. When I slide open the patio doors to step outside, I see that Marcia has fallen back asleep, and that the whimpers are coming from Gene.

"I'm sorry," he tells me. "I never do this."

"You earned it," I reply. I don't think many people have seen Gene in such a vulnerable state. Probably not even my brother. "Here, give me your hand."

Gene winces as I take it. "Good thing she didn't get my fingers." He feigns fingerpicking a guitar with his right hand.

I gently dab at the wound that, while raw, isn't very deep and shouldn't take much time to heal. As I wrap the bandage around the broken skin, a few more tears escape.

"It's gonna be okay," I assure him.

"Thank you, Jimmy. I don't know what I'd do without you."

"Hey, you'd do the same for me."

"I'm not just talking about right now. You and Eddie, man—they broke the mold." Gene is still under the impression that my tour begins sometime in the distant future. If I intend to speak up, now is the time.

"About this tour," I begin. "See, the way it's scheduled, I'll have to miss the Liverpool contest."

Gene laughs, unable to comprehend that I could even entertain such a thought. When I fail to crack a smile, his demeanor flips. "Shit. You're serious."

I nod. He doesn't move or say anything for a good twenty seconds. Finally, he acknowledges what is happening. "It's okay. Do what you need to do."

I wait for his reevaluation, and the inevitable fireworks, but neither are forthcoming. Gene's words have been delivered without malice or sarcasm; he really is giving me his blessing.

"I've got five other Pauls I've reached out to—" I start to show him the list, but he's not interested, at least for now.

"Don't worry about it," Gene says, trying, without success, to hold back the next batch of tears. There's nothing phony about these either. I put my arm around him. The tears turn to sobs. Never did I imagine that I would one day find myself comforting the phenom who had inspired both my brother and me to become musicians, and that he would let me leave his orbit without a fight.

I'm patting his shoulder when it sounds like my name is being called. I look up and see Marcia gazing in my direction. She, too, is tearing up. My first thought is that she must have made another garbled noise that sounded like "Jimmy," and is crying because there's sad music coming from next door. It turns out Gene isn't the only unpredictable Klein. The woman who gave birth to Long Island's premier fake John Lennon sharpens her gaze, looks straight into my eyes, and speaks, this time with just enough precision to leave no doubt.

"Jimmy ... please ..."

THE FAB FOURTEEN

When I tell Donny I'm unable to join the tour until after the second weekend in August, his tepid reaction does little to indicate our business relationship has a future. Nevertheless, I express regret for having to miss the opportunity, and submit an open invitation for my services down the line. Donny says he appreciates that, but the look on his face suggests he's already banished Jimmy Kozlowski to the distant memory file. While I've been deported to that place before, the sting of this exile is going to take a lot longer to heal.

Meanwhile, the march to Liverpool continues. The band rehearses as Gene commands, agreeing to whatever setlists he happens to put together, as long as none of the selections include vocals by Jasmine. Over the next few weeks, the vibe between the two of them grows so tense, they seem like they've been married for fifty years. She puts him down, and Gene sucks it up, because he still values having a devoted companion who's younger than his mother. But he begins to set some limits. Anything regarding the music is a line that must not be crossed. It isn't for Jasmine to decide which version of "Revolution" we should present to the judges.

The most significant development is that, despite Gene's optimism, his mother's health continues to decline. She refuses to eat much of the time, most of her hours are spent sleeping, and Gene has begun to question whether she still knows who he is. The original plan for Marcia to come to Liverpool becomes more and more unrealistic as her situation deteriorates. One night, at our regular JP Murphy's gig, a solemn Gene reveals the likelihood of Jasmine having to stay back to care for her charge.

Mikey and Prem are as fond of Marcia as I am, and the last thing any of us would want is for her to suffer. We're also aware that seeing her son perform at the contest, win or lose, meant the world to her. Yet what lands with the most impact is the potential for a Jasmine-less weekend. The picture of what that might look like, not having to suffer a fifth wheel, lightens the mood for all of us, including Gene. He invites the band out for fish-and-chips in anticipation of winning the trip to England, and the excursion sparks some genuine camaraderie. It's a jolly time for all: Mikey buying rounds of beers, Prem challenging the rest of us at darts, and Gene refusing to answer Jasmine's incessant phone calls.

"If it's about me mum, she'll text me," he says, breaking into a bit of offstage Liverpudlian.

Gene raises a glass. "Where are we goin' fellas?" he says, doing his best John.

"To the top, Johnny," we reply in unison.

"Where's that, fellas?"

"The toppermost of the poppermost."

As the glasses clink, three native Long Islanders and one Indian, ranging in age from forty to late sixties, get an inkling of what life must have felt like for four much younger dreamers in 1961.

Gene schedules one more meeting at his house to review last minute details for the Beatle Battle. He says he's tempted to ride up with the rest of us but thinks the more sensible choice would be to drive separately, in case something happens with Marcia and he has to hightail it back home. Then he opens a large cardboard box and removes a stack of "information packets" for the weekend. It seems Jasmine has had some computer training, and was able to compile all the relevant facts, as well as a spreadsheet sporting detailed stats on the competition. The pages are not only beautifully printed, but color-coded.

According to the packet, the fourteen entrants include bands from all over America, and some from other countries. They're a representative cross-section of the thousand-plus tribute acts that haven't achieved the marquee status of the Fab Four, the Fab Faux, Rain, or Ticket to Ride. Gene is of the opinion that Help! would be a marquee band if the others hadn't gotten to the party first. There are only so many big-bucks reenactments a saturated market can bear, but the local bar scenes are hopping with people who want to hear this music, especially without a cover charge.

This weekend, our foes will run the gamut from high-end second-tier bands like Revolution 2.0 to more exotic fare like Rubber Seoul (Korean mop tops), the Sheatles (unclear as to whether they are all-female or trans), and a quartet of octogenarians who call themselves Golden

Slumbers. The spreadsheet rates all the Pauls, Georges, Johns, and Ringos from one to five stars based on Gene and Jasmine's extensive YouTube research, note-taking, and cataloguing.

Gene summarizes the results of their findings. "We're in the top five, no doubt, maybe the top three. As far as I can see, the bands to look out for are Revolution 2.0 and the Hello Goodbyes, unless Golden Slumbers slides in on a sympathy vote. We hear their John is on a respirator, so if he can pull it off, the Slumbers will be a fan favorite."

"Here's my question," Mikey says. "Either way, we're going to hit that stage and kick as much ass as we have in us. How does getting this intel on the other bands make a difference?"

"That's a great question," Gene replies. "If you look at the 'Strengths and Weaknesses' section, you'll see that some of the bands are at their best when they play early Beatles, and others are late-period specialists. I like to think we do both well, with a slight edge toward the later stuff. So, let's say we make the quarterfinals against three early Beatles entries. We might want to play a killer late-period set just to differentiate ourselves."

Prem references one of the other pages, which has extensive biographies of the judges. He wonders whether we are supposed to mingle with them or are even allowed to. Gene indicates the absence of a "no mingling" clause in the rules and guidelines, so, as far as he's concerned, making new friends is fair game.

"And by the way, Prem," he adds, "one of the judges is from Pakistan, so schmooze him up good."

"India and Pakistan hate each other," Prem informs him.

"Exactly," Gene says, as if he knew this. "George was a spiritual guy who would reach out to the other side. I mean, Bangladesh wasn't India either, am I right?"

I am obliged to add my two cents. "Gene, I don't know if it helps our cause to be up the judges' asses. It might be seen as stepping over the line and disqualify us."

Gene responds that all *he* is saying is give peace a chance. It's a no-brainer that we're in great shape musically, and if we can bring India and Pakistan a little closer together in the course of our work, it's good press.

All in all, the meeting is pointless, save for Gene and the rest of the band coming away from it mostly on the same side, and feeling positive about the next few days.

It's only a four-and-a-half-hour drive from Long Island to the Syracuse suburb of Liverpool, but the guys and I get an early start since it's a Friday, and there's a VIP meet-and-greet cocktail hour at five for the deep-pocketed fans who crave face time with their fake idols. Our route begins with the usual hassle of negotiating the Bronx and Jersey, but, soon enough, we're past the worst of the turnpike and headed north into Pennsylvania. When you've been off the road as many years as I have, it seems like a chill field trip. An added perk is that we don't have to lug our own amps. Since the idea is to play like the Beatles, the sound people set up the amplification system exactly as the Beatles set up theirs, and all the musicians need to do is plug in.

I knew Prem loved to drive, but nobody told me that his favorite thing to do when Jaya isn't around is to stop at greasy spoons and eat crap. Diners, donut shops, hoagie stands—he's Yelped them all, with the locations printed up in almost as organized a fashion as Jasmine's packet. Mikey and I will keep our junk food bingeing to a minimum because we know we have our first performance later tonight, but Prem is so used to eating spicy and oily food that he sees no reason not to indulge. Two chili cheeseburgers, a taco pizza, and three corn dogs later, he pulls up to the Liverpool Ramada Inn. We carry our bags and guitars to the front desk and inquire as to whether Gene has checked in yet. He has not, which strikes me as out of character for a man who's been known to show up an hour and a half early to tease out his wigs. Nevertheless, the guys and I welcome a little extra relaxation time before we need to trot out the boots and suits.

As I carry my stuff into the room, I'm grateful to Marcia for having been kind enough to book us individual accommodations. The standard business hotel room feels like heaven because it isn't packed wall-to-wall with guitars and amps. I stretch out on the bed, close my eyes, and flash on the Washington Heights gig with Chuchita. It seems like another lifetime. I got to be "the guy" for one night. Now I'm back to my regular role as itinerant guest worker. I remind myself that I'm not exactly hunched over in a field, picking strawberries. I've got a nice, relaxing room, and two large bottles of complimentary water. I open one of the bottles and go to look out the window. It's a third-floor view of the front entrance, so I see a whole bunch of fake Beatles arriving with their guitars. Then I see what looks like Gene's van pulling up.

I'm a bit puzzled when Gene springs out of the passenger side door. My confusion turns to dread when the driver gets out, and I see it's Jasmine. Things continue to get weirder. Gene goes to the rear of the van and removes a wheelchair. He carries it over to the rear left door, at which point another caregiver exits from the right back seat to take the wheelchair. The next thing I see is Marcia emerging from the van and being helped into the chair. Even more bizarre is that the other caregiver looks familiar. It takes me a second to realize what's going on, because I've never seen her in scrubs, but Marcia's helper is the person who's been avoiding me for the past few weeks—my beach buddy, Christina.

I down the bottle of water in one gulp, unsure as to which part of this picture is more unsettling. The abrupt intrusion of Jasmine is galling, to be sure, but hardly a surprise given her history. Christina showing up in caregiver mode, however, is a puzzle I can't even begin to piece together. Even if Jasmine is indeed one of her good friends, and she volunteered to help as a favor, why wouldn't she have texted me a heads-up? What's more, if Christina has decided that she doesn't want me in her personal life, why would she come to a place where we're guaranteed to run into each other? Unless she's not trying to avoid me. Maybe Christina is using Jasmine's offer as an excuse to ditch Hubby for the weekend and hang with me.

Mikey and Prem are livid when told that Jasmine is back in the mix, but they also feel bad for Gene. He seemed fine with leaving his mom at home, his mood better than it had been in months. For a few fleeting hours, it looked as if this was going to be an old-fashioned Beatles guy trip. Then hopes were dashed, doubtless on account of Fake Yoko's inability to stay away from the action. The three of us agree to wait and let Gene contact us with the news. The band is due downstairs at the VIP meet-and-greet in a couple of hours, so, for the time being, we're just going to relax in our rooms before getting into wardrobe. Lying down for a quick nap, I make my first slip, fantasizing about a knock on the door that turns out to be Christina. This is exactly the sort of thing I must eliminate from my consciousness.

I manage to doze off for a little while, and, soon enough, it's time to start putting on my early-era suit with the collarless jacket. The outfits are Gene's bait-and-switch idea—let them think we're going early Beatles at the cocktail party, then do a late-period costume change for the show tonight. It seems like a waste of bait to me, but whatever. Of more significance is that there have been no phone calls or texts since I saw Gene from the window. Perhaps he's too upset, or too embarrassed, to talk about it. I'll do my best to pump him up at the mixer. There's also a better than even chance that the attention he receives from the VIP fans will get him where he needs to be.

The VIP crowd appears to consist of more band members than fans, and there's a lot of "checking each other out" going on. The promoter has required us to wear "Hello" labels that say, "My name is Paul, Help!, My name is Ringo, Brian Epstein Massacre," etc., so it feels as if we're salespeople at an insurance underwriters' convention. As it happens, the Massacre is the only other Long Island band to have entered, and one of the first people I run into is Dennis O'Malley, who Gene had been threatening to poach and install as Prem's replacement. Prem and Dennis know one another and are, in fact, quite friendly. Mikey, meanwhile, has been cornered by a sixty-something fanboy who's trying to wow him with his impression of Ringo flashing the "peace" sign.

"Chin up, two Flying V's, scan the room with a smile." He pats Mikey on the back. "You can use that," he tells him.

"Thanks for the tip," Mikey says, shooting me an eye-roll.

I look to my right and spot a sixtyish woman, dressed in some sort of service uniform, winking at me. I wave back. She comes racing over.

"Hello, Paul," she says with a smile. "You really are the cute one."

"Thank you, dearie," I reply, inexplicably adopting a British accent and hating myself for it. "And what would be your name, luv?"

"Guess," she says, striking a series of poses in her nondescript uniform.

"Marilyn Monroe?"

"Oh, come on, silly," she says. "I winked at you, I'm wearing this uniform, and I'm … lovely."

"Rita," I answer. "How could I be so daft?"

"My real name is Estelle Schwartzman. Tell me, will you be playing my song?"

"We'll just have to wait and see, won't we, luv?" I fire back with a wink of my own.

She blushes and moves off to approach more fake Beatles.

It all seems innocuous enough until an argument breaks out at one of the tables. An unassuming nerd named Mitchell has gone rogue, declaring his preference for the song sequencing on the American version of "Rubber Soul" to the UK release. "You can't tell me 'Drive My Car' is a better lead-in to 'Norwegian Wood' than 'I've Just Seen a Face!'"

The nerds occupying the chairs on either side are outraged, reminding him that changing the American sequencing was the record label's idea, not the band's.

"I'm not talking about who made the choice, I'm talking about the emotional effect of how the songs complement each other."

"You probably like those instrumental fillers on 'A Hard Day's Night' too."

The other nerds laugh. One of them mutters "asshole" in Mitchell's direction.

Mitchell responds by throwing a Klaus Voorman bobblehead at the guy. It looks as if a fight is about to ensue when a burly, bespectacled six-foot-six security guy steps in to break it up. Later, I realize this isn't a security guy at all, but a fan dressed as the late Mal Evans, the Beatles' road manager/bodyguard.

We're thirty minutes into the cocktail party and there's still no sign of Gene. First I worry if something's happened to Marcia, then I begin to wonder if I imagined what I saw outside the window. Whether or not he brought his mother with him, or even if she's taken a turn for the worse, this is not an event Gene Klein would ever think of blowing off. I make my way through a cluster of George fanboys to grab some food off the hors d'oeuvres table. It's filled with selections like "Glass Onion" tarts and a giant "Yellow Submarine" sandwich, cut into canape-size portions. I grab a piece of sub sandwich and walk over to the condiments table (featuring "Mean Mr. Mustard" and "Mayo-bla-di-bla-da") when I hear a collective gasp. Into a sea of goofy-looking band members and Beatle foamers enters a bearded, long-haired, white-suited John Lennon, accompanied by a large-breasted and braless Yoko Ono. Gene has apparently bagged his collarless jacket to make an instant splash, and Jasmine has added to the drama, either with recent surgery or some very convincing prosthetics. The stunt works like a charm, with fans abandoning a roomful of indistinguishable imitators to greet the only two people in the room who stand out.

I try to gauge whether there will be any sort of anti-Yoko backlash among the VIPs. Considering what a hated figure she was, it's remarkable not to see a shred of disrespect being aimed her way. Rather, the group reacts in awe to the couple's convincing characterizations. Gene struts around like a peacock, slinging sarcastic remarks at anyone and everyone, while Jasmine follows in silence, gazing at him in a command performance that exudes unshakable devotion. I notice a couple of John fanboys talking about going over to make conversation with her, but they all chicken out, even the one who claims to know Japanese. Jasmine doesn't look anything close to Japanese, but it makes no difference to the VIPs. They are looking for an excuse to be awed, and Long Island's own John and Yoko have delivered the goods.

I look up to see Prem and Mikey smiling at me, as if to say, "This crazy fuck pulled it off again."

They're right, at least for now, but it's a long weekend, and the Yoko meter could veer into the red at any moment, especially if she overstays her welcome or, God forbid, sings. I have to imagine that she'll be checking in on Marcia from time to time, but, for all I know, that's Christina's 24/7 weekend job. I think about ducking out of the cocktail hour to find Marcia's room and say hello to my long-lost beach buddy, if only to assure her that I'm cool with however she wants the weekend, and our friendship, to go. That's when I'm tapped on the shoulder by another woman who looks familiar.

"Mr. McCartney?"

"Whoa, it's you," I say. It's the Paul collector from Carmine's who was super into me until I made the egregious mistake of using the word "groupie." "How're you doing?"

"Amy. I'm sure you forgot my name."

"What are you talking about? I did not forget."

"We'll never know now, will we? I hope you do really well this weekend, Jimmy."

"Thank you. I appreciate that." I feel like I should give her a hug, but before I get the chance, Gene calls out for me to join him in the corner.

"Excuse me, Amy. I'm sure we'll talk again over the next few days."

"Don't be a stranger."

I nod, glad to be going into the competition without any known enemies in the room. I then approach Gene for the first time since he showed up with a surprise entourage.

"Hey."

"Hey, man." He flashes me an embarrassed grin. "You're probably wondering what's going on, right?"

"Kudos on the big entrance. Totally worked. As far as putting your mother in the back of a van for four hours—"

"Jasmine told me if I didn't bring my mom, I'd regret it for the rest of my life."

"Is Marcia in any kind of shape to come to the shows?"

"Probably not. She's not awake very much."

That being the case, I want to ask what the point is of having hauled her here. But I know this will only stir things up, and I don't want to make him any more anxious than he already is. Instead, I ask how he's holding up. He says he's feeling positive, both about being here, and our chances of taking the whole thing. "The Doctor Roberts from Ann Arbor are out," he announces with glee. Apparently, the only Beatles cover band comprised solely of MDs has been forced to cancel, as their cardiologist John Lennon had to stay back in Michigan to perform a coronary bypass. "We got this, Jimmy, I can feel it."

"We don't want to get overconfident," I say, before getting to the question on the rest of the band's minds. "So, what exactly is Jasmine going to do while we're playing?"

"It all depends on what Mom needs. If Christina can handle her, Jasmine will be sitting on the floor of the stage next to me. She brought her tambourine."

That stupid tambourine? Is he fucking kidding? "So, no early Beatles at all then?"

"Right. Everybody knows you can't have Yoko, pre-1966. But if Jasmine suddenly needs to go up to Mom's room, we can switch things up however we want."

It's bad enough Jasmine showed up; now our entire slate of weekend performances will be orchestrated based on the availability of someone who sits on the floor and shakes a tambourine. I want to tell him what a total Mickey Mouse move this is. Instead, I voice a quiet "I think we've got a good shot." This far in, why inject the slightest bit of negativity into the proceedings? Especially since Jasmine is not about to back down without a fight. The more practical choice is to keep Gene excited and let him believe we're all going into the weekend with equal enthusiasm. I do think we have a shot, but a bunch of the other bands probably do as well. And we're traveling with a deck full of wild cards.

SHIRLEY'S WILD ACCORDION

In the hours leading up to show time, the members of Help! are back in our hotel rooms, relaxing and showering before we change into our late-period wigs and outfits. In typical Gene fashion, Mikey, Prem, and I were left in the dark as to which songs we'd be playing tonight until we saw the handout at the mixer. No surprise: our Battle of the Beatle Bands debut will feature two Lennon songs, one of which is "Come Together." I'm pleased to see the other is the bold choice I championed, "Happiness is a Warm Gun." Even if these picks were a function of Jasmine wanting her man to hog the spotlight, they are beyond solid. Watching him in his white suit, belting out the oddities of Ol' Flat Top with the joo joo eyeball and mojo filter, is so convincing, you'll swear Mark Chapman's bullet missed its target. As for "Happiness is a Warm Gun," in addition to Gene kicking absolute butt on it, it's been said that no tribute band other than the Fab Faux has done justice to the song live. Once Help! puts its version out to the universe, that assessment will change. I think we're in a good place. Musically, anyway.

I'm in my bathrobe, holding off taking a shower because I forgot my toothbrush, and housekeeping is on their way to bring me one. While I'm waiting, I grab my iPad to check out a video from tonight's show opener, Shirley's Wild Accordion. The band's unorthodox name comes from a scrapped "Magical Mystery Tour" instrumental track, and its coveted opening slot from being the first to send in a security deposit. They are not good. In fact, if there were a URL that warranted shutting down the internet for eternity, the link of the Shirleys playing "I Want to Hold Your Hand" would be in the top ten. Four pimply-looking clods who nobody would want to touch, much less hold hands with, reveling in terrible musicianship and off-key vocals. The video is even more bizarre than my first impression of them stuffing their faces with "yellow submarine."

Midway through the second verse, the blessed door-knock comes. I put down the iPad to go retrieve my toothbrush. When I open the door, I see it being pointed at my face, but not by a member of the cleaning staff.

"You called for one of these?" asks Christina.

"I did. I heard you were a part-time caregiver. I didn't know you were a part-time housekeeper too."

Christina laughs. "I saw the cleaning person coming to your room, and I asked if I could make the delivery for her."

"You do good work. Come on in."

She moves forward and the door closes behind her. All I can think of in this moment is that heaven is a Ramada Inn. "Please, have a seat." I offer up the desk chair, and go to sit on the bed, facing her. "Sorry about the bathrobe. I have a show to do in a little while and I was about to get in the shower."

"It won't take long." Christina sighs. "I'm sorry I never answered your texts."

"You were busy. I get it."

"It wasn't right. I owe you an explanation."

"So, you traveled four and a half hours to give it to me? Impressive." I'm only half joking.

"I came to help Jasmine with Marcia. I was a little nervous about it because I knew I would see you, and I felt embarrassed. Then I decided I shouldn't be afraid to tell you—" She shakes her head and starts to tear up.

"What, Christina? What's wrong?"

After a couple of breaths, she steadies herself and continues. "I was supposed to take a vacation. To see my family in Cebu. But my husband—"

Hubby has turned into husband, portending an unexpected chapter in their storybook citizenship romance.

"—he wouldn't let me go."

"What does that mean, he wouldn't *let* you?"

"He said he needs me to be home to cook and manage things. I offered to hire someone to be there while I was gone. He refused to have a stranger in the house."

"Did you ever think of going anyway?" I ask, at the same time realizing how difficult it must be for her to go against the wishes of the person who rescued her from a hard life with few opportunities.

"I couldn't just leave. He didn't want me to take Lito with me because he's in school, but he also didn't want to take care of him by himself."

"And since he wouldn't let you hire anyone to help, you were stuck."

Christina nods. "That's what happened. After that—I don't know— I shut down. I told my family I had too much work. That I was unable to make the trip. Then I tried to forget how upset I was by staying at Pineview for long hours and locking myself in the office. I didn't want to talk to anyone."

"Does your husband know you're here?"

"Yes. He doesn't mind me going away for a weekend, especially if I'm bringing home some extra money."

"I'm really sorry. I wish there were something I could do."

She looks up at me. "You listened. That's something."

"I'll hear anything you have to say," I tell her. "Good news or bad."

"Thank you." She manages the smallest but sweetest of smiles, which reminds me how she started occupying so many of my thoughts in the first place.

I want to get up and give her a hug, but since we're alone in my hotel room and I'm in a bathrobe, I can't risk a malfunction. I try not to stare at her, but I'm finding it hard to avert my eyes. She seems to understand this and is okay with it.

"I haven't told anyone else … what I told you," she says.

"I'm glad you felt comfortable enough to share it with me."

"You're easy to talk to." Christina rises from the chair. "I'd better get back to Marcia. And you have to get ready."

"I hope we can talk some more," I tell her. "I mean, damn. We're both here for the next forty-eight hours, right?"

"We are. I hope we can talk more too."

I follow her to the door to open it. As I reach my hand out to grab the knob, Christina turns around and gently moves my arm down. I'm not quite sure what's going on until I feel her mouth on mine. This can't be happening, and yet it is. The lips are pillow-top soft, and the fit exceeds anything my subconscious has been able to invent. "Christina," I whisper, needing to say her name as I've imagined saying it for so long. I feel the bathrobe's grip growing ever more tenuous.

She doesn't answer my whisper with words, but instead pulls me back into another deep kiss. In my mind, we're back on Jones beach, frolicking between trash cans as we chase more kisses, until we drop to the downy sand and into each other's arms.

"I want to go with you to Cebu," I say.

Christina smiles. "That's sweet. But you've got a show to do, and I've got a patient to take care of."

"When do I see you again?"

"Whenever Jasmine gives me time off," she says. "I know where you live."

And with a wink and a smile, the woman I'd long assumed had written me out of her life is gone again, but this time with the will to return. I take a moment to process this. What it signifies in the big picture is unclear, but, right now, it seems as if my whole world has changed. It's time to crack open the cocoon of containment. I must commit to a life makeover, roll with the punches, and overcome my fears of a full-on crash-and-burn. I've been headed down this road for a while, but Christina's kisses have nudged me that last step forward. It seems Jimmy Kozlowski still has enough juice in him to shoot for the stars.

The Ramada Inn Ballroom B, which last weekend played host to the Northeastern New York Knights of Columbus, is now filled with a hundred and fifty rabid Beatles fans, as well as fifty-two fake Beatles occupying the two long rows of folding chairs closest to the stage. Per contest rules, all band members must be present for the entire show, so there isn't a problem with latecomers or people ducking out early. In addition, all fake Beatles are required to check their phones at the door because mobile phones didn't come into existence until 1973, three years after the Beatles broke up. Johns, Pauls, Georges, and Ringos are permitted to applaud their colleagues, but must otherwise remain seated in their chairs unless they need a bathroom break. These behavioral rules come on top of a lengthy list of dos and don'ts regarding the bands' onstage performances, right down to the mandatory authenticity of the wardrobe. In the early going, the room projects an uptight vibe reminiscent of a fourth-grade assembly. I take a quick look around for signs of Christina, but neither she, Jasmine, nor Marcia seem to be in attendance. I can only guess that Marcia's in no condition to come down.

The moment is upon us. Battle of the Beatle Bands promoter Lloyd Jorgenson has stepped up to the stage to greet the crowd. He's fortyish, slightly overweight, and sports a JFK-like pompadour wig. As the fans applaud, a few begin to chant "Sid! Sid! Sid! Sid!"

To the uninitiated this is both confusing and meaningless, but for the diehards, seeing a promoter who's made the effort to emcee the event dressed as Sid Bernstein, the Beatles' original US concert promoter, is the mark of someone who cares. Fake Sid goes on to reference the Ed Sullivan Show and Shea Stadium, after which he pleads with the audience to keep their screams down so they can hear the music. In a New York accent that sounds nothing like the real Sid, he reminds them that the "winnah will get to play in the othah Livahpool." From there, he ramps up his introduction, sliding into an ill-advised Ed Sullivan impression. "And now, ladies and gentlemen, on our stage, please welcome … Shirley's Wild Accordion."

The crowd screams to the best of its ability, but, as the median age here is north of fifty, the volume dips quickly.

The key difference between this show and my fourth-grade assemblies is that every one of those nine-year-old performers had more natural talent than the members of Shirley's Wild Accordion. One would not be the least bit surprised to learn that their wretched rendition of "All My Loving" fostered its own dedicated hate group. The strangest part is that the fans don't seem fazed by this musical abomination. Half the room is smiling, while the rest snap pictures of a lead singer who looks more like Shrek than Paul. It's a hodgepodge of sloppy drum work, wrong bass notes, and a tragic experiment with falsetto in the last chorus.

Most humans of sound mind would assume the Shirleys will be history as of tomorrow afternoon, unless those humans, like me, were present to witness their "All My Loving" receive thunderous applause, and their vomit-inducing "Do You Want to Know a Secret?" get a standing ovation.

I eventually put two and two together. Just as Gene has carved out a heavily skewed late-Beatles niche to differentiate us in this contest, the Shirleys are the pioneers of tribute camp. The only band to take a *Mystery Science Theater* approach to the work, they are much beloved as a result. According to one fanboy's algorithm, their steadfast awfulness could even translate into victory should the good tribute bands split the vote and cancel each other out.

The next band, Sea of Green, takes the stage. The group is solid, if unremarkable, their Ringo serving up a yeoman-like version of "Matchbox," followed by an overly earnest Paul mugging the shit out of "Things We Said Today." I give them extra points for not drawing out their bows and stage exits, but I'm not sure if that counts for anything with the judges.

The Sheatles come next. Thanks to their early-period short wigs and suits, there is the not-unexpected chatter as to whether they identify as trans or lesbian, but two bars into "Baby's in Black," nobody cares what gender they are because they're so damn good. I look over at Gene to see if their proficiency is rattling him, but he seems chill. Either he doesn't think they're a threat, he's appreciating their talent like the rest of us, or he upped his Lexapro. Whatever the reason, it's a welcome change to see him in a relaxed frame of mind.

Bands four through eight are a mixed bag, among them the promising Blue Jay Way, the expectedly lethargic

Golden Slumbers, and the stellar Revolution 2.0, who, as far as I know, is the first tribute band to perform "Within You, Without You" with a real sitar mastered by an albino George. Gene whispers something to me about how lucky we are to have the only Indian, insinuating that a brown George playing the sitar might have assured a Revolution 2.0 victory. I want to point out that the original George was white, not brown, but the bands are not supposed to be talking.

When band number eight, the unremarkable Liverpool Skiffle, finishes with "That's All Right, Mama," Help! prepares to go on. As we take our places, I see Jasmine come out of nowhere to sit down on the corner of the stage floor, where she can make moony eyes at Gene. Gene appears to be relishing the moment as he steps up to the microphone. "Ladies and gents," he starts off, in his finest Liverpudlian, "say hello to me best girl, Yoko." Prem and Mikey move into full cringe mode, but it seems Jasmine has made a favorable enough impression with the VIPs to collect applause, and the general admission fans join in. Then, just as I play the opening notes of "Come Together," I see Christina wheeling in a comatose-looking Marcia. She rolls her to the side of the stage closest to Gene, so Marcia can have the best view of her son should she happen to regain consciousness.

Gene is in all his glory, touting the likes of toe jam football, monkey finger, and one and one and one equaling three. His energy feeds off the enthusiastic audience, and I can tell the wheels are spinning. I'm proven correct when he decides to mix things up for the last verse. Opting for a bit of improv none of us had previously discussed, he switches out his hollow-body Epiphone for the Martin D-28 to close out "Come Together." The idea is to transition directly into "Happiness is a Warm Gun" before the audience even gets a chance to clap. He's betting the seamless segue will have a more powerful effect than letting the songs be separated by applause and equipment changes. He's also aware that no tribute band on the program has dared try anything like this, and that a well-executed surprise can make all the difference in the outcome. Why? Because tweaking protocol is something a *real* band would do.

It sends the audience soaring. Tonight, Gene is the closest thing these fans have to John Lennon going off on the royals or jamming with Keith Richards. His moxie beckons the room to sing along with him.

Marcia snoozes straight through to the finish, but I think her presence, conscious or not, has helped Gene ascend to this level. Help! gets a standing ovation, and Christina applauds heartily, throwing me a big smile before wheeling Marcia back up to her room. For the rest of the night, no other band, including the technically unmatched "Hello, Goodbyes," comes close to the excitement generated by Gene Klein. It's not enough to make Prem, Mikey, or me excited about staying fake Beatles for much longer, but, while we're still at it, we couldn't ask for a better result.

After the obligatory postgame schmoozing with the hoi polloi, and some nice compliments from the mixer VIPs, I get to my room around midnight. I immediately text Christina in the hope her shift has ended and we can meet up. She's sorry to tell me that Jasmine has her working through the night, so she won't be able to get together. Emphatic that she's not avoiding me, the graveyard-shift CNA goes on about how much she loved watching me onstage.

I bring up the idea of sneaking down to Marcia's room just to say hi, but Christina doesn't think it's a good idea. She tells me to get some sleep because I'll be doing as many as three shows tomorrow, which she's sure will be the case because she knows we're going to win. She signs off with a "sleep tight," followed by what I now believe to be the most meaningful symbol in the history of human civilization—the heart emoji.

As my head hits the pillow, Chuchita, Donny Delgado, and any possibility of my having a solo career are the furthest things from my mind. Right now, everything is about Christina, whose growing connection to me raises the one question with the potential to keep me up all night.

Do the two of us have a future?

Not wanting to be the drowsy Beatle for tomorrow's performances, I pop a five-milligram melatonin, which knocks me out before I get the chance to craft a strategy for going forward.

In the dream, my father has dragged me into the bank for the purpose of dressing down my mother, who is manning her station at the teller's window. "You think what they pay you at this place is going to make a difference?" he shouts.

"Not here, Lou," my mother says. I'm praying my father will listen.

He doesn't. "You know why it doesn't make a difference, Irene? It has nothing to do with the money."

"Lou please—"

"It doesn't make a difference because I'm not fucking happy. Are you happy?"

My father is creating a suburban malaise remake of Dog Day Afternoon, *and the bank manager is none too thrilled about it. Seeing customers back away, he accosts my father and tells him to take it outside. Lou proceeds to punch the bank manager in the face, and the two of them topple to the floor. Amid the scuffle, I hear a knocking sound, but I can't figure out where it's coming from …*

I wake up and shuffle to the door, half-expecting it to be Gene indulging his insomnia, but unless this is a cruel dream double feature, salvation has arrived in the form of Christina. I take her hand and bring her inside, where our mouths engage for probably five full minutes before I ask how she was able to break free from her job.

"Marcia's breathing became more forced," Christina explains. "When I texted Jasmine, she came to the room, gave her some meds, and told me she'd take over."

"Is Marcia gonna be okay?"

"Jasmine seems to think so," Christina says. "I don't know if it was the best idea to bring her here."

"I thought Gene was fine with Jasmine taking care of her at home."

Christina shakes her head. "I don't think Jasmine was okay with staying home."

"So, she painted a more positive picture of Marcia's health to him than she should have?"

"I don't know what she said. All I know is, I was hired to work, and now I've been told not to."

"And are you unhappy about that?"

"What do you think, Jimmy?"

Hearing her say my name out loud is so unexpected it feels like I've won the lottery. We fall onto the bed and begin the delicate dance of integrating our initial, tentative explorations with the removal of clothing. Mine consists of a Radiohead T-shirt and boxers, and Christina's, a simple cotton dress over a lacy white bra and thong that show off her golden-brown skin to heart-racing effect. I'm not anxious to make any of this go too fast, since I may never get to experience it again. It's like discovering the most perfect piece of music ever written and wanting to linger as long as possible on the individual notes in each measure. I consider whether my snail's-pace approach makes me the tantric Beatle. Christina is on board—up to a point. Eventually, her actions make it known that undergarments must be removed. I oblige.

Whatever conservative qualities I had ascribed to this woman, based on her desk job and one day at the beach, appear to have been fiction. We now take turns out-devouring one another, with plentiful moans and a few tears thrown in the mix. In this sacred, arguably sinful, moment in time, she is neither married nor confused, and I am not poor or adrift. We are two imperfect souls who have soldiered through long, barren stretches, brought together by the need to treasure, and *be* treasured.

I will go to my grave cherishing the night the Siren from Cebu brought me a replacement toothbrush.

GOOD DAY, SUNSHINE

I awaken a little before seven, sun streaming into the hotel room, and the other side of the bed, empty. Based on past history, and no physical evidence to the contrary, there is a persuasive argument to be made that last night's bliss existed in my subconscious, like every other Christina dream. Then I inhale. Her scent is everywhere. My first thought is to reach over to the nightstand and put the housekeeping card on the bed, informing the Ramada Inn staff that I, too, care deeply about the environment, so there's no need to change the sheets. Then I look over at my phone and find a text from Christina.

Back helping Jasmine. Marcia very weak.
Xoxoxo

The news and the sign-off make for a strange combination. I'm having trouble balancing my concern for Gene's mom with the afterglow of having been with Christina. After a bit of soul-searching, I decide that, since there's nothing I can do for Marcia, I may as well go all-in on the latter. I move my head from the pillow behind me to the one next to me and bury my face in it for a good ten minutes before getting up.

It's a busy morning, with the 9:30 a.m. show running two plus hours, followed by the judges' decision on the nine surviving bands. Both Jasmine and Christina are no-shows, missing my well-received "Get Back," Gene's stellar "I'm Only Sleeping," and the thunderous applause following the announcement that Help! has advanced to the next round. Shirley's Wild Accordion is still in the mix, as are The Sheatles. The Liverpool Skiffle, to no one's surprise, will be packing their bags and, in a shocking early exit, Revolution 2.0 will join them.

The next order of business is mingling with the attendees at the mandatory fish-and-chips buffet luncheon. Prem and I somehow catch a break, as the focus at our table is split between Gene, and which brand of vinegar the Beatles drizzled on their chips. I'm trying to figure out where Gene's head is at, with his mom in such a fragile condition. Another mystery is why many of the questions he's being asked by the fans are about "Yoko."

"Will she be appearing at your performance in the next round?"

"Does her singing voice sound like the real Yoko's, and, if so, does that diminish your sexual attraction?"

"Will you be playing anything from *Milk and Honey*?"

Gene is either doing a great job of disguising his concern, or in such a deep state of denial that he expects Marcia to suddenly come bouncing back and reclaim her head cheerleader position. I find myself wondering what my father would have been like had he been able to "bounce back" from dementia. Maybe he would have returned with a new perspective on life. Perhaps he'd finally understand that Gene, whom he detested for so many years, didn't kill Eddie. There might even be a chance he'd feel empathy for his former protégé; appreciate how hard it must be for him to carry on while his mother wastes away.

My eyes are getting watery when I feel a tap on my shoulder. I turn to see Amy, the Long Island Paul-o-phile, smiling at me. "You are really good," she says. "I mean, you're always great at Carmine's, but this is another level."

"Thanks, Amy. I appreciate that."

"You remember my name. Nice. I mean, you should, seeing as how I'm probably the only fan who followed you all the way to Liverpool."

"Seriously? You came here because of me?"

"Not totally. There are couple of other Pauls I came to see, but you're the only one I already met in person. FYI, if any of my Pauls win, I'm planning to go to the real Liverpool."

I have an alternate suggestion for her. "Just a question, and I'm not trying to be cute or anything. Did you ever think that, if you saved your money, you could go see the *real* Paul? Probably three or four times."

"The real Paul gets plenty of love, Jimmy. My thing is supporting the everyday Pauls. The guys in the trenches, doing the heavy lifting." Amy wishes me luck in the next round and says to text her if I want to hang later. I nod, certain this will never happen.

Round Three says goodbye to Shirley's Wild Accordion, who, even for a comedy act, seemed to overstep their bounds with a version of "A Day in the Life" that evoked Fats Domino in the A-part and Black Flag in the B-part. The Sheatles have hung on and made it to the Super Six, along with the energetic Koreans, Rubber Seoul, The Hello Goodbyes, the Parisian band, Sun Kings, the surging Blue Jay Way, and us. The surviving bands are not required to go to the Saturday night fan dinner, the thought being that they need to save their energy for the crucial evening performance that determines tomorrow's Final Four. Our guys plan to retreat to their rooms to get some private time, and will order in food if they're hungry. I'm hoping to meet up with Christina, but it seems Jasmine wants her with Marcia, so she can be with Gene in their room.

I text:

I really want to see you,

I know.

She doesn't say the feeling is mutual. A tinge of paranoia begins to surface, so I have to ask:

Do you want to see me?

Very much.

I'm not dead yet. I finish picking at a limp Chinese chicken salad and get ready for the evening performance, the last of the day. We'll play another four songs, which will make it a total of ten since we took the stage this morning. A ten-song Beatles set usually runs forty-five minutes tops, but with the hours spent sitting in the ballroom, plus the fan interaction, it seems like a twenty-hour shift. I want to call Christina so I can hear her voice, but I hold back. I can't be too pushy and make her uncomfortable.

One would think that after so many shows in the identical room, there'd be a "same ol', same ol'" vibe by now, but tonight's energy suggests otherwise. Now that the contest is down to the Super Six, the excitement is palpable, and the bands rise to the occasion. Blue Jay Way kicks the shit out of "Taxman," which does not go unnoticed by Prem. The Sheatles' "If I Fell" is performed with harmonies so pitch-perfect that nobody wants it to end.

The room is buzzing as we take the stage. While we're plugging in, there's a huge roar from the crowd. I'm mystified, until I start hearing them chant "Give Peace A Chance."

Yoko, a.k.a. Jasmine, is headed for her spot at the corner of the stage, and the audience eats it up. She graces them with a gentle wave. We burst into a killer "One After 909," Gene's smile conveying his enjoyment of the way our two voices blend. From there, it's his aching "Don't Let Me Down," followed by Prem's exquisite "Something." We're slated to close it out with "Across the Universe," but Long Island's most unpredictable Smart Beatle engineers an impromptu change of plans, barreling into the opening chords of "The Ballad of John and Yoko." Jasmine rises, the audience applauds, and, before long, Gene has the entire

Ramada Inn Ballroom B up on its feet, singing a spirited refrain about a man preparing to be crucified.

There is no doubt that Help! will make it to the Final Four. I'm happy for Gene, but also worried about what's happening with Marcia, and how Christina is handling it.

The minute the surviving bands are announced, and Gene and Jasmine start basking in the adulation of their fans, I get my butt upstairs and knock on Marcia's door. There's no answer. I text Christina but get no reply. I try knocking a few more times, and finally the door opens, revealing not Christina, but a heavyset Latina, dressed in scrubs, and wearing a name tag that reads "Bianca." Unbeknownst to me, and possibly even Gene, Jasmine has hired another caregiver. I ask where Christina is, and what's going on, but the woman keeps repeating "No Inglés."

"I want to say a quick hello to Marcia," I tell her. I start into the room, but the caregiver blocks me, braying in Spanish that I'm not allowed in.

"I need to make sure she's all right," I insist, managing to poke my head in far enough to get a glimpse of the body lying in bed. Marcia looks like she's breathing, but barely.

"Has anyone called a doctor?" I ask.

Bianca responds by picking up an umbrella, pointing it at me, and shouting "Rajá de acá! Fuera! Fuera!" The caregiver backs me up far enough to where she can shut the door in my face and triple-lock it.

I wonder if I should call an ambulance. Or the police. Instead, I go back to my room and call Christina, praying she'll answer and tell me what is going on. It seems odd that she didn't text to let me know what happened, so I hope she's okay. After ten minutes of not hearing anything back, I decide to go downstairs and confront Jasmine. By the time I get there, she's gone. I manage to pull Gene away from his fans long enough to hear that Jasmine is back up in Marcia's room, administering the loving care only she knows how to give.

"When was the last time you saw your mom?" I ask.

"At the show last night. She needed to rest today, but Jasmine says she'll be ready for the finals tomorrow. I want to make her proud, Jimmy."

"You've already done that," I say. "Seeing she gets the proper care is what matters now."

"Of course. That's why Jasmine went back to the room. And why she hired an extra CNA."

"Did you know Christina's not there anymore? There's somebody new working with your mom."

"If Jasmine hired her, I'm sure she's good."

Christina's welfare is of no concern to Gene. To him, she's just a roadie who switches out catheters instead of guitars. Roadies get replaced all the time.

"Gene, do you think maybe you should get the advice of a doctor?"

"Absolutely," he nods. "If Jasmine says we need one, we'll get the best doc in Liverpool. You know, we have a few doctors here in the crowd." He points to a bald guy who looks to be in his late sixties or so. "Jerry over there is a dermatologist. Loves my solo work."

Naturally, Gene is referring to the real John Lennon's solo work, but since he's clearly the most lauded John of the weekend, it's no surprise to find him appropriating the praise. I want to ask if he's made any kind of arrangements for Marcia if, God forbid, the worst should happen, but by then he's been pulled aside by a fan who wants a selfie with him. I look around for Prem and Mikey, but they're nowhere to be found. My guess is that once I took my early leave, they decided it was acceptable to get out of there too.

It's nearly one-thirty when I climb into bed, my head a jumble of thoughts, none of them comforting. I turn off the light on the nightstand and try, without success, to think about how to repair whatever relationship I have left with Donny Delgado. Minutes later the phone rings. I'm positive it's Gene calling to let me know that Marcia's life has come to its tragic end in a Ramada Inn, but the name on my phone says "Christina."

Thank God. "You're okay, I was so worried—"

She's not okay. She's crying. "Jimmy—"

"Where are you? What's wrong?"

She tells me she's sitting in a twenty-four-hour diner in Sayville, not far from her house on Long Island.

"What? When did you leave here?"

"Earlier tonight. I wanted Jasmine to call a doctor, but she wouldn't. Then she fired me and sent me back in an Uber. I'm too upset to go home right now."

"You should have just come up to my room and hid out. You could have driven back with me and the guys tomorrow."

"I wasn't thinking straight," she says. "I'm still not."

"You can't stay at the diner all night."

"I know. I'll go home. I just need to figure out a few things."

"I understand. I hope I see you soon."
"Wednesday. Pineview. You're coming to work, right?"
"Right."
"So, you'll see me then. Bye, Jimmy."
"Bye."

I start to obsess on what Wednesday is going to look like. Are we going to settle in for a reset, and turn back the clock to where we just work and flirt? Or is the flirting over too? It's a dispiriting possibility, but she, as a married woman and mother, is the one who'll have to call the shots. If she votes "reset," I'll have to find a way to respect that.

If, on the other hand, she should dare to make a move, I will do everything in my power to insure she isn't sorry. Her son may be reluctant to bond with me, but I'll keep reaching out until he comes around. We'll go to baseball games, I'll teach him guitar—whatever it takes to show him, and his mother, how much I have to offer. Thanks to Liverpool weekend, I know I'm ready to give it all.

THE TOPPERMOST

Sid Bernstein, a.k.a. Lloyd Jorgenson, introduces Final Four Morning with the gravitas of a pastor delivering his Easter sermon. The subject of the promoter's homily, delivered in the most grating of Brooklyn accents, is not the return of Christ, but the miracle of the Beatles having been resurrected in a chain hotel outside of Syracuse, all because of him. After some clichéd pontificating on the timelessness of *Rubbah Soul*, *Revolvah*, and *Sgt. Peppah*, Lloyd reminds the fans to sign up for next year's Beatle Battle before they leave, as Early Birds are entitled to a twenty percent discount and a free Cavern Club tote bag. Maybe it's me, but by the time the promoter gets around to introducing the Final Four, he seems to have exhausted the lion's share of his euphoria on hawking swag.

Norwegian Wood and Rubber Seoul have both been eliminated, leaving Blue Jay Way, The Sheatles, The Hello, Goodbyes and us to duke it out for the Grand Prize. Help! is set to open the festivities with a mixed bag of "Across the Universe," "Rain," "Yes it Is," and "Lady Madonna," but Jasmine has not yet come down from the room, so Gene decides to switch out the Yoko-period "Across the Universe" for "Bad Boy," an early-Beatles Larry Williams cover. If he's nervous about Marcia, he's not letting on. Gene proceeds to shred his Rickenbacker, revving up the crowd each time he bellows for Junior to behave himself. That Gene is comfortable enough to throw in an early-period number, despite his previous game plan, speaks to his confidence in our ability to crush any song in the catalogue. His hunch is well founded. The rest of Help's set is up to the gold standard he's squeezed out of us.

I do wonder what he's thinking when he sings the line from "Rain" about people who might as well be dead. It seems you don't have to look very far to find a death reference in this music. Fortunately, "Yes it Is" and "Lady Madonna" don't mention the word, so the morbidity quotient won't spike any higher. The good news is that Gene seems thrilled with our performance. He looks as happy as a fake Beatle could possibly be under the circumstances.

Both Blue Jay Way and The Hello, Goodbyes are beyond reproach, the former submitting an ebullient turn on "Lovely Rita," to the delight of attendee Rita/Estelle Schwartzman. The revelation of the morning is The Sheatles. As bold and innovative as Gene considers his take on the canon, this band has found a variation all its own. As a tip of the hat to the super deluxe box set, they'll be performing the vocal tracks only from the *Abbey Road* medley. Hearing these songs in perfect a cappella harmony, while watching it happen right in front of you, is enough to wring tears out of anyone. I notice a couple of the judges getting misty-eyed, and Gene himself fighting back a sniffle or two.

As the judges retire to the adjacent conference room where decisions are made, the audience stands, stretches, and schmoozes, keeping a respectful distance from the bands because they know how much is at stake. The musicians are still without cell phones, so Gene is unable to check on his mom, and I can't text Christina to keep her up to date. I'm thinking we have a good shot, considering our overall track record for the weekend, but if the judges base their decision solely on this morning's performance, it's all up for grabs. The Hello, Goodbyes, who have emitted nothing but buoyancy since we've been here, now seem tense and worried. The guys in Blue Jay Way are immersed in some early-Beatles horsing around, but their antics come off as artificial and forced. I think I hear Mikey and Prem whispering about playing some gigs together down the road, but I'm not sure. Gene, meanwhile, is either in poker-face mode or has, as a survival tactic, zoned out completely.

The lights in the room begin to flicker on and off, signaling the return of the judges and the imminent announcement of who will compete for a trip to the only Liverpool that matters. The room goes dead silent as Lloyd makes his way to the stage. When he reaches the mic, Fake Sid Bernstein offers his thanks to both the fans, and the hardworking bands "who gave it all to honor the greatest musical act ever to rock the planet." And then, the moment arrives.

"Ladies and Gentlemen, please give it up for your Battle of the Beatle Tribute Bands finalist, The Sheatles!"

No one is surprised, yet the room erupts with a standing ovation and boisterous applause. The Sheatles themselves are moved to tears, as am I. It is both unexpected and gratifying to see an event dedicated to mimicking a cultural phenomenon from almost sixty years ago acknowledge that the culture has progressed. I know the real Paul and Ringo would love it, and if there exists an "up above," John and George are smiling from there. In the middle of my reverie, Lloyd announces that the other finalist for the Grand Prize is... Help!

Gene, in a life-skills first, looks humbled, even more so when the applause is louder than what had been extended to our uber-talented competition. He gives Mikey and Prem each a hug. When it's my turn, he holds the hug a bit longer, whispering two words I can't remember ever hearing Gene Klein say.

"Thank you."

He's not done.

"Let's win this for Eddie."

I nod my head. Sheatles tears morph into Eddie tears.

The two triumphant bands are served a quiet lunch in the judges' lounge, after which we're permitted to return to our rooms to freshen up before the finals, if we so choose. Gene has asked Prem, Mikey, and me to stay and hang with him on the first floor. He obviously doesn't want to cloud his focus with what's happening upstairs until the show is over. Part of him is still hoping Marcia will make it down for our last set, which he plans to close with "Strawberry Fields Forever," featuring Prem's elaborate effects. Since the band put off premiering it on Long Island because Marcia was too weak to be there, it will be a fitting finale.

With Help! having opened the semi-finals, The Sheatles are tapped to start the championship round. They seem a little frazzled as they begin their first song, which is being performed as "And I Love Him." The gender-switch in Beatles songs is difficult for anybody to pull off, much less a band that's already challenging gender norms. People are so used to hearing the lyrics a certain way that what might seem like a minor tweak takes them completely out of the moment. I think The Sheatles feel this from the crowd and, perhaps, regret their choice of opener. What one can't help but appreciate, though, is a group unafraid to go big, and put everything on the line for their art. I'm happy to see them settle in for the rest of their set, which builds to a gut-wrenching finish, the flawless three-part harmony of "This Boy."

Maybe the best thing about the finals is the stark contrast in material the two bands have assembled. The Sheatles played to their strengths, showing off a refined vocal talent surpassing any Beatles tribute band I've ever heard, including the ones that are too big for a contest like this. Help! on the other hand, has decided to put all its eggs in the raw power basket, kicking it off with "Everybody's Got Something to Hide 'Cept for Me and My Monkey," and moving on to "Helter-Skelter," "I Want You," and "Yer Blues," before closing with "Strawberry Fields Forever." Everything seems to be going according to plan. The one question mark is that we're already halfway through "I Want You," and have seen no sign of Marcia, or even Jasmine. One would think that if Gene's mom were in anywhere near stable condition, Jasmine would have left her with Bianca and come down for the big finish. I'm sure Gene's stomach is churning, but his precise attack betrays none of his angst. This is further supported by the seamless transition he makes into a blistering "Yer Blues."

An aura of exhilaration envelops the room as Gene soars higher and higher. He nods to the band, letting us know he's going to take a guitar break when the verse ends. The blond Epiphone screams, as Gene closes his eyes to concentrate on each note of the solo.

It is when he opens them back up that everything changes. Jasmine has entered the ballroom, wheeling in a sleeping Marcia, who's so stiff and pallid she seems ready to be embalmed. Gene looks horrified. We're heading toward the end of the tune when his voice starts to crack.

If I ain't dead already, girl, you know the reason why ...

Jasmine is smiling at him, trying to keep the mood elevated, but Gene can't muster anything close to a positive expression based on what he sees. The crowd's enthusiastic response as the song ends also fails to get a rise out of him. He signals to the band that he wants to speak to the audience before they play their last song. It's anybody's guess how he plans to address the personal drama unfolding before him.

"If I could have your attention, ladies and gentlemen." He points to the wheelchair.

"This is me mum, over here. She's been having a bit of a dodgy time of late, so maybe if you show her some love, it'll 'elp lift her spirits."

The audience answers with huge applause. A resigned Gene turns to the band and tells us we won't be ending with "Strawberry Fields" after all. He picks up his acoustic guitar and tells us to follow along.

"You're very kind," Gene tells the crowd, suddenly dropping the Liverpool accent. "We're going to end with a song that's very special to Marcia. Sometimes she even hears it playing in her head when there's no music on. It's also special because I learned it from a gifted musician who never got credit for how talented he was."

And with that, Gene picks some notes that sound classical, or flamenco, or Italian.

And then he starts singing:

> *Volare, oh oh*
> *Cantare, oh oh oh oh*
> *No wonder my happy heart sings …*

It takes me a minute to realize what's going on. Gene Klein has just given a shout-out to my father, not only for his unheralded musical expertise, but for teaching him the very song Lou identified as a symbol of his own failure. Even more bizarre is that this MOR anthem, first made popular by Italian singer Domenico Modugno, and later in America by Dean Martin, has become the crowning benediction to three days of Beatle worship.

Gene as Dean is not embarrassing in the least, his smooth-as-silk "Volare" croon a respectable fit for any retro piano bar. Mikey and Prem supply sweet and subtle support as I fill in the bass notes. Gene is solely focused on his mom, his eyes not straying, even for a second, to look up at Jasmine. From where I stand, Caretaker/Fake Yoko appears horrified. She is, no doubt, thinking about all her efforts to get Gene this far, only to see him sabotage them by turning John into a lounge singer. The fab fans, however, look like they're enjoying the extemporaneous switcheroo. Perhaps it's in deference to the ailing Marcia, or the good will Gene has accrued as the weekend's peerless Lennon doppelgänger, but there's no doubt the crowd is with him. Suddenly, as if his fluid, rat-pack warbling weren't enough, he ups the shock-and-awe ante by singing the second verse in Italian. For the third stanza, he bids arrivederci to Roma, but his assured delivery proves equally lilting in English.

And then it happens. In keeping with the already surreal sequence of events, his gamble pays off. For the first time since our arrival in the bastard cousin of real Liverpool, Marcia's eyes open all the way, accompanied by the slightest hint of a smile. Just as remarkable is the sight of bred-for-showbiz Gene Klein stripping away the artifice of stage performer to assert his humanity, something he's never before dared in public. Watching his tears of joy, it's as if the wig, the Beatle wardrobe and, most notably, Jasmine, don't exist. The audience stands in reverence, swaying from side to side as they drink in the emotion of this Olympian denouement. Once the last note is struck, Gene blows kisses to the crowd and receives, hands-down, the loudest applause of the contest.

Help's! leader would love nothing more than to soak up the praise and gather us for a group bow, but time is of the essence. He leaps off the stage to give Marcia an extended hug. When he finally breaks away, he sees her eyes close again, which prompts him to pull the wheelchair away from Jasmine and begin escorting his mother out of the ballroom. Jasmine, unsure whether to stay for the announcement of the winner, or tend to her other job, hesitates for a split second before ordering me to text her the results. She goes to catch up with Gene and Marcia.

The three remaining members of Help! stay for the awards ceremony. Based on Gene's unassailable talent, as well as the raw honesty he exhibited in our finale, we are the obvious fan favorite. Yet we also know, as do Gene and Jasmine, that among the myriad Battle of the Beatle Tribute Bands rules is the one that reads:

ALL SONGS PERFORMED MUST BE
SONGS PREVIOUSLY PERFORMED
OR RECORDED BY THE BEATLES.

The judges, who are the most seasoned of Beatle nerds and sticklers for doing things by the book, delay the announcement of the winner so they can perform their due diligence. This means manning their laptops in search of a clue as to whether an early Beatles setlist, or even a joking-around-in-the-studio outtake, might have included a line from "Volare."

Forty-five minutes later, they are ready to announce their decision. Lloyd Jorgenson steps up to the mic, makes one last pitch for discounted pre-enrollment in next year's festivities, and the moment of truth arrives.

"I want to thank all the bands and the fans one more time. You've made this a greater success than anything we ever could have imagined. The weekend has offered many surprises, resulting in outcomes none of us could have predicted when we wrote the rule book. Frankly, it's been a bit of a wake-up call and, as a result, we've decided to make some changes … for next year."

This year, sad to say, finds no documented evidence of the Beatles having ever played "Volare," so the Sheatles are the uncontested champions. I am happy for them, and I think Prem and Mikey are too. On a certain level, we're relieved that we won't have to cross the pond as a Long Island tribute band, with Jasmine nipping at our heels. Liverpool, New York has been a fitting last hurrah. If it is indeed true that, in the end, the love you take is equal to the love you make, we did our best to honor the Beatles' influence in the most loving way we knew how. Now we can move on to new musical spaces, and I can bury Fake Paul in the spirit of closure, rather than in a fit of anger. The three of us decide to hit the hotel bar and raise a glass to the incorrigible Gene Klein.

AND IN THE END...

The funeral takes place barely five days after the contest; ironically, on the morning of my fiftieth birthday, which I hadn't made plans to celebrate anyway. It is a modest-sized affair, as most of Marcia's friends and family have previously rolled up for the eternal Magical Mystery Tour, as Gene explains in his eulogy. Out of respect for our grieving leader, the band has decided to delay turning in its formal resignation until he's had some time to regain his footing. Meanwhile, Jasmine is nowhere to be found, with the Beatle Battle finale having served as Gene's come-to-Jesus moment. The faux Yoko's questionable caregiving, as well as her near emptying of Marcia's personal checking account, formalized the end of a partnership that had gotten far more acceptance from Help! fans than the real Yoko ever got from anybody.

Christina, on the other hand, has taken time out of her busy work schedule to come pay her respects. I'm not prepared for the instant level of comfort I feel when our eyes meet. She seems equally at ease, all of which is remarkable in light of our impassioned cries at the Liverpool Ramada Inn. I was sure we'd be filled with anxiety about what that night meant, both then, and going forward. How is it possible for us to be so calm? My only guess is that Christina and I have come to an intuitive, if unspoken, understanding.

Irrespective of how things play out based on the practicalities of life, the love we feel for one another is real. Even should our relationship end tomorrow, the value of the connection we made will never diminish.

I'm not a mind reader, so there's a decent chance I'm projecting my own wishful thinking onto her, but, right now, it's all I've got. As Christina said after I listened to her story about the Philippines, "it's something."

After the rabbi's Kaddish, the mourners add shovels full of earth to Marcia's grave. Then Christina says goodbye to Gene, and comes over to me.

"This must be hard for you too," she says.

"It is. One more piece of the past."

"I'm sorry."

"Thanks for being here."

Christina nods, then pulls a small, framed picture out of her handbag. "Happy Birthday, Jimmy," she says.

It's a selfie of her in mid-figure-eight, from our day at Jones Beach.

The perfect gift. "Thank you. I can't tell you how much I love this."

"It's okay. I don't have time to listen. I need to get back to the office."

"Wait. You don't do social media. How did you even know it was my birthday?"

"That little application form you had to fill out at Pineview—"

"You're a sneaky one."

"Bye, you." She gives me a quick hug and is on her way, my gaze following her until she's in the car, and pulling out of view.

The rest of us head over to Gene's house to reminisce and eat deli food. It is here, in the very place where Gene sharpened his Beatle skills for over fifty years, that he tells the rest of the band how sorry he is to break the sad news. He's bowing out of the tribute scene. Help! is over. Mikey and Prem do their best to hide their relief, having now been spared the awkward task of quitting. I, on the other hand, am strangely rattled because I can't imagine how Gene envisions his life from here on out. He tells me how fortunate he is to have cut things off with Jasmine before she could abscond with all his mother's money. Now he can retire if he wants. He knows he probably won't, but at least he can take some time to think things through before making his next move. Much to Mikey and Prem's consternation, I tell him not to make any rash decisions about the band in his current state. Gene assures me that his grief is not preventing him from thinking clearly. He'd already made up his mind to retire Help! after Liverpool. He hoped it would be after Liverpool, England, but since that wasn't in the cards, the time is now.

It's hard to fathom, but in the aftermath of his mother's death, Gene sounds healthier than he has in the entire time I've known him.

On the drive home I realize that Gene isn't the only one who's going to have to make a major adjustment to a world without Help! I'll need to figure out some modifications of my own because, over and above the steady gigs and round-the-clock noodging, Gene Klein is my last connection to a life that is no more. His able but silly-looking tribute band, whose raison d'être was nostalgia, had provided me the opportunity to tap into what made me who I am. There wasn't one night of playing with Gene that I didn't reflect on my brother, and the places life might have taken him had he made it into his forties and beyond. Visions of Eddie got me thinking about Mom, and how much shit she had to endure from a husband who could never find the strength to rise above his misery. Ironically, it took till the very end of Help! for me to uncover the deepest revelation of all, and I had nothing to do with it. It was Gene Klein who revived his mother with a tribute to his mentor, Lou Kozlowski. Thanks to Gene, I finally understood that my father had a lot more to do with all of us being talented musicians than anybody realized, including my father.

I pull up to my basement entrance, wiping away tears. As a freelance musician, I'm accustomed to change, but this one doesn't go down so easy. Just as Gene has lost Marcia, I'm grieving for my departed family all over again. Jaco's still here, though, meowing like crazy and rubbing up against me as I walk in. It's annoying a lot of the time, but not today. Who knows? Maybe somewhere along the line, forces will conspire to have Christina become a part of our little mixed species home, but, in the meantime, it's extra salmon for this dude.

Since it's already a day of tectonic shifts, I decide to shake up everything at once and place a call to Donny Delgado. If he threatens me with a restraining order, I'll take it as a sign to investigate other options.

Donny doesn't pick up. I leave a message for him and proceed to stream a couple of *Seinfeld* reruns. The goal is to lighten my mood, but, for the first time, the babka episode isn't cutting it. It's hard to figure out what will bring me some semblance of peace. I grab the *Tortilla Curtain* paperback I took to California to give to Kaylie, but rereading a tragic tale of income inequality between Mexican immigrants and rich white folks does little to relieve my angst. I need to get out of this basement. I just don't know where to go. Jaco is certainly not about to come up with any suggestions. Finally, for no reason that makes sense, I decide to get a cup of coffee at the Roslyn Diner.

I'm in the car, on my way to a place that will only make me sad because all the people I enjoyed going there with are dead. *What was I thinking?* I'm about to turn around and head back home when the phone rings. It's Delgado. I pull into a gas station, so I'll be able to hear him clearly when he tells me to stop calling, and that he never wants anything to do with me.

"Hey, Donny, thanks for calling back," I say.

"How did your commitment go?" he wants to know.

"How much time you got?"

"I'm losing money every minute I talk to you. But I want to know what you're doing for the next few months."

Unbelievable. "Chuchita still wants me to open?"

"No, you're dead to her," Donny assures me. "But I'm more reasonable. I'm offering you a chance to tour with "The Rick James Experience.""

"You want me to open for a Rick James tribute band?"

"The hottest Rick James tribute band out there. A huge cash cow."

"I'm confused," I tell Donny. "I thought your whole thing was cutting edge original material."

"It is. But what do you think subsidizes the acts I love that don't make a dime? Casino gigs with bands like Fred Zeppelin. Fred's a great guy by the way. Gets more tail than Plant."

"I don't mean to sound ungrateful. It's just that I spent more than ten years in a Beatles tribute band."

"Exactly. So this time you get to be the cutting-edge guy."

"But these audiences aren't looking for anything new or different."

"Correct. Which means that if they like you, you've really got something. Hey, I'm not gonna twist your arm. You ever hear of a guy named Wayne Weinberg? I hear he's good."

"He's a Barry Manilow impersonator."

"Never mind."

"Do I have some time to think about this?" I ask.

"Three weeks. I gotta say, Jimmy, you're awful picky for a guy who plays casuals in a nursing home." He hangs up.

I'm not going to make any decisions right away. There's no way I buy into Donny's theory that opening for a tribute act will be good for my career, but I can't overlook the reality that Jaco needs a roof over his turds. The good news is, I've got a little breathing room to see what I can scare up.

In short order, I manage to book a few session gigs, help score a low-budget movie, and land a slot at the club in Sea Cliff where I had originally planned to debut my solo material. Reprising the set we played in Washington Heights, I once again have Tracy singing harmony, Prem playing bass, Raji on keys, and I've added Mikey on drums. To top it off, I have Christina in the audience, sans Hubby. We're back to being friends, but my interpretation of our unspoken understanding seems to have been a fair assessment. The future is still to be written.

Unlike the Chuchita gig, where I needed the help of Tracy, and the star herself, to get the crowd on board, these guys feel us from the start. The songs are so well received, and flow with such ease, that an unsuspecting patron might mistake them for rock standards—my Nursing Home Performance Theory writ large. Looking out at the enthusiastic audience, I have an epiphany:

I am the only one in my immediate musical universe, going back to Lou Kozlowski, who was able to entertain a crowd with all original compositions. I hear Eddie's voice in my head.

See, little bro. You always thought I was the talented one.

As we begin the second set, a disheveled-looking older dude shuffles into the place and waves at the band. After twenty seconds or so, I realize it's Gene. He doesn't look dirty or homeless, but this is not the fastidious bandleader I've known since I was a kid. I haven't seen him since the funeral, which I've felt kind of bad about. I'm also not sure how he found out about the gig, but he doesn't look mad or unhappy. I see him ask Christina if he can sit down at her table. She welcomes him, though I'm certain he has no idea who she is. Gene turns toward the stage to take in the music. Based on his facial expressions, he seems to like it. The crowd is totally with us, so I'll go home loving this night no matter what he thinks. We play two or three more songs, and I figure, what the hell? I invite Gene to sit in on the last tune, and he gives me the thumbs up. Prem hands him one of his guitars.

As impossible as it is to comprehend, Gene Klein is not only playing backup on one of my originals, he seems grateful to be a part of it. No bandleader ego, no prima donna shit, just Gene, for the first time in his life, applying his talent to support somebody else's thing. It dawns on me that there has been a cosmic reversal. Now that the last of Gene's family is gone, I am *his* only connection to a life that is no more. I feel his pain like it's my own, because it's been my own for so long.

I ask Gene to do the encore with us. As soon as he agrees, I pick up one acoustic guitar and hand him another. What could be more fitting than to end with one of my favorite Beatles tunes? Especially one that's a duet. I start fingerpicking the intro, and then … it's just Jimmy and Gene harmonizing on "Two of Us," and sounding almost as badass as the original. Gene's relaxed, I'm smiling, and the two of us are going out on a better note than the real John and Paul could manage. The audience approves. After handing back the guitar he used, Gene gives me an awkward hug, waves to the crowd, and proceeds to stumble out of the club. I make a note to call him in a couple of days, but, for now, I want to shake some hands, and greet my one and only VIP.

I reach Christina's table, and she jumps into my arms, hugging me like she doesn't want to let go. When she finally breaks, she looks into my eyes and says, "I have news."

I feel my legs weakening. "Maybe I'd better sit down." I slide into Gene's former chair, waiting for the words I've been longing to hear from the moment we met.

She starts … "Jimmy, being with you changed everything for me."

"It did?"

She nods. "The way you listened. The things you said. And I made up my mind to do something about it."

"I can't tell you how happy this makes me."

"I figured it would. Thanks to you, I told my husband I'm going back to Cebu by myself, and he can take responsibility for things at home. I'll be with my family for two weeks. I leave at the end of the month."

"That's great," I say, holding my breath for the second part of the reveal.

There is no Part Two. She reiterates that she never would have been able to stand up for herself without my encouragement.

There's an uncomfortable silence. At least it's uncomfortable for me. I realize that I can't let this moment go by without standing up for what I want, and who I am. So, I let it fly.

"I love you, Christina."

"I know."

"And?"

"I have a lot of thinking to do."

"But you don't … love …"

"Would I be doing so much thinking if I didn't?"

I smile.

"I should be getting back home," she says.

I thank her for coming. She tells me she loves my original songs. Then she gives me a quick kiss and makes her way out the door. I head back to the stage to help the others pack up, knowing that I leave here with no assurances other than the truths that have already been shared.

Once everything's ready to go, I turn my phone back on, only to find a message from Kaylie. I'm careful not to read too much into it, having learned my lesson and then some. Turns out, she's sent a video of herself in her apartment. I press "play."

A smiling, makeup-less twenty-five-year-old waves to camera. "Hey, Dad. I just wanted to share this with you. I guess it kind of spoke to me. Don't worry, I'm okay and everything. I just love how it's so … unafraid, I guess."

She proceeds to pick up her guitar and starts to strum awkwardly, launching into Billie Eilish's "Happier Than Ever." It's the confessional of a woman who's been burned by a man and couldn't be happier now that he's gone. Kaylie plays like the beginner she is, sings slightly off-key—and I love it. My fast-tracking, bottle-service-loving daughter is paying attention to the words and music that move her. The lyrics of this song touched her so deeply she needed to sing them herself. What's more, she felt compelled to sing them for me, playing the guitar I strung for her.

It's something.

THE END

ACKNOWLEDGMENTS

I am grateful beyond measure for those who believed in a quirky little novel that, with the benefit of their wisdom, dug deeper with each revision. First and foremost, a huge thank-you to publisher Lou Aronica and his entire staff at the Story Plant. After a lockdown-assisted stint in solitary confinement, the best gift an author can receive is a talented team of collaborators. Your knowledge, insight, professionalism, and organizational skills made the process a joy. Marc Weingarten, your passion for music informed keen editorial notes that couldn't have been unearthed by anyone else. Thank you to early readers Elliot Shoenman, Roy Teicher, and David Kukoff for your candor, letting me know when passages went on too long, or just plain sucked. Also, a big shout-out to Sabrina Dax, who pushed me forward to find a home for this book, and another one to David Pierce, who helped smooth out the details.

As someone who came to fiction writing after two decades of working in television, I am indebted to the new colleagues I've met along the way, writers whose prose and poetry always challenge me to do better. I count among them John Andrew Fredrick, Scott Bradfield, David Kukoff, Michaela Carter, Jim Natal, Ben Loory, and John Densmore—and there are many more.

Jian Huang, you are a marvel. Thank you for clearing my path in the social media/internet jungle, and making sure people hear about my books.

I Buried Paul would not exist without the brilliant musicians who inspired it. Obviously, John, Paul, George, and Ringo played their parts, but the ones who first drew me to this story were a lot less famous. I have always been moved by the exceptional artists all over the world who ply their musical trade without ever landing a big payday. I've seen many of them deliver superstar-quality thrills to audiences, as you probably have. If nothing else, perhaps this novel is a reminder of how much working musicians add to our lives; how deserving they are of our respect and support. As for the tribute bands? I spent a good part of my youth trying to figure out how to play Beatles songs, but no matter how many hours I labored, making them sound even passable was beyond my reach. Today there are legions of acts that can replicate much of the Beatles' canon note for note. Mimicry and commercial ambition aside, their talent and commitment has rendered them the singing, strumming archivists of this essential musical history.

I Buried Paul also owes a debt to the unsung heroes of nursing home health care, many of whom were part of my family's life for the last fifteen years. Their dedication, especially in the fiercest stages of COVID, was nothing short of miraculous.

A final and most important thank-you to my wife and children. We've faced many difficult challenges together, and it has been a gift to be able to count on each other for love and support. Lyn, you are the rock, the glue, the selfless nurturer who lifts us all. We are forever blessed to have you in our lives. Especially me.